beautiful
chaos

ALEX
USA TODAY BESTSELLING AUTHOR
GRAYSON

Beautiful Chaos

Copyright © 2023 by Alex Grayson.

All rights reserved.

Cover Design by Cover Me Darling.

Interior Formatting by Alex Grayson.

Editing by Edits by Erin.

All rights reserved. No part of this publication may be reproduced, distributed, or transmitted in any form or by any means, including photocopying, recording, or other electronic or mechanical methods, without the prior written permission of the publisher, except in the case of brief quotations embodied in critical reviews and certain other noncommercial uses permitted by copyright law.

The scanning, uploading, and/or distribution of this document via the internet or via any other means without the permission of the publisher is illegal and is punishable by law.

Please purchase only authorized editions and do not participate in or encourage electronic piracy of copyrightable materials.

All characters and events appearing in this work are fictitious. Any resemblance to real events or persons, living or dead, is purely coincidental.

To anyone who's ever felt like escaping.

CONTENT WARNING

Please be advised, this is not a light and fluffy read. There are some situations that may be triggering. I highly suggest taking heed of the warning below.

This book contains scenes that may depict, mention, or discuss: assault, attempted murder, attempted rape, blood, cheating, child abuse, child death, death, hostages, incest, murder, pedophilia, physical abuse, poisoning, PTSD, rape, self-harm, sexual abuse, sexual assault, suicide, torture

Chapter One
Caterina

I jerk upright in bed, my eyes darting around the dark room as the echoes of screams bounce around in my head. There's a tightness in my chest, as if a boulder sits on my sternum, and my throat convulses, making it difficult for me to breathe. The eerie sounds felt so real that I half expected to find someone across the room, their haunted eyes watching me.

Warm breath fans over my shoulder seconds before a hand touches my back, running soothingly up and down my spine. Taking a deep breath, I close my eyes, letting the comforting touch calm my rattled nerves.

"Shh...," a deep voice rumbles. "I've got you."

I release the tight grip on my hands in my lap, and my shoulders hunch forward. Tears prick the back of my eyes and my nose stings.

"Another dream?" Hunter asks, pressing his lips against my shoulder.

"Yes," I croak through dry lips.

Hunter slides his arm around my waist and pulls me closer. "Come here," he murmurs. Lying down, he pulls me so I'm lying on his chest, placing my head directly over his heart. My only relief from these strange nightmares is hearing his steady heartbeat and having his arms around me, our legs tangled together.

Finally, the screams begin to subside.

"Do you remember anything?"

I always give the same answer to this question.

My fingers curl against the coarse hairs on his chest. "Screams. Only the screams."

He tightens his hold around me, pulling our bodies so close that not an inch of space is between us.

The dreams started five years ago. I wouldn't even consider them dreams, more like nightmares, since all I remember are the screams. There are no faces, no settings, and I have no idea who is making the horrible, painful sounds. My heart aches for the person, as it's obvious they're in a lot of pain.

In the beginning, the screams filled my head almost every night. In those early days, I felt like I was going insane. As a result, I became so afraid of falling asleep that I saw a psychologist. Thankfully, they've lessened over the years. It's now only once or twice a week that I have them. I might get a full week without one if I'm lucky.

Focusing on Hunter's heartbeat, my own begins to slow down, and the tightness in my chest starts to loosen. When I draw air in, it's not so painful, and the tense muscles in my arms and legs slowly relax.

"Sleep, baby," Hunter whispers, his breath moving the hairs on top of my head. "I've got you. No more dreams tonight."

Chapter Two
Hunter

Walking into the kitchen, I come to a stop when I see the girl sitting at the table eating a banana, a half-full glass of orange juice in front of her. She's wearing a purple romper with white polka dots and her long, dark hair is in two braids, both hanging over her shoulders. Her chin is propped on one of her hands with her elbow on the table as she stares out the backdoor window.

I clear my throat as I continue across the room to the coffee pot already filled with coffee.

"Good morning, Presley," I say to the preteen girl. "What brings you by so early?"

I glance over my shoulder just in time to see her smile. "Nothing special. I just wanted to say hello."

"Where's Cat?"

Before answering, Presley bites into her banana. "Dunno."

"How did you get in?"

"Cat gave me the alarm code a while back."

I nod, turning my attention back to the coffee and pour some of the black brew into two cups. After I drop a spoonful of sugar in mine, I add two to Cat's and then a splash of creamer. I stir both, then take mine to the table, leaving Cat's on the counter.

"How's life treating you?" I ask, taking a sip of the hot brew.

Presley lifts her shoulder in a careless shrug typical of preteens. "It's okay."

"Anything new going on?"

"Nope," she chirps as she pulls back the last of the banana peel and sets it on her napkin. Happiness sparkles in her eyes as she looks at me. "Except for this cute boy who just moved in down the street."

My jaw tightens unconsciously, and a flare of irritation sours my stomach. As a twelve-year-old, Presley shouldn't be noticing boys yet.

Even though she isn't our daughter, I still feel responsible for her. It never made sense to me why, but Presley started showing up at our house at random times after moving into our neighborhood a few years ago. It's never for a specific reason. She just likes to hang out. Her visits are always brief, lasting no more than a few minutes. It doesn't bother me when she's here though. She's a cute kid and sometimes quite entertaining. Just not when she's talking about boys.

"Aren't you too young to be thinking about boys?" I ask the question with as much calm as I can muster.

The sparkle in her eyes doesn't dim at all. Instead, she giggles, and despite my suddenly peevish mood, my heart warms.

"It's not like I want to kiss him and stuff. I just think he's cute. But not as cute as you, of course," she adds quickly, her grin widening until all of her teeth flash.

Despite her young age, Presley is a flirt. It doesn't bother me because I know her crush is the innocent kind most kids her age have on adult figures.

"Stay away from boys, Presley. They're bad news."

She rolls her eyes and replies sarcastically, "Yes, Dad."

I grunt while holding my cup to my lips.

"What are you up to today?" The rest of the banana gets stuffed into her mouth as she waits for my answer.

"Work."

Her pert little nose wrinkles adorably. "You mean that place where girls get naked and shake their butts?"

"How do you know about Slate?" I ask, mildly surprised.

She grabs the end of her braid and rubs it over her cheek while muttering, "I hear stuff."

My eyes narrow. "What kind of stuff?"

"Just stuff. Gross grown-up stuff." She drops her braid, tilting her head curiously, "Do you... like that kind of stuff?"

Nope, not going there.

I set my cup down. "That, little girl, is none of your business."

A tiny sparkle appears in her eyes, indicating she knows exactly what she's doing and is enjoying it. "Fine. I'll ask Cat."

"You'll do no such thing. That information is too delicate for your young ears."

Once again, her eyes roll upward before returning to me. "You're no fun."

"And you act older than you are."

"Whatever."

Huffing, Presley carries the napkin and banana peel to the trash, rinses out her glass, then deposits it in the dishwasher.

She starts for the kitchen door. "It's time for me to go. I'll see you later, Hunter."

With that, she leaves without saying another word. Standing up from my seat, I watch her skip down the hall and disappear into the living room. The door closes a second later.

Amused by Presley's abrupt departure, I walk over to the stack of papers she left behind. Presley, like Cat, enjoys writing, except her stories are innocent and sweet about her daily life at home with her parents and little brother. They're more like journal entries, and she likes to share them with Cat.

After I carry my cup to the counter and refresh it, I slip Cat's in the microwave to rewarm. I leave it on the counter where she'll see it, along with the stack of papers, and take my cup out to the back porch. Taking a seat on one of the loungers, I prop my feet on the railing and gaze off into the woods and the high mountains beyond them.

Tennessee is beautiful this time of year. It's the start of fall, so the leaves are just starting to change into deep oranges, lush reds, and bright yellows. It won't be long until the trees are bare and the chill becomes bitter.

The door behind me opens, and a second later, Cat steps beside my chair with her own coffee cup. Dropping my legs from the rail, I grab her cup and set it on the table between the chairs before she can take the seat beside me. Wrapping my hands around her waist, I pull her down on my lap.

She laughs lightly as she settles herself sideways. Her arm circles my shoulders and she drops her lips to mine, exactly what I wanted.

"Morning, gorgeous," I rumble against her lips.

"Morning."

I lay my arm across her lap and my hand moves to the back of her upper thigh, right below her ass.

"Presley was here?" she asks.

"Yeah. She left a few minutes ago." I press a kiss against the side of her head, then hand her her cup of coffee. "Any plans for the day?"

"Catch up on work. Darren is hounding me about the first draft."

Cat is a fictional thriller author. As a child, she dreamed of becoming a writer, and with the encouragement of her parents, she sold her first manuscript to a publishing house before she graduated from high school. Within weeks of its release, it topped the charts, much to Cat's and her parents' surprise. In the years since then, she has written and published nine bestselling books.

"You still have a month before your deadline hits, right?"

"Yeah," she sighs, lifting her cup to her lips. "It'll be close, but I'm confident I can finish in time."

"Anything I can do to help?"

"Unless you can make the voices in my head cooperate, there's nothing anyone can do." She takes another sip of her coffee before balancing the cup on her knee.

"I'm sure you'll whip them into shape in no time," I tell her. "How are you feeling this morning?"

My eyes are drawn to her hands as they tighten around her cup. Bringing up her nightmares isn't something I like to do, but I need to reassure myself that she's okay. I hate that she's still having them, and I hate even more that I can't make them go away. With all the power I have at my fingertips, not being able to help my wife makes me feel fucking powerless.

As a line forms between her brows, she answers quietly, her gaze drifting to the backyard. "What time are you leaving this morning?" she asks, changing the subject. It's nothing new for her to avoid talking about her nightmares. I always let her because I know how much they get to her. But I watch her eyes to make sure she's not concealing some emotion. For now, they appear clear.

Lifting my arm, I check my watch. "In about five minutes." Grabbing her chin, I turn her head so I have access to her lips.

After dropping a lingering kiss on them, I pull away. "Which means, I should get going now before I decide to blow off work today."

She laughs. "Okay."

I help her up from my lap, but before I grab my coffee cup, I drag her into my arms for a more heated kiss. Reluctantly, and with a deep groan, I retreat. My cock throbs beneath the fly of my slacks, making me wish I had an extra hour so I could carry Cat back to our bed and slide into the warm depths of her pussy.

Keeping her arms loosely wrapped around my shoulders, her fingers play with the hair on the back of my neck. She tips her head back to look at me. The sensual curve of her lips and the desire in her beautiful blue eyes do nothing to lessen my desire for her. "Behave, Mr. St. James, or *I'll* be the one keeping you from work."

My molars grind, and I will my wayward dick to behave.

"Yeah, yeah," I grumble, dropping my head for another brief kiss before letting her go.

She follows me to the kitchen, where I rinse then place my cup in the dishwasher. I grab my wallet, phone, and keys from the kitchen island.

"Don't forget we have dinner plans with my parents tonight," she reminds me. Depositing her cup on the counter, she walks me to the front door. "And don't forget to pick up wine on your way home."

"Yes, ma'am."

I turn to her with a grin once I'm at the door. Rolling to her toes, she gives me one last kiss before stepping back. "Love you."

"Love you back."

When the door closes behind me, I wait for the lock to click and the alarm to sound before making my way to my SUV. Every time I leave Cat at home, I listen for those two things. It's a habit I've developed over the years, and I don't intend to change it. Leaving her at home alone is already difficult. There's not a chance in hell I would without those precautions.

Before pulling out of the driveway, I dial Cat's parents' number on my phone, transferring the call to Bluetooth so I can talk while driving. Peggy, Cat's mom, answers on the third ring.

"Hello? Hunter? Is everything okay?"

Peggy always answers the same way, like she's expecting something to be wrong when I call.

"Everything's fine. I was just calling to make sure the house is ready for our visit this evening."

"Oh." Her sigh of relief comes over the car speakers. "Yes, honey, everything's ready."

"Great. We should be there by seven."

"Max, Emily, and Skylar will be here."

"They're driving down?"

"Yes," Peggy answers. "They won't be able to make it for Christmas this year, so they're making a trip down now."

Max is Cat's older brother and Emily is his wife. Skylar is their daughter. Ginger is Cat and Max's younger sister. She's married to Mason, and they have five-year-old twin boys, Aiden and Joshua. They live in a neighboring county, while Max lives in Montana with his family.

"Cat will be happy to see everyone. It's been too long since we've all been together."

"It'll be nice to have everyone in the same house. We haven't had that since last Christmas."

After switching on my blinker, I turn right onto the road that leads to Slate, the exclusive nightclub I own with my partner. We talk for a bit longer before we end our call.

After parking beside Silas's truck, I get out of my SUV and engage the locks with my key fob. Unlocking the back door to the building, I step inside, making sure to relock it. The keys jingle when I stuff them into my pocket as I walk down the hall to the private stairs that lead to the second floor. Seeing Silas's open door, I decide to check with him before going to my office.

Just inside the threshold, I stop. Silas, my business partner and best friend, has Katie, who looks after the girls at Slate, bent over his desk. The woman's skirt is hiked up around her waist and the black string of her thong is pulled to the side, digging into her ass cheek. Silas's pants sag beneath his ass as he pounds into her pussy, one hand holding her still while the other grasps her hair, pulling her head up so far that her back is bowed. With each powerful thrust, the massive desk they are against inches forward.

"God, yes, Silas. Right there," Katie moans, digging her nails into the hardwood.

Rather than quietly backing out of the room to give them privacy, I lean against the door frame. Not for the pleasure of the show, but because I'm here already. There is no point in leaving only to return when they're finished. Seeing Silas fuck a woman isn't something I haven't seen before, just as he has seen me take my fair share back in the day. Hell, we've even shared a few.

With grunts and squeals of pleasure filling the room, I pull out my phone to scroll through some emails.

A few minutes later, Katie lets out a loud cry, followed closely by Silas's deep growl. I repocket my phone and look up just as Silas tucks his cock back into his slacks and Katie shimmies her skirt back down. She glances at me briefly, her cheeks flushed, but not with embarrassment. Katie doesn't get embarrassed and she has not one shy bone in her body.

"Enjoy the show?" Silas asks. His question is for me, but his gaze is firmly fixed on Katie as she stands in front of a mirror, fixing her makeup and hair.

Once upon a time, I would have answered yes. It doesn't matter who you are. Watching a man rail a woman from behind would make the holiest of men pop a stiffy. Since I met Cat, the only thing I need is her. Now it's only mildly entertaining to watch other people have sex.

Standing against the doorframe, I lift my shoulder. "Not particularly."

Silas chuckles as he fixes the mess they made on his desk. "You used to be more fun," he remarks dryly.

That may be true for him, but I'm happy with my life and have plenty of fun with Cat.

"You get the email I sent over last night about the girls coming in for an interview?"

"Yes. Katie marked off a couple of them."

Katie turns away from the mirror and saunters over to Silas's desk, leaning a hip against the side. "I didn't like the look of a couple. They're shooting up."

We have a rule at Slate. We hire only *clean* employees. Physicals and drug tests are part of the hiring process. Drug tests are continued monthly, and if they're found to be using after being hired, they'll be terminated without notice. We don't accept second chances or excuses.

But if you stay clean, Slate takes damn good care of you.

Two stage girls came in high off their asses last week, and since drugs turn people into fucking morons, they turned on each other when they both wanted the same man's attention. Our girls aren't required to sleep with customers, but Slate has rooms in the back in case they want to earn extra money. We'd rather have them fuck customers here where we can make sure things stay consensual, instead of them taking men home or a back alley and run the risk of things turning sour.

Men taking something from a woman they don't want to give is something we don't tolerate, and is a sure way to end up on our bad side. And you don't want to end up there. Bad shit happens.

Katie continues, "The three remaining girls are coming in later today. Kurt's going to sit in on the interviews since neither of you can make it."

I nod. Kurt is our head bouncer and takes his job of protecting the girls very seriously. At seven feet and built like a bull, he could crush someone's skull without breaking a sweat. Silas and I trust him implicitly.

Katie walks up to Silas and curls her fingers into his shirt, pulling his tall frame down until his lips seal over hers. "If either of you need anything, I'll be downstairs," she says demurely, smoothing out the wrinkles in his dress shirt. "See you later, Hunter."

I tip my chin at her as she passes by me.

Turning my head, I see Silas watching Katie leave the room, lust still lingering. Once she's gone, his gaze moves to me. "You've got shit timing," he says, turning and walking around his desk to take a seat. "I wasn't nearly done with her."

I drop down in the seat in front of the desk, propping an ankle over the opposite knee and placing my laced hands over my stomach. "I'm sure you'll survive. Besides, my standing there wouldn't have stopped you from continuing."

Grunting, he opens one of the drawers in his desk and grabs something. He glances at the door before tossing a small black box on top.

My brows lift when I reach for it. The ring tucked into the black velvet bed sparkles when the light hits it. I close the box and set it on the desk. Silas grabs it and puts it back in the drawer.

"When do you plan to ask her?" I keep my voice low.

Leaning back in his chair, he steeples his fingers together and places his hands behind his head. "This weekend."

"Shit, I never thought I'd see the day that Silas Ward would tie himself to one woman."

"Fuck off," he mutters. "I still have to convince her to say yes."

"Is there any doubt she will?" I ask, arching a brow. "The woman's fucking mad about you."

Several years ago, we hired Katie as a stripper. The first few months were rocky between her and Silas. After she caught him railing a woman in his office the first time she met him, she immediately disliked him and thought he took advantage of our girls. He made it worse by continuing to fuck the girl while she watched, frozen in the doorway. Her assumption couldn't have been further from the truth. He may have been a man whore, but he did not touch our girls. The woman in question wasn't an employee, but a random club guest. It took months before Katie stopped looking at him like he was gum stuck to the bottom of her high-heeled shoes. As far as I know, he's kept his dick in his pants, except when Katie pulls it out to play with.

"Let's hope you're right, because if she says no, I may be charged with kidnapping."

The thing with Silas is, he's not joking. If Katie rejects his proposal, he'll damn sure hold her captive until she relents. Whenever it comes to the blonde bombshell, the man is fucking bonkers.

"Have you heard any word from Marcus?" I ask.

"Fuck no," he growls, his chair creaking as he abruptly sits forward. "Last I heard he was tracking Timothy in West Virginia."

Timothy used to be a member of Slate. He cornered Katie in the alley out back and attempted to rape her.

My teeth gnash together and the muscles in my jaw tense, tired of fucking waiting for the bastard to be brought in. As it is, the fucker has already continued to breathe past his expiration point. The longer that man lives, the harsher his death will be.

As much as I'd like to take a few licks, he's Silas's to do with as he likes. However, I'll be there to enjoy the show.

Since Katie was the one Timothy injured, she was given first dibs, but she refused, leaving the deed to Silas. While Katie has the stomach for it, she knows Timothy will suffer more under Silas's hand.

I head to my office, two doors down, and take a seat behind my desk. The doors of Slate were opened by Silas and me fourteen years ago, and since then, it has thrived. It's an exclusive club catering only to the rich and entitled. You have to be a member to walk in the doors, and to get a membership, you must submit to a full background check. Silas and I aren't dense. We know deals are made and cash is exchanged within these walls, but as long as we don't hear about it, it's not our business. If it does become our business, we deal with it appropriately. Or what we consider appropriate. Silas and I have built a reputation in River Heights. Don't fuck with our shit, and you keep your hands. If you do, you'll be lucky—depending on your transgression—to walk away with your life.

However, when it comes to harming a woman or a child, all bets are off. Your time is up and the reaper comes out to play.

As I recline back in my office chair, my eyes are drawn to the photo on my desk. Cat's smiling eyes shine back at me. She knows everything I've done and still do, but I keep her away from it. There's no part of my life she doesn't know about. Well, except for one. She's already been touched by the evil the world has to offer and it nearly destroyed us both.

Grief, rage, but mostly guilt tighten my gut when I think about what happened to her. What happened to our family. I usually push those thoughts away, but at times, I let them consume my mind.

I use those moments as self-punishment. They serve as a reminder of my failures. As a result, I use them to feed the rage building inside me to ensure that I never fail her again.

Chapter Three
Hunter

L ater that evening, I follow Cat into her parents' house. The door is barely closed before little patters of feet come running across the hardwood floor, and Cat's bombarded by two dark-haired boys.

"Aunt Cat!" they both screech before they launch themselves at her legs.

Laughing, Cat squats to give them both a hug. Their embraces are so forceful, she's pushed back until she lands on her ass.

"Wow!" Her eyes sparkle as she grins at her nephews. "You act like I haven't seen you in ages."

"But it feels like forever," Aiden, the more outspoken of the two, replies.

"Well, we'll have to make sure we see each other more often then, huh?"

Josh, who's always been quieter than his twin, nods his head with a shy smile.

After Cat kisses both boys on their cheeks, I chuckle and help her to her feet. Ginger stands just inside the living room doorway, smiling softly. Cat walks to her and they hug.

"What have you been feeding those boys? I swear they've grown half a foot since we last saw them," Cat remarks.

Ginger replies with an easy laugh. "They take after their father too much. They're already towering over all the other kids in kindergarten. I wouldn't be surprised if they're taller than me before they hit their teens."

"What am I being accused of now?" a deep voice asks seconds before Mason appears. He walks to Ginger and stops behind her with a hand on her waist.

She looks over her shoulder at him, her eyes glinting with laughter. "Just that our boys are going to be giants like you."

Considering Ginger's short stature, the giant comment is accurate. Mason towers over his petite wife by well over a foot.

"You know what they say about tall men, right?" He wiggles his brows.

Ginger gives him a disgruntled look while jabbing her elbow in his ribs. "Behave."

We all laugh and follow Ginger and Mason to the large open kitchen. Peggy and Emily are looking into one of the steaming pots on the stove. Jacob, Peggy's husband, and Max are sitting at the table playing what looks like Go Fish with Skylar.

Max spots us first and gets up from his seat, moving to Cat with a tender expression.

"Hey, sis." He pulls her into his arms for a tight hug.

Cat and her family have always been close. Max moved to Montana several years ago, so we don't see him as often as we used to. The last time was almost a year ago. His first wife died during childbirth. Skylar was a year old when Max hired Emily as a nanny. They danced around each other for two years, pretending they didn't care about each other. Emily became her stepmother four years ago. Emily and Skylar adore each other, and Max fiercely loves them both.

Cat moves to Skylar next and the little girl gets up from the table, already expecting the hug and cheek kiss she gets from her aunt.

Cat cups Skylar's cheeks and stares down at her. "Oh my, you are simply gorgeous."

Skylar blushes as her cheeks puff out with her grin. "Thanks, Aunt Cat."

After dropping a kiss on her forehead, she steps up to Emily next. I hold my hand out to Jacob, then do the same with Max.

"How long are you guys here for?" I ask Max.

"A week. Pretty sure anything less than that and Mom would have my hide."

"I heard that," Peggy calls over her shoulder.

"Wasn't trying to hide it," he retorts, his lips twitching.

As Cat helps Peggy, Emily, and Ginger finish dinner, I join the kids at the large table for a game of Go Fish. Aiden sits in the chair beside me, and I help him with his cards. Josh is by Jacob and he does the same.

With the exception of Max, Cat's family is clueless to the more sinister side of my life, which is the way I prefer it. Max only knows because he caught me beating the shit out of a guy when I was trying to get answers from him. Max knew who the guy was, what he did, and the answers I was looking for. He didn't say a word, and even watched with a blank expression, as the guy begged and pleaded for his life. A plea that was ignored.

My attention is drawn back to the room by peals of laughter and giggles. When I've lost all my cards, to the kids' delight, I glance over at Cat. She's leaning against the counter, facing the table, her gaze unfocused. Her furrowed brows and the lost look fill me with dread. This is because I know her thoughts are moving to places that lead to bad things.

Before I can get up from the table and go to her, her gaze moves to me and the look fades with her smile, like the disturbing expression was never there. As the knot in my chest loosens, I smile back. She turns to the stove, but I keep a watchful eye on her in case she has another moment like she did seconds ago.

Once the food is done and the cards are put away, dinner is set out on the table in the dining room. Despite the abundance of food, everyone attacks the dishes like they're starving and may miss out on something. Peggy is a damn good cook, a result of the many years she spent working at the restaurant she and Jacob owned before they retired.

Small talk is made as we all catch up on each other's lives. It's rare that we're all together like this anymore, so there's a lot to go over. Max, who owns a ranch with Emily, talks about the extra help he had to hire because the corn production did so well this year. Emily gives horseback riding lessons, and she talks about the foal that was born a few weeks ago. The kids are mesmerized by the pictures on her phone.

Skylar grins proudly as she tells everyone that her mother let her watch from outside the stall. "The foal came out with a lot of yucky stuff, but after she was cleaned, she was beautiful. She has a cute little star-shaped spot on her forehead. Mama said I could name her, and Daddy said she'll be my new pony."

"I wanna ride a horse, Mama," Aiden says, looking imploringly up at Ginger.

She ruffles the top of his head. "We'll see about it the next time we visit Uncle Max and Aunt Emily."

His grin takes up his whole face.

"Mama, I need to go to the restroom," Skylar says, tugging on her mother's shirt sleeve.

"Go ahead, sweetie. Just make sure you wash your hands afterward."

Hopping from her chair, she takes off down the hallway.

"So, Cat," Ginger says, drawing everyone's attention. "When can I expect to get my hands on your next book?" She rubs her palms together, a gleeful expression filling her face.

Cat laughs. "It's going to be a while. It's not due to my agent for another month, and it's usually nine months or more after that before it releases."

Ginger gives her a sly look. "You could always give me what you have so far, and I could be a beta reader, or whatever it's called."

Cat's eyes shine with mirth. "Nice try, but you know I don't let anyone read my manuscripts before they're finished. But you'll be the first to get it before I send it to Darren. Well, the second." Her eyes slide to me, and I toss her a wink.

I'm proud to call myself Cat's number one fan. Ginger is a close second. We're both proud as fuck of Cat's accomplishments and success in her career. Her whole family is.

Ginger wrinkles her nose in disappointment. "Fine. I suppose I can wait until then."

Cat never lets anyone near her manuscript while she's writing. She much prefers to finish the story before anyone reads it.

"Hey, Mama, who are these kids?"

Everyone at the table turns quiet, and we jerk our gazes at Skylar as she walks back into the room. Her eyes are fixed on the framed picture she holds in her hand. My stomach drops just as everyone in the room, except for Cat, stiffens. All of us know what that picture represents, and we know what it might do to Cat.

Skylar, unaware of the turmoil her innocent act could cause, wedges herself between Emily and Cat's chair and holds the frame up for her mother to see. Unfortunately, it's at an angle where Cat can see it too.

Watching Cat's expression, I tense, prepared to intervene if necessary. Leaning closer, she seems unfazed by the image, but that could change at any moment.

Emily looks at the picture then quickly darts her gaze around the room to each person before she takes it from Skylar. Taking care not to alert Cat, she looks at her daughter while turning the frame away from her.

"Where did you get this?"

"The closet in the hallway."

Emily's voice is gentle. "You know you're not supposed to go through people's things."

Worry creases Skylar's forehead. "I didn't, Mama, I swear. I dropped my ring," she holds up her hand, showing off the pink plastic ring on her finger, "and it slid under the door. When I opened it to grab it, I saw the picture."

"Can I see it, Emily?" Cat asks, her voice low and filled with something that sends a ball of lead to my stomach.

Such an innocent question about something that should be a harmless act. One eight-by-ten image set in an elegant metal frame. The people in the image are just as innocent and so very precious. They should never be hidden away, but for now, it's for the best.

Before I can come up with an excuse to keep the picture out of Cat's hands, Peggy lets out a loud gasp and jumps from her chair. The front of her white blouse is soaked with tea.

"Well, shoot," she grumbles as she pulls her shirt away from her chest. "I'm so clumsy." She lifts her gaze to Cat. "Can you help me, honey? I don't want this to stain, and I know you have that special recipe you use. I can never get it right."

"Sure, Mom."

Cat tosses her napkin on the table and stands, unaware her mother just played the situation to distract her from the picture. She only got away with it because Cat allowed it. Or rather, her subconscious did.

My eyes meet Peggy's before she leaves the room, silently thanking her for her quick thinking.

As soon as they leave the room, Emily hands me the picture with an apologetic look, and I get up from the table. As a rule, I don't invade people's privacy—their bedrooms are theirs alone—but I do go into Jacob and Peggy's room and straight to their closets. There are a few more picture frames on a shelf at the top. Looking at the picture in my hand, I let my eyes linger on the two children. A beautiful young girl, not quite a teenager, with curly brown hair, is sitting in a wicker chair holding a toddler. She has her head down so her cheek is pressed against her little brother's. Both of them are smiling into the camera, their eyes filled with joy.

My throat tightens and the ache in my chest that never goes away, doubles in pain. Lifting the picture, I bring it to my lips and kiss it before placing it on top of the others.

THE RIDE BACK TO THE HOUSE IS QUIET. TOO QUIET. IT makes me worry. With a sideways glance, I see Cat staring out the passenger window. I don't know where her thoughts are, and not knowing is making me twitchy.

When they returned to the table after taking care of Peggy's shirt, she acted as if nothing had happened. Maybe I was wrong though. Perhaps that's why she looks so pensive.

Reaching over the console, I lace my fingers through hers.

"Hey," I call, grabbing her attention from the window. "You okay?"

From the streetlights we drive past, I see the small smile that curls her lips. "I'm fine. Just a little tired, and I feel a headache coming on."

"How about you take a pain pill while I draw you a bath when we get home?"

I take my eyes off the road long enough to see her shifting in her seat so she's facing me more.

"That sounds heavenly."

I bring the back of her hand to my lips. "Done."

Some of the stiffness in my shoulders loosens as I continue to navigate the streets. Over the years, I've perfected reading Cat's emotions pretty well, and I don't get the sense from her that she's not feeling more than what she claims.

But something tells me I'm wrong.

Chapter Four
Hunter

The tall, white double doors loom before me as I walk up the wide stairs leading to the front porch that wraps around to the sides. The building is old, dating back to the mid-eighteen hundreds, and the owners have done well with keeping the Victorian feel over the years. A wooden sign with bold script that reads The Grove is to the right of the doors.

Up until a few years ago, the place was run down. The staff who watched over the patients residing here, save for a few good apples, took advantage of the people who depended on them in disgusting ways. The Grove is now considered the top private psychiatric facility in the state and only houses ten or so carefully selected patients.

Pulling one of the doors open, I walk inside and go straight for the receptionist's desk. An older woman sits behind a computer, and the moment she sees me, she offers a friendly smile.

"Good morning, Mr. St. James. How are you today?"

"I'm fine, Katherine." I shove my hands into my slacks pockets. "And yourself?"

"Nothing to complain about so far." Using the mouse, she clicks something on the computer screen before getting up from her seat. "I'll take you back. She's been waiting for you."

"How is she today?"

She pauses, her head swiveling around to give me a look I know well. "She seems more gloomy than usual, but I'm sure that'll change once she sees you."

With my silent nod, she turns and leads me down a wide hallway toward the back of the facility. The house is over ten-thousand square feet, has twenty bedrooms—only half being used—and sits on twenty acres of land. A third of those acres are wooded. Back in the day, the place was an inn that catered to weary travelers.

When we reach a large room, which has been converted into a recreation area, my eyes are drawn to the woman I'm here to see. She's sitting at the same small, round table she always chooses when she's in this particular room. Her head is bent, the thick mass of dark hair a mess and tangled around her face. A deep look of concentration is pulling her features down as she slowly traces the design on the tabletop.

Just as it always does, a dull ache forms behind my sternum as I gaze at the thick bandages wrapped around her wrists.

I barely noticed Katherine's announcement that she'll be back in a short while to check on us. I pull out the chair across from the woman and take a seat. She still hasn't lifted her head or acknowledged my presence.

"Athena."

It's not until I softly call her name that she lifts her head. A moment passes before recognition dawns. Slowly, her dull, despondent expression gives way to a charming smile.

"Hunter," she breathes, a brilliant light shining in her eyes.

Reaching across the table, I gently take one of her cold hands. Her hands are always icy cold, no matter how warm it is. "How are you this morning, honey?"

Her eyes drop to our clasped hands as she lifts a slender shoulder. "I'm okay, I guess." Her voice is soft and lyrical.

"You want to tell me what you were thinking about just now?" I ask, slowly rubbing my thumb on the back of her hand just as she likes. "You seemed pretty deep in thought."

"It was nothing." She raises her eyes to me. "Just thinking about what's for dinner tonight."

Deflection. That's what Athena does. If she doesn't want to answer a question, there's no forcing her to. I learned the hard way not to repeat questions she doesn't want to answer. The one time I did, it ended with Athena being restrained and injected with a sedative. I never want to see that hysterical look on her face again. The pain of it brought me to my knees as I helplessly watched the staff try to calm her.

"What did you have for breakfast?" I ask, trying to maintain a calm voice despite the turmoil raging inside of me.

"Eggs and bacon with blueberry pancakes."

"That sounds good," I remark.

I stop stroking the back of her hand for a split second, and her expression tightens. I immediately restart the soft movement and her features once again relax.

Athena loves it when I touch her hand. I'm not sure why, but any time I visit her, she wants me to hold her hand. I've spoken with her doctor about it, and he believes the gentle way I touch her is comforting. It doesn't bother me. Anything to bring her peace, I'm willing to do.

Keeping her gaze steady on me, she props her chin in her palm with her elbow on the table. Again, my eyes are drawn to the stark-white bandage before returning to hers. I want to ask her about the bandages, but again, that's a no-go subject.

"How long can you stay?" she asks out of the blue.

I give her an easy smile. "For as long as you want me here."

"Would you stay forever if I asked you to?"

Unconsciously, my smile slips a bit. "Is that what you want? Do you want to stay here forever?"

I've been coming here to see Athena for years. My first encounter with her was by accident. I was here to see Dr. Armani when I spotted Athena being led into one of the patient rooms. Before she and the nurse could step through the doorway, her head lifted and our eyes met. A strange connection formed between us that day. She became agitated when the nurse tried to get her to enter the room, so I approached the pair. I sat with her for an hour that day, and I've been visiting her ever since. Other than me, she doesn't have any other visitors.

"I don't know." Sadness creeps across Athena's face, and her eyes drift from me to stare blankly across the room. "I think I deserve to stay here forever."

I squeeze her fingers to bring her eyes back to me. They look desolate when they do.

"Why do you think you deserve to be here, Athena?" I ask, keeping my voice low and even despite my growing disquiet.

Her tongue comes out to run across her lips. "Because I did something horrible," she whispers, as if she's ashamed.

It takes everything in me to not yank the woman into my arms and demand she wipe those thoughts from her head. It's only the reaction I know I would get that keeps me in my seat. While she loves it when I hold her hand and gently rub the back with my thumb, that's the only touch she'll allow. Anything more, she'll turn distraught. Not because she abhors my touch, but because she feels like she doesn't deserve it.

"What happened was not your fault," I tell her sternly.

Angry heat flashes in her eyes, and for a moment, I think she's about to pull her hand away, but she doesn't. Instead, her fingers wrap tighter around my palm, as if my touch is the only thing keeping her sane and grounded. Like if the connection was broken, she would fall to so many pieces there would be no hope of putting her back together.

"It *was* my fault," she replies vehemently.

"Athena—"

"No!" she yells, jumping to her feet, this time dislodging our connection. She bends at the waist, her hands gripping her wild hair, tugging the strands, and her expression contorts into pain. "It was my fault!" She hits her chest with a closed fist. "Mine!"

Slowly, I get up as an orderly and a nurse watch our exchange, preparing to intervene if necessary. I try my best to calm Athena down. The last thing I want is for her to be drugged out of her mind.

"Athena, sweetie—"

Again, I'm cut off, but at least she's not screaming anymore. Some of the ire and pain in her expression has faded when she looks at me coolly.

"I want you to leave."

A small crack forms in my heart with her emotionless demand. I don't want to leave her like this, but I know if I stay, there's a chance I could make it worse.

I stare at her. Her arms are crossed tightly over her chest and her back is ramrod straight. Athena is done. She's closed herself off from me.

This happens every time I try to tell her that what happened to cause her to be in this place wasn't her fault. I know she wants to believe it, I see the desperation in her eyes, but a dark place inside her won't allow her to.

I stuff my hands into my pockets to keep myself from reaching out to her. "If that's what you want."

Her nod is stiff. "It is."

Swallowing past the thick knot in my throat, I tell her the same thing I tell her every time before I leave, no matter if I leave on a good note or a bad one. "I'll be back next time."

I'm not sure if she realizes the flash of relief she reveals on her face, but I hang on to that look with desperate hope.

Gritting my teeth, I turn and walk away. The nurse and orderly I pass, two faces I've seen hundreds of times, as well as many others, give me sympathetic looks. I don't acknowledge them. I don't acknowledge anyone as I leave. All of my focus is on keeping my feet moving forward. Because if I don't, I'll never have the strength to walk out the door.

When I step outside, the sky is gray and dreary, matching my somber mood. I keep my head down as I trek across the gravel parking lot to my SUV. Once I climb inside, I grip the steering wheel, my eyes automatically going back to the building where I just left part of my heart.

Guilt churns in my stomach.

Guilt for leaving Athena.

Guilt for what I'm doing to Cat by being here.

For as long as I've been making these visits, I've never told Cat. She wouldn't understand my need to be near Athena. She wouldn't understand the feelings I've developed for the woman. I love Cat with everything inside me, but Athena has a part of me too.

Athena doesn't know about Cat either. I've kept both women a secret from each other. It's better this way.

Because I know in my heart that if one knows about the other, I very well may lose them both.

Chapter Five
Caterina

Carrying a laundry basket full of clean clothes upstairs, I walk past the two closed doors on either side of the hallway and go into Hunter's and my room. I set the basket on the bed and grab Hunter's socks and boxer briefs and take them to the dresser to put away.

As I pull out a stack of t-shirts from the basket, my eyes land on the framed picture on Hunter's nightstand. A smile curls my lips as I walk around and pick it up.

Sitting on our bed, I stare at one of my favorite pictures of Hunter and me. It was taken a few years ago when we went to Montana for Max and Emily's wedding. The ceremony was held outside on Max's ranch. With my hair swept up, I wore a lavender satin gown that showed off my shoulders. Hunter looked devilishly handsome in his black tux. The look on his face as he dipped me backward during our dance will forever be one of my favorites. Anyone looking at him would see the absolute devotion in his eyes as he gazed down at me. My own expression was full of every ounce of love I have for the man holding me. Mom took the picture, and she couldn't have captured it at a more perfect moment.

I thank God every day for my best friend, Megan, because she's the reason Hunter and I met. We were both in our third year of college and had just finished finals. After stressing over classes for a week, I wanted to sleep for days, but Megan dragged me out of the house to celebrate. A friend of ours had a membership with Slate and managed to get us inside. We had been to the club once before and we liked the atmosphere.

We danced, we laughed, we drank, and even met a couple of guys who were charming. Or, we thought they were. It wasn't until I left Megan on the dance floor to grab a drink that the guy who had attached himself to me handed me a glass. Before I could take the first sip, the drink was ripped from my hands and the guy flew backward. He landed on his ass with blood gushing from his broken nose. Seconds later, he was hauled up by the back of his shirt by another man with huge, beefy arms, and he and his friend were tossed out of Slate.

Dazed and stunned by what had happened, I turned to the man who caused the ruckus, prepared to give him hell. I'll never forget that moment. He wore black slacks and a black button-up dress shirt with the sleeves rolled up to his elbows. His dark hair, long enough on top to run your fingers through, was a bit messy. His face was shaved, but a hint of stubble was starting to form. It was his eyes that left me speechless. Even in the dim light of the club, they held me captive. They were a beautiful green that reminded me of fresh-mown grass.

"Don't ever take a drink from someone you aren't well acquainted with."

It took me a moment to process his words and recognize his

anger. I had to blink the haze of his good looks away before I could respond.

"Excuse me?"

"That bastard slipped something in the glass you were about to down," he explained. "Had I not been watching, you'd be out in the alley right now with your back scratched to hell while he fucked you, and you'd have no clue what happened tomorrow."

"You were watching me?"

Yes, *that's* what I asked. My first concern and thought was that this man, with ungodly looks, was watching me. Not that I was nearly drugged and more than likely would have been raped.

It wasn't until later that night, after Megan and I were home, and I told her what had happened, that I realized the dangerous situation I managed to dodge. And only because Hunter had been watching me. In fact, he noticed me the first time Megan and I were at Slate, and even told his bouncers if I showed up again to let him know.

That was the beginning of Hunter and me. He stole my heart that night and he never gave it back. A year later, we were married.

With that memory in mind, I gently set the picture back on his nightstand and continue putting the clothes away.

A couple of hours later, with the laundry done, the dishes put away, and only a thousand more words written on my manuscript —thank you writer's block—I'm sliding out homemade biscuits from the oven.

I've just put the pan on the stovetop when I feel strong arms wrap around my middle and a hard chest presses against my back. I smile as sandalwood invades my senses.

"Mmm... my favorite," Hunter mumbles with his face buried in the crook of my neck.

I tip my head to the side and grin. "That's why I make them. Because I know you love them so much."

"Not the biscuits," he responds huskily before he sucks my sensitive skin into his mouth.

A giggle escapes, and I press my ass into his groin. My hands curl into fists against the counter as a pulse begins in my clit.

He slips his hands beneath my shirt and trails them up my stomach, stopping just below my breasts. His lips release the suction on my neck and move to my ear.

"How is it possible, Mrs. St. James, that I've had you damn near every day for nearly two decades, and I can't seem to ever get enough?" he whispers.

My breath becomes choppy. "I don't know," I pant. "But please don't ever get enough."

"Never," he growls in that sexy voice that always sends a tingle between my legs.

One of his hands continues its trek until he's cupping my breast over my bra, while his other hand moves south. My breath catches in anticipation, and I moan when his fingers slip beneath the waistband of my leggings. His fingers tickle the spot just above my clit. So close, but not close enough.

"Please, Hunter," I whimper, shifting my legs apart to get his fingers where I want them.

"What do you need?" His voice is guttural, like he's struggling for control.

"Touch me. Please touch me."

"Where?"

My nails dig into my palms, and I lift to my toes, becoming desperate, as I seek out his touch.

"You know where," I moan.

"Yeah, baby, I do." He licks a path up to my ear while he tweaks one of my nipples between his fingers. "But I want to hear you say it."

"My pussy." My face heats and moisture leaks from me. He loves hearing me say dirty words, even if it does embarrass me.

The words barely escape my lips before Hunter lets out a low growl and flicks his fingers wickedly over my clit. I cry out, instant pleasure making the sound hoarse. Sparks shoot from my clit and crawl through my limbs.

"Yes!" I hiss. "There. Oh God, please don't stop."

He does stop, but only to move his fingers further down to my drenched hole. While he hooks two fingers inside, he grinds the heel of his palm against my clit. I buck against his fingers, and his hips follow my movement, grinding his hardness against my ass.

"You're soaked," he groans. "Always so wet for me."

As he continues to send my body into a frenzy, I toss my head back against his shoulder, my mouth falling open on a silent moan. My orgasm builds, tightening the muscles in my legs and my lower stomach.

I'm seconds away from reaching my peak when his hands leave me. A protest falls from my lips, and I'm about to turn around and demand he continue, but then my leggings are being yanked down. Hunter steps on the crotch of them.

"Pull your foot out," he grunts, his hands now gripping my waist.

I only get one foot out before I'm spun around. The lustful look in his eyes has my desire ramping up.

Grabbing my hips, he spins us both so my back is to the island. Then I'm hoisted up until my bare ass is resting on the counter. He yanks me to the edge with one arm, grabs a handful of my hair, and smashes his lips against mine. My legs lock around his waist, and the denim of his jeans rubs deliciously against my aching center.

Our tongues slash together, his groan and my moan filling the room. Grabbing his T-shirt, I quickly pull the material up and our lips separate just long enough for him to pull it over his head. My nails score the rock-hard plains of his chest.

When his hands move between our bodies, I loosen my legs so he can unsnap his jeans.

I yank my lips from his when the head of his cock touches my wet pussy. Our gaze locks as he slowly slides inside.

"So goddamn tight; you take my breath away," he breathes out roughly, never moving his eyes from mine.

"Take me, Hunter," I rasp. "Remind me I'm yours."

The muscles in his jaw twitch and the lust in his eyes flares. Pulling out slowly, he returns just as leisurely.

What was once a mad dash to get him inside me as soon as possible has turned into something sweet and unhurried.

"Don't ever doubt you're mine, Cat. You'll always be mine."

Locking my ankles together, I dig my heels into his ass, begging him with the movement to go deeper. With his cock buried inside my snug heat, his slow thrusts stop. He grinds his pubic bone against my clit, and I let out a whimper.

"And you're mine. Only mine," I whisper against his lips.

A hissed breath pushes past his lips and he growls, "Yes. Only yours. Always."

"Always."

His movements become more frantic, his pelvis slamming against mine. Each thrust forward has him hitting my clit, sending me higher and higher. Our bodies slap together and my cries get louder, his grunts grow deeper. A bead of sweat slides down the side of his face and drips between our bodies.

Within minutes, after hitting a particularly sensitive spot inside me, the walls of my pussy clamp down on Hunter. Spasms ravage my body as sparks of white light drift through my closed eyes.

"Give me your eyes, Cat." I give Hunter what he wants. "That's it, baby," he whispers.

I hold his gaze through my orgasm, loving the intensity in his eyes as he watches me.

Just as my release begins to fade, Hunter's thrusts pick up speed and he finds his own. Buried to the hilt inside me, he grinds his pelvis against mine, knowing the added stimulation mixed with my lingering orgasm will bring on another.

Hunter rests his sweaty forehead against mine, and we stay like that for several long moments as we catch our breath. His hands run up and down my thighs, the rough texture of the calluses on his palms abrading my skin.

"I guess you had a good day at work," I remark, a smile on my lips as I press them against Hunter's.

The corner of his mouth quirks up, his eyes drifting down between our bodies as he slowly slides out of me. "Something like that."

I stay on the counter where I know Hunter wants me. I watch him grab a rag from the cabinet and wet it with warm water at the sink. He brings it to me, and I lean back on my hands, my legs spread, as he runs it over my swollen pussy. This is another thing Hunter likes to do. I asked him once why he always cleans me afterward and he said it's his job as my husband. From the look of contented concentration on his face, he not only feels it's his duty, but it's one he enjoys immensely.

"I love you," I whisper softly.

He looks up at me, his lips curving into the smile I adore. He throws the rag into the sink behind him and wraps his arms around my waist. Mine go around his neck.

"I love you too, baby," he replies just as softly.

Chapter Six
Hunter

The floorboards creak when I step up to the last window downstairs. I check the lock needlessly, since I already know it's securely latched, just like it is every night. I move to the front door and once again, make sure the alarm is set. For years, this has been my nightly routine. Not only for Cat's peace of mind, but for mine as well.

I take the stairs two at a time to the second floor. As I pass the first closed door, my steps slow, and I run my knuckles across the wood. I do the same to the door across the hall from it.

Cat's already in bed, leaning against a pile of pillows, the blanket pulled to her waist, her eyes on me. Like she's been waiting for me. She watches as I turn off the light and stride across the room to the bed.

"Did you check the windows?" she asks as I place my gun on the nightstand. I'm never without my gun. It's an extension of myself. It's what separates Cat from anyone who may want to harm her.

I've lost count of how many people I've killed over the years. I don't take the lives of innocents. Only people who I consider unworthy of their living status. Consequently, because of that, I've made plenty of enemies. Sometimes those enemies grow bigger balls than what they're capable of carrying and think they can take or harm what belongs to me.

There's only been once they've succeeded, and I'll kill every motherfucker walking the earth before I let it happen again.

"Yeah, baby, I did," I tell Cat.

"Even the one above the sink?"

I get into bed, pulling the covers over my waist. Cat moves to my side, wrapping her arm around my torso, and laying her head on my chest. I pull her closer, needing my girl as close to me as possible.

I kiss the top of her head. "You know I checked it."

"Okay," is her quiet reply.

Cat tucks her face deeper into my chest and tosses one leg over mine. I pick up her hand and bring the inside of her palm to my lips. I get a kiss on my chest in return.

"Love you, Hunter."

I've heard those words thousands of times, but they never cease to amaze me how I got so lucky to have found a woman like my Caterina. She's special in so many ways, and is the strongest woman I've ever known. My life would be a blank void if I didn't have her, and I thank God every day that I do.

"I love you too, baby," I reply roughly.

Cat's the only person who can bring out the softer side of me. Before I met her, I didn't have a soft side.

Both of my parents died when I was two. After they passed, I was tossed around from one foster home to another. At thirteen years old, I left the last foster home behind and moved my ass to the streets. I could take care of myself a fuck of a lot better and was happier as a homeless kid than I ever was living under some sick fuck's roof.

During the next several years, I stole, fought, and slept behind the same dumpsters I dug in for food. I ran drugs for a couple of different thugs and beat the hell out of those who thought they could fuck those same thugs over. I was scrappy and learned early on how to fight and stand up for myself. Because on the streets, if you didn't, you'd end up someone's bitch or in a body bag.

Nine months shy of turning eighteen, Thomas Myers found me breaking into his car and took me home to his wife, Sandra. Thomas gave me a choice. I could either stay with them until I reached legal age or he would report me to the cops for attempted burglary. I chose option A, which left me in a warm bed at night and food in my belly. However, I remained wary of the couple.

I don't know why Thomas invited me into his house where I was around his wife. The only thing he knew about me was that I lived on the streets and was a thief. No matter how cautious I was around them or how withdrawn I was, Thomas and Sandra never let it bother them.

By the time I turned eighteen, my guard around them had slipped. While I didn't fully trust them, I wasn't as worried about their ulterior motives.

A week after my birthday and the night before I decided it was time for me to leave, Thomas and Sandra pulled me into Thomas's office. They had a secret. A fucking huge secret. It wasn't a coincidence that brought me into their lives. Apparently, they knew my parents. Not only did they know them, but they were very close friends. However, that wasn't the biggest shocker. My parents had left me an inheritance, which equaled more money than I could ever spend in a lifetime. A week after they delivered that news, they were both killed in a car accident.

I went from being a homeless street rat with nothing to his name, to having a bank account fatter than most. The money was only accessible if I went to college or when I reached twenty-one. Although I had no desire to further my education, I got my GED, and my ass went to college.

During our sophomore year, Silas and I began planning Slate and opened its doors three years later. As a kid on the streets, I built a reputation for being harsh and merciless. I took what I needed, stayed out of others' business, and brutally protected what was mine. As long as you didn't fuck with my shit and didn't prey on the innocent, we'd have no problems. My reputation remained intact and strengthened once we opened Slate.

Cat shifting against me pulls me out of the past and back to the present. A contented sigh escapes her lips as she tucks her face into the crook of my neck. I tilt my head down and breathe in the vanilla and rose scent of her hair.

My life began the day I met Cat. Not only that, but she saved me from heading down a dark path I'm not sure I would have found my way back from.

I IMMEDIATELY WAKE UP WHEN I HEAR A LOW WHIMPER. My instincts know exactly what it is before I open my eyes. Cat's captured in one of her nightmares. Her sweat-drenched body is still draped over mine, her small hand balled into a fist on my chest. The look of pain on her face tears a jagged hole in my chest.

Usually, Cat wakes up as soon as the nightmares begin, but sometimes she gets trapped in them.

Rolling to my side, I slowly move my hand up and down her

stiff back. My other hand slides through her hair and cups her cheek, lifting her head so I can see her face better.

"Cat," I call softly.

Her eyes stay closed and her face pinches in more pain.

"Cat, baby, wake up," I plead in a guttural tone. I press my lips against hers when I don't get a response. "Caterina, please, baby."

I fucking hate these nightmares. I feel so goddamn helpless when she has them. There's nothing I can do to stop them. My only consolation is that when she wakes up, she only remembers the screams. If she remembered more, I'm not sure her mind would be able to handle it.

I become desperate when Cat stays lost in her nightmare. Just as I'm about to shake her, her eyes snap open. They instantly lock on mine, tears filling them to the brim and spilling over.

It's times like these when I feel like I've failed as a husband. A husband should be able to protect his wife from the horrors of life. He should be able to take away the pain and absorb it himself.

"Do you remember anything?" I ask.

I always ask this question, then hold my breath as I wait for her answer. A part of me wants her answer to be different from what it usually is. That she remembers the nightmares. Maybe if she did, she could work on moving past them. Yet another part of me fears losing Cat forever if she ever remembers the night we lost everything.

More tears fall from her eyes, and I swipe them away with my thumb.

"Only the screams. Oh God, Hunter, they were horrible." She hiccups.

Gathering her in my arms, she turns her head to the side

when I pull her closer. Her cheek, wet from her tears, presses against my sternum, and her arms lock around me.

"I'm so sorry," I croak through a tight throat. "So fucking sorry."

It takes a long time for Cat's breathing to even out and her body to relax. There's no way in hell I'll be able to sleep again, so I don't even try.

I simply lay there, holding the love of my life, and damning myself for not being strong enough to take away her pain.

Chapter Seven
Hunter

The slick sound of the knife sliding out of flesh and howls of pain mix with the tone of an incoming text. Dropping the knife on the table beside me, I whip out my phone and turn away from a crying, pale-faced Lenny.

The pulse in my temple throbs when I see the message.

After sending a reply, I shove the slim device into my pocket and turn back to Lenny. "Looks like it's your lucky day, my friend," I comment, observing the sniveling piece of shit.

Lenny's one of River Heights's newest drug dealers who's trying to make a name for himself. So far, he's kept his business out of Slate, but I doubt that'll last long. It's rumored he's dabbling in prostitution. Except the women he's been recruiting haven't been willing participants. Lenny also has connections, or rather the people he knows do. And those connections could include names.

As I stare at the man, I curl my lip in disgust. Streams of snot run from his nose and into his mouth, only to flow back out in a slobbering mess. His face is drained of color, probably from the copious amount of blood on the floor below him, and there's more skin covered in slash marks than there's not.

Naked except for a pair of tighty whities that aren't so white anymore and hanging from the ceiling from a rope wrapped around his wrists, Lenny looks pretty fucking pathetic, which is just the way I like him.

Correction, I'll like him even more when the pigs at the farm outside of town start chomping on his remains. Anything they don't eat, gets soaked in lye until it dissolves.

Lenny lifts his head, or rather he tries to, and looks at me with dull, bloodshot eyes. "Please, man," he whines. "I got nothin' else to give you."

I pick up a rusty flathead screwdriver and scrape it along one of the many open wounds on his stomach. "That's where you're wrong, Lenny boy. You still have plenty to give. You're still breathing, right? And I don't have the name I seek."

Before he can protest further, I stop at one of the cuts and slowly push the flathead between two ribs. Lenny thrashes and screams, trying to get away from the bite of pain, but with only the tips of his toes barely grazing the floor, he has no traction. He only manages to wiggle the tool around, making it worse.

"Regardless," I look into his shit-brown sunken eyes, "you just got a temporary reprieve. Not to worry though, I'll be back to pick up where we left off." I twist the flathead and dig it in deeper, angling it just right so I don't puncture a vital organ. I can't have Lenny dying before I get what I want. "And when I do return, I expect you to sing the fucking name I want."

I leave Lenny hanging limply by his arms, whimpers filling the room and the tool still lodged between two ribs. Kurt's standing just outside the steel door when I walk through it.

"Make sure he doesn't die," I tell him.

"You got it," the big man replies.

Not only is he Slate's head bouncer, but as an ex-Army combat medic, he knows how to patch Lenny up enough to keep him breathing.

I take the stairs from the basement of Slate to the main floor. I stop by the employee bathroom to scrub my hands before I go out the back door where my SUV is parked. Impatient to get to where I'm going, I break all kinds of traffic laws as I speed through town.

By the time I pull up to the two-story house, the sun has already set and the shadows have come out to play. I'm usually getting home around this time, so I text Cat to let her know I'll be a couple more hours.

I find the key I want, and unlock the door. The eerie silence that greets me when I push the door open would send many people scurrying away, but it only adds fuel to the fire slowly simmering inside me. The absence of any sound and the lack of light come as no surprise, since the person who lives here prefers to be in the dark anyway.

After taking off my wedding band, I drop it along with my keys and wallet on the small table beside the door. Passing the stairs leading to the second floor, I go to the kitchen. Once there, I head straight for the cabinet where the liquor is stashed and pour myself three fingers of whiskey. Tossing it back, I pour another. Twice more, I fill the glass.

As I stare out the window above the sink, I allow the effects of the alcohol to relax my tense muscles and wash away the guilt I feel.

Unclenching my hand from around the glass, I rinse it out and put it and the bottle back in the cabinet. My eyes adjust to the darkness as I ascend the stairs and walk down the dark hallway. It wouldn't matter if it was pitch black and I couldn't see anything. I could navigate the house with my eyes closed.

The closer I get to the last room at the end of the hall, the faster my blood pumps. The door is wide open when I approach, and only the moonlight shines inside the room. Across the room, fifteen feet away, is a big king-size bed, and on it is Scarlett.

My cock hardens and rubs against the seam of my slacks as I take in the woman. She wears a black lace bra that barely covers her cherry nipples and a scrap of material that hides the small patch of hair over her pussy and slides between the globes of her plump ass. Her long, raven hair with red streaks throughout falls over her shoulders and back.

She sits on the center of the mattress on her knees, her ass against her heels. Her chest juts out, her back ramrod straight, and her shoulders are squared. Her head is tilted down, her gaze on the bed before her, and her hands are palms down on her thighs. Two of her fingers, the right ring finger and the left thumb, carry silver rings. On her wrists are several wide, black leather bands. Her knees are spread about a foot apart, and if I were closer, I'd see dampness glistening on her thighs.

She is, without a doubt, a vision that would bring any man to his knees, and that includes me.

I take a couple of steps into the room and start working the buttons of my shirt through the narrow holes, before tossing the material away. My undershirt is next to come off. My hands move to the snap on my pants, but I only undo the button, leaving the zipper alone.

Scarlett doesn't move an inch, not even a hitch of breath or a flutter of her eyelashes, giving no indication that she knows I'm in the room. But she does. She always knows when I'm near.

I turn on the small lamp on the nightstand before walking to the end of the bed. I take a long moment to simply stare at her, my eyes roaming over every inch of flesh exposed.

"Come closer, Scarlett," I command.

"Yes, Sir."

My cock jerks at the sweet cadence of her voice.

Rising to her knees, she slowly shuffles forward until she's only an inch away from me, then drops her ass back to her heels. My head fills with the aroma of her intoxicating natural scent.

Her face is still bent down, blocking my view of her, which I don't like.

Wrapping my fingers around her delicate throat, I tilt her head back with my thumb. The pulse beneath my hand flutters wildly. Beautiful eyes, lined with black eyeliner and lashes thickened with mascara, stare up at me.

"You know the rules, Scarlett. Your eyes remain on me." I flex my fingers, tightening them fractionally. Her face turns a light shade of red. "You don't ever hide them from me."

Her gaze flickers with fear as she runs her tongue over her lips, but something else lies behind it. Something dark and needy. Something sinister and twisted. Something Scarlett searches for and only I can give her.

"Sorry, Sir," she whispers. "It won't happen again."

Yes, it will. Like every time I come to her, she will continue to hide her face until I demand otherwise. It's one of my rules, and she always breaks it because she loves being punished.

"Make sure you don't," I grunt, "or your punishment will be swift and not pleasant."

Again, her eyes are filled with dark anticipation. Seeing the expression has my cock jerking.

Using my hand around her neck, I pull her face closer, then drop my mouth to hers for a rough, brutal kiss. My lips slam against hers so hard I taste the coppery tang of blood seconds later. She doesn't mind. In fact, she moans and presses closer.

Yanking my mouth away from hers, I glare down at her.

"Take my cock out. I want it in your throat," I growl.

She immediately complies, reaching for the zipper before the words fully leave my lips. She's careful as she slides the metal tab down. My cock springs free, slapping against her hands, and she pushes my pants over my ass just enough so my balls hang out.

I watch as she tries to wrap her small hand around my shaft. I'm too big for her fingers to touch.

"I didn't say use your hands, Scarlett. What did I tell you?"

Lifting her head, she peeks at me through her thick lashes. "My throat," she answers, a quiver in her voice.

"Then give me your fucking throat," I hiss between my teeth, unable to conceal my anger or the unequivocal need in my tone. "And keep your hands on the bed."

My cock, already so hard I could hammer fucking nails, is angled upward, so she doesn't have to fish for it. The moment her warm breath flutters over the head, my balls draw up. The touch of her soft lips is heaven. But it's the feel of her sliding my shaft into her warm mouth and the head meeting the tightness of her throat that almost has me losing control.

"Jesus fucking Christ," I groan, baring my teeth.

Gathering her hair in one hand, I fist it in my grip and slowly slide her off my cock. When just the head is left inside, I give her no warning before I'm ramming my hips forward, wedging myself further down her tight throat. All of her oxygen is cut off, so she can't make a sound, but I feel the ripple effect of her throat convulsing as she gags. It damn near drives me mad.

Once her airway is clear, she lets out a moan of pleasure. She gets just as much pleasure, if not more, from me using her throat like a fuck toy.

With each forceful thrust, I push a little bit further down. I hold her head still, her nose smashed against my pelvic bone and her chin rests against my tight balls. Her nails dig into the comforter as her throat convulses around me. She tries to pull her head back, needing to draw in air, but I don't allow it. I smash her face against me, releasing a deep growl as the tightness nearly strangles the head of my cock.

My eyes are drawn to the layering of scars on her back. The small raised dots are no bigger than the tip of a ballpoint pen. They range in color from a light peach for the older ones to a deeper shade of red for the newer ones. All made by my hands after Scarlett begged me to give them to her.

I shouldn't be here. I should be home with Cat. My sweet, beautiful, gentle Cat.

But I'm not. I'm here. Doing something I shouldn't. Fulfilling a need that was dormant until Scarlett appeared in my life. A need that eats away tiny bits of my soul each time I'm with her. I'm a different person when I'm with this woman. The person I used to be. A person I'm not when I'm near my beautiful Cat. I hate this part of me. I hate it, but I can't help but relish in it when I'm with Scarlett.

"Enough!" I bark, yanking Scarlett's mouth away. She falls back on her ass and lifts her head, her teary eyes meeting mine. Black streaks from her mascara and eyeliner run down her cheeks. She looks so fucking beautiful it's almost painful to set my eyes on her.

Anger slithers up my spine, making my movements jerky. Scarlett looks up at me, her eyes imploring, begging for something only I can provide. The look pisses me off. My anger isn't directed at her, but at myself. I'm the one who's guilty here. Scarlett is innocent, despite the darkness that resides in her that makes her the way she is. Despite the temptation she represents. *I* pursued her all those years ago, not the other way around. *I'm* the one who gave in. *I'm* the one who's betraying his spouse.

Shaking my head, I push all thoughts of Cat from my mind. For this to continue, I can't think about my wife. And I want to continue this thing that Scarlett and I have. I need it like I need my next breath.

"Turn around," I tell her in a harsh tone. "Stay on your hands and knees."

She complies, presenting her ass to me, and I reward her by stroking my callused palm over her smooth cheeks. She moans and arches her back, her hair hanging over one shoulder.

Keeping my gaze on her, I raise my hand and swing it forward. I slap her right ass cheek so hard that my palm stings. It's not a love tap that a lot of couples do for sexual gratification. It's hard enough to leave an angry red handprint from just one slap. Most people would scurry away. Scarlett doesn't. She tugs on her bottom lip with her teeth as her eyes light up with fire.

I slap her twice more in the same place. I glance down and see the evidence of her desire leaking from her pussy. She's so wet, the thin material covering her can't hold all of the juices, so her thighs glisten with her arousal.

Pain is what gets Scarlett off. It's what she needs. And I'm willing to give it to her because I can let out the darker side of my desires which I refuse to inflict on Cat. Mutual satisfaction.

"Tell me what you want, Scarlett," I demand, delivering another blow that has her hoarse cries filling the room. "You want more?"

"Yes," she hisses breathlessly. "I want more. I want it harder. Make me hurt, Hunter."

Gritting my teeth, I slap her other cheek. The one I've just abandoned is bright red. Her other cheek needs to match it.

As her left cheek becomes as red as her right, Scarlett pants, little sounds of pleasure coming from her parted lips. My palm stings like a bitch and my heart beats like it's trying to escape my chest.

Holding Scarlett by the waist, I pull her until her sore ass meets my hard cock. It wedges itself between the globes of her ass and the soaked material of her thong rubs against my shaft. I yank the material away, pushing it past her ass and planting the length of my cock between her cheeks.

Leaning over her back, I grip her hair and yank her head back. "Where do you want it?" I growl the question in her ear.

"My ass," she answers.

My tongue lashes with hers, craving her. I love the taste of Scarlett on my tongue. Almost as much as I love the taste of Cat.

Again, I force Cat from my mind. It's wrong of me to think of one woman while I'm with another.

Leaning away from Scarlett, I grab the base of my cock and angle the leaking tip at her entrance, sliding it through the juices seeping from her.

Scarlett tries to buck her hips, but I keep her in place by wrapping my hand around her waist, digging my fingers into her flesh. "Stay still," I bark.

"Not there," she begs, looking at me over her shoulder.

"I'll take you however I want, Scarlett. In this, you have no choice."

Tears appear in her eyes, and I almost stop. The nature of our relationship is purely sexual. Despite my feelings for the woman, emotions have no place here. Showing any form of affection will push Scarlett away, and I refuse to give up my time with her.

So, I harden my resolve and push forward, sliding in every fucking inch until I can't go any further. The tight grip of her has me throwing my head back and hissing out a breath between my clenched teeth.

Fucking hell, she's unbelievably tight and feels so goddamn good.

Scarlett cries out, trying to shift her body forward to dislodge my cock. I keep her in place. Ignoring the pleas leaving her lips, I hold her still and fuck her hard and deep. Sliding out to the tip, I hammer back inside until her snug heat envelopes me.

The utter pain in her expression has me closing my eyes and blocking out her whimpers. Taking her the way I am isn't what she wants, but I'll be damned if I give in. This is what *I* need to give her what *she* needs.

I slow my movements and pray for patience and the strength to keep my release at bay. Scarlett may bristle and abhor me taking her pussy, but her body can't lie. She gets wetter and tighter the longer I'm inside her.

After several minutes, I can't take the sound of her low cries anymore, so I reluctantly pull from her warm sheath. She relaxes when she feels the broad head of my cock at her other hole. Her scrunched expression smooths out and she lets out a sigh of relief.

With my hands around Scarlett's waist, I ram my hips forward, not giving her time to adjust to my size. A sharp pain licks up my spine as I force my cock against such unprepared tight muscles. The only form of lubrication Scarlett allows is what I get from fucking her pussy, which still isn't enough to slide inside her with ease.

Scarlett's sudden cry is filled with pain and my soul shrivels just a little. Within seconds, I hear a low moan and her hips shove back against me, silently demanding more. I've never been able to deny her anything.

"Is this what you wanted?" My voice is deep, punctuating each word with a hard thrust. "To force you? To hurt you? To rip you from the inside" She doesn't respond. "Answer me, goddammit!"

"Yes!" she shouts. She fists the blankets and meets every thrust with ferocity. "Make it hurt!"

"I fucking hate you for this," I growl, digging my fingers into her flesh so hard it'll leave marks behind. When I pull back, the wetness coating my cock is tinted pink with blood. "I hate you for making me like this."

I don't hate her. What I feel for Scarlett is anything but hate. What I hate is myself for needing her so much. For needing to give us both what we crave. For putting us in this situation we're in. I should have told her no the first time I met her. I should have been strong enough to stay away from her after the first depraved time I fucked her. But she's become an addiction I can't break.

I take her ass with no mercy, forcing my cock in and out of her tight muscles. When I feel her tighten even further around me, I pull my cock free. Before she can protest, I flip her to her back. After shoving my pants off the rest of the way, along with my socks and shoes, I latch my hands around her thighs and lift her hips, ramming my cock back inside her ass.

She moans loudly, her mouth dropping open in ecstasy, her eyes glazing over, as if having me in her ass is the best thing she's ever felt. Despite knowing damn well that my roughness hurts her, she doesn't show it. Instead, she fucking loves it.

I hold still and wait for her eyes to meet mine. Only then do I drop forward, wrapping my fingers around her neck. Her eyes bulge and her face turns a deep shade of red when I tighten my fingers, cutting off most of her oxygen. She can still breathe, but only barely. Her tongue pops out, running across her plump lips, the only indication she's still enjoying what I'm doing.

My hips hit the back of her thighs. Only my grip on her throat prevents Scarlett from sliding up the bed with my forceful thrusts. Her nails dig into my forearms and her legs tighten around my waist.

I push my face closer to hers. "Goddamn you," I seethe heatedly.

When I recognize the glazed look in her eyes that tells me she's about to pass out at any second, I release her neck. I don't give her a chance to catch her breath before my lips seal over hers. I force my tongue into her mouth, and she meets my kiss with a passion I've only ever felt with Scarlett.

Snaking my arm between her back and the mattress, I lift the bottom half of her body and grind my hips downward, hitting a spot within Scarlett that has the muscles in her ass clamping down on me as she releases a loud shout. Her release is too much for me, and I find my own. My cock erupts, spurting jet after jet of cum deep inside her.

Chapter Eight
Hunter

Reclining back on the pillows with my hand thrown behind my head, I watch Scarlett quietly leave the room, the door left open behind her. Neither of us spoke after I pulled out my cock and rolled off her. I long to hold her in my arms. To run my hands gently over her body to try and soothe away the physical pain I know she's feeling. But I don't. It would only lead her deeper into her dark thoughts. It's best to leave Scarlett alone after our rough fucking.

The sudden silence in the room has my thoughts going to places I don't want them to, but I can't stop them.

Cat, my wife.

My eyes close when an image of her pops into my head. Instead of fighting the guilt, I let it wash over me. This is my punishment. I deserve every bit of self-hatred and loathing I feel toward myself. What I've just done, what I've been doing for years, is unforgivable. To be absent today, of all days...

Getting up from the bed, I dress, and then sit on the rumpled sheets to put on my socks and shoes. With my elbows on my knees, I roughly run my fingers through my hair and let out a deep sigh before getting up.

Weariness has my shoulders slumped as I leave the bedroom. I don't come across Scarlett as I grab my shit from the small table by the door and leave the house. I slip my ring back on my finger as I walk to my SUV. I take the long way home, needing the extra time to myself to gather my courage to face Cat. No matter how much guilt I feel after my time with Scarlett, I always go back. Deep down, I know I always will.

Cat's bright-red car is in the driveway when I pull up to the house forty minutes later. I take a moment to make sure my hair doesn't look like I've just gone through a round of rough sex before I climb out and go inside. After disarming and resetting the alarm, I turn to face the rest of the house. It's quiet and dark, which means Cat's in her office or in our bedroom. I make my usual check of the downstairs windows, leaving Cat's office for last. She's not there, so I go up the stairs.

Typically, once I get home after visiting Scarlett, I head straight for the shower to wash away any evidence of our time together. Tonight is different. I need to see Cat. I have to make sure she's okay. To see for myself that today, and what it represents, hasn't taken her away from me more than it already has.

Our bedroom door is ajar and light from inside floods the hallway. However, it's the door before it that captures my attention. It's cracked open. It's never open. Occasionally, I enter the room and the one across from it when I need a reminder of what we had and what we lost, but Cat never does. To her, neither of them exist.

As I approach the door, my gut drops to my toes. It's silent as I push it the rest of the way open. Despite the darkness, it only takes me a second to recognize Cat's shadowy form by the window. She's turned away from me, so I can't see her face to determine what's running through her head.

My eyes are drawn to the single-sized canopy bed in the middle of the room. I don't need light to know the comforter draped across it is a soft pink. There's a nightstand beside the bed with several books stacked on top. At the end of the bed is a chest with a couple of decorative pillows placed on top. Against one wall is a vanity with a lighted mirror and chair. On the vanity is a pretty purple container holding some of Cat's old make-up. Posters of boy bands hang on the walls, and there are other girly items throughout the room.

My throat convulses as I take in the space, and I swear the innocent scent of lavender still lingers in the air.

Silently, I walk across the room and stop behind Cat. She's staring out the window, as still as a person can be while still breathing. I'm hesitant as I reach out and place a hand on her waist. She gives no indication that she feels my touch. I'm scared to move too fast or make too much noise, because I don't know what state of mind she's in.

Stepping closer, I lightly press my chest against her back. I look over her shoulder and see the stuffed alligator she's holding in one hand and an old purple silk cloth in the other. This alligator means she was also in the other room. Both are clutched tightly to her chest.

"Cat," I say her name softly, and it's only then that I feel the slightest movement in her body. Her lungs deflate and refill with air, her shoulders moving slowly up and down.

I remain quiet after that, letting her take the lead on how this encounter will go. She's silent for several long minutes. I keep my eyes on the side of her face, while she continues to stare out the window.

"Whose room is this?" she asks, filling the silence.

I wrap both arms around her waist, placing my hands on her lower stomach. "You know who it belongs to."

She shakes her head. "I don't want to say their names. It hurts too much to say them."

I close my eyes, the pain in her voice tearing through my insides. Cat knows what happened the night our lives changed forever. She just doesn't like to remember, so she forces it all back, including the memories of them before that night, into a secret compartment in her head. I can count on one hand the times she's allowed herself to remember them over the last five years.

"Eliana," I say hoarsely.

Her fingers tighten around the silk cloth in her hand. "And the other room?"

I force the next name out through a dry throat. "Ryder."

Her breath catches as the name leaves my lips.

She brings the silk material to her nose and inhales deeply. "I remember when I gave her this."

Her voice cracks, like she's forcing the words out past the tears that are streaming down her cheeks. I want so badly to turn her around and take her into my arms. But it's so rare for her to talk about the two children we lost. The only reason she's doing so now is because today marks the anniversary of when we lost them.

"She was a year old. She always loved the feel of the silk nightshirts I wore." Her fingers glide over the material as she talks. "I ended up cutting a square out of one of them and hemming it before I gave it to her to sleep with." She looks down at the silk square, a tear falling and wetting the material. "She slept with it every night, up until...."

Her words trail off, but there's no need to finish her sentence.

A soft sob leaves her lips and it nearly buckles my knees.

"Cat—"

"He was so fascinated with alligators," she continues, holding the stuffed alligator up so we can both see it. "Gator was one of the first words he said. Mama and dada were his first."

"Cat, please, baby—"

"I haven't forgotten about them," she says, interrupting me again. "It's just too painful to remember." She pulls the alligator and silk back to her chest and embraces them tightly. "I miss them so much, Hunter. So damn much. Sometimes I wish I could be where they are. It's not fair for me to live while they don't."

Unable to listen to any more of her torturous words, I spin her around. Her cheeks glisten with her tears, and I know mine look the same.

Bending my knees, I put my face close to hers. Her hands and the items she's holding are smashed between us. "You are exactly where you're supposed to be, Caterina."

She's already shaking her head before the words fully leave my lips. "No. It should have been me who was taken. I didn't save them. I tried, but I couldn't do what they wanted. I wasn't strong enough."

Her face crumples into a mask of profound pain. For so many years, my beautiful Cat has suffered through things she should never have endured. Her experience was so horrific, it would have driven anyone insane. Guilt, no matter how many times and ways myself, our families, and her doctor have told her she shouldn't feel, consumes her. It is the same guilt that rests squarely on my shoulders. *I* couldn't save our children. *I* wasn't there to protect them. It was *my* job, and *I* failed. Not only our beautiful children, but also my wife.

My grip tightens around her waist. "No one could have made

that decision. No one, Cat. What they asked of you was evil and wrong. You are not to blame for any of it."

She sniffles, her teary eyes meeting mine. "Like you don't blame yourself?" My jaw clenches, but I hold her gaze. "You aren't to blame either, Hunter."

This is something we will never agree on. I will never stop blaming myself for Eli and Ryder's deaths. The most important job in my life is to protect and care for my family, and I did neither.

Cat switches the silk material to her other hand and lays her palm against my cheek. Her thumb swipes away a tear.

"You tell me not to blame myself, but you ignore the fact that you aren't to blame either."

I say nothing, because what she's claiming is simply not true. There is nothing anyone could say to make me believe otherwise.

"Come shower with me," I say instead, needing the focus off me. What I feel for my part in losing our precious children is deserved. What Cat feels is not.

After a moment of her staring at me like she wants to say more, she nods. As she approaches the bed, she brings the silk material up to her nose and inhales deeply. She then places it on top of the pillow where it usually lays. Years have passed since we lost Eli and Ryder, but their bedrooms remain the same. Even the notebook Eli was using for her English assignment sits on her desk, open to the last page she was writing on.

A heavy weight settles in my chest as we leave our daughter's room and make our way to Ryder's. I stay right behind Cat as she walks to his bed. She places a kiss on top of the alligator before she sets it down on the pillow. After the first year, I suggested that we pack up their belongings. Cat about lost her mind, and I haven't suggested it since. Eventually we will, but only when she's ready.

With Cat's hand in mine, I lead her to our bathroom. It feels wrong to shower and wash Scarlett's scent off my body while Cat is with me. But I can't bear the thought of leaving her alone right now. She needs me just as much as I need her.

I turn the shower on to warm up. Before I can strip either of us, Cat walks to me and wraps her arms around my waist, burying her face against my chest. I hold her for several minutes, loving the feeling of her in my arms. It's my favorite place for her to be.

She sniffs then pulls her head back, her eyes on my chest. A frown wrinkles her brow, and I tense, fearing she might smell Scarlett on me. But after a moment, she blinks and the frown smooths out. I wait another moment, hoping and praying she doesn't ask me questions I have no way of answering.

When she doesn't, I grab the hem of her shirt and pull it over her head, exposing her yellow lace bra. Next, I reach behind her to unsnap it. The straps on her shoulders loosen, and I pull them down her arms. The sight of her beautiful breasts is enough to make my mouth water.

"How was work?" she asks after I've stripped off my own shirt. "Did you get the issue you were having with an employee taken care of?"

My hands pause as they reach for the snap on Cat's jeans. A problem at work was my excuse for being out so late.

While I continue to work on Cat's jeans, I lift my eyes to her, gauging her expression for anything I should be concerned about. Does she suspect anything? Did she smell Scarlett after all and is now fishing for answers?

Fortunately, I don't sense a hidden meaning behind her question. She looks genuinely curious, and not in a suspicious way.

Slipping my fingers under the waistband of her jeans and

panties, I squat in front of her as I slide them down her legs. "Yes. We took care of the problem."

Cat's fingers sift through my hair while I help her the rest of the way out of her jeans. "Sometimes you work too hard."

I grunt, dropping my eyes to concentrate on my task. As I stand, I run my hands up the sides of her legs.

Cat stands before me, completely naked. My cock, which is currently being strangled in my pants, jerks at the stunning view. Toned legs and a flat stomach with curvy hips. Stretch marks line her lower stomach; the only visible evidence that she carried the two children we lost. Her breasts are full with hard, deep-red nipples.

She's simply the most beautiful woman I've ever met.

Her eyes drop to my hands, which are working on my own pants. Once my cock is free and my slacks are shoved away, her tongue darts out to swipe across the seam of her lips. Like she's picturing taking my cock in her mouth.

She moves forward, reaching for me, but I catch her by the waist and lift her into the shower. I immediately move us under the water. I need to wash away any traces of Scarlett before I allow Cat to touch me. What I'm doing is depraved enough. The least I can do is clean myself before taking my wife.

"I want to touch you," she says in a low, needy voice.

All signs of the intense moments we spent in Eli and Ryder's bedrooms are gone. Her mind has already shut them out again. Not because of our current situation, but because she hides their memories. For months, even years, at a time, it's like they never existed. It's what she needs to cope, so it's what I give her.

Before she can reach for me again, I turn her around and press her back against my chest. "In a minute. Let me wash you first." I reach for the sponge and soap on the shelf and pour on a generous amount. Creating a lather, I run it over her body, paying attention to her breasts since I know she likes it.

Next, I run the soapy sponge over her ass and down her legs. On my way back up, I take extra care between her legs. Ordinarily, I would take even more time cleaning her, building her arousal to a feverish pitch, but tonight I'm impatient to have her tight pussy surrounding my cock, and I still have to wash myself.

I quickly wash my own body, giving my cock a thorough rinse, before carelessly dropping the sponge. Cat is already facing me, her eyes hooded with desire. She runs her hand, with nails painted red, over my pecs, flicking my nipples before scraping them down my abs. My stomach muscles clench and my cock bounces.

"I love the feel of you," she says with reverence, her eyes following the movement of her hands. "You're so hard, but soft and smooth at the same time."

Her fingers slide through the happy trail on my lower stomach, taking her time working her way down to where I want her.

"Baby, please. You're killing me here."

A small smile curves her lips. "Now you know how I feel when you tease me."

"You like my teasing though."

Her head cocks to the side, and she looks at me through thick lashes. "Are you saying you don't like what I'm doing?"

"I fucking love it," I grunt. "But I'd love it more with your hands actually on my cock and not just close to it."

"You mean like this?" Her hand wraps around my shaft, causing a hiss to escape my mouth. She slides it down to the root then back to the tip.

My knees damn near buckle, so I slap a hand on the shower wall to hold myself up. "Fuck yes."

Cat steps closer, tilting her head back so she can still look at me. "I want you in my mouth."

A pearly drop of precum seeps from the tip of my cock. When Cat begins to drop to her knees, I let the wall go and grab her hips. As fucked up as it is, I've already had a mouth around my cock tonight. Right now, all I want is Cat's tight pussy strangling me.

"You can suck me later." Sliding my hands down to her ass, I pick her up and her legs automatically wrap around my waist. "I can't wait, baby. I need to be inside you."

Her hands move to the back of my hair as she stares down at me with eyes filled with so much love.

I'm going to hell, I say to myself as I slowly lower her down my cock.

Chapter Nine
Caterina

Drumming my fingers on the desk, I stare at the blinking cursor on my computer screen. For the past thirty minutes, I've been trying to figure out how to lead to the story's climax. I love my job. Having free rein of creativity. Manipulating readers into believing one thing when the truth is the total opposite. Building my own worlds. Influencing the emotions of others. In a way, authors are gods of their own universes.

Needing a break to let my mind rest and regroup, I grab my empty coffee mug and carry it to the kitchen. It's almost lunch time, so I decide to make myself a sandwich.

I'm sitting at the bar in the kitchen when my eyes catch on the laundry basket on the floor just outside the laundry room door. Hunter's shirt on top of the pile of clothes reminds me of last night when Hunter and I were waiting to shower. As I stood in front of him with my face pressed against his chest, I thought I caught a hint of a feminine scent. It was barely noticeable, but one that was oddly familiar.

If Hunter were any other man, I would doubt his fidelity, but

I have complete trust in him. I know with absolute certainty that he will never cheat on me. I know how lucky I am, because a lot of women can't say the same.

There must be another explanation as to why Hunter would have the scent of another woman on him. It could easily be Katie's. Or any number of the other women he works with daily at Slate. I know he would never willingly touch one of them, but that doesn't mean he doesn't come into close contact with them.

Although I'm confident Hunter would never cheat on me, I still don't like that another woman's scent was on him. When it comes to my husband, I'm possessive. I'm not a violent person, but just the thought of another woman touching Hunter has a red haze wanting to cloud my vision. I love him more than I thought was possible for a person to love someone. He's my heart and soul, and I'd be utterly lost without him.

My phone ringing on the counter pulls me out of my dark thoughts. I lean to the side and look at the screen without putting my sandwich down. I smile when I see the name.

I press the answer button and hit the speaker. "Hey, Megs," I greet my best friend.

The line is quiet on her end for a moment before her voice comes through.

"Oh, good. I wasn't sure if you... would be available," she finishes slowly.

"Why wouldn't I be? I'm pretty much always available. That's one of the perks of working from home." I laugh.

"Yeah, well, I don't know. I wasn't sure if you were busy writing or whatever else you authors do in front of a computer."

"I always have time for my best friend." I prop my chin on my hand. "So, what's up?"

"I was calling to see how you were doing."

"I'm fine. Why wouldn't I be?"

Another pause on her end. "Never mind," she finally mutters. "Just ignore me."

"Okay." I draw out the word, setting my sandwich down and brushing the crumbs off my hands. "Now you have *me* worried about *you*."

She laughs, but I know it's one of her fake ones. Megan has never been good at acting. I should know, I was in the one middle school play she participated in. To say it was a disaster is an understatement.

"Don't worry about me," she says, trying her best to sound sincere. "I'm just peachy."

"Your horrible acting skills are no better than they used to be," I inform her. "Now, why don't you tell me the truth?"

The speaker crackles, like she just let out a huff of air. "Fine. Just some stupid shit at work. Nothing I can't handle."

"Uh oh." I grin. "Is Mr. CEO giving you trouble again?"

Wyatt Foster, Megan's boss and head of the company she works for, has been giving her grief since he took over the company a year ago. She has a major crush on him and he won't give her the time of day, despite the heated glances she claims he gives her on occasion. When he's forced to communicate with her, his words are clipped and filled with animosity.

"Yes!" Megan answers a bit too quickly. "Trouble with the asshole again."

Something tells me she's lying and is using my guess as an excuse. I want to call her out on it and demand she tell me the truth, but decide to remain silent. For whatever reason, she doesn't want to talk about what's bothering her. As close as Megan and I are—for the most part, we've always told each other everything—I know there are times when a person just needs to work through their own issues.

"Whatever it is, Megs, I'm always here when you're ready to talk," I say quietly.

"You know I'm here for you too, don't you, Cat?"

"Of course. That's what best friends are for." I get up from my stool and carry my plate to the sink. "So, when are you coming to visit me?"

Megan and I met in kindergarten and were thick as thieves all through school. A few years ago, she moved an hour away for her current job. I don't get to see her as often, and although we talk on the phone regularly, I miss seeing my best friend in person.

"I'll be in town in a couple of weeks. Think you can wait that long?" she asks in amusement.

I let out a long dramatic sigh. "Fine. If I must."

She laughs, which brings out my own smile.

"How's Hunter doing?"

"He's great."

"Everything okay between you two?"

"Yes," I reply slowly, my brows dropping low. "Megan, what is go—"

"Sorry," she says, interrupting me. "I've got to go. I'll call you in a few days."

My frown is still in place as I stare down at the phone, watching the words "Call Ended" blink on the screen.

What in the hell was that about?

I shake my head. There's no telling with Megan. I love my best friend, but she can be a bit weird sometimes.

With my mind refreshed and the hunger ache in my stomach gone, I head back to my office to tackle my characters once again.

Later that afternoon, I've just shut down my computer when I hear the front door open and the beeping of the alarm as Hunter disengages then resets it. The alarm system we had installed years ago is always set when we're in the house. Hunter is adamant about it, which suits me just fine. It's the only thing that makes me feel secure and safe when Hunter isn't here.

I leave my office before he has the chance to hunt me down. I find it so sweet that he looks for me as soon as he gets home. As if he's missed me throughout the day and can't wait to see me again.

I walk right into his arms and roll to my toes for a kiss. It's not until I pull back that I see the prominent stress lines between his eyes.

My fingers curl around his biceps as I lean back. "What's wrong?"

The lines smooth out, but I've already seen them. "Nothing that you need to worry about."

First Megan called acting bizarre, and now Hunter is doing the same. I feel like they know something that I don't.

My nails dig into his arms. "Something is clearly bothering you. Please tell me what it is."

He sighs, his head dropping momentarily to glance at his feet. When he lifts his head again, I spot a barely noticeable tic in his jaw.

"I have to leave town. I may be gone overnight."

It's like a rope suddenly snaps around my throat, restricting my airflow and nearly choking me. The hair on the back of my head prickles and a flush feeling spreads over my skin, like I ran through a steam room, and a hazy blackness slowly fills the edges of my vision. I stare up at Hunter through the haze, my gaze frozen on his face. I try to force myself to breathe, but it's like every part of my body, organs and all, has forgotten how to work.

"Shit," I hear muttered right before I'm weightless and lifted off my feet.

The next thing I know, my head is being forced between my knees and Hunter is squatting in front of me, his hand moving up and down my back.

"Slow breaths, Cat. In and out. You got it, baby."

It's his calming voice that has the remnants of a panic attack slowly fading. While concentrating on the feel of his hand on my back, I take a deep breath and slowly exhale. In and out. In and out. The black haze recedes and my throat opens.

When I finally feel confident I'm not going to pass out, I lift my head. His concerned gaze meets mine. "What happened?"

"Panic attack. You almost blacked out."

"I'm sorry," I croak.

"No, baby." He wedges himself between my legs to bring us closer. "Don't ever be sorry. This isn't your fault."

I nod, even though I know it's not true. For years, I've had panic attacks, and I don't know why. I hate them because they make me feel weak. Like I don't have control over my own body and mind.

Remembering what brought on the attack, I suck in a deep breath and ask, "When do you leave?"

Instead of answering me right away, he gets up and sits beside me. He picks me up and places me on his lap sideways, my back against the arm of the couch. Taking my hand in his, he brings it to his chest and presses it against his heart. Feeling the heavy thump of the beat calms me more.

"I leave as soon as I pack a bag. There's a guy I've been hunting, and I want to get to him before he's warned and takes off."

I nod numbly.

I'm aware of Hunter and Silas's extracurricular activities. I also understand that by most standards what they do is wrong and unethical, not to mention it could land them in prison for decades. I don't worry about them getting caught. They know what they're doing and how to do it without leaving any evidence behind. Their methods are ruthless and vile, but what they do protects others. They aren't vigilantes who seek out these sick people, but if they hear of one, they also don't let them live much longer.

Perhaps that makes me a terrible person. To be so uncaring if a person dies. Most of the time, the notion goes against everything I believe in. But the way I see it, those beings aren't people. They're monsters, and who wants to walk among monsters?

His hand moves to my lower thigh and his thumb rubs back and forth over my knee. "You know I wouldn't go unless it was important."

I force a smile on my face. "I know. I'm being stupid. Don't worry about me. I just want you to be careful."

"I'll be back as soon as I can. Jacob and Peggy are coming over to stay with you while I'm gone."

I shake my head. "There's no need for my parents to be here, Hunter. I'll be fine on my own."

A look passes over his face, but it's gone before I can analyze it. "They always come over when I'm away from the house at night. I feel better knowing you have someone here with you. Please do it for me."

My shoulders sag and a ragged breath leaves me. "Fine."

His eyes fill with relief, and for the first time since he walked into the house, his features appear less tense.

My fear of Hunter being away from home overnight is a mystery to me. It's also ridiculous. Hunter leaves me alone at home almost every day while he goes to work, and I'm fine, so long as the alarm is set and the doors are locked. But just the thought of him being gone overnight nearly paralyzes me with fear. It's pathetic.

What kind of woman can't be away from her husband for more than a few hours?

Chapter Ten
Hunter

"Fuck!" I roar as my fist slams against the wall of the building and rage nearly blinds me. I was so goddamn close, I swear I could feel the heat of the person I want to slaughter the most against my fingertips.

For more than four years I've been looking for the person known as Whisper, and every time I get close, he manages to slip from my grasp. It's fucking maddening.

Whisper is the person who took half of my family, and the reason the family I have left is barely holding on to her sanity.

He was given the moniker Whisper because there are only whispers of the man. No one knows who the real person is behind the proverbial mask. And if someone gets close enough to uncover his true identity, they suddenly disappear, never to be seen again. Not a single person I've interrogated over the years has been able to give me a name. Either they don't know it, or they fear him more than me. Which is a testament to the shit Whisper can do to a person, because my methods of interrogation aren't gentle and are oftentimes lethal.

"Fuck!" The expletive grates past my clenched teeth. I aim

my fist at the wooden sign by the door. I pull my hand back and barely register the mangled mess of my knuckles.

"Lock it down, Hunt," Silas growls, anger giving his voice a sinister vibe. "He can only hide for so long. This bastard is walking on borrowed time and he knows it."

That may be true, but fuck all if it helps my mood. I want that asshole found now.

I gave Lenny two days to think over his options before I returned to finish what I started with him in the basement of Slate. He knew either way he wasn't leaving that room still breathing. Not after I found him in the process of attempting to rape a woman who was passed out from the drugs he had given her. It was up to him whether his death would be painfully slow or quick with a bullet between the eyes. It was unfortunate for him that he thought Whisper's wrath would be harsher than mine.

It wasn't until all of his fingernails had been ripped off, one eyeball plucked from its socket, and I was sawing off his dick with a rusty knife that he finally gave in. It seems that Whisper enjoys visiting Mad Town, a sex dungeon-type place with rooms in the basement where select clients can indulge in their darkest fantasies. It's rumored that sometimes the girls aren't quite so willing.

Whisper was due to visit Mad Town. He always enters the establishment through the back door in the alley. Silas and I have been here all night at the other end of the alley, waiting for him to show. At three in the morning, a black BMW pulled down the darkened street and parked. We were too far away to see the person who emerged from the car and walked inside the building. However, we did see enough to be able to recognize the figure if we saw him inside. Like a druggy shooting up heroin, adrenaline pumped through my veins. We searched every fucking inch of that place, including the basement, and the bastard was nowhere to be found. When we returned to the alley, his car was already gone, and a handwritten note was left on the windshield of my SUV.

Say hi to your wife for me.

The goddamn asshole somehow figured out we were on him, and now he's playing games. I'm sure he knew we were there the whole time, and even showed up just to fuck with me. He was probably hiding in the hallway where the alley door is and watched us from the fucking shadows as we crept inside.

I crumple the piece of paper in my hand and throw my fist against the wall one more time.

"Let's go," I bark at Silas and yank open my door, climbing behind the wheel. The paper gets tossed into the console as I speed down the alley and onto the street.

Even though I've left prints all over it, I'll give Marcus the note to check for fingerprints or DNA. Marcus is a former detective with connections within the department. While I don't think Whisper would leave evidence behind, damn if I won't have it checked.

Silas and I don't talk as we head out of town back to River Heights, but the silence in the vehicle is loaded with pent-up aggression. Silas keeps quiet because he knows I'm on the verge of losing my shit, and my own thoughts are filled with what our next move should be. No one can stay hidden forever. No matter how good Whisper is, there will be a time he makes a mistake.

And I'll be there fucking waiting.

Thirty minutes later, I park behind Cat's car in the driveway. Jacob and Peggy's car is next to hers. I owe them an expensive bottle of wine for staying with Cat while I've been gone. Of course, they won't accept it. They worry just as much as I do about her being alone.

The house is dark when I walk through the door, except for a small lamp in the living room. Going in to turn it off, I notice a dark lump on the couch. I walk toward it, already knowing who it is. Cat lays curled up on her side, one hand tucked beneath her cheek, and a throw blanket pulled up and tucked under her arm. She should look peaceful in sleep, but I don't miss the tiny stress lines between her eyes, as if, even in slumber, she's worried.

Pulling the blanket off of her, I lay it on the back of the couch, then bend and pick her up. I look down at her face just as her eyes crack open. A soft smile curls her lips at the corners, and she wraps an arm around my shoulders.

"I missed you," she whispers sleepily.

I drop my head and lay a tender kiss on her lips. "I missed you too, baby."

I carry her up the stairs to our bedroom. After setting her down on her side of the bed, I flip on the bedside lamp. I'm reaching for the belt of her silk robe when her eyes drop and she notices my busted hand.

She sucks in a startled breath and immediately reaches out to gingerly grab my wrist.

"What in the world did you do to your hand?" she asks, lifting it closer to get a better look.

"Nothing," I say, trying again to unwrap my wife from her robe.

She lets my wrist go and bats my other hand away from the belt I'm tugging on. Pressing her palms against my chest, she pushes me back enough for her to stand. Reclaiming my wrist, she pulls me behind her to the bathroom, then I'm shoved down on the closed toilet.

The whole time, I watch Cat with a smirk. I'm more than capable of taking care of my hand and was intending to do just that after I got her into bed, but I let her do her thing. It's not the first time she's treated my wounds, and it won't be the last.

She leaves me long enough to grab a first aid kit from the bathroom cabinet before returning. She bumps her legs against my knees, and I widen them so she can fit herself between them. A deep V forms on her forehead as she picks up my hand to inspect it.

"I don't like seeing you hurt," she says quietly.

"I'm not hurt, baby." I flex my fingers to show her I'm not in any pain.

"Stop that," she grumbles, reaching for a pair of tweezers.

As she begins plucking out the small grains of grit and splinters of wood embedded in the open cuts, I drop my eyes to her chest. While I hadn't managed to untie the belt of her robe, I did loosen it enough that a small amount of cleavage peeks through the parted material. There is no part of Cat that I love more than the others. Every fucking inch of her is perfect. But seeing the hidden valley between her breasts makes my mouth water. I want to bury my face there and never come up for air.

While she concentrates on her task, I lift my other hand to the back of her thigh. After a brief pause at my touch, she continues working. Slowly, I inch my palm up her smooth leg, my gaze already shifted to her face to watch her. Satisfaction fills me when her lips slightly part and her breathing comes a little faster. She doesn't look away from my hand, seemingly still focused on cleaning my knuckles, but she can't hide the fact that what I'm doing is getting to her.

I stop my hand when I reach the curve of her ass and chuckle when a barely audible whimper slips past her lips.

Her eyes move to me and her tongue darts out to lick the corner of her mouth. "Behave," she mumbles.

Flashing her a wicked grin, I don't respond verbally. Instead my hand continues its trek north, over the little silk panties covering her ass.

"Hunter," she whines breathlessly.

"Continue what you're doing, Cat," I tell her.

Flattening her lips, determination enters her eyes and she drops them back to my hand.

Reaching the top of her panties, I wiggle my fingers underneath the band and slide them over one of her luscious ass cheeks. Her breath catches and her eyes flutter when my finger trails down the line of her ass crack. I've never taken Cat's ass before. Not because I haven't wanted to, but because she hasn't shown any interest in the carnal act. It's not something I need from her, so I've never pressed her for it.

Unbidden, an image of Scarlett on her knees in front of me, my cock buried deep in her tight little asshole, flashes through my mind. I force the image away, unwilling to let my experiences with the two women mix together. Cat is who I'm with right now, and she deserves every bit of my attention.

Sliding past her back hole, my fingers encounter the slick juices seeping from Cat's pussy. My cock, which is already trying to punch a hole through my slacks, jerks, begging to be set free. I slip just the tip of my middle finger inside her, the ring of her entrance clenching me tight.

Cat stops pretending she's still cleaning my hand and curls her fingers around my shoulder, her nails biting into the flesh.

"Why did you stop?" I ask, then hold back a grin when she glares at me.

"You know why," she growls in the only way my pretty little Cat can growl.

One of my brows angles up. "Do you want me to stop?" I wiggle the tip of my finger inside her.

"No!" The word comes out in a rush and this time I can't hide my grin.

"Then continue. We don't want it to get infected, do we?"

Sometimes I can be an asshole, even though it's done in fun.

Cat wiggles her shoulders, likes she loosening them before a fight, and blows out a breath. The action draws a chuckle from me, but she ignores it.

After dropping the tweezers on the counter, she grabs a cotton swab and soaks it in alcohol. I barely register the sting when she begins dabbing it over my knuckles.

Pulling my finger from her slick pussy, I drag it back up her ass crack, momentarily pressing the pad against her other hole, curious to see her reaction. Her breath stutters and her eyes flutter closed. Hmm... Maybe she wouldn't be as opposed to anal as I thought.

I slip my hand out of her panties. The plea barely has time to form on her lips before it's quickly replaced with a sigh of relief when I begin sliding her panties down her legs. They stop at her knees.

"Feet further apart, baby," I coax and she immediately widens her stance, stretching the material of her satin panties.

My hand moves back to her pussy, poising one finger at her entrance. I watch her face as I push the digit inside, not stopping until the outside of her pussy prevents me from going any further. I pull it out, then shove two fingers inside.

"Oh God, Hunter," she moans and her ministrations on my hand stop again. I flex my fingers to remind her to get back to work.

Daggers shoot from her eyes and the look only intensifies my need. I pump my fingers in and out of her and add a third finger. She's so fucking tight, I have to force the digits inside.

Cat grabs a roll of gauze, quickly rolls it around my hand, and rips off a piece of medical tape with her teeth before securing the cloth.

She drops the tape in the sink, but before it has a chance to hit the porcelain bowl, I'm already up from the toilet. Grabbing her hips, I spin her to face the sink and bend to press her hands on the edge.

"Keep your hands there," I demand huskily. "Don't let go."

My cock is out within seconds. With one hand gripping one of her ass cheeks and the other holding the root of my dick, I notch the head at her slick entrance. I slip just the tip inside, and fuck, I'm already on the verge of exploding. Keeping my eyes down, I slowly and steadily slide through the tight walls of her pussy. It's hot as fuck to watch my cock disappear inside her.

Once I'm all the way in with my pelvis against her ass, I lift my head. My gaze clashes with Cat's in the mirror. Her eyes look glazed, a red blush coats her cheeks, and her bottom lip is tucked between her teeth. Her expression is filled with intense pleasure, pure love, and absolute trust.

And by some miracle I'll never understand, those emotions are directed at me.

Chapter Eleven
Hunter

"I'll be down in a few minutes," Cat says after I kiss the back of her head. I leave her in the bathroom to get dressed.

It's the morning after I returned from looking for Whisper. Surprisingly, Cat didn't have a nightmare last night. I expected her to because of the stress of me being gone most of the night. She slept like the dead, never moving an inch from the position we fell asleep in.

When I walk into the kitchen, I'm surprised to find Peggy and Jacob still here. Peggy is frying bacon and eggs at the stove, if my nose is correct. Jacob is sitting at the table reading a newspaper. Their appearance makes me laugh, because they look like a typical married couple from an old movie.

I never had this growing up. Every foster home I lived in had shitty parents who weren't the loving type. I was with the Clark's, the last foster family, for six months before "Daddy Clark"—yes, that's what Mr. Clark required all the foster kids to call him—started looking at me leeringly. It was fucking gross, and I knew if I stayed, it wouldn't be long before those looks turned into touches. At that point, I had grown into an angry kid and just wanted to be left alone because of all the shit I'd gone through in the system.

In the dead of night and with a hundred bucks stolen from Mrs. Clark's purse, I left out my bedroom window.

"Morning, honey," Peggy says, pulling me from my thoughts. "Breakfast should be ready soon. Grab a cup of coffee and take a seat."

I walk over to the coffee pot and grab two mugs from the cabinet above it. "I really appreciate you staying with Cat," I tell them. "I figured the two of you would be gone by now."

As she takes the bacon from the frying pan, she replies, "You never have to thank us for staying with Cat. She's our baby." She dumps the eggs into a glass serving dish. "And we heard you come in late last night. I figured you'd appreciate waking up to some bacon and eggs."

Peggy, always the caretaker.

"That's nice of you. Thank you." I pour coffee into both mugs and add the right amount of creamer and sugar. "And speaking of Cat, there's—"

I'm cut off by the sweet, innocent voice of Presley. "Hey."

Our eyes turn to the doorway to see the little girl standing there wearing a purple jumpsuit and pigtails. It takes Peggy and Jacob a second to recognize her, and while their expressions hold surprise for a moment, they both offer her a soft smile.

"Hey, Presley," Peggy says, walking to her as she wipes her hands on the towel hanging over her shoulder. Taking the girl in her arms, she holds her tightly for a moment. She lets her go and takes a step back. "My, my, don't you look pretty today?"

Presley beams at the compliment. "Thanks, Mrs. G."

"Like I told you last time, there's no need to call me Mrs. G. It's Peggy."

Presley giggles and flashes her dimples. "I'll try to remember."

Jacob and Peggy have been here a few times when Presley has visited. When Peggy first saw the little girl, she captured her heart. She claims it's because she reminds her of Cat when she was a child. Even I can admit that Presley has something about her that draws people in. She brings out the protective instincts of everyone she meets.

"Hey there, Presley," Jacob says, his newspaper now lying on the table before him. "We haven't seen you in a while. Where have you been hiding?"

"I was here last week. I just haven't felt like visiting as much."

I share a look with Peggy and Jacob before I turn to Presley. "Is everything okay?"

"Yep," she chirps, her pigtails bouncing as she skips over to the counter to steal some bacon. She munches on it while answering. "Sometimes I don't feel like going out."

"Well, it's a pleasure to see you," Peggy comments.

"I like seeing you too. You and Jacob remind me of my parents."

"We do?" Peggy asks, keeping an eye on Presley as she grabs plates from the cabinet. "How so?"

Presley's shoulder lifts. "I don't know. You're just motherly and fatherly like my mom and dad. And you make the best eggs like her."

A smile pulls at Peggy's lips.

Presley casually walks to the two mugs sitting on the counter and picks up the one I made for Cat. Before she can bring it to her lips, I stop her by gently taking it away.

"You know better than that, Presley," I tell her, my lips twitching. It's not the first time she's tried sneaking a cup of coffee.

"Besides, that's Cat's cup, and we both know how she is when she doesn't get her caffeine."

Her lips drop into a fake pout, and I have to force back a laugh.

"You're mean."

It's my turn to shrug. "Call it what you want, but you're still not getting any."

"Fine," she grumbles.

"Will you be joining us for breakfast?" Peggy asks Presley.

"Not this morning. I have to go home and do chores or else Mom might make me listen to one of her lectures." She shudders like it's the worst thing ever.

Peggy lets out a sputtered laugh, her eyes shining with mischief. "Well, I'm sure you want to avoid that at all costs."

Presley nods, her expression turning serious. "I do. I always feel so bad when I disappoint her and Dad."

Peggy's good-natured composure melts into sadness as she takes in the girl's words and her sudden change of expression.

"I can't imagine that happening often. I bet both of your parents are very proud of you."

"You really think so?" Presley looks at Peggy hopefully.

Peggy smiles and walks over to her. She takes her into her arms, and I barely make out what Peggy says. "I don't think so. I can pretty much guarantee it."

"Thanks, Peggy. I hate the thought of disappointing them." She kisses Peggy on the cheek before stepping back. "It's time for me to go. I'll see you next time."

Before she walks away, she comes to me and pulls out a rolled stack of papers from her back pocket and holds it out. Her latest story to Cat.

"Make sure Cat gets these."

The three of us watch her walk out of the kitchen, each deep in our own thoughts of the little girl. Sadness seeps into my veins, because as young and innocent as Presley is, she's been through more than any one person should ever go through. I want to hold onto her, protect her with all my might, but the only thing I can do is be there for her when she visits and hope she comes out on the other side as a whole person.

Several hours later, after saying goodbye to Cat's parents, we're snuggled up on the couch. My back is against the arm of the couch and Cat is on her side between my legs. Her long hair, which was pulled into a high ponytail when she first came into the kitchen earlier, is now down, lying over one of her shoulders.

Her cheeks are puffed out from the big smile on her face as she reads Presley's latest story. With a laugh, she sets the papers down on the coffee table.

"What's so funny?" I ask, twirling a lock of her hair between my fingers.

"Presley was helping her mom change her little brother's diaper and he peed on her. Of course, she freaked out, which was highly entertaining to her brother. While she was busy throwing off her top, her brother was on the changing table giggling his head off. Presley, the sweet big sister that she is, couldn't help but be charmed by his giggles, so she ended up in hysterics with him."

I chuckle. "That girl is something else."

"She really is. It's so cute how much she loves her baby brother."

"What do you want to do for your birthday?" I ask.

"It doesn't matter to me," she answers drowsily. "Just as long as I'm with you."

Crooking my finger under her chin, I tip her head back and look down at her with a smile. "There's nothing that would take me away from you on your birthday."

Leaning up, she returns my smile and presses her lips against mine. "You couldn't be a better husband," she murmurs against my lips. "I was blessed beyond measure the day I stepped into Slate."

I remember that day vividly.

I was getting ready to leave for the night, but I needed to speak with Silas first. While I was looking for him at the bar, I happened to glance at the dance floor. Right fucking there, with her hands sliding through her long, dark hair, her hips swaying to the soft beat of the music, wearing a short skirt barely covering her ass and a shirt that had slipped off one shoulder, was the woman I knew to the very depths of my soul, I would make mine. I didn't leave like I had planned to. I rooted my ass into a chair, and I watched her. For hours, I sat there and watched her and her friend, looking like they were having the time of their lives. I almost followed them when they left, but I resisted the urge to learn more about the woman who so completely captured my attention.

They returned a couple of weeks later. I had informed Kurt that I wanted to be informed as soon as she walked in the door, so I had more time to observe her. Once again, I sat in the shadows and watched my girl swing her hips while laughing with her friend. Twice I almost beat the fuck out of a couple of guys who dared approach her. Their faces were saved only because she didn't show much interest in them.

Later that night, things changed. That's when I saw an

asshole spike her drink. After breaking his nose, I had Kurt throw him and his friend out of the club. That wasn't the end of it though. I found out who the guy was a week later, and he had an unpleasant ending. The pigs were happy though, as they fed on his corpse.

"You got that backward, baby," I say, switching my thoughts back to the present. "I was the one blessed that day."

She smiles against my lips. "You're too good for me."

That earns her a grunt. "You got *that* wrong as well. You're too good *for* me."

Cat would never know how true my statement is. With everything I've done in the past and everything I'm still doing, I will never be good enough for her.

Chapter Twelve
Caterina

Hunter grabs the back of my shirt and spins me around. I laugh as I fall against his chest, but it dies when his lips drop to mine for a heated kiss. I moan against his mouth, my body quickly lighting on fire, just as it always does with Hunter pressed against me. The man knows exactly what to do to get my heart rate up. Hell, he doesn't even have to *do* anything. A simple look at his green eyes can make me want to climb him like a tree. It's been that way since the first time I saw him and the desire has only grown since then.

"I don't want you to go," he says against my lips. "I want you here so I can do wicked things to you."

A giggle slips free, and I shove my hands into the back pockets of his jeans, squeezing his ass. "You know if I don't go, Megan will hunt me down."

A deep growl rumbles from his throat. "Fine, but hurry back. I know how to hunt down people too."

I roll to my toes and kiss Hunter again before grabbing my purse from the hook by the door. I pull out my keys from an inside pocket.

"You can last a couple of hours without me," I tell him.

He lets out a dramatic sigh. "Only if I must."

With another laugh, I blow him a kiss, then wiggle my fingers at him. "Love you."

"Love you back."

Hunter opens the door for me, and I step out onto the porch. I feel him watching me as I make my way to my car. Looking back at him as I open the driver's side door, he gives me the smile he reserves only for me. The one that's proof that he loves me just as much as he claims.

I turn on the radio, keeping the volume low, as I drive the ten minutes to the restaurant where I'm meeting Megan. Since she's in town visiting her parents, we decided to have lunch together.

I spot Megan sitting in a window booth when I walk into the restaurant. After pointing her out to the hostess, I walk over to her. She gets up from her seat and we hug.

"It feels like it's been ten years since I saw you," she says after we take our seats.

I laugh. "It's only been a month."

"Really? It seems longer."

I pick up the menu sitting on the table and look at her over the top, my eyes glinting playfully. "Probably because you've had your head full of Mr. CEO."

Her eyes roll heavenward and she snorts. "That's not the only thing that's been full of Mr. CEO," she mutters, avoiding my gaze.

I slap the menu down on the table, and lean across it, my interest more than piqued. "Um, excuse me. You care to elaborate on that statement?"

Slowly, her lips curve into a smile that takes over her entire face. "Yeah, so, I slept with Wyatt."

I grin back at her. "When? How did it happen? Was he any

good?" I feel like a teenager bombarding her girlfriend with all of these questions, but damn, I'm almost as invested in what happens between them as she is.

She laughs, but before she can answer, our waitress walks up. After giving her my drink order, I impatiently wait for Megan to give hers.

"Spill," I demand the moment the waitress is out of ear shot.

Her dimples pop out with her big grin. "It happened a few nights ago. How it happened is cliché as hell. And, girl," now it's her turn to lean over the table as she lowers her voice, "good doesn't even come close to how well that man fucks. Today is the first day I've been able to walk properly since it happened."

"A few nights ago? Why are you just now telling me?"

"I wanted to tell you in person."

I can understand that. It's always better to tell your best friend juicy details face to face.

"Fine. I'll let that slide." I roll my hand in a gesture for her to continue. "Now tell me how it happened. I don't care how cliché it sounds."

"Let's order first. This may take a while, and I'm starving."

After we call the waitress back over, she takes our order, and brings our drinks, Megan begins her story.

"A few nights ago, I stayed late to finish some reports due the next day. Everyone had left for the night, or so I thought. I was in the elevator leaving when a hand appeared between the closing doors."

"Let me guess. It was Wyatt."

She plays with the ring around the cloth napkin, rolling it around. "He said some pretty nasty things to me earlier in the day, so I ignored him. I was done with his uncaring ass. No more secret crush. As far as I was concerned, he could jump off a high-rise building for all I cared. My silence apparently didn't bother him, because he didn't acknowledge my presence in the elevator."

When she frowns, I reach across the table and grab her hand. "What happened?"

The concentrated look disappears and she looks at me. "We were a few floors from the first when the elevator suddenly stopped. I looked over and saw him with his finger on the emergency stop button. After what he had said earlier that day, I was angry that he would entrap me in an elevator with him and figured he was taking the opportunity to spew more hatred at me. Furious, I walked across that damn elevator and stood in front of him. When I demanded he start it again, he only said "No."" She mimics a deep voice. "That's when I decided I'd had enough and lifted my hand to smack the shit out of him."

"Oh damn." I laugh. "I bet he didn't take that too kindly. Not that he didn't deserve it."

"It never happened," she tells me. "He caught my hand, and the next thing I knew, I was up against the elevator wall with my legs around his waist and his mouth devouring mine."

"Holy crap."

"You got that right. I was just as shocked as you are." She laughs. "It wasn't long before we were ripping off each other's clothes. After what he said to me earlier, I still had a lot of pent-up anger, and you can believe I took it out on him. The sex was rough, raw, and aggressive." She sighs. "But it was the best sex I had ever had in my entire fucking life. I left without saying a word to him, and I haven't seen him since. He was out of the office the last couple of days."

"Has he tried calling you?"

"A couple of times, but I let them go to voicemail."

"Are you planning to see him again? I mean, obviously besides seeing him at work."

"I don't know." She slides her hands over the table and laces her fingers together. "The asshole needs to pay for how he's treated me. I think I'm going to make him stew for a bit. I want to know if he's really interested or if I was just a convenient hole to stick his dick in."

"Good for you. Maybe bringing him down a peg or two will teach him a lesson."

She nods. "I really hope so, because I can't imagine never having that kind of sex again."

That makes me laugh. "I'm sure he'll see the error of his ways and come crawling back to you, begging for your forgiveness."

"I guess we'll see." She sits quietly for a moment, her eyes locked on mine, her expression thoughtful. "So, how are you doing? Anything exciting going on?"

"We're good. Nothing too exciting. Hunter was gone most of the night a couple of nights ago."

"Oh yeah?" Her brow rises. "How did that go?"

Megan is aware of my anxiety when Hunter is away. I have spoken to her many times about why I get so stressed out. She's calmed me down several times during panic attacks.

"It was okay." I pick at the cuticle on my thumb nail. "Mom and Dad stayed with me. It's ridiculous that, as a grown woman in her thirties, I freak out when my husband is away overnight."

Megan stops my cuticle picking by grabbing my hand. "It's not ridiculous at all, Cat. Some people just don't do well being alone."

"Yeah, but why am I like that?" I give her a questioning look. "I wasn't like this when I was younger."

A wrinkle forms on her forehead as her hand squeezes mine.

"There's no telling what caused it. Have you spoken to your doctor about it? Maybe the nightmares have something to do with it."

I stare sightlessly at my hand in hers. "Maybe," I murmur.

Our conversation is interrupted when the waitress approaches with our food. Megan and I chat about mundane things while we eat. I miss seeing my friend regularly. She's only an hour away, but between our schedules, we don't see each other as often as I'd like.

"How are your parents and brothers? Is Noah still enjoying college?"

In middle school, Megan and her older brother, Dean, were surprised by the news that their parents were expecting another child. Their parents were just as shocked, especially since Dean Senior had a vasectomy after Megan was born. There was never a question about whether their mother had cheated. Their parents are a lot like mine. You can just see the love radiating between them. If anyone did doubt Meredith's fidelity, it was soon put to rest when Noah came out the spitting image of Dean Senior.

"He's fine. Ready for graduation next year. He already has a job lined up for next summer."

"That's great. He's been a lifesaver to me a couple of times when my computer went kaput. I love the man, but Hunter's computer illiterate."

Megan laughs. "I've put him to use several times myself." Megan wipes her mouth with her napkin and places it on her plate. "Izzy found out she's pregnant. Dean's over the moon."

I smile, happiness spreading through me for Dean and his wife. "Really? I can just imagine how happy they must be. I know they've been trying for years."

"The news came out of nowhere. Izzy went for an endoscopy

for some digestive problems she had been having. A pregnancy test was required because of the medicine they give you to knock you out. The test came back positive. I'm pretty sure Dean passed out when he heard the news, but of course, he'd never admit it."

I giggle, not surprised Dean wouldn't admit to something so unmanly. Neither would Hunter. I think it's a man thing.

We spend the next hour catching up before I insist on paying the bill. I walk with Megan to her car to give me the gift she bought me since she won't be here for my birthday next week. My eyes well up with tears when I unwrap a painting she commissioned of Hunter and me on our wedding day. We're facing each other beneath a weeping willow tree. Hunter's head is tilted down, and mine is tilted back. We're in our wedding clothes. The attention to detail is stunning.

After a long hug, we part ways, and I get into my car after carefully placing the painting in the trunk. I know the perfect place to put it. I'm not sure why I never put pictures there, but there's a blank space on the wall in the living room where it would look perfect.

Chapter Thirteen
Hunter

I'm leaving the floral shop where I picked up a dozen purple peonies, Cat's favorite. I asked her to be ready by five. I'm taking her to our favorite restaurant for her birthday. Afterwards, we'll head to Willow Lake, which was where we made love for the first time under the stars. I have a blanket laid out and wine in a cooler waiting for us. In my pocket is a silver key on a silver chain.

I get behind the wheel of my SUV and start the engine. I'm heading home to pick up my beautiful wife. Tonight I have her all to myself. This weekend I'll share her with her parents, where we'll have dinner at their place with her sister and her crew.

Just as I shift into drive, my phone buzzes with a text. I put the vehicle back in park and check the device.

My gut drops, and I grip my phone so tightly it creaks.

> Scarlett: I need you.

My eyes slide to the flowers in the passenger seat, and the box in my pocket feels like lava against my thigh.

When Scarlett texts me, I can't ignore her. But she's never

needed me this early in the day. It's usually in the evening, after the sun has set, when her demons plague her. Something must have happened for her to need me right now. My stomach churns at what that something could be.

I ignore the suffocating pain in the center of my chest and the guilt that consumes me for ruining Cat's birthday.

I quickly type a reply.

> Me: I'm on my way.

I then send a message to Cat.

> Me: Got caught up at Slate. I'll be a couple of hours late getting home. I'm so sorry, baby.

Again, ignoring my guilt, I throw my phone into the center console and speed out of the parking lot. Fifteen minutes later, I'm pulling into the driveway of the old house. It's strange to see it in the light. I haven't paid much attention to the outside of the house in years. Just like the other older homes along the street, the lawn is well-kept.

After setting my wedding band in the console with my phone, I exit my vehicle. I take the steps two at a time and use the key I acquired years ago to open the front door. It comes as no surprise when I find the house quiet. It's rare that I see Scarlett outside of the bedroom. Our time together is always spent in the room upstairs.

Instead of heading straight to Scarlett, I go for my customary drink. I don't know if Scarlett orders my favorite whiskey on purpose or if it is just a coincidence. I throw back three shots before the harsh liquid calms my nerves.

Everything inside me screams for me to leave this dark place. I shouldn't be here. I should be with Cat, celebrating her birthday. Instead, I'm here, adding to my list of sins.

Rinsing my glass, I set it and the bottle back inside the barren cabinet.

Scarlett waits for me on the bed, in her usual position. My cock immediately fills with blood, and my hands move to the buttons on my shirt.

Today, she's wearing a blood-red bra and thong set, the bright color matching her name. Her black and red hair shines from the sunlight filtering in from the window. She wears the same thick leather bands on her wrists and rings on her fingers. She's even more beautiful in the daylight.

She holds completely still in her submission position as I approach the bed. While I've rarely been here during the day, Scarlett acts the same as she does when I'm here at night.

I order her to come closer and she scoots on her knees to the end of the bed. Wrapping my fingers around her delicate throat, I tilt her face upward. Black streaks trail down her cheeks from her eyeliner and mascara, as if she has been crying. Her appearance has me loosening my grip on her neck.

"No!" she shouts, her hand flying to mine and holding it there, reapplying the pressure I had just released.

"Why have you been crying?" I ask, keeping my voice firm.

Her tear-filled eyes lock onto mine. "I need to feel the pain," she whispers brokenly. "I need to be punished."

I come closer to the bed and my knees knock against the edge. "Why? What happened?"

She shakes her head despite my tight grip around her neck. Her throat convulses against my palm. "I can't talk about it. Please don't ask me to."

Gritting my teeth, and against my better judgment, I give her a tight nod. "Tell me what you need."

The question barely leaves my lips when I spot something over her shoulder on the bed. A black-handled whip with long leather strands. I return my eyes to Scarlet and she looks at me with a dark sense of need.

"Are you sure?" I ask, my voice deepening.

Her tongue darts out and rubs against her red lips. "Yes. You have to, Hunter. It's the only way to make them go away."

Scarlett's demons.

Sometimes they visit her as often as once or twice a week, and sometimes only once or twice a month. It seems like they've been present more lately, and that really concerns me.

To keep our sanity, denying her request isn't an option for either of us. She'll end up more of a mess than she already is, and seeing that isn't something I can handle. These "punishments" help her release the pain she harbors inside her.

When I release her throat, her chest rises and falls rapidly. She flips around to her hands and knees in front of me without needing to be told.

After taking off my shirt, I drop it on the floor. Walking to the side of the bed, I grab the whip, the familiar touch of the handle is cool and smooth in my palm. This won't be the first time I've used it on her, and it won't be the last. When Scarlett's thoughts become too dark, the whip is brought out.

Each time I give her these types of punishments, a part of me dies. How much longer before there's nothing left of me?

I grip the handle of the whip tightly and go back to the end of the bed. "You know the drill, Scarlett. Put your chest against the bed and turn your head to the left. Count each lash."

When she complies, I take a step to the left, making sure her face is visible. My heart pounds in my chest as I raise the whip. Gritting my teeth, I slam my arm forward hard. Scarlett won't accept anything less. She needs to feel the bite of pain. The more it hurts, the faster her demons recede back to the darkness in her head. The thin tails of the whip land against her lower back.

"One."

I'm not sure what I hate more; the low pain-filled moan with a hint of pleasure that comes from Scarlett as she counts, or the thin marks left on her back.

It only takes a few seconds for the marks on her back to open up and small red dots to appear. It's not the leather strips that break the skin, but rather the small metal pieces attached to the tails. Scarlett had the whip custom made.

The first time she asked me to use it on her, I refused. In response, she said she would find someone else. There was no way in hell I was allowing that to happen, so I gave in. Imagining someone else wielding this weapon against her, someone who wouldn't care about her, had violent thoughts filling my head. I wanted to kill the faceless man.

My jaw twitches when I pull my arm back and swing it forward a second time. As more red dots appear, those from the first strike begin to smear across her back.

"Two," Scarlett croaks.

Tears steadily stream down her cheeks, and I force myself to ignore them. The sooner I get to five, the sooner it'll be over.

Two strikes later, her lower back, ass, and upper thighs are covered with red lines and bloody dots. I'm panting and sweat drips down my face and chest. Scarlett simply lays there, taking each lash with barely any notice, except for the small whimpers leaving her lips when she counts each strike.

I hate that she feels she deserves these beatings. This woman should be cherished and loved with a gentle hand, not degraded on her knees while her lover marks her permanently.

After I deliver the fifth strike, I immediately drop the whip to the floor like a hot iron. I feel disgusted at myself, but I know this isn't over yet.

Knowing and uncaring that it reveals a softness toward her that she won't welcome, I lay a soft kiss against her spine. Blood coats my lips when I raise my head, and I run my tongue over them to lick it away. Scarlett's breath hitches as she slowly rises from her hands to sit before me on her knees. She watches me take off the rest of my clothes with wary eyes.

When she makes a move to lay down, I stop her.

"No," I say, my voice harsh. "Stay there."

Scarlett took her lashes without showing any signs of real pain, but I know she must be hurting. I'll be damned if I take her on her back.

Stalking to the side of the bed, I lay back on the mattress. She licks her lips as she takes in my hard cock jutting upward. As fucked up as it may be because of what I just did to her, I'm still hard as a fucking rock. It's Scarlett. I don't even have to be around her to want her.

"You got what you wanted with that fucking whip. It's my turn. You want my cock? You'll have to take it yourself."

Her eyes light up with anticipation as she crawls across the bed and throws a leg over my hips. I grab the side of her thong and tear the material away. As she lowers herself, her wet pussy glides across my stiff shaft, causing me to jerk. When she wraps her fingers around the base and guides the tip to her ass, I stop her by grabbing her waist.

"You know that isn't how this works, Scarlett." I growl. "You want it in the ass, you give me your pussy first."

She wants to argue. The words are on the tip of her tongue. But seeing the determination on my face, she decides against it. I've never given in on this point, so she knows better than to try anymore.

Notching the head of my cock at her tight entrance, she slowly sinks down. She's so wet that I slide inside her easily. Her bottom lip is tucked between her teeth, a look of discomfort darkening her eyes. No matter how much pleasure she gets from having me inside her pussy, she won't allow herself to enjoy it.

I hiss out a harsh breath. She feels like fucking heaven. I'd stay in her tight pussy forever if I could.

She only allows me to fill her pussy for a few strokes before she lifts herself off me. I want to demand we continue the way we are, but I know she needs what comes next. Only the pain of being fucked anally gives her relief.

"Go slow," I demand.

A look of complete bliss fills Scarlett's face as the head pops past the tight ring of muscles. Her head tilts back, the tips of her long hair tickling my thighs, and her mouth falls open with a low moan. My hands tense on her thighs because the pleasure is almost more than I can bear.

In the next moment, one I should have foreseen coming, she drops down, taking the full length of my cock in one fucking stroke.

"Fuck, Scarlett," I growl, moving my hands to her waist to hold her still. "I told you to go slow."

Her head falls forward, her hair nearly hiding her face from me, and her eyes are filled with pain as they look straight into mine. "I don't want slow," she says, a stubborn tilt to her chin. "Slow doesn't give me what I need. You know fast, hard, and rough is the only way I take it."

Gritting my teeth, I allow her to slide up my cock until the head is left inside, only to drop back down quickly. Her tight muscles grip me and leave me on the verge of exploding. It's only my own will power and determination to have her come first that keeps me from falling over the edge.

I lie there, breathing heavily, fighting back my orgasm, and watch as Scarlett destroys both of us.

Chapter Fourteen
Caterina

I put the lipstick back in the tube after swiping the soft peach color across my lips. Leaning closer to the mirror, I rub my lips together to even it out, and use my pinkie to swipe away a smudge from the corner of my mouth.

Over my shoulder, in the mirror, Hunter appears in the bathroom doorway. A small smile plays on his lips as he leans against the frame. I spin around and give him a big grin.

"Sorry I'm late." His eyes sweep up and down my body. I'm wearing a tight, deep lavender dress with thin shoulder straps. The hem stops a couple of inches above my knees. On my feet are a pair of strappy sandals with low heels. My black hair is swept up and pinned at the top of my head with a few loose pieces falling around my face. "You look absolutely stunning."

"Thank you."

He steps forward, coming to a stop in front of me. His arm whips out from behind his back, revealing a beautiful bouquet of my favorite flowers.

"For you, Mrs. St. James."

Lowering my head, I bury my nose in the sweet-smelling flowers. "They're beautiful. Thank you."

"Anything for my beautiful wife." With the flowers between us, he drops his head and lays a tender kiss against my lips.

When he lifts his head, I keep mine tilted back to look at him. I've known Hunter since I was twenty-one years old. I've learned all of his expressions and can tell his mood just by looking at him. As he stares down at me, I see love shining in his eyes. It's a look I've seen on his face every day since he first told me he loved me, only weeks after we met. I love the look, and it always manages to make my stomach flutter.

However, underneath the love, something else lurks. An emotion I'm not sure I know the name of. It almost looks like sadness and remorse, and maybe even a hint of guilt.

I frown and reach up to trace my finger over the line between his eyes. "What's wrong? Something's bothering you."

The line smooths out and his eyes skitter away from me for a brief moment before returning. "Nothing. Just work stuff."

Something heavy settles in my stomach, making a knot of dread form. "You don't have to leave again, do you?"

"No." His expression softens, and he tightens his arm around me, squashing the flowers. "I won't be doing that again for a while."

Relief floods through me, loosening my tense muscles. "Is there anything I can do?"

"Just being here with you is all I need." He drops another kiss on my lips. "Why don't you put these in a vase while I shower? I'll be ready in fifteen minutes tops."

I laugh. "Men are so lucky. Fifteen minutes isn't long enough to shower, let alone get dressed and do my hair and make-up."

"You could be in rags with not a stitch of make-up and your

hair dull and flat, and I'd still think you're the most gorgeous woman I've ever met."

My heart flutters with his compliment. It's even more special because I really believe him.

With another quick kiss on my lips, he hands me the flowers and gently pushes me toward the door. "Now go. I was able to reschedule our reservation, but I doubt they'll hold it if we don't show up on time."

With a smile, I leave him and go to the kitchen. After grabbing a vase from one of the cabinets, I set the flowers on the counter and remove the wrapping. Once the stems are cut at an angle, I fill the vase with water and place the flowers inside. Carrying it over to the sink, I set it on the window sill so I can look at them while I'm in the kitchen.

I'm rearranging the flowers when something outside catches my eye. It's dark outside and the back porch light isn't on, but the light from the window I'm in front of illuminates a small patch of yard.

My lungs freeze and my heart stutters to a halt when one of the shadows suddenly moves. Someone is in our backyard.

An ear-piercing scream fills my head. It's only when I'm out of breath and sucking in more air to scream again that I realize the sound is coming from me.

"Caterina!" Hunter's voice shouts from behind me. He's at my side in an instant, gripping my arm and turning me to face him. "Baby, what's wrong?"

Numbly, I notice the gun in his hand. The only thing he's wearing is a pair of slacks with the button undone.

My breathing is stuttering and I'm shaking like a leaf.

"Cat." Hunter's harsh voice snaps my gaze back to his.

"S-someone's out there." I dart my eyes to the window. "I saw a sh-shadow."

His jaw hardens and his eyes become alert as he stares out the window. In the next moment, Hunter ushers me to a door in the kitchen and he practically drags me down the stairs to the basement. I feel numb, like I'm not really in my body, as I'm shuffled to a steel door. After keying in a number on the keypad, Hunter drags me inside and straight to a chair in a corner.

He squats in front of me. "Stay in here," he orders. Pointing to one of the computer monitors set on a big desk across the room, he continues. "Don't open the door unless you see me on the screen." He shakes me gently when I don't respond. "Cat," he barks my name. "Baby, are you listening?"

"Y-yes," I croak.

"Only my face, okay? I'm going to go check things out."

When he stands, I scramble to my feet and clutch his arm. "No!" I shriek, wincing at the desperate sound. "Don't leave me. You can't go out there. What if they hurt you? Stay here with me. Please, Hunter. We'll call the cops."

His face twists painfully, but he gently pushes me back into the chair.

"Nothing will happen to me, Cat." He holds up the gun. "I have protection."

Hunter is very much capable of protecting himself. Not only is he proficient at using a gun, he works out daily and has a black belt in two different martial arts. Knowing this, it still doesn't alleviate my fear of him getting hurt. There's always the possibility that someone will have more skills than him.

I squeeze my eyes shut, blocking out the image of Hunter lying in the grass, blood soaking the dirt beneath him, and his eyes staring sightlessly at the star-filled sky.

"Baby, look at me." I open my eyes and get snared in Hunter's. "I'll be okay as long as I know you're safe in this room. If I feel like I'm in danger, I'll come back to the house and come straight to you."

It's the best concession I'm going to get. No matter how much I plead with Hunter, I know he won't listen. He has this unreserved need to protect me at all costs. While I love that about him, it also scares me because I'm absolutely certain he'd put his own life on the line to protect me. The thing is though, I would do the same for him. We'd both fall apart if something happened to the other.

"Good girl," he says when I nod, then presses a hard kiss against my lips. "Only my face, okay?"

With a knot the size of a bowling ball stuck in my throat, I nod again. "Please be careful."

"You know I will."

Standing, he walks to the steel door. It bangs loudly when he slams it shut behind him. As soon as the lock automatically engages, I rush over to the bank of computers and sit in one of the chairs. Looking from screen to screen, I don't relax until I spot Hunter in the kitchen. He's holding his gun up with one hand and rests the butt of it in his other.

I keep my eyes glued to the screen as he slowly walks across the room. I'm forced to switch to another monitor when he enters the dining room where the back door is. Although the video has audio, not a sound comes through the speaker as he opens the door and steps outside.

On another screen, Hunter slowly descends the steps of the back porch. The porch light is still off, but the cameras are equipped with night vision.

When Hunter suddenly takes off running, I tense in my chair

and all the air in my lungs whooshes out. One minute I see him on the edge of the camera and the next, he's gone. I look at each screen we have outside, but no matter how much I wish it, he doesn't reappear. My airway becomes blocked and tingles form on my scalp. I clutch the edge of the desk and lean over it to look closer at the screens, as if I can mentally command him to appear.

Dark memories try to worm their way past the formidable walls I've built in my head. Memories I've buried so deep, they'd burn if they saw the light of day.

I strengthen those walls, adding steel barriers in front of them and pouring concrete in the small cracks trying to form. I can't let those memories out. If I do, I know deep down, my mind will fracture, and I'm afraid there will be no piecing it back together.

Tears pool in my eyes and leak down my cheeks the longer I look at the screens and don't see Hunter. It feels like my soul is oozing from my pores as I'm forced to wait. I keep conjuring up horrific scenarios of what could be happening to him, and it's driving me insane.

I should never have let him go out there. I should have made him stay in the safe room with me. In here, nothing can get to us. In here, we're completely safe.

What feels like hours later, but could only be minutes, Hunter finally reappears on the camera centered on the back porch. He looks whole and unharmed as he walks up the steps, the gun resting at his side, and goes to the back door. I sag in my chair, covering my face with my hands as deep sobs wrack my body. Nausea rolls in my stomach, and I'm forced to swallow back the bile.

"Cat," Hunter's voice calls through the speaker. "Open the door."

I scramble up from the chair and smash the required numbers

on the panel beside it. It takes me three times to get it right because my hands are shaking so badly.

Once the door is wide enough for me to squeeze through, I throw myself into Hunter's arms. He catches me, and it's only once I feel him holding me that I truly believe he's safe.

"Shh, baby, I've got you," he croons in my ear. "Everything's okay."

I can't stop the pathetic noises coming from me. I clutch his back, digging my nails into the skin, knowing I'm leaving marks, but uncaring at the moment. Suddenly, I'm lifted off my feet and carried out of the basement. The whole time my face stays buried in his neck, breathing in his sandalwood scent.

He settles down on the couch and forces my face out of his neck. My cheeks are caught in his big palms and his thumbs under my jaw lift my head up so I'm looking at him.

"Cat, you're breaking my heart," he says hoarsely. "I'm okay."

I stare at him helplessly. "When you disappeared from the screen, I wasn't sure what happened to you."

"Nothing happened. I heard a noise and ran after it."

That does not help my frightful mood, and from the tightening of his jaw, he knows it.

"It was just the neighbor. Their dog got loose and ran through our backyard. The shadow you saw was Jordan looking for him."

"Oh."

His lips quirk up. "You scared the shit out of Jordan when he heard you scream."

Mortification stings my cheeks. Jordan is a thirteen-year-old boy who lives with his parents and younger sister across the street from us. Both he and his sister are sweet kids. Jordan has mowed our lawn a few times to earn extra money.

"I'm such an idiot for overreacting."

The smirk on Hunter's face straightens and his hands still around my cheeks brings my face closer. "Don't ever think you overreact. I'd much rather you overreact when you shouldn't than not react the way you should when you need to."

"I feel horrible. His parents must hate me."

"I've already spoken with them, and they're fine. Judy knew you would feel this way and she said you shouldn't. Jordan should have knocked on the door instead of wandering into the backyard."

I nod, but I still feel horrible for scaring him. The issues I have are my own. They shouldn't affect the people around me.

He wipes away the wetness on my cheeks with his thumbs. "Do you still want to go out for dinner?"

"Do you mind if we stay in instead? We can go out tomorrow."

"Whatever you want, baby." Leaning forward, he gives me a tender kiss. "We'll order takeout and have a nice quiet night in."

"That sounds perfect."

Chapter Fifteen
Hunter

"Why didn't you call me as soon as the judge announced the order?" I snap into my phone, my blood running hot and my vision blurred from the red seeping through it. "You should have called me yourself."

"I was intending to, but I got called away before I could. I told one of my officers to do it. I'm not sure why he didn't. My guess is there was miscommunication somehow."

"That's not an acceptable excuse, Trevor, and you damn well know it. It's my wife's life at stake here," I growl through gritted teeth. "The incompetence of the police department has put her in danger."

Trevor is the chief of police and is considered a good friend. At least he was until this massive fuck up.

Trevor sighs heavily over the line. "There's no reason to believe Henry will go after Cat, Hunter. He left town immediately after being released two days ago. According to my sources, he has no plans to come back." He pauses for a moment. "If it helps, I'll have a couple of officers patrol the neighborhood for the next few weeks."

"Fuck you, Trevor. I'll hire my own people. I'll be damned if I let the idiots at the department watch over my wife. They can't even follow orders and pick up the phone to inform me that one of the men who almost murdered Cat and succeeded in murdering my children is out on the streets. What makes you think they'd be any better at protection?"

"It was a mistake that won't happen again. I give you my word."

The comment only irritates me more. This shit should not have happened in the first place. Not to mention, the fucking bastard should never have been released. "Your word doesn't mean shit if you can't control the assholes who work under you."

Silas walks into my office with his eyebrows raised, no doubt wondering what all the shouting is about. He folds his large frame into the chair in front of my desk.

"Did you at least get the letter that was sent out?" Trevor asks.

"What letter?" I bark.

"The Court of Appeals sent one out the day the conviction was overturned."

I bite back a curse. "I haven't seen one, but that doesn't mean Cat didn't come across it first."

The thought of Cat seeing that letter when I wasn't there sends a murderous rage through me. Not that she doesn't have the right to know that one of her attackers was released from prison. However, I would have preferred to tell her myself. If she has seen the letter, she hasn't mentioned it. Which isn't surprising, since Cat tends to repress anything to do with that night.

"I'm sorry about this, Hunter. Please let me know if there is anything the department can do. Rest assured, I plan to find out why you weren't notified."

"Yeah," is all I grunt before I smash the End Call button.

My phone skitters across the desk when I angrily toss it down.

"What's going on?" Silas asks, catching my phone before it can slide off the edge of the desk.

"Henry Stephens was released from prison two days ago."

His relaxed posture stiffens. "What the fuck?"

I nod grimly. "Fucking Trevor was supposed to call me, but there was some fuck up and the call never came."

"How in the hell did he manage to get out?"

"A technicality." Anger makes my voice come out a deep growl. "Apparently, there was a discrepancy with his DNA results found at the scene."

"Shit," Silas mutters.

"Trevor claims Henry left town and isn't expected to return." Now that Henry's been released, he's within my grasp. "I want the bastard found and brought to me."

"I'll get a couple of guys on it. Are you heading home?" he asks.

"Yes. I want to check on Cat." I snatch up my phone and start scrolling through names, looking for a particular one. "I'm calling Mathias and having him put a couple guys on Cat. I don't think Henry is smart enough to stay the fuck away. Especially with Whisper catching wind I'm onto him."

"Good idea." He gets up from his seat. "How's Cat doing?"

"She was fine when I left this morning. What happened last night really shook her, but I think she was more embarrassed than anything when I told her it was only the neighbor she saw."

If Cat found and read the letter with the news about Henry, it would explain her extreme reaction to seeing a shadow in our backyard last night. It's not the first time she's reacted in such a way. There have been other instances where she thought she saw something that wasn't there.

PTSD is a vicious beast that Cat will always have to face.

The safe room in our basement took three months to construct, and it only added a small sense of security once it was completed. There is nothing that can totally remove Cat's fear of being attacked again. Just as nothing can take away my own fear of something happening to her.

The men who broke into our home and terrorized my family were caught and sentenced to prison for seventy years. However, the crime wasn't random. My children didn't die and my wife wasn't brutalized because the sick bastards happened on our house by accident and decided to have some twisted fun.

My family was specifically targeted, and no matter how much the criminals were interrogated, the person who ordered it was never found. They only gave a single name. Whisper. According to them, Whisper always contacted them by phone with an untraceable number. There's no way to verify whether their claims are true.

Now one of the men is walking the fucking streets.

After calling Mathias and having a couple of his men shadow Cat, I slam through the back door of Slate. I climb behind the wheel of my SUV and take off, headed for home. As I navigate the busy streets, my body is still vibrating with rage. Knowing Henry Stephens has been free for two days without my knowledge has my fists strangling the steering wheel, imagining it's his fucking neck.

By the time I pull into the driveway, I've calmed down enough to walk into the house without letting Cat know something's wrong. She must already know. The letter would have been addressed to both of us. The return address on the top left corner would have prompted her to open it. She would have opened it, read it, and then hid it. Not to keep the news from me, but to prevent herself from seeing it again. Cat's mind can't handle anything that reminds her of that night. That's why all of our family photos are kept in a box in the closet. It's also why her parents take down picture frames of our kids when we visit them. I hate that we can't display the memories of our beautiful family, but I won't let what we once had destroy Cat's mind. My memories of them will forever remain in my head, and that is how I cherish them. They also live on in Cat and me.

I hear music playing when I walk into the house and reset the alarm. Despite the bad news I received today, a smile tugs at my lips. Following the soft beat of the music, I find Cat in the kitchen. Standing at the counter, she smashes dough with her hands. Her hips sway and her head bobs up and down as Bon Jovi plays on her phone. Bon Jovi has been her favorite band since she was a teenager.

I let all thoughts of Henry drift from my mind as I walk up behind her. Her lips tip up when she turns her head a fraction to the side, sensing me before I reach her. Wrapping my arms around her waist, I press my chest against her back, placing a kiss on the soft column of her neck.

"You're home early," she comments, turning her head so I have access to her lips. "Not that I'm complaining."

"What can I say? I was anxious to get back to you."

A smile spreads across her face as she looks over her shoulder at me. "It's amazing how you always know what to say to make my stomach flutter."

My lips twitch with amusement as I lift my brow. "You aren't used to it by now?"

Her laughter is light and full of happiness. "I'll never get used to it."

Resting my chin on her shoulder, I look down at the dough on the counter. "What cookies are you making?"

"Do you have to ask? Do I ever make anything other than your favorite? It's a good thing I also love Snickerdoodles."

I chuckle. "And it's a good thing I like to share."

That earns me a giggle. The contrast of the Cat from last night to the Cat today still amazes me. There's not a hint of stress from the night before visible on her face. It's as if the incident never happened at all.

I adore all sides of Cat, but the playful side holds a special place in my heart. It reminds me of our younger days, before darkness touched our lives.

Seeing a cooling rack with baked cookies on top, I grab one. I lift it to Cat's mouth first, then pop what's left in mine. I moan at the delicious sugary cinnamon taste. Cat's snickerdoodles rival those of professional bakers.

"Our reservation is in a couple of hours," I tell her. "Is this the last batch?"

"Yes. I'll be done in about fifteen minutes."

"Meet me in the shower?"

She wiggles her ass against my cock, which quickly begins filling with blood. "You betcha."

Grabbing her chin, I turn her head enough so I can steal a kiss before I let her go with a light smack on her butt.

I leave her laughing in the kitchen and head upstairs. Rather than going straight to the shower, I move to the closet and pull out the lock box shoved to the back on the floor. After punching in the code, I lift the lid. When I see the white envelope on top, my jaw clenches painfully. My anger isn't due to Cat hiding the letter. It's solely focused on what the envelope represents and the reason it was sent.

I pull the envelope from the box, close the lid, and shove it back before walking out of the closet. Snatching the paper out, I unfold it. My blood boils with every word I read. I knew Henry's lawyer has been trying to get his client released on the technicality, but I didn't expect it to actually work. I'd love to get my hands around the neck of the asshole who fucked up the DNA test and squeeze until I see the life fade from their eyes.

Henry Stephens, Terry Fletcher, and Howard Leeway, all sixteen at the time, wore masks the night they broke into my house and terrorized my family. After murdering my children and leaving my wife for dead, the boys exited my home and went on their merry fucking way. By pure luck, Jimmy Simons, a homeless man digging through trash in the neighborhood at the time, witnessed the three teens leaving the house. After seeing blood on their clothing, he decided to investigate. That man saved my wife's life. While I can never thank him enough, I started by getting him an apartment, paying his bills for the first three months, and assisting him with finding a job. To this day, I visit him regularly and he comes by the house often. Cat's met him as her rescuer. However, when she started repressing her memories when they became too much for her mind to cope with, he became just a guy I met and became friends with.

I shove the paper back into the envelope and stuff it in a banker's box under the bed.

God help Henry if he ever comes back to town. He and the other two fucks who decimated my family were safe only because of the prison bars they were put behind. Now that one is free, there won't be an inch of him that's recognizable once I get my hands on him.

Chapter Sixteen
Caterina

I can't contain my smile as Hunter leads me, with my hand in his, from the SUV to our spot close to the lake's edge. Willow Lake will always hold a special place in my heart. It was here that I gave myself to him for the first time and where he proposed to me two months later.

The moon shines brightly above us, so we aren't in complete darkness. The added reflection on the lake helps as we approach the blanket already set out on the ground with a small cooler nearby.

My heart pitter patters in my chest as I take in the set up.

I turn to Hunter. "If you were with me all night, how did you set this up?"

His lips quirk into a smirk. "I had help from Silas and Katie."

"You seem to think you're getting lucky tonight." We stop at the edge of the blanket. "Sure are confident of yourself, aren't you, Mr. St. James?"

"You planning to say no?" He drops to his knees in front of me and pulls off my shoes one at a time, his head tilted back to keep his eyes on me.

I run my fingers through his thick hair. "I could never resist you." My voice is scratchy from the emotions he pulls from me.

He smiles as he leans forward, kissing my lower abdomen through my dress. He runs his hands up the outside of my thighs under my dress, and when he reaches my hips, he pulls me down on the blanket with him.

Once I'm seated beside him and his own shoes are thrown to the side, he reaches for the cooler and pulls out a bottle of wine and two wine glasses.

"I'm sorry we couldn't do this yesterday," he says after popping the cork. He fills a glass and hands it to me.

"Tonight is the perfect night to be out here." I gaze up at the full moon. "The sky was overcast yesterday, so we wouldn't have had this beautiful sight."

While sipping my wine, I enjoy the breeze drifting past us. It really is a beautiful night, especially considering it's the beginning of fall and usually a little cooler this time of year in the evenings.

I glance over at Hunter and find his steady, green gaze on me. I've counted myself lucky so many times over the years for having Hunter as my husband. I don't need to wonder how my life would be if I hadn't met him. However glorious that life might have been, I don't want any part of it. It's impossible to imagine anything better than what I have now.

Hunter takes my glass from me and places it beside his on the cooler lid. Reaching into his pocket, he pulls out a small black box. It brings back memories of him doing this before. But instead of a diamond ring, I find a small silver key hanging from a chain, both twinkling in the bright moonlight. Leaning forward, I take a closer look.

"You took possession of my heart the first time I saw you in Slate all those years ago, Cat. I never wanted or asked for it back.

It belongs to you forever, because I know you will always treasure it." Tears spring to my eyes when he holds up the key dangling from the necklace. "The key is unnecessary, because my heart hasn't been my own for years, but it still belongs to you."

A tear blazes a path down my cheek as I reach out for the key, touched beyond measure by Hunter's words. After angling the key just right, I see the words written in Italian on the side: *Per Sempre Vostri*. Forever Yours.

"It's beautiful." I lift my eyes to him. "Thank you. Help me put it on?"

I spin around, giving Hunter my back and lifting my hair out of the way. The key is cool against my heated flesh when it settles just above my cleavage.

Warm breath fans across the back of my neck seconds before Hunter's lips touch the spot. Shivers run through my body as goosebumps appear on my arms. I look at Hunter over my shoulder and he immediately captures my lips in a kiss. Without breaking away from him, I turn around so I'm facing him. I meant to climb on his lap, but he has me on my back with his body poised above me in the next breath.

One long finger traces the curve of my cheek. I can't see his face because he's cast in shadow, but I know his expression is full of love.

"If God gave me the ability to build the perfect woman, I couldn't have done any better than He did with you."

"Hunter," I whisper his name, emotions clogging my throat.

"You give me life, Cat, and there's not a day that goes by that I'm not thankful and humbled for that." His finger moves to my lips, and I open my mouth as he gently rubs the bottom one. "I don't know what I did to deserve you, but never doubt that I know what a rare gift I have in you."

Unable to take anymore of Hunter's sweet words before I burst into a blubbering mess, I fist my hands into the back of his hair and yank his head down. He thinks I'm the special one, and to him I may be, but it's Hunter who's truly the special one.

With our mouths pressed together, I try to put every bit of love I feel for him into the kiss. Words would never be enough, although Hunter's loving speech comes close.

Hunter lifts his body just enough for me to spread my legs and he settles between them. His hand travels up my thigh and raises the skirt of my dress as he goes. His hand is warm and slightly callused, the roughened skin fueling the fire already burning within me. My thigh is lifted higher, and I moan when the hard length of his cock, through his slacks, rubs against my wet center. In search of a firmer touch, I clutch Hunter's shoulders and lift my hips.

Our mouths separate and he trails his lips down my neck to the valley of my breasts. Once there, he lifts his head and tugs down the flimsy material of my dress and bra. The cool breeze blowing across my nipples, coupled with the intense desire Hunter brings out in me, has the peaks turning into stiff little points.

"You look absolutely stunning in the moonlight," he rumbles, his voice filled with appreciation. "Like an innocent angel on the verge of committing her first filthy sin. I could look at you for a lifetime like this and never get my fill."

"Hunter, please," I plead. I gently grip the strands of his hair, pulling him closer.

I arch beneath him when he pulls a hardened nipple into his mouth. "Yes," I shout, caught up in the moment. People rarely come to the lake at night, so I'm not too worried someone will hear us. Even if they did, I wouldn't care. My head is too full of Hunter to worry about being seen or heard.

He pays homage to one breast while kneading the other. Then he switches to the opposite and does the same. Need and desire blaze through me like a hurricane wreaking havoc, leaving me desperate to have Hunter's mouth on other places.

As if hearing my thoughts, he moves his mouth south. Lifting my dress so my bottom half is completely exposed, he leaves light kisses behind as he makes his way to the top of my panties. Expecting him to pull the lace material down my legs or hook his finger and pull them to the side, I release a deep moan when he sucks my clit through the silky material instead.

"Damn, baby, you're fucking soaked," he growls.

I wiggle my hips and release his hair, moving my hands to the thin straps on the side of my panties.

"Off," I pant. "Take them off, Hunter. I want your mouth on my bare skin."

"You want me to fuck you with my tongue?"

"God, yes," I moan desperately.

He takes pity on me and slides the material down my legs. As I'm spread out before him, my bare pussy inches from his face, he places his palms on the underside of my thighs and pushes them back, so my knees are close to my head. Before I can be embarrassed by the position, my mouth drops open, and I let out a delirious scream of pleasure.

Hunter feasts on my bare pussy, deep, growly rumbles leaving him, as if the slick juices leaking from me is the most delicious thing he's ever tasted.

I thrash my head from side to side, nearly overwhelmed by the intense feelings coursing through me. My orgasm comes out of the blue, taking control of my body in a way that only Hunter can elicit.

He laps up every drop that seeps from me.

Looking down my body, I find Hunter's dark gaze, a look of satisfaction sparking in his eyes. My arousal glistens on his lips and chin, which should embarrass me, but it only intensifies my desire.

"My turn," I tell him.

He gets to his knees as the hunger in his eyes darkens further. "You want my cock in your mouth?"

"Yes, please."

My polite reply causes his lips to twitch, and he reaches for the button on his slacks. He grabs my hand to help me sit up after releasing his engorged cock, but I shake my head.

"I want you up here." I lick my lips, my eyes darting to his long length as he strokes it in his fist. "I want you to feed it to me."

"Fuck, Cat," he growls, his jaw clenched. "Are you trying to make me come prematurely?"

I smile saucily at him. "Only if you aim it at my mouth. I want to taste you."

"Shit," he mutters.

A husky giggle escapes me as he quickly straddles my waist and scoots up my torso. My mouth waters as I see a pearly drop of pre-cum clinging to the slit at the tip. My tongue snakes out to swipe it away, and Hunter hisses out a breath.

With one hand, he angles himself down toward my mouth, and with the other, he slides his fingers through my hair and helps me lift my head. When I open my mouth, he slides the tip inside, and I latch my lips around it. Another strangled groan leaves Hunter.

My mouth stretches as he presses his hand against the back of my head.

My eyes open when he hits the back of my throat. Hunter is staring at me with his head angled down. He looks as if he's barely holding onto his control. Like he's on the verge of ramming his hips forward and forcing his cock down my throat. Moisture gushes between my legs at the thought. Hunter has always been gentle when taking my mouth, never forcing me to take more than I can handle. Sex between us is a little more rough. I love it when he grabs me and positions me how he wants me, the look in his eyes revealing his deep need. Like he'll die if he doesn't have me right then.

The mere image of him forcing his cock down my throat sends a wave of desire so intense it nearly blinds me.

I let Hunter's cock pop free of my mouth. "Fuck me," I whisper to him. "No," I add when he makes a move to leave his position. I dig my fingers into the muscles of his ass. "My mouth. I want you to fuck my mouth."

His green eyes blaze. Despite the heated look and the need I can see he's trying to hide, he says, "Baby, I don't want to hurt you."

Lifting my head, I run my tongue along the underside of his cock. "But wouldn't it feel incredible if my throat spasmed against your cock?" I taunt him, watching the thread of his control unravel. "How tight it would feel." I scrape my teeth over the head and his fingers flex against my scalp. "How sexy it'll look to see the bulge of your cock and the spit dribbling from the corners of my mouth." I lap at the drop of pre-cum leaking from the slit. "I want you to, Hunter. I want to know what it feels like to have you force your cock down my throat until I choke on it."

The snarl that escapes him has my clit pulsing and my legs

scissoring to try and relieve the ache. Nothing is more satisfying than hearing Hunter make all those needy noises. I'm pretty sure the blanket below me is soaked with the arousal pouring out of me. I've always had a secret desire for Hunter to take me roughly. For his iron-clad control to snap. For him to pound my mouth, my pussy, and even my ass with no remorse or concern that he's being too rough. I want him to dominate me.

And from the intense need in his eyes, it's something he wants too.

"Open your mouth wide," he demands in a husky whisper.

I comply and he slips the head back inside my mouth. He releases my hair to catch himself when he falls forward. The changed position allows me to open my mouth wider, and he slips further inside. When he bumps the back of my throat, I fight against my gag reflex. He pumps his hips slowly before picking up speed. With each thrust forward, he goes in further. Hunter isn't a small guy by any means, so even though he's already partially wedged in my throat, I still have a few inches to go.

"Goddamn, baby, that feels so fucking good," he groans.

My throat and mouth have become sore, but it's the delicious kind. I stretch my neck back and look at his face. An intense thrill rushes through me when I notice how delirious his eyes are. I work my throat muscles the best that I can with something thick lodged inside it.

He grunts and thrusts deeper, shoving even more of him down my throat. This time I can't hold back my gag, which only tightens the muscles gripping his cock.

He pulls his hips back, but I only allow him far enough for me to suck in a much needed breath before I'm tugging him back by digging my fingers into his ass. I take the full length of him, my nose pressing into his pubic bone, his balls against my chin.

"Motherfucker," he curses darkly. His hand moves back to my hair and he grips the strands tightly in a fist. He forces my head back, only to slam forward again. He uses my hair to control the speed at which he fucks my mouth

My hips lift into the air as I search for a touch I'm desperate for. One hand leaves his ass and my fingers seek out the swollen folds of my pussy. I insert one finger into my slick hole then bring the tip to my clit, desperately flicking the tight bundle of nerves.

"I'm gonna come, Cat," he grits out. "You want it?"

With my mouth full of his cock, I hum in the back of my throat and nod.

The sound barely leaves me before he pulls back a couple of inches, and a blast of hot cum spurts out of him, coating my throat. I greedily swallow the bitter saltiness down. After licking every drop from his cock, I let him slide out of my mouth with a pop.

He still hovers over me, his shoulders rising rapidly as he tries to catch his breath.

"Fucking hell, baby," he mumbles. "That was incredible."

I can't help the cheesy grin that stretches my lips. "It was my pleasure."

Chuckling, he scoots down until he's once again between my legs. He grabs my hips and lifts me so he's on his knees and I'm straddling him, my arms around his neck. A low moan slips from my lips as my wet pussy presses against his rigid shaft.

God bless Hunter's stamina.

"My little Cat needs to be filled, doesn't she?" he asks, nuzzling his lips against my neck.

"Yes," I whimper, tilting my head to the side.

Without warning, he lifts me enough to notch his head at my opening and pulls my body down on his shaft. The sudden intrusion pinches a bit, but the delicious fullness overrides the slight pain.

Hunter uses my body the same way he used my mouth. Slowly at first, then picking up speed. I hold on tight and relish the divine ride he's giving me.

Chapter Seventeen
Hunter

I spring awake when I hear the whimpers beside me, my instincts on high alert. I'm on my side, facing Cat, and my eyes immediately move to her face. Her expression is pinched in pain and her head tosses back and forth on the pillow.

"Oh, God, please," she cries in her sleep, the broken tenor of her voice shattering my soul. "Please don't hurt them. Take me instead."

Throwing the blanket off both of us, I sit up and slip my arms under her shoulders and knees. She's still stuck in her nightmare as I settle her on my lap.

"Please don't make me," she whimpers.

"Cat, baby, wake up." I kiss her damp forehead. It's destroying me to hear her pleas, but I'm afraid of waking her up too quickly. These fucking nightmares are slowly sucking the soul out of my body.

Suddenly, she stiffens and lets out a godawful cry. "NOOO!"

The sound still echoes in the room when her eyes snap open. I see the events of that night still lingering in her gaze before the protective barrier in her mind takes over and the look fades, the memories receding.

"Hunter," she croaks dryly. Her arms band around my neck and her face falls to my chest, where she sits for several minutes, great sobs shaking her entire body.

With my knees slightly raised, I pull her closer against me. I feel like my chest is collapsing in on itself as my eyes become moist.

"It's okay. I've got you," I whisper against her ear. "Was it the same?"

It takes her a moment to calm down so she can lift her head. Her eyes are swollen, her face is red, and her cheeks are streaked with tears.

"Yes," she says, her voice scratchy. "But...."

She trails off and her eyes fall away from me to look at her clenched hand resting on my chest.

Fear seizes my lungs, making breathing impossible. What else did she see? She usually never sees anything. She only remembers the screams. From her descriptions, it always sounds like a combination of her screams and those of our babies. Of course, she doesn't acknowledge they're our children's cries. Only that it belongs to her and to someone else.

I gently lift her head by her chin. "Tell me," I urge softly, needing to know what she remembers.

She squeezes her eyes shut, shaking her head as more tears trail down her cheeks. Her eyes look haunted when she opens them again.

"I-I was tied to a chair." Her throat bobs when she swallows. "There was a m-man holding a knife. The mask he was wearing looked so evil, Hunter." Her face crumples with a hiccupping sob. "H-he asked me a question, but I can't remember what it was."

It feels like my heart is trying to claw its way out of my chest. I remember the first time Cat mentioned the question she was asked while she and our children were held captive. Exactly like then, I experience a blinding rage unlike anything else I've ever known. Locking down that feeling and keeping it from Cat takes almost more effort than I possess. My body vibrates and my skin heats to such a degree that should burn anywhere Cat touches. The need to find Henry and completely eliminate him floods my system. The other two men are unattainable since they're in prison, but Henry isn't. He's free and available to quench my thirst for murder. Whisper is next on my list as soon as I find him.

Slamming my eyes shut and taking a deep breath, I quell the violence that's trying to overwhelm me and refocus my attention on Cat. She needs my full attention on her, so I need to stop thinking about all the ways I will slaughter Henry and Whisper.

"It was just a nightmare, baby," I whisper hoarsely, running my hand up and down Cat's leg. "Nothing and no one can hurt you." *Not as long as I draw breath*, I silently add.

The nightmares are getting worse, and I don't know what that means. Dr. Armani has told me repeatedly that we need to let Cat remember the events of that night on her own. Forcing it could cause irreversible mental damage. For a few months after the break-in, she remembered, but one morning it was as if the incident never happened. Any memory of that night, including having children, simply vanished, as if her brain said "*Enough.*" Now the mere mention of our children or that night causes her to break down and she becomes hysterical.

No one, especially me, blames Cat for what happened that night. However, she blames herself, and it's that misplaced guilt that prevents her from truly healing.

There's not a damn thing I can do to convince her that there was nothing she could have done to save our children. Those teens entered our house with the intent of killing my wife and children. There was nothing she could have done to change the outcome. Cat surviving was a miracle.

Henry is living on borrowed time. And eventually I'll find a way to get to Terry Fletcher and Howard Leeway.

And then there's Whisper. I'll enjoy killing him the most.

Chapter Eighteen
Hunter

> Cat: Can you pick up a carton of my ice cream on your way home?

I smile as I read the text message I received thirty minutes ago. I should have expected to receive this message today, since she ate the last of the butter pecan ice cream last night. Cat always keeps it in the freezer. The woman is obsessed with the stuff.

I shoot off a quick reply.

> Me: You got it, baby.

After exiting the text app, I get up from my chair, having already shut down my computer. Paperwork is one of the things I hate most about owning a business. The majority of the work can be delegated, but there are some financial things Silas and I need to handle ourselves.

I leave my office and head to Silas's to tell him I'm leaving. It's rare for me to be here at night when the place is packed. As Silas prefers the nightlife, he tends to be here during the late hours more often than not. Sometimes, like today, he's here when I arrive in the morning.

Katie is sitting in Silas's chair when I enter the office. He's standing behind her, one hand resting on the desk and the other on the back of her chair as she shows him something on her computer.

"What do you think?" she asks as I walk into the room. Neither of them notice me. "It's perfect, right?"

"Anywhere you pick will be perfect, so long as it has a bed, and I get to spend the majority of my time in it with you."

She snorts and rolls her eyes. "Sex. It's all you think about."

Fisting a handful of her hair, he pulls her head back, leaving only a couple of inches between their faces. "Not my fault you've ensnared me with your tight-as-fuck pussy. It's damn near all I can think about."

She sneers, though it's hard to miss the shiver that shakes her body in response to the dominant action. "Don't be so crass, Silas. It's not an attractive look."

Silas laughs before dropping a hard kiss against her lips and letting her hair go. "You like my crassness. Admit it. It makes you wet."

"I'll admit to no such thing." She pats her hair, fixing the mess Silas made of it, while giving him a disgruntled look. "I have no idea why I put up with you."

"Because you're addicted to my big cock just as much as I'm addicted to your tight little pussy."

She gets up from the chair. "Whatever," she mutters. "If you hate the place I pick, don't blame me."

I walk further into the room, interrupting their playful spat. "Haven't even tied the knot yet and you're already bickering like an old married couple," I say with a chuckle.

It came as no surprise when Silas told me Katie had accepted his proposal.

"Shut your mouth," Katie says, a fake scowl forming on her face. "We'll never act like a typical married couple."

"If you say so," I reply, then turn to Silas. "I'm heading out. You good here?"

"Yes."

"How are the new girls doing?"

It's Katie who answers. "They're both good. Learning the ropes. I like them, especially Trixie. She's got moves that even turn me on."

Her statement earns a grunt from Silas and she glares at him. "Get that shit out of your head because it's not happening."

While she says it like she means it, we know if Silas really wanted Trixie to join them for a bit of fun, Katie would be on her back with her legs spread wide as Trixie went to town on her. Silas and Katie may be devoted to each other, but they also like to play, and that includes adding a third. And they don't discriminate. Men and women are welcome.

After leaving the pair, I stroll down the hallway and take the stairs to the first floor, the soft beat of music getting louder. As I pass by one of the rooms the girls use to get ready for the night, one of them steps out into the hallway. She's wearing a skimpy red bikini that exposes more than it conceals. I keep my eyes on her face.

"Oh, hey, Hunter," she says, a cheerful smile curving her lips.

Annika has worked at Slate for four years as an exotic dancer.

When she came to us, she had just graduated high school and had just left home, where she had been abused for years by her father. The desperate look in her eyes and the fresh bruises on her neck spurred Silas and I to offer her a job. The next night, Silas and I visited her father. Our night ended with the sounds of grunting pigs devouring the bastard.

Annika's currently in college, working her way toward a master's degree in social services. She's a good girl and a hard worker. She brings in a lot of regular clients due to her sweet and innocent girl-next-door looks.

"Hey, Anni," I greet with a smile as I slip my keys from my pocket. "How's school going?"

She tucks a long strand of her red hair behind her ear. "Good. I've got finals coming up, so I've been spending a lot of time studying."

"Grades still good?"

"Yep. A 3.7 GPA."

Slate offers to pay college tuition for any girl who works for us. The only requirement is that they keep a GPA of at least 3.0 and remain clean.

I tip my chin up. "That's good."

"Tell Cat I said hi."

"Will do."

Cat doesn't come to Slate as much as she used to, but she knows most of the girls. Annika has always been her favorite.

I go out to the alley and get into my SUV. My phone rings just as I start the engine. Tension tightens the lines around my eyes when I see the number.

"Hunter speaking."

"Hey, Hunter, it's Katherine at The Grove," the woman

answers, like she hasn't called me a hundred times before, and I wouldn't know the number. "You're needed."

Nothing further needs to be said. Athena is the only reason Katherine would call.

"I'll be there in ten minutes."

After ending the call, I drop the phone in the console and speed out of the alley. Eight minutes later, I pull to a stop in a parking spot and hop out of my SUV. Katherine is waiting for me when I walk inside, her expression grim. Without a word, she spins on her heels, and I follow.

"Is it bad?" I ask in a low, deep voice filled with dread.

Instead of leading me toward the community room where I usually sit with Athena, she heads up the stairs to the second floor where the patient rooms are.

As she ascends the stairs, she glances over her shoulder at me. "It's been worse, but she's not having a good day."

My jaw clenches with my tight nod.

At the top of the stairs, we turn left and stop at the third door on the right. With the curtains open, the room is bright and sunny. The walls are a soft yellow and the ceiling is white, both adding to the brightness. A single bed with a nightstand is against one wall and a rocking chair sits by the window. Opposite the bed is a simple dresser. On top of it is a bouquet of flowers I had delivered a few days ago. The flowers are a constant. Every week, a fresh bouquet is delivered to replace the old one. It's to give Athena something pretty to look at when she's in her room.

I walk past Katherine and enter the room. On the bed, Athena sits with her legs drawn up to her chest, her chin resting on her knees. She appears to be thinking about something unpleasant, judging by her somber expression.

I partially close the door behind me, giving us some privacy.

Athena's head slowly turns toward me as I approach the bed. The haunted look in her eyes sends chills down my spine.

"Athena." I keep my voice light. Taking her cold hand into mine, I sit next to her on the bed. Some of the darkness that coats my world lightens when relief flashes in her eyes at my touch. "How are you feeling today?"

As she gazes at our hands, her lips curve down slightly. "Lonely," she whispers, the single word carrying a note of immense sadness.

"You know you aren't alone, right?" I ask gently. "You've got me. And there are other people who care about you."

Her head lifts again and her eyes meet mine. "I miss them."

My heart thumps heavily in my chest. "Who, Athena?"

"My family."

If I were standing, my legs would fucking buckle at her reply. The words come out with utter despair.

The tragic loss of her family years ago left Athena broken. The pain that shadows her is the reason I'm here whenever she needs me. She reminds me of Cat on the rare occasions she allows herself to remember.

What Athena doesn't realize, what she won't admit to herself, is that she has me. I'm her family now. She'll have me for as long as she exists.

My eyes are drawn to the white bandages on her wrist. Athena came to The Grove after she threatened to cut her veins to stop the pain of her loss. My first encounter with her was the day she was admitted. She followed through with her threat two days later, sawing through her wrists with a plastic butter knife she had stolen from the kitchen. It left behind jagged scars. Since then, her wrists are always covered with gauze. Seeing the evidence of her helplessness in dealing with her pain always manages to hit me in the chest like a sledgehammer.

Rather than respond to her whispered words, I move an inch closer to her, afraid of setting her off. Apart from my hand, I don't let any other part of me touch her.

"Your family loved you, and I know they miss you just as much. I bet right now, they're looking down at you, wishing they could be here."

Her eyes hold hope. "You really think so?"

A smile forms on my lips, even though contentment is the last thing I feel right now. "I do."

"You don't think they hate me?"

My molars grind, and it takes almost more effort than I have to keep from yanking the woman into my arms.

"No, Athena." My voice comes out hoarse, forcing me to clear my throat. "They don't hate you."

"You promise?"

"I promise."

When she smiles, it seems like the sun peeks out from behind a dark cloud, bathing the room in brilliant light. It's amazing to witness the transformation from a broken woman to one who is looking at me with sparkles in her eyes. I don't get to see many of Athena's smiles, but on the rare occasion that I do, all I can do is stare. The woman is utterly gorgeous.

Before I freak her out by my stupefied expression, I drop my eyes from her. "Want to go for a walk outside?"

"Okay."

I get up from the bed, letting her hand go for a moment. The instant our connection is broken, a frown appears between her eyes.

"Hey," I murmur and her eyes lift. "I'm right here."

Her tongue slips out to run along the edge of her lips, and her head dips into a nod.

I'm not sure why Athena has attached herself to me. Perhaps she feels the same deep connection with me as I do with her. Maybe she senses that, in a way, I'm broken too. Regardless of the reason, I'm glad she chose me. There is no one else I trust to treat her with the same care I do. Athena is special in so many ways, and no one but me will ever see that.

When she's out of bed and her shoes are on, I take hold of her hand and we walk down the stairs together. After telling Katherine we're going for a walk, I lead Athena out the front door. We take the stairs on the side of the porch that lead to the backyard. There are numerous flower beds filled with colorful flowers that are just starting to droop because of the cooler weather. Throughout the area, there are large trees with low-hanging branches. Here and there, benches and picnic tables offer patients a place to sit and relax in the open air. The area is picturesque and relaxing. A few patients are currently enjoying the freedom of the outdoors with some nurses and orderlies watching over them.

I tug Athena behind me over to one of the benches by a flower bed filled with daisies. The moment she sits down, she tips her head back, her expression serene, as if luxuriating in the heat of the sun. Taking advantage of the opportunity, I stare at her unabashedly.

Her long dark hair flows down her back in a tangled mess, as if it hasn't been brushed in weeks. Her cheeks are sun kissed, and her nose and cheeks are sprinkled with freckles. With her eyes closed, her long, thick lashes rest against her cheeks. A smile tips up her full, peach-colored lips.

I'm not sure if I've ever seen her more beautiful and at peace.

As free as she is at the moment from her dark thoughts, I know it won't last. These precious moments never do. They're so special, which is why I try so hard to see them when I'm with her.

Her head drops after a few moments, and she looks down at our hands. Her gaze lingers for a few seconds before lifting. I shift in my seat as she looks at me, her brows pinched together, as if she's searching for something specific on my face.

"Why do you visit me?" she asks quietly.

"Do you not want me here?"

Her tangled hair swishes when she shakes her head. "Seeing you is the best part of being here. I just wonder why. You didn't know me before and have no ties to me now. Why would you spend time with a stranger?"

I look across the back yard, trying to come up with a way to explain why I'm compelled to come here. I can't quite put into words how I feel about Athena. Even in my own mind, the emotions I feel when I think about her are complicated and complex.

I turn my eyes back to her. "I... care about you." I use the word care because what I really want to say might unnerve her. "I don't like the thought of you being here alone."

She ponders my answer for a moment before she pierces my heart with her next words. "I hope you never stop coming." She looks down at her bandaged wrists. "You keep the voices quiet when they scream at me to end the pain forever."

Fucking. Hell.

Never have I struggled so hard to keep my hands to myself. My muscles literally tense with the need to reach out and gather her against my chest.

What she just revealed is one of the main reasons I come to The Grove. My head can't handle the thought of Athena taking her own life. If that were to happen, it would be me who took up residence in her room here, because it would drive me insane. Or worse yet, I may follow her into the afterlife.

My fingers tighten around her hand as I turn on the bench, wanting her to hear me loud and clear. Having her full attention, I look into her eyes imploringly, letting her see how much pain her words have caused.

"You listen to me, Athena," I say, my voice hard and not giving a fuck. "You tell those voices to fuck off. When they plague you, you think of me. You think of what would happen to me if you no longer existed. Because I'm telling you, God as my witness, I swear on everything I hold dear, if something happened to you, it would destroy every fucking part of me."

My shoulders rise and fall with my heavy breathing and my chest aches like I was punched in the solar plexus, stealing every ounce of breath in my body. *That's* what it does to me when I envision Athena being gone. There's no way in hell I'll be able to cope with that reality.

It's evident from her shocked expression that I surprised her. Hopefully it'll be enough to knock out any thoughts of ending her life.

I huff out a breath and turn so I'm not facing her anymore. Using my free hand, I run it roughly through my hair, gripping the strands hard as they pass through. Blood flows hot and cold through my veins.

I need to calm my shit down before I look at her again, because I'm sure my eyes look crazed at the moment. Breathing deeply, I wait for my heartbeat to slow down and for my thoughts of losing her to fade.

Looking back at her, she has her bottom lip wedged between her teeth, and it seems like *she* is worried about *me* now.

I give her hand a soft tug. "I'm okay." I don't know if I'm saying it for her benefit or mine. Maybe both.

She bobs her head slowly, but her eyes remain filled with concern. I force my lips to form a semblance of a smile. "Tell me something good that happened today."

Thankfully, her eyes clear and her lip bounces free of her teeth. She holds out her free hand and wiggles her fingers. "I had my nails painted."

I look at her newly painted nails. Hunter green. My lips quirk at the color, and a part of me wonders if she chose it because of its name.

"They look beautiful."

She looks at me shyly. "Thank you. I had my toenails done too." She lifts a leg out in front of us, stretching her foot. "But you can't see those."

"I bet they look just as good as your nails."

The next thirty minutes are spent talking about nonsensical topics. Athena has never been one to talk about her personal life, and I've never pushed, since I don't talk about mine. Some of my visits are spent in silence. Sometimes we talk about mundane things. The harder visits are when I spend my time talking Athena off a cliff only she can see.

When she releases a yawn, I know it's time for me to leave. I stand and gently pull her up with me.

"You look like you could use a nap."

Her chin dips to her chest before rising again. "I am kinda tired."

"Come on. Let's get you back inside."

We head inside, straight to her room. She falls to the bed like her legs are unable to handle her weight. Her eyes drift closed seconds later, and a moment after that, her breathing evens out. It gives me comfort to see the peacefulness relaxing her features. I often wonder if dreams plague her like the nightmares that cripple Cat, and pray that they don't.

Bending at the waist, I carefully whisper my lips over her temple, closing my eyes as her sweet, subtle scent drifts through my senses.

"Sweet dreams, Athena," I say softly. "Until next time."

Chapter Nineteen
Caterina

As soon as I press send, I sit back in my chair and exhale a sigh of relief. A manuscript that should have taken me three months to complete turned into five months. But it's finally finished and is currently traveling through cyberspace on its way to my agent for approval. If Darren comes back with big changes, I'm going to use the papers he printed my words on and give him a thousand papercuts. Make no mistake, I love my characters, but this book was a beast to write and was emotionally draining. I'm done looking at it.

I plan to take a month off from writing, but I tell myself that every time I finish a book. It never pans out. I'm lucky if I go two weeks before the need to start my next story drives me crazy, and I'm back behind my desk with a fresh Word document pulled up. I can already hear the voices clamoring in my head, begging for freedom.

The doorbell rings, and I pull up the camera app on my phone. Ginger waves at me, knowing I always check before I come to the door. Her two adorable boys follow suit.

Swiveling in my chair, I grab my coffee cup and drop it off at the bar on my way to the front door. I quickly disengage the alarm and yank the door open. Aiden and Josh immediately barrel their way inside and attach themselves to my legs.

Ginger sighs, walking inside at a slower pace. "I swear they love you more than me. I never get that reaction when I pick them up from kindergarten."

As I gaze down at the boys, I place my hands lovingly atop their heads. "It's just because they see you every day. I'm the shiny toy they only get to see every so often."

"Same ole, same ole mom, huh, stinker one and stinker two?" Ginger says, making them giggle. "Sorry to disappoint you, but you only get one, so get used to it."

Ginger closes the door, I re-engage the alarm, the security system beeping to let me know it's set.

"What brings you by today?" I ask, turning to Ginger.

"Ice cream!" Aiden shouts and Josh bobs his head up and down dramatically.

With a grin, I bop the ends of their noses with my finger. "Ice cream, huh? Is that all I'm good for?"

With an amused eye roll, Ginger remarks with mock authority, "We did not come to see your aunt for ice cream." She looks at me. "We were in town for their five-year check-up, and I figured we'd stop by and see what you were up to."

"But, Mom," Aiden says before I can reply. He lets my leg go to hold up his arm, showing off a Spiderman Band-Aid on his skinny bicep. "We got shots today. You said we would get ice cream if we were good. We didn't cry. Not even a little bit."

I laugh at his pleading look. His brother matches the look, even though he keeps quiet.

"Sorry, Ginger, but I can't say no to that. Especially if it's a promise." I ruffle both boys' heads. "And it just so happens, I have an almost full carton of ice cream in my freezer."

"Yah!" Aiden turns his beseeching eyes to his mom. "Can we, Mom?"

She tries to pull off an irritated look, but she can't hide the twitch of her lips. "Fine. A small bowl for each."

They run, hellbent on getting to the kitchen. We laugh and shake our heads as we follow them down the hallway. We find them already sitting at the kitchen table, their legs swinging joyfully and their eyes filled with anticipation as they gaze at the freezer.

As I grab the carton of ice cream and two bowls and spoons from the cabinet, I can't help but laugh. The minute the bowls are placed before them, they snatch up the spoons and shovel cold bits into their mouths.

"From the looks of them, you'd think they never get the stuff," Ginger says dryly, grabbing a water bottle from the fridge.

"You know getting ice cream from someone else's house is so much better than what you get at home." Ginger lets out a short laugh before she tips the mouth of the bottle to her lips. "Or that's the logic for kids, at least."

"Nope." She recaps the water. "I've just got spoiled kids. I blame it all on Mason."

"Whatever. Those boys are adorable, and you know it," I tell her.

"Oh, I know it all right, and they're already taking after their father and using their cuteness to get what they want." Her amused eyes slide to me. "Them at your table eating your favorite ice cream is proof of that."

I lift a shoulder. "What can I say? They're my favorite nephews."

"They're your only nephews."

"Eh. You got me there." Smiling at our banter, I put the ice cream back in the freezer and pull out a package of steaks to grill later.

Ginger and I grew up as close as two sisters could be. We were each other's best friends before we started to make friends of our own. I still consider her my best friend, she's just not my only best friend anymore.

"Have you talked to Mom today?" She takes a seat on one of the stools at the bar.

I pull out the one next to her and sit. "No. She called earlier, but I was in the middle of finishing up my manuscript. I haven't had time to call her back."

"Her and Dad are talking about buying a yacht and living on it part of the year. They want to sail up and down the east coast."

"Wow, really?" This news surprises me. My parents have never expressed an interest in living on a boat. "That's out of the blue. What made them come up with that idea?"

"Not sure how she met her, but I guess she's been talking to this woman online for a while. She and her husband have been living on a boat full time for the last ten years. I guess all the stories she's told Mom have piqued their interest. Her and Dad are planning a trip down to Florida this summer to meet the couple in person. They're going to stay with them on the boat for a week."

My brows jump up. "Wait. Are you serious? How well does Mom really know these people? They could be serial killers who lure people out on their boat and they're never seen again."

Ginger laughs as she picks at the label on her water bottle. "You really ought to lay off the thrillers for a while, Cat. Your imagination is a bit scary at times."

"Oh come on," I huff, turning in my seat to face Ginger. "You can't tell me you're really okay with this. What does Max think about it?"

Her eyes come to me and her lips twist. "He has the same concerns as you. But neither of you are giving our parents credit. They aren't stupid, you know. Dad is an excellent judge of character, and you know he won't risk Mom's safety if he felt an inkling of doubt. He's already having the couple checked out."

"Well, that makes me feel somewhat better," I grumble, still not totally appeased.

Ginger's hand lands on mine, squeezing my fingers. "Don't worry. They'll be safe."

I nod and decide to change the subject. I'll talk to Mom later and hear from her what precautions she and Dad are taking.

"Did Mason make partner?"

Ginger grins, letting my hand go to continue picking at the label. "He did," she answers happily. "In two weeks, the name Hart will be alongside Spencer, Mullens, and Thatcher."

"Oh my God! That's wonderful!" I reach over and hug Ginger. "I'm so excited for you both!"

Mason started at the bottom of Spencer, Mullens, and Thatcher, one of the top corporate law firms in the country. He's been with the firm for five years. Although it's not common, it's not unheard of to become a partner after only five years. Mason has worked his ass off and is a damn competent lawyer.

"Let me know if you want Hunter and me to watch the kids so you can go out and celebrate," I offer.

"I may take you up on that. Our lives are going to be hectic for a while. He's expected to put in some hellacious hours, not that he hasn't already."

"Well, we're here when you need us," I say.

"Thanks, sis."

Ginger and the boys hang out for a while longer before she takes her crew and heads out. I make a mental note to order a bottle of wine this week and have it delivered to my sister and Mason.

After locking and setting the alarm after they leave, I return to the kitchen and grab the bottle of pain pills from the cabinet above the stove. I've been getting migraines for years, and I feel one coming on. I want to head it off before the worst of it comes. The sooner I take the prescribed medicine, the less it will cripple me.

After swallowing the pill with some water, I go upstairs and wet a rag with cold water. Besides taking the medicine, the best thing I can do during a migraine is to lay down and sleep.

After crawling between the cool sheets, I lay the rag over my forehead and eyes.

Chapter Twenty
Hunter

Dropping my keys and phone on the desk, I sit in my chair and start looking through the few pieces of company mail Katie left for me. Most of it is the usual shit. However, it's the small padded envelope that catches my eye. Flipping it over, I see my name typed on the front. It doesn't have a return address, which gives me pause. It's never pleasant when you get a mysterious piece of mail with no return address. It means the sender is concealing their identity for some reason.

When I open the envelope, I find a thumb drive inside. A sense of foreboding has the hair on the back of my neck standing up. A thumb drive sent anonymously through the mail is notorious for holding information. In most cases, that information isn't good. Instinct tells me I'm not going to like what's on this one.

I tip the envelope, letting the thumb drive fall to my desk, and then grab my laptop. Once it's booted up, I insert the drive into the USB port. Sitting stiffly in my chair, I prepare myself for whatever I'm about to see.

The name of the file that pops up doesn't help the uneasy feeling forming in my gut.

FunWithKitty.

The file is a video. After I double-click the icon, a black screen pops up. Once the screen changes, I immediately recognize where the video was taken.

It's my fucking house.

I tense, preparing to spring up from my chair, at first thinking the video was recently recorded. That means the person who sent this could be inside my house right now. As soon as I see the picture on the wall, I stop in my tracks. It hasn't been there for years. Five years, to be precise. It's a family photo of Cat, Eliana, Ryder, and me. All of our family photos have been hidden away. The paint behind the picture had also been changed a couple of years ago, so the person taking the video couldn't have found the picture and rehung it.

I hear heavy breathing at first, like the person holding the camera has just finished a marathon. They move from the hallway into the living room. A bookshelf filled with Cat's published books comes into view, and the person heads straight for it. The camera is turned and placed on a shelf facing the room. From this new angle, it looks like it sits on the second one from the top. It gives the camera a clear view of the rest of the room.

A person wearing a black plastic mask with electric blue X's on its eyes and mouth appears. Immediately, I recognize who it is. Rather, he's one of the three teens who broke into my house years ago.

Ice shards form in my blood. My temples pound so hard that I can barely hear the faint noises coming from the speakers. Screams of terror and muffled cries. My vision clouds and my teeth nearly snap in two from clenching them so hard.

The masked teen walks away, back across the room, and meets another teen with a mask—the same design, except the X's are neon green—who is struggling to bring Cat into the room. No matter how much she fights, her attempts are weak. Probably from one of the many hits to the head she received. Her eyes are wide with terror, and a piece of tape covers her mouth, but it doesn't muffle her screams much.

Following the boy holding my wife is another, this time with purple X's. As he holds my two-year-old son like a football, he drags a screaming and kicking Eliana by her hair with the other hand.

The full force of unrestrained rage consumes every fucking fiber of my being. My body vibrates and my nails leave little crescent marks on my palms.

Not fucking once did Henry, Terry, or Howard mention there was a video of the night they attacked my family. I've only lived that night through Cat's words. It was difficult to hear what she and our kids went through.

I watch them each being tied to a chair. Seeing this firsthand is going to destroy a part of me that I'll never get back.

I want to close my computer and burn the thumb drive. I want to forget I ever got it and pretend I haven't watched what I have so far, because I know this is only the beginning. I know it gets much fucking worse.

This is my punishment. Cat had no choice but to endure this nightmare. She had no choice but to watch the destruction of our family. Because of that, I force myself to continue.

I watch as they start on my wife. My eyes are glued to the scene as each one of them takes turns brutally raping her in front of our children. Not just with their bodies, but with random objects they find in the room. Then they take her all at once.

Cat's muffled screams fill my ears, the same as those she makes in her nightmares as she relives this night over and over again. I want to jam screwdrivers in my ears until they puncture my eardrums. The sounds that leave her throat will haunt me forever.

What seems like hours later, they leave Cat on the floor, naked and covered in her own blood. She's deathly still, and I'm not sure if it's because she's passed out or is in too much pain to move. However, when they turn to Eliana and my twelve-year-old daughter starts to scream, Cat stirs.

My jaw locks, the muscle cramping, when Cat struggles to get to her hands and knees. Blood coats her bare thighs, the color too fucking bright, and her tangled hair falls around her shoulders. Her face is nearly unrecognizable from the damage the bastards inflicted on her while they were raping her. With a hoarse voice, she begs the boys to leave our daughter alone as she crawls toward them. She offers herself, her strangled pleas blistering my ears.

One of the boys leaves the others and walks to Cat, picking her up and throwing her into a chair. She's bound to it by her arms and legs and has another piece of tape slapped over her mouth. After that, he rejoins his friends.

What they do to Eliana is no better than what they did to Cat. In fact, it appears that they're enjoying it more. Whether it's her young age or the rise they're getting out of Cat as she watches our daughter being used in such a horrible way, I don't know.

They laugh and jeer as they savagely defile my precious daughter in ways that will brand my brain for the rest of my life. No wonder Cat's nightmares are so intense, and she tries to forget what she saw and experienced.

A sane person would be driven mad if he or she remembered this.

As they leave Eliana lying on the floor, barely alive, her small body shivering, I feel bile rise in my throat. They move to Ryder next.

It's when they strip my sobbing toddler of his clothes and one man strokes his soiled dick that I can't watch any longer. I slam the laptop closed so forcefully that I hear the screen crack.

I've seen the autopsy reports. I know exactly what those bastards did to my family. How battered their bodies were after they were finished with them.

It wasn't Eliana and Ryder's rape that killed them, however harsh their perversions were. The coroner says they would have more than likely died from their internal injuries from the sexual abuse if given the opportunity. But the bastards ended their lives in another way before their brutalized bodies could give up on their own.

Cat was stabbed in the torso six times before they left, one of those wounds a mere centimeter from her heart. All things considered, she should also have died that night. It was considered a miracle that she survived. But I know it was her sheer will to live. She wishes she hadn't, but I thank God every fucking day that she wasn't taken from me too.

But after watching that video, I understand. After experiencing that, no one would want to live.

My chair slams back against the shelf behind me, knocking several items to the floor. The crash of glass barely registers, the rage filling my body taking control and filling all of my senses.

My body works on autopilot as I grip the edge of my desk and drop my head. My chest pumps as I pull in air and let it out slowly. Blackness seeps into my vision, and I try to push it away. When I close my eyes and try to center my thoughts, images from that fucking video flash through my mind.

And with them, the sudden urge to do damage is too

compelling to ignore. Because I don't have the sick bastards in front of me, I take my anger out on my office. Everything I fucking touch will be destroyed.

A deafening roar erupts from my throat as I flip my desk. It crashes on its front, launching its contents everywhere. Mindlessly, I pick up my chair, and with another bellow of rage, I launch it across the room. The shit on the shelf behind me gets thrown. My fist slams against the wall. As I repeat the move over and over again, I barely feel my bones crack and my skin split open.

No matter how much I try, I can't get the images out of my head. I'll never be able to get them out. They've super glued themselves to the walls of my brain to stay forever.

This was Whisper's doing. Henry could have sent it since he's out of prison, but I know it wasn't him. He sent me that goddamn thumb drive knowing how it would affect me. I nearly caught up with him so he's fucking with me. It's a reminder of what he did to my family, and what he could still do.

My chest feels tight and my head beats a crazy, unhinged beat when I'm done destroying my office. Shit lays everywhere. I want to do more. I *need* to do more, but there's nothing fucking left for me to demolish.

As I spin around, looking for something to grab, I see Silas and Katie standing in the doorway to my office. Kurt stands behind them. While Katie's eyes are wide, Silas and Kurt's faces are expressionless.

I take a deep breath through my nose, like a bull ready to charge, and my hands are fisted at my sides. My shoulders lift and drop, and I'm sure my eyes look wild. It feels like I'm coming apart at the seams.

"You want to explain what the fuck that was?" Silas asks, stepping into my office, his cautious eyes assessing me.

"Later," I grunt, my voice rough from yelling.

I start kicking shit out of my way, looking for my laptop. After spotting it under some papers, I pick it up, not surprised to find the back case cracked. When I pull out the thumb drive, part of me hopes it's also destroyed.

After finding my keys across the room and my phone, which is surprisingly not broken, under another pile of papers, I shove them both into my pocket. Katie quickly steps out of the doorway when I stalk toward her, and I feel her weary gaze as I walk down the hallway.

"Hunter!" Silas calls, following me down the stairs.

I don't stop, just growl over my shoulder. "I said fucking later."

Slamming through the back door of Slate, I pull Mathias's name up on my phone and tap it. He answers on the second ring.

"I need a status report on my house right now," I bark into the receiver.

"One sec," he replies.

I switch over to my SUV's Bluetooth and peel out from behind Slate as I wait for Mathias to talk to his man.

A week after Cat's attack, I had Mathias put a man on her. I've known the man since my time on the streets when I was a teen. He's three years older and was a ruffian like me. We parted ways when I went to live with Thomas and Sandra Myers, but we met back up again about ten years ago. He joined the Army and served as an Army Ranger for four years before he left the service. As soon as he was out, he founded his own security company.

With the mastermind behind the attack free, I wasn't taking any chances. It's been quiet for five years. Whisper has never made his presence known. No matter how hard I searched or who I beat the shit out of, no information could be found. It was like the guy was a fucking ghost.

Until a couple of months ago when Silas heard the name Whisper mentioned in Slate.

"Damon says a black Toyota just pulled up to your house," Mathias says, pulling me from my thoughts. "Jimmy Simons got out and approached the house, but he was waylaid by Presley."

Only a few people are allowed on my property when I'm not around. Cat's family is a given. Silas and Katie are another. And Presley, of course. Jimmy doesn't come by often and usually calls before he does, but I've added him to the list.

"Presley will keep him company until I get there. Let Damon know I'm on my way, but keep vigilant."

"Anything I should know about?" he asks.

"I received a thumb drive containing a video of the night of the attack. I don't know what Whisper's next move is."

"I'll inform my men to be extra cautious."

"Thanks," I mutter before ending the call.

I press down on the gas pedal, speeding through a red light when I see no cars coming. At the moment, my sole purpose is to get to Cat. I need to see her. To feel her in my arms to ensure myself she's really okay.

I SEE JIMMY AND PRESLEY SITTING ON THE STEPS OF THE porch when I pull up to the house. With clenched teeth, I step out of my SUV and approach the pair. I stuff my hand with torn knuckles in the pocket of my slacks to keep them from asking questions.

Normally, I wouldn't mind Jimmy stopping by and even encourage him to do so. At the moment, however, he's keeping me from reaching Cat, something I need to do to calm the waves of rage running through me. Presley is with him, but I can never be irritated by her.

Jimmy gets up from the steps when I walk up. "Hey, Hunter."

While he's only a handful of years older than me, he looks older after living on the streets for so long.

"How's it going?"

"Can't complain." He turns his head to the girl beside him. "Presley was just keeping me company."

"That so?" I cock an eyebrow at Presley. "Are you behaving?"

"I don't know what you mean," she answers haughtily, her eyes sparkling with laughter. "I'm always good."

I snort, which earns me a giggle.

"Too bad you weren't home sooner," she sasses, getting up from the step and brushing her butt with her hands. "Now I only have time to give this to you before I have to go."

She grabs the small stack of papers from the porch, and I take them with my uninjured hand.

"Perhaps if you'd given me a heads up, then I would have been," I say, part of me wishing she had, because I wouldn't have been at Slate and seen that fucking video.

Typical of a girl her age, she sticks out her tongue at me. My lips twitch.

"When have I ever given you a heads up? You're supposed to just know these things."

I grunt in response.

She turns to Jimmy, flashing a couple of dimples when she grins at him. "It was good seeing you again, Jimmy."

"You too, girl."

Jimmy and I watch as Presley skips down the driveway to the sidewalk. I swear, she never simply walks. She has to skip everywhere.

I face Jimmy, anxious to see what he wants so I can get him to leave. I don't feel bad about rushing him. I'm grateful for what he did for my family, but right now, I need to get inside to my wife. "What brings you by?"

"Nothin' particular. Just stopping by to check up on things since I haven't seen you both in a while."

"We're all good here. Things okay for you at work?"

"Yep. The boss man wants to make me a supervisor," he says, giving me a broad grin.

The smile I give him is genuine. "That's fucking great, Jimmy."

"Thanks. I wouldn't be here today if it weren't for you."

And my wife wouldn't be here today if it weren't for him. Cat survived that night only because Jimmy got to her in time. Just a few more minutes, and the doctors said she would not have survived.

I'd give my life for the man in front of me, since that's what he gave me. He saved my life by saving Cat. For a long time, I was barely living after what our kids suffered through. Had Cat died, I wouldn't have been able to live through it.

"You know I'll forever be in your debt, Jimmy," I say solemnly. "There's nothing I could ever do to make up for what you gave me."

Clearing his throat and looking off to one side, he appears uncomfortable. "Yeah, well," he mutters gruffly. "I'm just glad I was there for her."

With a nod, I let the subject go. Jimmy never feels comfortable when I express my gratitude for saving Cat. Though he says he doesn't need my thanks, I'll tell him until the day I die.

"Anyway, I better get going. I'm sure you're anxious to get inside."

"I'll tell Cat you stopped by. She'll be disappointed she missed you."

"I'll be back. Or you can bring her by my place."

"Will do."

We shake hands again before he gets in his car and takes off. As soon as he pulls out of the driveway, I head inside. My first stop is the downstairs bathroom to wash and bandage my hand, and then I head straight for the second floor, knowing Cat is lying down. She texted me earlier, saying she was getting a headache and wanted to try sleeping it off.

When I walk into the room, the thick, light-reflecting curtains are closed, so it's dark, but I can spot Cat sitting up in bed. As I sit on the side of the bed, some of the ire still radiating throughout my body fades. Cat is the only one who can ever calm me down when I'm drowning in the blackness of rage.

A soft smile curls her lips at the corners as her sleepy eyes meet mine. "Hey."

I cup the side of her face, smoothing my thumb along her cheek. "How's your head?"

Turning her head, she kisses my palm before looking back at me. "Better." Her eyes drop to the papers in my hand and she notices the bandage.

"What did you do this time?" she asks as her brows pucker into a frown.

I ignore her question and hold out the papers. "These are for you."

She nibbles her bottom lip as she takes them. Her mind is still on my hand, but I don't want to discuss it right now. Thankfully, she drops it and looks over the papers.

"I love Presley's stories." She flips through them. Seeing her delight has more of the fury blackening my soul drifting away. "I can't wait to read what other shenanigans she's come up with."

"With Presley, there's no telling," I say with a laugh.

"This is true."

Keeping my hand on her cheek, I pull her head forward and dip my lips closer to hers. My eyes close, and I savor the precious gift.

"How about we order in tonight and sit in front of the fireplace while we eat?"

"You truly are a man after my own heart," she answers with a smile.

"You got that wrong, baby," I say, rubbing my lips against hers. "I already own your heart, and I'm never letting it go."

Chapter Twenty-One
Caterina

An unexpected laugh bursts from my lips as I read about Presley dressing her baby brother in one of her doll outfits. The baby was barely three months old, still small enough to fit into the pink tutu and leotard. What makes it so funny is her father's reaction when he saw it. According to Presley's description, her dad nearly had a stroke, and the horrified look on his face made her and her mom laugh so hard they cried. Her dad scooped up the baby, informing his two girls that he was taking charge of dressing his son from now on.

The story continues to tell how Presley's mom went to her dad to apologize for what they did, and her dad's scowl only made things worse. Then she explains how her mom made it up to her dad by kissing him. It's amusing to read Presley's reaction to her parents' affection. She claims it grosses her out when they kiss with their tongues, but she also doesn't mind it. This is because it means they love each other like a mom and dad are supposed to.

I set the papers down on the coffee table with a smile on my face. Presley has been gifting me these stories for years, and every time I read one, I get a surge of love for her. Presley is pure innocence, and it shows in her writing.

I consider my own writing. It's the exact opposite of Presley's. Mine are filled with darkness and pain. While each story ends with a happy ending, the path my characters take before they reach that point is filled with heartache, misery, and hopelessness. I've tried writing fluffy stories. Ones where the characters laugh and smile and enjoy life, but they always seem so stale and boring. I need my characters to suffer horribly, feel lost, and have to fight tooth and nail for their happiness. They need to feel helpless and alone before they see the proverbial light at the end of the tunnel.

The doorbell rings, and I grab my phone to check the camera app. I see a young man holding a small box under one arm and a clipboard in his other hand. Tension stiffens my shoulders. I never answer the door if I don't recognize the person on the other side. A delivery is usually dropped off, and I wait until they leave before I grab whatever it is. This one, however, seems to require a signature.

Getting up from the couch, I cautiously approach the door, as if the person on the other side will hear me and try to break in. I know there's a reason why I'm so afraid, but I refuse to let the thought surface.

When I reach the speaker and screen attached to the alarm, I pressed a button. "Can I help you?" I ask, my voice wobbling as I speak.

On the screen, the man looks down at his clipboard. He must have noticed the camera above the door, because he tilts his head back and looks into its lens. "I have a delivery for Caterina St. James."

"You can leave it on the porch," I tell him.

"I'm sorry, Miss, but I need a signature."

I huff out a breath, fearing this might happen. "Would you mind slipping the clipboard through the mail slot? I don't open the door to strangers."

His eyes flash with irritation on the screen. I couldn't care less about whether he likes it or not. He can leave and take the package with him. I'm not expecting anything from anyone, so whatever's in the box, I'm sure I won't miss it.

"Fine," he finally grumbles.

When the edge of the clipboard appears in the slot, I pull it the rest of the way through. On the top of the paper, the logo of the company is displayed along with their contact information. Below that is the size of the box and the address where it came from. A post office box with no name.

I scribble my name on the signature line and shove the clipboard back through the slot.

I press the intercom button again. "Thanks. Just leave it outside."

After setting the box on the porch, the man spins away and walks down the steps. I wait until I hear an engine start and rev as he pulls away. After punching the alarm code, I open the door and grab the square box laying on the welcome mat. It's surprisingly light and small.

I reset the alarm and carry the box into the kitchen. Grabbing scissors from a drawer, I cut the tape. I don't know why, but my hands tremble as I pull back the flaps. There's a bunch of packing peanuts, so I grab handfuls and toss them on the counter. The first thing I see is something pink. I dig out more peanuts and white frilly lace comes into view.

A hollow feeling forms in my stomach as I reveal more of the box's contents. My hands are still shaking as I pull out a pink shirt with lace around the bottom hem. Another pink piece of material lays beneath it. I don't need to pull it out to know it's a pair of sleep shorts. The outfit is small, a size suitable for a young girl. The top has red splatters, like drops of blood, on the front.

When I throw the shirt back into the box, a cry rips through my lips.

Screams fill my ears, and I slap my hands over them, trying to block them out. As images of violence, blood, and pain float through my mind, I slam my eyes shut, trying to force them away.

Painful and anguished cries of a girl. Her broken body lying on the floor unmoving.

A toddler's scream of fear. Blood puddled beneath his mangled body.

A woman's plea to save them both and her wails of grief when she couldn't.

I can't let them in.

I can't remember.

I don't want to remember.

To remember is to relive it all over again.

A return to the past means revisiting the horrors and carnage, and experiencing the hurt of loss and helplessness. To remember that I wasn't strong enough to save them. To watch the brutality with devastation and to wish for death to come for me next.

I back away from the box and my back hits the counter so hard it jars me. The edge scrapes across my skin as I slide down until my butt hits the floor. I draw my knees to my chest. My hands still cover my ears and my eyes are squeezed shut as I scream, hoping the noise will drown out the cries in my head.

I scream so loud and so long that my throat goes raw and I sway to the side with dizziness. Another wail of grief erupts from my mouth.

My babies.

They're gone.

Not just gone, but taken in the most brutal way a child can be taken from a parent.

I couldn't save them. I let what happened to them happen because I wasn't strong enough to stop it. I was weak and unable to protect them as a mother should.

"Jesus fucking Christ," I think I hear whispered right before strong hands grab mine and try to pry them away from my ears.

I fight against the hold. I need to keep them where they are to help muffle the cries.

"No!" I yell when the hands continue to pull mine away.

"Cat!" A voice booms and it sounds familiar. "Tell me what the fuck happened!"

I open my eyes and my vision is filled with a pair of green ones. Hunter squats in front of me with his knees on either side of my feet, only inches from my face. A worried look fills his face. No, not worry. He looks terrified.

I curl my fingers around the top of my ears and a whimper crawls out of my throat. "I can't make them stop," I say, my voice hoarse from yelling. "Make the screams stop, Hunter. Please," I beg.

"I will, baby. I will," he answers in a gruff voice. His fingers gently uncurl my fingers from my ears. "Let go," he says softly.

I do, but only because I know Hunter will help me. He knows what to do. He'll make the screaming stop. He'll make the memories go away again.

The tips of my nails are bloody when I look down at them, and I feel a faint sting behind my ears. Although the sounds are still there, they're quieter, as if the people making them are further away. Hunter stands up and bends down to pick me up under my shoulders and knees. I bury my face in his neck, breathing in his scent.

"I don't ever want to remember," I cry.

"I know you don't, baby," he responds softly. "Shh... It's okay. I'll make them go away."

I hate the way his voice sounds. Like he's on the verge of losing his composure.

He carries me upstairs and places me on our bed. I tighten my hold around his neck, not ready to let him go yet. He lets me hold him for a moment before gently pulling my arms free. I curl on my side and press my lips together, trying and failing to hold my tears at bay. They still fall like a river from my eyes.

Sitting on the side of the bed, he pulls open the drawer of my nightstand. He takes out a bottle of pills and taps one in his hand.

"Take this," he says, holding the pill out to me. "It'll make the screams go away."

The way I snatch the pill from his palm and nearly shove it down my throat makes me feel like a drug addict. He hands me a bottle of water, and I greedily take a sip to wash the pill down.

The drugs will make me sleepy. I don't want to sleep right now, because I'm scared of my nightmares. I just want my mind clear of those awful cries, and I know the pills will help.

Once the pill is washed down, Hunter scoots me over so he can crawl into bed with me. I stay facing him, needing to be that much closer to him for as long as I can until sleep claims me.

His arms wrap around me, cocooning me in his safe embrace. I keep my arms in front of me and turn my face to press my cheek against his chest. His rapid heartbeat is soothing and helps drown out the lingering cries.

"I've got you, baby." His voice rumbles in my ear as tears still slide from my eyes. "Sleep. Everything will be better when you wake up."

I don't know if what he says is true. I can only pray that the walls I've built in my mind will rebuild themselves.

Because I'm not sure I can survive the alternative.

Chapter Twenty-Two
Hunter

My muscles tense as I draw Cat closer to me. My nerves are fucking shot to hell and back after finding her in the state she was in. Something happened, and it had to do with the box on the counter I briefly noticed when I rushed to her.

I close my eyes and take a deep breath. It's been years since she was this distraught. She left fucking bloody crescent marks behind her ears. She didn't have to tell me that her memories had a hold of her. I could see the demons in her eyes as she stared at me, silently begging me to make them go away. She was reliving her worst nightmare. Not only reliving it, but it was like she was right there in those fucking moments.

As much as it hurts that she doesn't acknowledge or remember our children, it hurts even more when she does, since I know how much it tortures her. Before her mind started protecting her, Cat had to be admitted twice to the hospital when the memories became too much for her to handle. The first time was two weeks, and the last time was ten days. One day during the second time, she woke up and seemed to have forgotten about that night and our children.

Making sure Cat is in a deep sleep, I carefully loosen my arms and slowly get up from the bed. The medicine will keep her in a dreamless sleep for hours, so I don't have to worry about her waking up while I'm not here. While she sleeps, her mind will repair its walls, and she'll wake up with the memories safely tucked away so they can't harm her anymore.

Standing beside the bed, I gaze at my beautiful wife. Her eyebrows are pinched together and her cheeks are splotchy red. Her hair is tangled from her gripping it earlier.

Unfolding the small throw blanket at the end of the bed, I pull it over Cat and tuck it around her shoulders. After brushing a lock of hair from her cheek, I lean over and kiss the spot. "I love you, baby," I whisper.

My heart lurches when I pull back and see the frown between her eyes slowly smooth out, as if my words give her comfort, even in sleep.

Walking across the hardwood floor, I leave the room, making sure the door stays open just in case she does wake up. I go down the stairs and head toward the kitchen. The closer I get, the tighter my muscles become.

I head straight for the box on the bar. Before looking inside, I check the outside for the address label. It's not surprising that the return address is a post office box. Getting a post office box is easy, and you don't even have to give a real name, so finding out who owns it is unlikely.

I don't worry about wearing gloves or contaminating any fingerprints. I don't intend to turn it over to the police. Since I never got the phone call about Henry being released, it's obvious I can't rely on them for shit anyway.

I'll give it to Marcus, but I don't expect he'll find any prints.

He didn't with the note left on my SUV at Mad Town, nor the envelope with the thumbdrive.

Pulling back the partly closed flaps on the box, I take out the pink piece of cloth. I recognize it immediately. Eliana wore an exact replica of this outfit the night she died. Under the shirt is the matching shorts. Both appear to have blood splatters. Since the outfit is too new, it can't be the same outfit she wore that night. Somehow, the sender found a matching set or had one made that's damn close.

Under the pink night outfit is another. My molars grind together as I pull out the blue and red Superman outfit. Again, it looks just like the one Ryder was wearing. Again, red spots dot the cloth.

I fist the material, the cuts on my knuckles from destroying my office yesterday popping open. The pulse in my temples pounds heavily as my body temperature rises.

Whisper is to blame. He may have Henry helping him, but this package came from Whisper.

In any case, it doesn't really matter. Both are dead men walking. It's only a matter of time before I get my hands on them. Cat and our children's suffering will be nothing compared to what I do to them.

I pull out the single piece of paper at the bottom of the box.

It's the same handwriting as the note left on my SUV a couple of weeks ago.

I hope you enjoy my gift. You can show your appreciation soon.

I ball the paper in my fist, barely controlling the rage filling every cell in my body.

Fucking games. I hate fucking games. And that's exactly what Whisper is doing. He's playing a game. The man isn't stupid. I have no doubt he can find out Cat's mental condition. He's taunting me because he knows how much I want his blood on my hands. He's doing the same to Cat to see how far he can push her before she completely breaks.

That shit is not happening. I'm done playing his games. He's taken far too much from my family.

My joints creak as I fist the paper and throw it back in the box, along with the clothes. After closing the flaps, I take the box out to the garage and shove it underneath a shelf where Cat won't see it.

As I walk back into the house, I take out my phone and dial Silas's number.

"Silas," he barks.

"Cat got a package today. It had the same outfits Eliana and Ryder were wearing that night. Red splatters all over them. And there was a note. Same writing as the one on my SUV. She flipped the fuck out, and I almost lost her."

"Shit," he curses.

"Pull every fucking resource we have," I growl, staring out the kitchen window. "Bring in every fucking guy we know who might have a connection to Whisper. I don't give a shit. I want this bastard found."

"You got it."

"I'm not leaving her. She's either at work with me or I'm here with her."

"I've got things covered here," he says. "Just take care of her. I'll call when I have something."

As soon as I hang up with Silas, I call Mathias and tell him I'll be sticking to Cat's side, but I still want his men around.

Cat is safe with me here, but I won't take any chances. I want as many men near Cat to protect her as I can get.

After that's taken care of, I carry my ass upstairs to our room. Cat's still in the same position as when I left her. After taking off my shirt and pants, I get into bed and wrap my body around hers. When I feel her warmth, my breathing becomes easier.

Chapter Twenty-Three
Hunter

I wake up to an empty bed and a dark room. Reaching out, I feel the sheets beside me, noting the coolness of the soft material. Cat rarely wakes up before me, and she never leaves the bed without my knowledge. The stress of the last few days must have knocked my ass out.

I hate not being aware of her waking up. Although I'm reasonably sure that her memories from earlier are safely tucked away in her head, I can't be sure until I see her.

I tilt my head to listen for movement in the house, but hear nothing. The silence is deafening, and I don't fucking like it. There should be music playing or footsteps on the stairs. A shower running or the sound of pots and pans clanking. Cat doesn't like the quiet. She says it makes her feel alone. So there's always some form of sound. Maybe the TV set on low or the soft lyrics of one of her favorite songs.

Quickly tossing the covers off me, I get out of bed, moving straight for the pants and shirt I threw off earlier.

If the house is silent, that means Cat's not in it, and that nearly has my bones freezing in fear.

Whisper's threat to Cat hovers in the back of my mind.

I don't know when or how, but he has plans to come after her. I won't let that shit happen, but with her out of the house, it may be out of my control.

My palm twitches to lash it against her ass. It's not her fault—the chances of her remembering the threat are slim—but I still want to punish her for putting herself in danger, whether she realizes it or not.

I'm snatching my phone from the nightstand when I see a note sitting beside it.

> *Going to Sunnyside. I'll be back in a couple of hours.*
>
> *Love you, Husband.*
> *Cat*

"Goddamn it," I growl and scowl down at the paper.

After shoving it into my pocket, I leave the room. Taking the stairs two at a time, I check my phone as I go. I have a couple of missed messages. The first is from Mathias. How in the fuck did I not hear my notification go off?

> Mathias: Cat took off. Damon and a couple others are trailing her.

As soon as I punch the alarm code, I leave the house and run to my SUV. Slamming my door, my anger and fear mounting, I pull up the second message. My jaw clenches as I read it.

> Scarlett: I need you.

Motherfucker.

I shoot off a reply to Mathias.

> Me: Keep a couple men on her, but send a couple back to the house to watch things.

> Mathias: Got it.

Using the app on my phone, I pull up the map that shows Cat's exact location. After a moment, it loads and shows her where she said she would be.

Next, I pull up the camera feed at Scarlett's house. Although the rooms are dark, the cameras are equipped with night vision. I switch from camera to camera until I find Scarlett wandering the halls of the house, making her way to the master bedroom.

The muscles in my jaw tense as I clip my phone into the holder so I can keep an eye on the screen. Backing out of my driveway and almost clipping a mailbox, I speed down the road.

For the moment, Cat is safe with Mathias's men watching over her. While I want to be with my wife and make sure she's safe, Scarlett needs me more right now.

AFTER ENTERING THE DARK HOUSE, I FORGO MY USUAL DRINK and head straight upstairs, where Scarlett is waiting for me.

I slip off my ring and slip it into my pants pocket. My shirt is ripped over my head and the button on my pants is unfastened when I make it to the room.

Using my foot, I kick the door open and it slams against the wall. I'm still angry with Cat for leaving the way she did. I'm angry with Scarlett for pulling me away from my wife. And I'm fucking pissed at myself for being so goddamn weak.

The loud bang of the door hitting the wall has the woman on the bed, wearing only a black thong, jerking up from her slouched position. Scarlett's eyes, wide with a hint of fear, watch me as I stalk across the room. I've never laid a hand on a woman out of anger. Scarlett is the only woman I've ever physically hurt, and she begs for it. Nevertheless, I'm fucking livid at this moment, needing to punish the woman in front of me. If not for her, I'd be with Cat right now. If not for her, I wouldn't have this twisted need to dole out the pain she craves. She allows me to show the darker side of my desires, but she pushes my limits. Since Scarlett entered my life, I've done things I would have never done before. She brings out the worst in me, and I keep coming back for more.

I don't stop until I'm at the end of the bed with my slacks sagging down my ass. I wrap my fingers around Scarlett's neck, my grip tighter than normal. In the dim light, her face turns red.

She doesn't have to tell me to make it hurt. I'll give her what she wants without her mouth begging for it.

I yank her head up and slam my lips against hers, the edge of my teeth sinking into the plump flesh of her bottom one. The taste of copper fills my mouth. My anger rises when she lets out a little moan at the bite of pain.

Using her neck, I yank her head back and scowl in her face. It kills me to see the desire in her eyes, knowing it's from the pain I've caused her.

Grabbing her hair, I shove her head down while pulling out my cock with my other hand.

"Open," I demand darkly, holding my cock in front of her face.

Her lips are barely parted before I force the head past them, not stopping until I reach the back of her throat.

"Jesus, fuck," I curse harshly, loving and hating the tight grip of her throat as she gags.

I pull back a couple of inches before slamming my hips forward and yanking her head toward me. I feel some of the strands of her hair snap, but I'm too far gone to care.

The woman has driven me to the brink of madness. I hate that I love her. But I also love that I hate her. She stands between me and my wife, and I'm helpless but to allow it. I've tried to leave her, but I'm always pulled back the moment I get one of her messages.

I slide the fingers of my other hand into her hair and use both to navigate how fast her head bobs. I fuck her mouth viciously, sawing in and out like it will be the last time I ever get my dick wet. I use her like a desperate man uses a whore. Leaving restraint behind, I slide in deep until her nose touches my groin and her chin rests against my balls, only to pull back out and repeat it.

My balls draw up, but I push my release away. No fucking way is Scarlett getting off so easily. She wants to be used and abused, and I'm in the fucking mood to give it to her.

Black streaks run down her cheeks as slobber drips down her chin and out of the corners of her mouth. As I push back into her mouth and her throat convulses again, she grabs my thigh and tries to push herself away. I slap her hand.

"Keep your hands to yourself," I growl, shoving her back down my cock. "Choke on my fucking cock like a good girl."

I grit my teeth, letting out a harsh breath as her throat tightens around the head. My glutes tense as I rock my hips back and forth, using her hair to force her to meet my thrusts. Her moans are cut off each time I hit the back of her throat.

"Goddamn that feels so good," I groan. "Your throat is so fucking tight. It's the best one I've ever had the pleasure of fucking."

Scarlett doesn't respond to my praise. She can't. She barely has time to take a breath before I steal it from her again.

I fuck her mouth over and over again until I'm so close to the edge that if I don't stop, I'll fill it with cum. I don't want to release in her mouth. My cum belongs in a different hole. Not the one I want to fill, but the one she demands I fill.

I yank her off my cock by her hair. Before she can fall backward, I grab her waist and pull her off the bed to stand in front of me. My hand goes back around her throat, and I use my thumb to tip her head back.

"You drive me fucking insane, you know that?" I grit between clenched teeth. "Fucking insane, Scarlett."

Her eyes, swirling with sorrow, stare up at me. "I'm sorry," she whispers.

I bark out a humorless laugh. "You're not fucking sorry. If you were, you wouldn't do this to me. You would let me go. You would br—"

My words are cut off by the tear that slides down her cheek. I feel that tear like it blazes its own fiery path down my cheek, and will leave a scar behind.

I bite the inside of my cheek and slam my eyes closed. I can't look at her. It hurts too much. It makes me wish that things were different. It makes me wish *I* could be different. That I could be exactly what she needs with nothing standing in our way.

No history.

No darkness.

No pain.

With my gut twisted into knots, I spin Scarlett around.

Putting my hand between her shoulder blades, I push her top half down so she bends over. Her ass, round and so fucking plump and delicious, sticks out, inviting me to take it.

I separate the globes, and pinpoint on the puckered hole. My cock twitches, knowing how tight it's going to feel around my shaft.

I never take Scarlett's ass without proper preparation, which includes coating my cock with her cunt juices first.

But right now, I'm strung too tight to insist I go easy. It makes me an asshole, but I want her to feel the pain. I want to punish her for what she's doing to me. Besides, she craves it anyway, so I won't be forcing it on her. I would never take from her what she isn't willing to give.

Keeping her cheeks spread, I drop spit on her little hole and smear it around with my thumb, slipping just the tip inside. After letting one of her cheeks go, I lick my palm, and slide it up and down my hard cock a few times. I aim the tip at her asshole. My jaw clenches when I press inside, her tight muscles gripping me.

Scarlett whimpers, and I glance at her face, satisfied to see she's turned her head to one side. Her bottom lip is caught between her teeth, and her eyes are filled with pain. I don't stop. I keep pressing forward, knowing from the sounds leaving her throat that she's getting pleasure from the pain cutting through her.

Once I'm a couple of inches from bottoming out inside her, I lean over her back. Grabbing a handful of her hair, I pull her head back roughly, causing her back to bow at an awkward angle, and put my lips at her ear.

"Does this feel good?" I whisper, anger making my voice come out a growl.

"Yes," she moans.

Her answer pisses me off further. My fingers tighten through the strands, and I use her hair to pull her back at the same time I slam the rest of the way inside.

"Fuck you, Scarlett," I snarl as I pull out and thrust forward. "Fuck you for making me like this. Fuck you for keeping me away from her."

Letting her hair go, I rest a fist beside her head and lay the other arm across her back, curling my fingers around her shoulder. I use my grip on her as leverage to pound her ass the way she likes.

I like it too. I like the way she sucks me inside of her. I like how tightly her muscles grip me, as if she never wants to let go. I like the pillowy softness of her insides. I like the way she whimpers and moans my name, her tone filled with both pain and pleasure.

"Motherfucking hell," I mutter. "Why in the fuck can't I ever get enough of you?"

I'm not really asking Scarlett, so I don't expect her to answer, but she does so anyway.

"Because I'm yours." My eyes fly to hers at her breathy reply. "You need me just as much as I need you. Because you're mine."

I grind my molars just as hard as I grind my hips into her ass, getting just a little bit deeper inside. I hate her answer because it's true. I can't live without Scarlett in my life.

I hold her eyes as I growl, "I hate you."

Her gaze softens and she licks her bottom lip. "You love me."

I bare my teeth and hiss, "I love you."

Sadness creeps across her face. "You hate me."

I drop my head and smash my lips against hers, taking her mouth in a brutal kiss. I pour every bit of love, hate, passion, and loathing I have for her into it, hoping she feels my turmoil.

I pull away and stand behind her, keeping one hand on the

small of her back as I fuck her relentlessly. I look down, seeing the scars dotting her back, hating myself for putting them there. Hating her for making me put them there.

"Play with your clit. I want to feel you squeezing my cock as you come," I grunt, slowing my thrusts before I blow my load.

Her hair slides over her shoulder when she shakes her head. "No. I need more."

Pushing all the way inside, I stop with my pelvis pressing against her ass. "Get your fucking hand down on your cunt, Scarlett," I growl. "Now, before I leave you laying here and go home." I grind my hips, hitting a spot that has her back arching. "You want that? You want me to walk away and take the pain with me?"

"No, please," she whimpers. Her fingers curl in the sheets, her knuckles turning white.

"Then do what I fucking said."

Shifting her weight, she slides her arm underneath her body. Her fingers graze the root of my shaft when she gathers the juice from her leaking pussy and brings them back to her clit.

I slide out slowly and thrust forward hard. My balls tighten, my impending release right on the edge, but I wait. I wait until she lets out a hoarse cry and her asshole spasms and tightens around me.

My movements become hurried and uncoordinated. Pulling out, I slam back inside. Over and over until I can't hold back any longer. My vision blurs and my jaw hurts from clenching my teeth.

Cum spurts from me and fills the tunnel of her ass.

I slide from her, bending down to pull my slacks up. I tuck myself inside and pull the zipper up, but leave the button unfastened.

Scarlett stays on her knees, her head now turned away from me, shielding her eyes.

I stand there and look at her, waiting for some type of reaction. She always leaves the room first when we're done. Immediately after I leave her body, she stands up and walks out the door without looking back.

This time though, she stays in her kneeled position, with her knees tucked against her stomach.

I loathe the way she looks right now. Like she's curled into herself and processing something terrible that just happened to her.

I wish I had the right to go to her. To gather her in my arms and push her head into my neck. To say I'm sorry for the things I do to her. To comfort her the way a man comforts the woman he loves.

Instead, I do as she wishes and leave. This time, I'm the one walking out first, and it feels wrong. My heart demands I go back inside and force my comfort on her. But my legs carry me downstairs, picking up my discarded shirt in the hallway, not bothering to put it on before I walk out the front door.

Chapter Twenty-Four
Caterina

Sweeping my leg out, I manage to take Hunter to the floor. A smirk curls my lips as I stand over him with my hands on my hips, one foot planted on either side of him.

A squeak escapes me, followed by a throaty laugh when I'm grabbed by my waist and flipped. My body tenses, waiting for the impact of the floor to jar me, but I should have known better. My back gently meets the padded floor and within a second, Hunter's straddling my waist. His face hovers a couple of inches above me, his fisted hands beside my head.

His dark hair, damp with sweat, falls over his forehead. The light scruff on his face, along with the proud look in his eyes, has my breath stuttering in my throat. He is without a doubt the sexiest man I have ever met.

"I finally got you," I say, smiling up at him.

His white teeth flash as he grins. "You sure did, baby." Doing a half push up, he places a kiss against my lips. "You're getting better every day. Before long, I'll be no match for you."

I snort. Hunter and I have sparred for years, and while I have gotten better, he's delusional if he thinks I'll ever be as good as him. He grew up fighting on the streets. It was necessary for him to learn if he wished to survive. "I appreciate the vote of confidence, but we both know I'll never be a match for you."

"I don't know. I'm pretty sure the kick you gave my thigh earlier will leave a hellacious bruise."

Now *that* has me rolling my eyes. Hunter doesn't bruise.

With my hands around his shoulders, I tunnel my fingers through his hair and pull his head down until his lips meet mine. I moan into the kiss, our tongues sliding together, and he matches the sound with a groan. I lift my hips, pressing my pelvis into the V of his legs.

Our moment is interrupted by the sound of the doorbell. With a muted growl against my mouth, he yanks his lips away. He lifts his head, a scowl narrowing his eyes as he stares at the stairs leading from the basement. Using his fists to leverage himself, he leaps up and extends a hand to assist me. He yanks hard enough for me to fall into his arms once I'm on my feet, where he presses another hard kiss against my lips.

"I'll change out the clothes in the washer and then make us a quick lunch," I tell him.

"Sounds good."

Walking up the stairs ahead of him, I laugh when he lightly smacks my ass when he leaves me in the laundry room. I transfer the sheets to the dryer before reloading the washer with clothes. Having it grilled into my head as a child from my mother, I always check pockets before I wash clothes. Hunter never leaves anything in his pockets, so I'm surprised to find something soft inside a pair of slacks. Frowning, I pull out the material. When I realize it's a thong, the pants fall from my hands.

A wave of nausea nearly causes me to heave as I feel my heart drop to my stomach.

Why are they in his pocket? Where did they come from? And to whom do they belong? All questions a woman would ask herself. All questions that point in the same direction. Hunter is having an affair.

The mere thought of that makes my chest feel like it's being clawed open and my heart gouged out.

It can't be true. There's no way Hunter, my beloved husband, is seeing another woman.

Touching her.

Kissing her.

Making love to her.

Whispering sweet words in her ear.

Making her body light on fire like he makes mine.

There has to be another explanation.

There has to be.

But what possible explanation could there be? What could he possibly say to explain why he has another woman's underwear in his pocket? There is no reason for it whatsoever. Nothing he can say can justify it.

I barely muffle the loud cry that erupts from my lips with my hand.

Never, in all the years that Hunter and I have been together, have I ever doubted his love and dedication to me. I knew to the marrow of my bones, to the depths of my soul, *with every fiber of my being*, that he would never touch another woman intimately.

How could I have been so wrong?

Could it be something I did? Is there something he gets from this other woman that he doesn't get from me? Am I not enough for him anymore? Do I no longer please him?

No answers to these questions would be acceptable excuses

for cheating. No reason is good enough. Nothing gives him the right to hurt me like this.

And this certainly hurts. The pain is so intense that I wouldn't be surprised if I looked down and saw my shredded heart on the floor at my feet. It hurts to breathe, so I hold my breath. Part of me wishes I could hold it forever until the blistering pain stops. It will never go away, though. I'll feel it for the rest of my life.

The ache grows and festers, becoming a permanent lesion on my soul. My eyes water, and my lips tremble.

Hearing the front door close, I blink and force back the tears. I'm not ready to confront him just yet. I shove the pain aside, refusing to let it cripple me just yet. I need time to think. I need time to process. Later, I can fall apart.

Putting the thong in my pocket, I haphazardly throw clothes into the washer, no longer willing to check pockets. What if I find more damning evidence?

Suddenly, a memory resurfaces. This isn't the first sign that Hunter has been with another woman. He came home with the scent of another woman a few weeks ago.

I made excuses then, since the alternative was unbelievable. But the thong? There is no plausible explanation for it. I can't even say they belong to one of the girls from the club. That maybe he found it randomly and it doesn't belong to someone he's been intimate with. If that were the case, he would have tossed them away. There's a reason why a man keeps a woman's panties. Because they mean something to him. There's only one reason why he would have them.

I also watched from the window a few weeks ago as he put his ring back on. Why would he have taken his wedding ring off?

Hurt weighs heavily on my shoulders and in my heart. But there's also anger. So much anger.

How dare he do this. How dare he destroy what I've always thought was special between us.

"Hey."

My shoulders stiffen when his deep, rumbly voice comes from behind me. I wipe all emotions from my face before turning to him. I must do a terrible job because he's in my face the next instant. My eyes well with tears when he cups my cheeks and looks at me like I'm the most important person in the world to him.

For years, I thought I was.

"What's wrong?" he demands, his tone deepened by worry that looks so genuine.

I paste on a fake smile, but I'm sure it looks more like a wince. "Nothing. I feel a headache coming on."

For the first time in my life, I'm able to make use of my headaches. And it's not a lie. I feel the beginnings of one in the back of my head.

He pulls my head forward and presses a kiss against my forehead. "How about you let me take care of this? We'll get you some medicine and you can lie down for a while."

"Okay," I mumble, too afraid to say more and give away the large lump in my throat.

We enter the kitchen, and I stand numbly while Hunter grabs a pain pill and a glass of water. After swallowing the pill, he leads me upstairs. I feel like I'm on autopilot. Walking naturally because that's what people do, but not caring or understanding where I'm going.

As the bed presses against the back of my legs, I automatically sink down.

"Let's get these off you," Hunter says, his voice sounding miles away.

When I lie down, I barely feel him remove my pants and place the cover over me. I let my head fall to the side, and I notice his phone on the nightstand hooked up to the charger.

I roll my head back to Hunter. "I left my phone downstairs. Can you grab it for me?"

"Sure, baby. I'll get a cool rag for you too."

Before he leaves, he places a soft kiss against my lips, and another flood of tears threatens. My eyes follow him out of the room. When I hear his footsteps on the stairs, I grab his phone from the nightstand and unlock it. I click on the text icon, scrolling past the people I know.

My heart thumps heavily as my finger hovers over an unfamiliar name.

Scarlett.

Before I can second guess the move, I push down on the name.

> Scarlett: I need you.

That was the last message sent, which was two days ago.

Before that, the same three-word message was sent ten days ago. Before that, it was two weeks. Hunter's response is always the same.

> I'm on my way.

Bile rises in my throat, and I barely manage to swallow it down.

So it's true. Hunter is seeing someone else.

A small part of me wished and hoped it was only a one-time occurrence. Not that once is even close to forgivable, but maybe it would hurt a tiny bit less if I knew it was a spur of the moment encounter. One that he regretted deeply.

But no. He's been seeing her for months. Possibly even longer. The messages sent and received indicate that it happens about once a week. From the looks of it, it seems that Scarlett is always asking him to come see her. He never initiates it.

My throat feels tight and a tear slips free. I dash it away angrily. Having seen enough on his phone, I carelessly return it to the nightstand. I roll away from the side of the bed, knowing that's the side Hunter will approach. I don't want to see his face right now.

When I hear the thumps of his feet on the stairs, I slam my eyes shut and try to regulate my breathing. He's only been gone a few minutes, not enough time for me to have fallen asleep, but long enough that I can pretend to be drowsy.

I feel rather than hear him come to the side of the bed. A shadow appears in front of my closed eyes as the mattress dips. I barely crack them open and see him hovering over me.

"Your phone is on the nightstand," he says quietly. "I'll be downstairs. Use your phone to call me if you need anything."

"Okay," I whisper.

He doesn't move with my answer, and I feel his eyes still on me. His lips touch my cheek a moment later. "Are you sure everything is okay?"

I push my tremulous emotions back and roll my head to the side so I can look up at him. I force my lips into a small smile. "Everything's fine. I'll be better once I sleep this headache off."

His eyes flicker back and forth between mine, looking for something I hope he can't see. I don't know if I hide my pain well, or if he's giving up for the time being. After a silent moment, he drops his head and gives me a gentle kiss.

He's not out the door before the tears start falling. I bury my face in the pillow, only realizing it's Hunter's when I'm suddenly engulfed in his scent.

Chapter Twenty-Five
Caterina

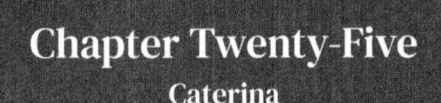

Two days later, I'm no closer to confronting Hunter. Any time I think about it, my chest threatens to cave in on itself.

I've avoided him as much as possible, but it's difficult to do that when he's always here. It's been five days since he's been to Slate. I asked him why he hadn't gone to the club and he said he was taking some time off. I could tell there was more to it, but didn't ask him to elaborate. It's already hard enough being around him—seeing his gorgeous face, smelling his delicious scent, hearing his deep gravelly voice, feeling his hands on me—I don't want to encourage conversation.

During the day, I spend most of my time in my office. I told him that inspiration for my next story has hit, and I want to get it down while it's fresh in my head. He knows I'm lying. I see the frown lines between his eyes whenever he looks at me. He knows me better than anyone else. I don't understand why he doesn't call me out on my lie. Maybe he's afraid of what I'll say. Maybe he suspects I know his secret and doesn't want to deal with the fallout.

The nights are the worst. After the sun has gone down and

Hunter and I are in bed. No matter how weak it makes me, I cling to him in the darkness of our room, pretending my heart isn't broken, and let him make love to me. I've loved Hunter for almost half my life. It's not an emotion I can simply turn off. He knows my body just as well as I know his. He knows exactly how to touch me, where to put his hands, how soft to kiss the sensitive spot on my neck, how gentle to slide his fingers down my side, the sexy words he whispers in my ear...

I soak up every single caress he gives and every word of love he speaks.

Afterwards, with his strong arms encircling me, my back pressed against his chest, and his heavy breathing in my ear, I let the tears flow. I soak my pillow with him none the wiser.

Hunter may suspect something is wrong, but he doesn't realize how wrong it is. For now, I prefer to keep it that way.

The time I've spent in my office the last two days hasn't been for nothing. I've used the time to type up all the feelings I've felt since discovering the panties. I have over five pages filled.

That's what I'm doing when I feel his presence enter the room. Stealing myself, I look across the room at the door. Hunter stands there, leaning against the door frame. His expression is intense, as if he's thinking about something important.

"I have to go to Slate to take care of something," he says, moving away from the door and walking toward me. He rounds my desk and slides a hand through my hair to the back of my head, gently pulling it back. "I'll be gone a couple of hours."

He's lying. As good as Hunter knows me, I know him just as well.

"Okay," I reply, trying hard not to reveal the boulder in my throat.

He's going to see her.

Scarlett.

He's leaving me to sleep with another woman. I recognize the look on his face. It's filled with guilt.

He bends over and gently presses his lips against mine. I close my eyes. Nausea rolls in my stomach, knowing he'll soon be using those same lips on *her*.

"I love you."

I don't know how I do it, but I manage to repeat his words without breaking down. "I love you."

His beautiful gaze, with a frown between them, lingers on me a moment longer before he turns and leaves the room.

My eyes sting and my throat convulses, threatening to drag me into a dark hole I'll never escape. I force myself out of my chair. I feel numb as I walk out of my office. I rush to grab my purse and keys as soon as the front door closes. I'm in such a hurry, I almost forget to disengage the alarm system. That would be just my luck. Getting caught by the alarm going off when I'm trying to be sneaky and follow my husband to his lover's house to confront them both.

After Hunter pulls out of the driveway, I rush to my car.

I must be stupid to do this. I'm asking for my heart to be shredded and handed to me on a platter by following him. I'm hoping against all hope that I'm wrong. That he really does have a legitimate excuse for having another woman's panties in his pocket.

If he heads to Slate as he said, I'll turn around and leave and wait for him to come home to ask about the panties. But if he goes somewhere else like I believe he is, then I need to see for myself. Maybe I'm a closeted masochist, wanting to feel the pain of seeing him with another woman. Maybe seeing it will turn that pain into anger, and I won't hurt anymore. If I see it first hand, there's no way he can explain it away.

I creep along behind Hunter's SUV, staying far enough back that he won't see me. My hands shake as I grip the steering wheel. When he makes a left at a green light instead of a right, my stomach drops. A right turn would have taken him to Slate.

I blink back tears and ignore the hollow sensation in my chest. After a few minutes, Hunter pulls up in front of a two-story home. I stop a few houses away and watch him as he gets out of the vehicle. He doesn't even look around as he walks out of view, heading into the house.

I bite the inside of my cheek until the coppery taste of blood fills my mouth. I take a deep breath of courage and let it go as I step out of my car. Besides Hunter's black SUV, there are no other vehicles in the driveway.

As I walk up the steps, my whole body shakes.

I'm a glutton for punishment as I go to the front door and check the doorknob, half hoping it won't turn, and I'll be forced to leave. I'm not sure whether luck is on my side or against me when it turns.

I stand there for a solid minute, the brass knob in my hand, but not pushing the door open.

Can I really do this? Do I really want to see the woman who may have broken up my marriage and stolen my husband? Do I want to witness Hunter touching someone other than me? To take the chance of walking in while they are in the middle of....

I close my eyes and shake my head. I have to do this. I *need* to. This is the only way I can be sure I'm getting the truth.

I cringe as I slowly open the door, thankful it doesn't make a sound. I close it just as quietly behind me and turn to face the room. It's not really a room, but a small entryway with a wall directly in front of me. I keep my steps silent when I round the wall and step into the living room. Surprise flickers through me when I notice the sparse furnishings. There is only one coffee table and one loveseat against one wall of the large room.

Leaving the room, I walk out through a double doorway. There's another hallway to the right, which appears to lead to the dining room and kitchen. On the left are stairs. My feet instinctively lead me to the stairs, knowing Hunter and Scarlett will be found on the second floor.

Halfway up the stairs, I force my legs to keep moving forward rather than running back out the front door. I don't want to be here. I want to rewind back to three days ago when I thought my life with Hunter was perfect.

No sound comes from the second floor, which I find intimidating and worrisome. As I reach the top of the stairs, I turn right, again, something compels me to go that way. There are no windows in the hall and the lights are off, so it's quite dark. At the end of the hall a door is cracked open, leaving a strip of light on the hardwood floor.

Despite not making a sound, I half expect Hunter to come barreling out of the room because my screams to leave seem so loud in my head.

Once I'm at the door, I peek through the crack, but all I see is a big bed. The light comes from a lamp on the nightstand. I fold my arms across my chest, my body tense, and my breathing becomes heavy with dreaded anticipation.

I wait and wait and wait. Waiting for Hunter to appear or for some woman to show herself. I feel like I stand there forever, and I wonder if maybe they're not up here afterall, but somewhere else in the house.

A tear slides down my cheek, followed closely by another. I

let them fall. There's no way I can stop them now. Not when I'm about to catch my husband with another woman. I do keep my crying silent though.

"You can come in, Cat."

My teeth cut into my tongue as I hear Hunter's deep voice coming from the room. I barely feel the literal bite of pain.

He knows I'm here. But how? Did he see me following him? Was I louder than I thought as I walked through the house? And where's Scarlett? Did he force her to leave when he realized I had followed him?

Dropping my arms to my sides, I take a couple deep breaths before pushing open the door. My eyes immediately focus on Hunter, sitting by a window in a chair. His legs are spread casually as he reclines back, still wearing the same jeans and black Henley he wore when he left. His arms are on the arms of the chair, one hand holding a short glass with an inch of amber liquid.

He lifts the glass to his lips and drains the rest of his drink while his green eyes remain fixed on me.

As relaxed as he appears, I know from the guilty look in his eyes he's about to completely decimate my heart.

Chapter Twenty-Six
Hunter

I knew this day would come, and no matter how much I tried to prepare myself for it, seeing the utter devastation in Cat's eyes will haunt me forever. Every time I close my eyes, I'll see the look of betrayal and stark pain on her beautiful face. This woman has suffered more pain in her life than any person should, and I hate myself for being one of the people who caused it.

"Why?" she croaks and wraps her arms around her middle like she's trying to hold herself together. Like if she doesn't, she'll fall apart at the seams.

My fingers tighten around the glass in my hand. "I love her," I say, knowing how much it will hurt, yet refusing to lie.

Her face scrunches and a sob escapes her. She throws one hand up to her mouth, but the sound still slips free.

When it looks like her knees are about to buckle, I set the glass on the floor and get up from the chair. I'm a couple of feet away when she throws a hand up in the air, her palm facing me.

"Stop!" she yells. "Don't come near me."

I ignore her request and move closer until her palm touches

my chest. Her face is red and her eyes are swollen, indicating that she's been crying longer than she's been in the room.

I push against her hand. "Let me explain. There are things you don't understand yet," I tell her.

"No," she says, strength coming into her voice. She moves back, but I just follow her. "There's no need. Your answer a moment ago was enough."

"Baby, no. There's more you need to know. It's not what it looks like."

Even to my own ears, my words sound pathetic and cliché as fuck. Don't all cheaters say the same?

This time she lets out a bitter laugh. "I don't need to know the details, Hunter." Anger enters her tone and her eyes flare. "I don't fucking care how you met. I don't need to fucking hear how you couldn't help yourself," she says mockingly. "Or how it was impossible to not fall in love. Or that you didn't mean to. Or whatever other garbage you want to say."

Cat's pissed. It's not often that she curses. Only when her emotions are high. Her anger is entirely justified. In her eyes, I've betrayed her in the most despicable way. And in a way, I did.

When she turns to leave, I grab her arm, and that's when she turns into a hellcat. She rounds on me, her other hand striking out to land across my face. I don't attempt to stop her. I want to feel the heat of her slap. It's nothing in comparison to what she's feeling right now, but it's a taste.

Her palm lands two more times against my face before I spin her around and bring her back against my chest. I wrap my arms tightly around her, trapping hers at her side. She struggles and bucks against me, attempting to stomp on my foot.

"Let me go, you bastard!" She shouts through the broken sobs still leaving her lips. "Let me go!"

"I can't," I croak, burying my face in her neck. "I can't lose you, Cat. I will never fucking let you go. You're mine."

She stops struggling, but her chest pumps rapidly. Her hot tears splash on my arm as she sniffs.

"You've already lost me." Her voice is low, but her words blast through my ears like she shouted them through a megaphone.

Her statement has a jagged hole tearing through my chest, and my breath is stolen from my lungs. This woman is my life, and she's telling me she's taking it away. Life without her would be unbearable. It's a life I refuse to live.

I tighten my arms around her, expecting her to struggle when I lift her from her feet and carry her to the chair. Surprisingly, she doesn't fight me. After I set her down, she refuses to look at me when I drop to my knees in front of her. Tears still stream from her bloodshot eyes as she presses her lips into a firm line.

In the next second, her features go lax and all emotion is wiped from her face as she continues to stare at the window.

Getting stabbed repeatedly with a rusty knife wouldn't hurt this bad. I know this look. I've seen it a hundred times. She's protecting herself from the pain by closing herself off. And there's no telling what will happen next.

Or rather, who she'll be.

I have to tread very carefully.

She lets me grab her cold hand in mine. Not a twitch or hitch of breath at the contact.

"How did you find out?" I ask quietly.

Her reply is mumbled and lacks feeling. "I found her thong in your pants pocket."

I already knew this. The day she had a headache, and I brought her to our room to lie down, I saw the material peeking out of her pocket when I pulled her pants off. I also saw her looking at my phone when I left the room and knew what she was looking for.

As much as I hated knowing what she was thinking, I can't deny that a rush of relief passed through me. Keeping Scarlett from her was tearing me apart.

I took a chance and a huge leap of faith in our love to set it up so she would follow me here today.

It was time Cat knew the truth. I didn't want her to think I was cheating on her. That's the last thing I would ever do.

"I also smelled her on you a couple of weeks ago. It wasn't the first time I smelled another woman on you."

Dropping my head, I close my eyes. Shame slides instantly through my body. For almost five years, I've kept Scarlett's existence hidden. Apparently, I've done a shit job of it lately.

"How long, Hunter?"

I look up at Cat, seeing her expressionless eyes watching me. My throat threatens to close, but I force the words past my lips. "Almost five years."

Her face shows nothing, but another tear slips free to glide down her pale cheek.

"How can you do this to us? How can you say with one breath that you love me, and with the next, say you love her?"

I tighten my fingers around hers. "Because I do. I love you both with every breath I take." I pull in a lungful of air and let it out slowly. "Just like I love Athena and Presley."

Her brows crease in confusion and her hand twitches in mine. "Presley?"

"Yes."

I watch as the name rolls around in her head, and I wonder what she's thinking. It only takes a moment for me to get my answer, and it's not what I expected. Her lips curl in disgust and she yanks her hand away, finally giving me more than a void look.

"What the fuck, Hunter?" She grabs the arms of the chair and tries to scoot back. She has nowhere to go though. "Please don't tell me you touched—"

I cut her off before she has a chance to finish, anger making my words come out harsh. "You know me better than that, Cat," I growl, appalled that the thought would even cross her mind.

"I have no idea who you are at all," she declares. "The man I knew, *the one I fell in love with*, would never touch another woman."

"What I feel for Presley is not the same as what I feel for you and Scarlett."

Her eyes narrow. "Who in the fuck is Athena? You say you *love*," she throws the word out with such hate, "her too. Where in the hell is she?"

I sit back on my heels, my hands resting on my thighs. "She's here."

Cat's eyes widen as she darts them toward the doorway.

"They're all here, Cat," I say quietly, carefully watching her face. My heart feels sluggish in my chest, like it's struggling to beat.

Fear lodges itself inside my chest. Fear of what this will do to Cat. I've kept this secret, because as strong as Cat is, in some ways she's fragile. I have no choice but to come clean now. I won't lose Cat because she believes I've been unfaithful.

Her eyes shoot back to mine. "What?"

"All of them."

"What in the hell are you saying, Hunter?"

"They're all here in this room."

She shoves me back and pushes her way out of the chair. I

catch myself before I fall on my ass, not expecting her sudden move, and get to my feet. I turn and face her. Now across the room from me, her hair looks wild, just as much as her eyes do. They dart around the room, like she's trying to find a way out.

"You're insane," she gasps. Her arms lift and she grabs handfuls of hair as she shakes her head. I don't know if she's trying to force away visions of the night that forever changed our lives, or other unwanted memories. "I don't see anyone else here."

I approach her slowly, not wanting to frighten her.

She knows what I'm saying. She may not want to admit it, but *she knows*.

When I'm only a couple of feet away, her head snaps up, her hands falling to her sides. I stop in my tracks, unsure where her mind is.

"What you're saying can't be true," she says shakily.

"It is, and deep down, you know it."

"No." She shakes her head. "You're lying. You're just saying it to get out of being caught."

"No, Cat."

"But you have to be. What you're saying is fucking crazy." Her voice dips and cracks, and more tears appear in her eyes. "I'm not insane. I'm not crazy."

"Baby." I close the gap between us, not giving a single fuck about whether she wants me near her or not. I'll be damned if I let her think she's anything less than the sane, beautiful woman that I love. She's a lot more sane than most people would be if they suffered even half as much as she has.

I don't stop until I'm almost in her face. I grab her cheeks and force her to look at me. "You listen to me, Cat, and hear me well. You *aren't* crazy. Never let that shit enter your mind. Understand?"

Her eyes glisten and her lips wobble. Her whole body fucking shakes, and feeling the trembles coming off of her has my jaw tensing and my own body vibrating in anger. Not at her, but at the bastards who made Cat the way she is today.

"Then why does it feel like it?" she asks, her words barely audible. Her eyes squeeze shut and a tear leaks out. I swipe it away with my thumb. "If what you're saying is true, how can you believe otherwise?"

I drop my head and press my lips against hers. "Because I know *you*," I say once I pull back. "Because nothing you've done indicates you are. Your mind does what it needs to do in order to protect itself. You are the bravest, strongest woman I've ever met. I'm in fucking awe of you, Cat, because you've handled a hell of a lot more than I would have been able to. That anyone would be able to handle."

"What does that mean?" Her hands come up to grip my wrists, her eyes imploring. "I don't understand. How can I be someone I don't remember?"

I let her cheeks go and bend down to pick her up. Carrying her over to the bed, I set her down on the end and sit beside her, turning my body so I'm facing her.

"Yes, you do," I state, grabbing her hand. "You know. You're just not ready to accept it yet. You've kept the truth locked away, because you're afraid to face it. And when that truth sneaks past the walls you've built in your mind, you hide and become someone else." I lock our fingers together. "You let Scarlett take over when you think you should be punished."

She bites her bottom lip and a line forms between her eyes. "Why would I feel that way?"

I don't answer her question. She's not ready for that information yet.

"Athena appears when the pain becomes too much and you need to escape it." I pause a moment. "She's a patient at The Grove."

Cat's breath catches and her hand jerks in mine. "What?"

"She checks herself in and stays for a few hours. The nurses call me when you show up, and I come to you there. To you, I'm just some guy who visits you."

I stop and let it sink in what I've told her so far.

"You mentioned Presley," she croaks a moment later. "Is she...."

"Yes." A smile tugs at my lips. "She's the innocent, yet feisty part of you. She's the one who sees the world how it should be, without all the heartache and darkness."

Her gaze falls to our entwined hands, and she's silent for so long I fear she won't speak. But then she lifts her head, and I see the haunted look in her eyes.

"Something bad happened, didn't it? Something that made me this way."

"Yes."

"I don't want to remember." She roughly shakes her head, her hair flying about her shoulders. "I'm not sure I ever want to remember. And I don't care if that makes me crazy or insane."

I hate hearing those words leave her lips. They shouldn't even be in her vocabulary.

"Baby, the only thing you've done that's crazy is think that I would ever touch another woman." I lift her hand to my lips. "*You* make my heart beat. *You* breathe life into me. *You* give me everything I need and are everything I could ever wish for. There's not a soul alive that could come even close to tempting me away from you. I will be yours and *only yours* until I take my last breath."

For years, I've felt profound guilt for hiding Scarlett from Cat.

Despite being the same person, I felt like I was betraying Cat by being with her when she was Scarlett. When I was with Athena, I felt the same guilt, but it wasn't as strong since our relationship wasn't sexual. As shocking as this news is to Cat, I'm glad she finally knows the truth.

"Do you believe me?"

She chews on her bottom lip a moment before letting it go. "I don't know. I want to, but...." She trails off, looking uncertain.

I don't let her doubt bother me. It would be difficult for anyone to believe.

What does bother me is the way her body stiffens slightly when I pull her into my arms. My jaw clenches, but still, I lock my arms around her, refusing to let her go. Thankfully, she allows the embrace, which gives me hope.

I close my eyes and breathe in deeply, pulling in the sweet scent of my wife.

Chapter Twenty-Seven
Caterina

I wake up to the steady thump of Hunter's heartbeat in my ear and the warmth of his body pressed underneath me. I wrinkle my nose when one of the coarse hairs on his chest tickles me.

"Good morning, beautiful."

I smile and tilt my head back to see his eyes. "Morning."

"How are you feeling today?"

My smile slips when I remember what happened yesterday. What I thought was going to be my world ending with me catching Hunter in the act of cheating on me, turned into something way different. It still changed my life, but not in the way I could have expected.

I'm still not sure if I truly believe him, but the alternative—which is him cheating on me—isn't something I *want* to believe.

Three different people.

The mere thought causes my chest muscles to spasm.

If I'm being truthful with myself, it's easier to believe what Hunter told me. Sometimes I hear them whispering to me. Way in the back of my mind, from a place I've kept hidden for years and discounted as fictional characters begging for their story to be told, I hear their voices talking to me. They aren't fictional. They're real, my own flesh and blood.

While Hunter insists I'm not crazy, I know many people would disagree. I mean, how could someone be one person one moment, then be someone else entirely in the next, and *not* be crazy? At the very least, it makes me unstable, which seems almost as bad.

"Hey." I slide my eyes back to Hunter. "Talk to me," he says, running his finger between my eyes where I'm sure there's a frown line. "Tell me what you're thinking."

"Will you... tell me about them?" I ask hesitantly. "These other... people."

Using the arm he has wrapped around my waist, he runs his hand gently up and down my side. He's quiet for a moment, as if he's gathering his thoughts and figuring out what he wants to say.

"Athena made an appearance first," he begins, his voice deep, but quiet. "She's the broken part of you. The part that feels she doesn't deserve love, so she hides herself away at The Grove. She doesn't let anyone close enough to touch her, except me, and she only lets me hold her hand. Anything else, you become agitated."

"And the facility just lets me walk in whenever I want?"

I know there are facilities that let people check themselves in, but it seems strange for them to allow it over and over again.

"They have no choice, since I own the place and demand it. Besides, they all know of your unique situation and have come to care for you. Only the most qualified staff are employed there."

"You *own* The Grove?" I ask incredulously, sitting up and facing him on my knees. I know the place and its stellar reputation. "Hunter, that's insane!"

He grabs me by the waist and slides me across the bed until I'm sitting on his lap. "Yes. I bought it the second time you showed up there. I wanted to have control of who worked there. Dr. Armani was already on staff. I offered an amount the owner couldn't refuse. I had each staff member vetted. If I didn't like what I saw, I replaced them." His hand moves to the side of my thigh, his fingers barely slipping beneath the edge of my shorts. "I wanted you to have the best care while you were there."

I sit there with my mouth open, not quite processing what he's saying. He bought a freaking medical facility because he wanted to make sure I was taken care of properly. How could any woman be so lucky to have a man so committed to the well-being of his wife that he'd *buy a medical facility* to ensure it?

I lick my lips and ask, "How often do I go there?"

"It varies. Sometimes once a week, sometimes a couple of times a month."

I nod, taking his word for it.

"Wait." My brows pucker. "Am I the reason Ginger works there?"

"Yes. I didn't want you to show up without someone who truly knows you. Sometimes I get warnings that Athena will appear soon, but sometimes it's random. I trust the medical staff, but I felt better knowing Ginger was there. She mostly stays in the background when you admit yourself. We don't want to cause a trigger for you, but she's there just in case I can't get to you right away."

"Wow." I let out a slow breath, unable to imagine being around my sister and not recognize her as such. Of course, I can't imagine the same with Hunter either.

"What about Presley?" I ask, eager to know more.

His lips curve into a soft smile. "Presley was the last person to make herself known. She's this sweet, but feisty, young girl who likes to try to steal coffee."

I can't help but laugh at that.

"It's weird." I tilt my head and close my eyes. "I can see her in my mind, but I don't see her as me. She's... separate," I say, finding it difficult to explain. "It's like I have her thoughts and memories, but they aren't mine, they're hers." I open my eyes. "How can that be?"

"Because to you, they are separate people. You just share the same body. Each of these people have their own personality, their own minds. Presley's thoughts may reside in your head, but they aren't your thoughts and actions. They're hers."

I shake my head. "It's still strange."

He grabs the front of my shirt and tugs me down until our lips are pressed together. My hair floats around us like a curtain. "It's you," he says against my lips. "And it makes you unique."

"I think I'd rather be unique in a different way. Like being able to lick my nose or have webbed toes or something."

Hunter chuckles and nips my lips playfully. "I happen to like you just the way you are."

Putting my hands against his chest, I push away from him to sit back on my heels. "Tell me about Scarlett," I demand. I'm most anxious to hear about her since she nearly broke my heart.

He doesn't reply right away. After pushing down on the bed, he sits up and leans against the headboard before positioning me so my legs straddle him. He stares over my shoulder, brows pinched together.

The lost look in his eyes makes me nervous. Scarlett has obviously affected him more than the others.

"Scarlett showed up at Slate. It was a night I happened to be there. I think she chose that night because subconsciously *you* knew I would be there. It seems like you always seek me out, no matter who you are." His eyes slide back to me. "Knowing that, even when you aren't yourself, you still feel connected to me has helped me deal with all of this."

His hands slide up my thighs until they meet the junction of my legs.

"Scarlett likes pain," he continues quietly. "Like Athena feels like she deserves to be alone, Scarlett feels like she deserves pain. It's what helps her deal with past traumas. *Your* past traumas."

I let those words slide past me, not willing to look further into them.

"My relationship with her is purely sexual. Or at least, it is on her part. I know she feels something more for me, or rather, I believe it's your own feelings trying to break through, but she won't let them out. Scarlett wants me to hurt her... while we have sex."

I barely refrain from flinching. It's difficult hearing my husband talking about sex with a woman whose name is not mine.

His eyes turn haunted, as if the thought of causing me pain causes *him* pain.

"I gave her what she wanted, what she needed." His eyes lift, and the color transforms from a sea green to a hunter green. I swallow at the intense look. "Because I would do anything to ease your pain. There's not a single fucking thing, Cat, that I wouldn't do for you, even if it tears me up inside while I do it."

"Hunter," I whisper his name, my voice turning hoarse from holding back tears. "I'm sorry I put you through all this."

He cups my cheeks, sliding his fingers through my hair and leaving his thumbs on my cheeks. The muscles in his jaw work as his eyes bore into me.

"If I never hear those words leave your lips again, it'll be too soon. I would deal with a thousand personalities for you, baby. I love Scarlett, Athena, and Presley just as strongly as I love you, because they are a part of you. They're now a part of me."

My head falls forward and my forehead thumps against his shoulder. I sniff, trying to hold back the tears, wanting to be strong for him. Lord knows this whole thing couldn't have been easy. I can't imagine being in his position. Being with him and him not knowing who I was. It would break me in ways I'm not sure I could ever recover from.

"Hey." He lifts my head until I'm looking at him. "I love you."

I smile and my heart turns to mush at the tender way he says it. "I love you."

Pulling my head toward him, he presses the softest of kisses against my lips. As I close my eyes, an image of him looming over me in the dark flashes behind my eyelids. It's so brief, I'm not sure if I actually saw it or if the vision was even real. However, something whispers in the back of my mind that says it *was* real. But it wasn't a moment Hunter and I shared. Technically, it was, but I wasn't myself. I was Scarlett.

The searing heat of jealousy flares inside me, which is stupid. It's not like Scarlett is a different person. It was my body that felt the pleasure she sought. I just didn't have control at the time and have no memories of it.

Even knowing this doesn't take away the green evilness of envy. Scarlett's experienced a part of Hunter that I never have. He's given her something he's never given me. I thought I knew all sides of Hunter, and while under normal circumstances he may not like that dark part of himself, he still had to have enjoyed it in some way.

Pulling my lips from his, I keep my head lowered so I can only see him through my eyelashes. I'm not sure I can look at him directly when I ask my next question.

"Did you like it?" My voice is small. "I mean, the things you did to Scarlett. Did you enjoy it?"

The muscle in his temple pulses and his lips form a straight line. He doesn't like the question any more than I liked asking it. But it's something I need to know.

He's so quiet that I worry he won't answer.

"You have to understand, Cat. All I saw when I looked at Scarlett was you. I only have to think of your name and my body reacts. You may have acted differently than my sweet Cat, but you were still the same. I knew you were hurting, and I understood what you needed to help with that pain. I hated every moment of it, because you had already suffered enough, and I hated adding to it." He pauses for a moment, gathering his thoughts before he continues, his voice like gravel. "But there were some parts I did enjoy. Not because it hurt you, but because it felt physically good."

I tug my bottom lip between my teeth. "Tell me some of the things you did."

"Baby, I don't think—"

I cut him off by pressing a finger against his lips. "I want to know. Please?"

Again, he's so quiet that I fear he won't tell me.

He blows out a sharp breath before he starts. "She liked to be taken hard in the ass," he says, and something tells me that's one of the things he said felt physically good. Hunter and I have had sex in many different ways, in many different positions, and in almost all of the rooms in the house. We've experimented, tested our limits, but anal is something we haven't done yet. Not because I haven't wanted to, but because Hunter has never shown interest. Based on the brief flash of pleasure I just saw, it's something he has definitely been interested in. I store that knowledge away.

I stay quiet so he can continue.

"She wouldn't let me use any lube. She wanted me to take her brutally and raw so it would hurt. Most of the time, I gave her no choice but to let me inside her pussy first." This time I can't hold back my flinch. He grabs my hand and lays it flat on his chest. His heart beats steadily beneath my palm, calming my nerves like usual. "I needed to take her that way to coat me before I took her the way she wanted. She didn't like it, but I gave her no choice."

"What else?"

It's torture to hear this, but I'm fascinated and curious to learn more. I need to know all aspects of Hunter's relationship with Scarlett.

Before he continues, he grabs my waist and pulls me further up his lap. I sit right over his cock, and if I am not mistaken, he's somewhat hard. To be honest, I'd be lying if I said a tiny part of me wasn't turned on myself.

He blows out a frustrated breath. "I'd use a whip on her," he says quietly, and I suck in a breath. "She liked to bleed."

I'm sure my expression shifts to horror. It's evident from his expression that this part of their relationship is one he did *not* enjoy.

"That can't have been easy for you."

He nods jerkily. "It isn't, but it's what you need. My own feelings don't factor in."

"Whose house were we at yesterday? I assume that's where you always meet Scarlett?"

"It's ours. When I found you at Slate, I needed a place to take you that wasn't home because I wasn't sure how you would react. The house belonged to Silas, but he was in the process of selling it. After that first night, you always went back there. When I realized the house was sort of a safe haven for you, I bought it from Silas."

As my body drains of energy from the overload of information, I slump forward, lying against his chest. His hand smooths up and down my back, and I soak up the comfort. I hate myself for putting Hunter through what I have. I hate that I don't have control of my own body and mind.

Squeezing my eyes shut, I vow to do better in the future. I may have three different people living inside me, but I'll be damned if they continue to control me. It's time I regain control over my life.

I send up a silent prayer, hoping that thought is something I can actually follow through on.

Chapter Twenty-Eight
Hunter

I walk up the stairs to the second floor in search of my wife a few days after Cat found out about the other people who inhabit her head. Thankfully, I believe she's come to accept the truth.

I left her asleep in bed an hour ago. In the room, the bed is already made and the bathroom door is wide open with the lights on. I head in that direction, coming to a stop in the doorway when I see Cat standing in front of the mirror over the sink. She hasn't noticed my appearance. My cock fills with blood because she's standing naked and a naked Cat always makes me hard. Curious, I lean against the frame of the door and watch her.

Only her eyes move as she sweeps them up and down her body, stopping briefly at each scar left by a knife wound on her torso. The marks usually go unnoticed because they symbolize something she refuses to acknowledge, so I'm surprised she's looking at them now.

My throat spasms when she turns and looks over her shoulder at the ones on her back and butt. I fucking hate them because these scars were left by me. It doesn't matter that Scarlett demanded I strike her with the whip until I broke her skin. It doesn't matter that I witnessed her relief as I complied with her request. I'll hate myself until the day I die for being one of the sources of her pain.

Cat has never asked about the scars covering her back and ass, even though she was Scarlett when I left them. I think subconsciously, like the ones on her chest and stomach, she knew where they came from so she pretended they weren't there. But now, after finding out what I told her the other day, she can't pretend anymore.

I don't blame her for being curious. Neither do I blame her for asking questions about Scarlett. It felt wrong talking to her about —what could amount to in her mind—me being with another woman. Every time I was with Scarlett, it felt like a betrayal to Cat. My guilt was made worse by the fact that I enjoyed some of the things Scarlett and I did together. Not the times I hurt her. I abhorred those moments. But the anal sex, forcing my cock down her tight throat until she gagged, stealing her breath with a hand around her throat, and being in control when I gave it back to her.

When my cock twitches, I shake my head to rid myself of those thoughts. There have been so many times I've imagined taking Cat while she was actually Cat in the same way. But I've put her through so much as Scarlett that I would never take her so harshly as Cat.

Returning to the mirror, she lifts both arms, revealing another set of scars. Again, she's never acknowledged these either.

I push away from the doorframe and approach Cat. Her eyes meet mine in the mirror. I can see the questions lingering in the blue orbs. It's not easy for me to talk about her scars, but she deserves to know the truth.

I pick up her hand and twist it so we can see the gnarly scar.

"A couple of days after you arrived at The Grove the second time, you broke into the kitchen and used a plastic butter knife." I trace the jagged lines with my finger, and my throat tightens. "It was the first time you became Athena. You scared the shit out of me." I lift her wrist and kiss the raised marks.

"Hunter," she whispers, her voice cracking on my name.

"Every time Athena took over and you showed up at The Grove, I was so terrified you'd try again and succeed." I look into her beautiful blue eyes. "But you never did. Only that one time. You still wore bandages when you became her though. It was like you were stuck in the same time period over and over again and you couldn't move past you trying to harm yourself."

I let her hand go. Keeping my eyes locked with hers through the mirror, I begin tracing the small puckered marks on her back

"These are from a whip," I tell her quietly. "The harder I hit Scarlett with it and the more blood I drew, the more it relaxed her. All along the tails of the whip there are little pieces of sharp metal."

She bites her bottom lip and her eyes well with tears. "I can't imagine how difficult that was for you."

"I hated every fucking second of it." I slide my hands around her waist, my hands coming to rest over one of the knife scars on her lower stomach. "But the alternative would have been worse. I didn't want you to turn away from me and possibly seek out pain in other ways or from someone else, so I gave Scarlett what she wanted. If I gave her what she needed, at least I had some control."

She leans her head back against my shoulder then turns her face to press a kiss against my neck. "I wouldn't have blamed you if it became too much and you left."

I tighten my arms around her. "There was no chance of that

ever happening. The thought never even crossed my mind. The vows I took when I married you, Cat, are the most sacred words I have ever spoken. Only death will separate us."

She spins around and places her hands on my shoulders. Wrapping my hands around her waist, I pick her up and place her on the counter by the sink before wedging my hips between her legs.

"You are the most incredible, patient, caring, and loving man, Hunter St. James." She tugs my head forward for a kiss. "Please don't ever change."

One hand slides up her spine until I reach the back of her head, fist her hair, and gently pull her head back. I drop my lips to hers and give her a kiss that I wish could lead to more.

Unfortunately, there's a reason why I came looking for Cat. Making love to my wife will have to wait until later.

With reluctance, I pull back. "I have to go to Slate to take care of something. I want you to come with me."

There's no way in hell I'm leaving her here alone with the threat of Whisper and Henry still looming.

"Is everything okay?" she asks, a frown appearing between her eyebrows.

While I don't talk about the darker sides of my life with Cat, I also don't hide it. Instead of lying, which I hate doing because I've already withheld enough information from her for years, I tell her the truth.

"A guy we've been hunting for weeks has been brought to Slate. Silas and I have...," I pause a moment, "things to discuss with him."

Cat isn't stupid. She knows there will be no "discussion" involved. Only flesh meeting flesh and a shit ton of bloodshed.

She nods slowly, worry lining her face.

"Get dressed. I'll be waiting downstairs."

Fifteen minutes later, Cat and I are in my SUV. Ten minutes after that, I'm pulling behind Slate. We enter through the back entrance, and I take her straight up to my office. Silas is vibrating with rage when he walks in seconds later. The tension emanating from him is palpable. His body is locked tight, like he's barely holding back the need to drive his fist through something.

I know the feeling.

Katie comes in directly behind him. Anger flares in her eyes, but it's not as pronounced as the concern. She's worried about Silas's temperament and what will happen when he faces the man who nearly raped her.

I turn to Cat. "You'll stay with Katie while Silas and I take care of this. We won't be gone long."

I'm pretty sure it won't take Silas long to lose control.

"Okay." She rolls to her toes to reach my lips. "Be safe."

"Always."

With my arms wrapped around Cat, I turn to Katie. "Thanks for staying with her."

Katie's eyes are soft when they move to Cat. "It's my pleasure. It's been too long since Cat and I have had girl time. We need to catch up."

After leaving the two women in my office, Silas and I make our way to the basement. It's dark and damp below Slate. The floor and walls are cement, and the temperature is lower than on the upper floors. One of the rooms, where Timothy was placed, has a drain centered in the floor. A hose is attached to a faucet that comes out of one wall. One corner of the room contains a table with rusty tools and rubber gloves.

A mostly naked Timothy hangs from the ceiling by his wrists directly in front of us. Sweat beads down his forehead and hollow cheeks despite the cold seeping from the walls. His naked chest is smeared with dirt, mixing in with the dark hair that covers his torso. The light-blue boxers he's wearing are soaked on the front. My lips curl at the disgusting sight.

Timothy lifts his head, his mop of dark hair sweat-soaked, and his wide, fearful eyes meet mine before he slides them to Silas beside me. He fears us both, but it's directed more at Silas, because it was his girlfriend he touched.

"S-Silas, m-man," he stutters pathetically. "I'm sorry. I didn't know she was your girl."

"Wouldn't fucking matter if she wasn't," Silas growls. "You'd still be right here, facing your executioner, had it been any other woman. But touching Katie just ensures it's going to be a hell of a lot more painful."

The chains clank as Timothy tries to step back, but they hold him in place. "Please. It was the drugs," he pleads. "I ain't never touched a woman like that before. It was the fucking drugs that made me do it."

"No?" Silas cocks a brow. "What about Kendra?"

Kendra is Timothy's younger sister. After he disappeared, we searched for his family to figure out where he could have hidden himself. Kendra is from Utah and was a bitch to track down. But when we did, we found out a shit ton about Timothy and his younger years.

"Kendra?" Timothy croaks. "That bitch asked for it. *Begged* me for it."

"She begged you to beat her black and blue? She begged you to get her pregnant and then beat her so badly she lost the baby? Is that what you're saying? We've seen the pictures, Timothy. We saw the goddamn video you took and she stole from you before she disappeared. You raped and beat your sister from the time she was fourteen until she ran away at sixteen."

His already pale face drains of more color. His mouth opens and closes like a fish out of water as he tries to come up with something to say. But there isn't shit he *can* say. We've seen the evidence, and we're certain he's raped other women as well. Even if he hadn't, it wouldn't matter. The bastard will pay for touching Katie alone.

"How many others, Timothy?" Silas asks, his gait casual as he walks over to the table of tools and starts examining them. Timothy's eyes stay glued to him. "How many other women *begged*," he sneers the word, "you to rape them, abuse them?"

"N-none," he whimpers.

Silas does a half turn, making sure to show Timothy what he's holding. It's a nasty looking meat hook. "Are you sure that's the answer you want to give me? The more you lie, the slower you'll bleed to ensure you don't die quickly."

"Fuck!" Timothy curses, spittle flying from his mouth, some of it drooling down his chin.

"What do you think, Hunter?" Silas turns to me. "Think he's telling the truth?"

Leaning back against the wall, I shove my hands into my pockets. "Only one way to find out. There's a pair of vise grips on that table. Bet he'd sing like a canary if they were clamped around one of his balls."

"Hmm." Silas turns back to the table, picking up said vise grips and flipping them over in his hands.

"You bastards!" Timothy yells, desperation and fear making his voice hoarse. "I don't know how many! I didn't fucking keep count!"

He's telling the truth, and while we already knew he had

raped more women than Kendra and his attempt against Katie, his answer still has my blood boiling. The stiffness in Silas's shoulders confirms that he feels the same way.

"Hunter," he growls, his blazing eyes meeting mine over his shoulder. "You still want your shots, get them in now."

I don't need to be told twice. As I step away from the wall, I pull my hands from my pockets. Timothy's gaze drops down and he sees the brass knuckles I'm fisting. His eyes widen and panic sets in. Laughing, I slowly stalk toward him, enjoying the pathetic noises he makes as he wiggles against his bonds.

"Please, Hunter. I swear, man, I won't touch another woman for as long as I live."

I flash him my teeth. "You're right about that. You won't touch anyone again."

The first punch I throw lands in his gut. He falls slack, his arms pulled as taut as they can as his natural reaction is to huddle into a ball. With his head hanging forward, I deliver an uppercut. Blood spews from between his lips, slinging across the room, some of it landing on my shoes. My next strike, I aim for his kidneys. He grunts in pain, his body too weak to hold him up, so his arms bear his full weight.

As I take in Timothy's pathetic form, I'm not nearly satisfied, but I leave the rest to Silas.

I take a step back, my eyes turning to Silas. "He's all yours," I grunt.

Anticipation flares in his eyes seconds before he plunges a knife into one of Timothy's thighs, making sure not to hit a vital artery.

For the next thirty minutes, I watch Silas work him over thoroughly, not feeling a smidgen of remorse for the man slowly being tortured to death. It's people like Timothy the world needs to be rid of. If it were up to me, I'd kill every single one, starting with Whisper, then moving on to Henry, Terry, and Howard. Rotting in prison isn't good enough for the two bastards who are still there. If they're alive, then they have a chance of being put back into society, just like Henry, and that shit doesn't work for me.

A knock comes at the door I'm leaning against. Timothy has long since become quiet, only occasionally letting out whimpers of pain. Upon hearing the knock, Silas pauses in his pursuit of removing Timothy's other ear and glances over at me.

"Continue. I'll find out what they want," I tell him.

Giving me a chin lift, he goes back to work, and I turn to the door. The basement is strictly forbidden to most of the staff. In order to even open the door, you need a code, so there's only so many options for who's on the other side.

When I open the door, a grim-faced Kurt stares back at me. I step out and close it behind me.

"Got a problem, boss."

"What is it?" I ask.

"Katie sent me down here to tell you that Presley is here. No clue who that is, but from the look on her face, I take it she's not supposed to be here."

"Shit," I mutter, my gut pulling tight. Of all the times for Presley to make an appearance, right now couldn't have been a worse one. "Tell her I'm on my way. And do *not* let her out of my office or let anyone in. If you see Cat, don't ask questions. I'll explain later."

Kurt has never met Presley before, and he's only met Scarlett once. It was the night she appeared at Slate, dressed in a revealing outfit Cat would never wear. Kurt was understandably confused by the changes in my wife. I had already noticed her and was making my way to her when Kurt found me. Because I trust Kurt implicitly, the next day I told him about Cat's personality condition. There was no need to tell him about Presley and Athena because I never thought either of them would show up here. Athena only comes out at The Grove and Presley only appears at the house.

Kurt walks away to do my bidding, and I return to the room. There's so much blood on the floor beneath Timothy, he looks only a few drops away from bleeding out completely.

"Presley's here," I state and Silas whips his head around, his shocked gaze meeting mine. "You finish up here. I'm going to my wife."

"Go," he demands.

Without another word or a spared glance at Timothy, I leave the room. The whole trek up to the second floor, my nerves are shot. Why is Presley showing up now? What brought her forward? She usually only appears when Cat's emotions are heightened and she needs a reprieve from her dark thoughts or reminders of her past. There's a part of me that isn't surprised though. None of Cat's other personalities have emerged since the night she found out about them. I expected maybe Scarlett would appear, possibly even Athena, but not innocent Presley. Slate is not a place she should ever be. My only consolation is that she's in my office with Katie.

The door is closed when I approach my office. Kurt stands guard outside, like he knows my whole life lies behind that door and he's determined to protect it without being told.

"Thanks, Kurt. You can head back downstairs."

After he leaves, I grip the knob and push the door open. Katie sits on the edge of the leather couch against the wall, her body stiff, but her expression composed. She's doing an excellent job of not showing the concern I know she must be feeling.

My eyes dart across the room to my desk. Presley sits in my chair, spinning it in circles. When she makes it back around and her eyes land on me, her lips break out into a beautiful smile.

It's incredibly difficult to keep my body under control when I'm around Presley. She's Cat in looks, and I've never had a problem getting hard even thinking about my wife. Although Presley looks like Cat, her mannerisms are those of a twelve-year-old girl. It seems wrong and sours my stomach to envision getting turned on when Presley takes over.

It's weird to see her like this. Presley is usually dressed as any twelve year old girl would, but right now, she's wearing what Cat put on this morning; a pair of black leggings that mold to her curves and an off-the-shoulder lavender top that shows a glimpse of cleavage that no young girl would have.

"Hunter!" Presley yells, getting up from the chair and skipping her way around my desk.

"Katie," I call. "Thank you for keeping Presley company while I was away. Silas won't be long, and I'm sure he would love to see you in his office when he gets there."

"Yeah." Katie gets up from her seat and walks over to me, giving my arm a squeeze. She looks at Presley, her lips pulled up into a smile. "It was a pleasure seeing you again, Presley."

"You too, Katie." Presley beams a brilliant smile at Katie.

I wait until the door clicks closed behind me before I face Presley. "What are you doing here, Presley?"

Some of the joy fades from her face. "You're not happy to see me?"

Despite my strung nerves, I relax my features and soften my voice. "I'm always happy to see you. I just never expected you to show up here."

"Oh." Her eyes light up again and she bounces on her toes. "I wanted to surprise you. Did it work?"

I grab her hand and lead her over to the couch. I keep a few inches of space between us as we sit.

"You did. But this isn't a place for young girls."

Presley's bottom lip sticks out in a cute pout. "I'm not a little girl. I'll be thirteen soon."

She's been saying she'll be thirteen for years. Presley never ages.

"Regardless, this isn't the place for you," I say, keeping my tone gentle.

"Can you take me downstairs?"

"Absolutely not." My gentle tone falls to the wayside.

She laughs. "You really *are* no fun."

"Regardless, you will not be going downstairs." I pause. "Why are you here, Presley?"

"I wanted to see you. You weren't at home, and I didn't know how long you would be." She lifts her shirt, revealing her trim stomach, and pulls out a single piece of paper tucked into the waistband of her leggings. I recognize the stationary as the same as I keep on my desk. She must have written it before I made it upstairs. "And anyway, you need to give this to Cat. It's super important that she gets it." She thrusts the paper at me.

I grab it and briefly look down at the writing. "Why is it so important that Cat gets this?"

Presley lifts her shoulder, causing the shirt to slide down her arm even further. It takes effort to keep my eyes on her face and not dip to the amount of cleavage that's now on display.

"Because it's time," she says cryptically.

My eyes narrow. "Time for what?"

An unusual somberness fills Presley's eyes and it has my gut twisting. "Time for her to remember them. They can't stay in the shadows anymore. They need to be brought into the light again."

Anxiety has my back straightening. There is nothing I would like more than for Cat to acknowledge our children. To remember the good times we shared with them. To fill our walls with their pictures. But the fear of what it could do to Cat if she remembered, damn near brings me to my knees.

"Presley—"

I cut myself off when Presley's eyes become dazed, the muscles in her face going slack. It only lasts for a moment before she blinks and awareness returns. They move to me and her brows dip.

"Hunter?" Just from her voice, I know Presley is gone and my Cat is back. "You're finished already?"

Rather than answering, I pull her into my arms, needing her close to me. She doesn't hesitate when her arms wrap around my waist. Behind her back, I shove the piece of paper between the cushions of the couch.

Since finding out the truth about Presley, Scarlett, and Athena, Cat hasn't pressed for the reason why she is the way she is. In the back of her mind, she knows, but her subconscious is still protecting her. I haven't forced the issue because I'm not ready to face what the truth will do to her.

One day I will be, but not yet.

Chapter Twenty-Nine
Caterina

I snap awake, a loud piercing scream filling my ears. I slap my hands over them, trying to block out the horrible noise. My throat feels scratchy and raw, and it's only then that I realize I'm the source of the eerie sound.

"Cat!" A voice barks and then a face appears in front of me.

Hunter.

He's so close I can feel the heat of his heavy breathing. My mouth snaps shut and the screaming abruptly stops.

"Jesus Christ, baby," he mutters, pulling my hands down from my ears.

"Hunter," I croak. Even just that single word makes my throat ache.

He turns the lamp on and it momentarily blinds me. Then he's back in front of me, his big, rough hands framing my face.

"What in the fuck was that?" he asks, his own voice hoarse. "You've never screamed like that before."

Tears start streaming down my face like rivers as my bottom lip wobbles. Visions from my nightmare flash through my mind.

Visions I don't want to see and refuse to acknowledge. Ones I've fought so hard to hide from.

I shake my head hard, dislodging his hands from my cheeks. I put my hands on his chest and push him back. Catching him by surprise, he falls to his back, and before he can sit up, I've crawled my way on top of him, straddling his waist.

"Cat?" he questions. "What are you doing?"

I lean down until my face is only inches from him. "Fuck me, Hunter." A tear drops and lands on his cheek. "It hurts. Make me forget. Make everything go away again."

His expression softens as understanding dawns. He lifts a hand and curls it against the side of my face, sliding his fingers through my hair. "Baby," he whispers. So much feeling is in that single word.

"P-please," I whimper. "I'm not ready yet. I need more time."

I know my time living in a blissful make-believe world is coming to an end. The whispers of memories have been trying to push past the wall in my mind more and more lately. I've hidden from them for so long, refusing to allow them to see the light of day. I'm afraid to let them out. I'm afraid they'll drag me down into a black abyss from which I won't be able to escape. But no matter how much I fear them, I know I need to let them out. It's time for me to release them and face them. It's the only way I'll ever be whole again. It's the only way to be the wife Hunter truly deserves.

Grabbing my waist, Hunter rolls me so that I'm on my back and he's hovering above me. He's barely settled between my legs when I jerk my tank top off. My movements are frantic as I reach for my sleep shorts.

"Slow down, Cat," he says calmly.

"No," I shake my head heedlessly. "I can't wait. I need you right now."

He sits back on his heels, his hands moving to mine as I wiggle the shorts down my legs.

"Baby, I'll give you what you want. Just give me a minute."

I shake my head again. "No. I don't want to wait. I don't want soft. I don't want slow. I want you to fuck me. Take me like you take Scarlett."

He frowns and a small amount of surprise fills his eyes. I didn't mean to say that last part out loud, but now that the words are out, I don't want to take them back. I want Hunter raw. Unrestrained. So delirious with lust that he loses control. It pains me to know Scarlett has had him that way when I've secretly fantasized about it for years. I love Hunter's gentle side, especially because I know for most of his life he's been forced to be hard, but sometimes a woman just wants to be manhandled. To be taken roughly by her lover.

I want that right now. I crave it so badly that I ache for it. And I need it to rid myself of the demons in my head.

"I will not take you like I take her," he says, his tone harsh, as if just the thought of it is abhorrent to him. "It's brutal, Cat. Nothing Scarlett and I do is loving. It's pure, raw need, with no emotion."

"I don't care," I reply stubbornly. Now that the thought has entered my mind, I can't get it out. I reach for his cock, wrapping my fingers around his thick length. He's hard, giving away the fact that, even if he doesn't want to admit it, he likes the idea of taking me hard and rough.

He hisses when I squeeze him. "You love me, Hunter. I know how much. I know you'd do anything for me and you hate to see me hurt. All of those things, I feel for you too. Manhandling me, forcing me to submit, taking me without control won't change that." I stare up at him imploringly. "Please. This is what I want. What I need from you right now."

I'm wearing him down. I can see it in the indecision in his eyes, the naked need he can't hide, but he still holds back.

"I can't," he says quietly. "I've hurt you too much already. You're not in the right frame of mind to know what you're asking."

I rub my thumb across the tip of his cock, smearing a small drop of pre-cum. He hisses, baring his teeth.

"I *do* know what I'm asking." I push up on my elbows and slide my body down the few inches I need so he's poised at my entrance. "This isn't out of the blue," I tell him. "I wanted this before I knew about Scarlett. I've just been too afraid to ask for it. I want you to leave bruises on my hips and thighs from grabbing me so hard. I want to be sore between my legs from your forceful thrusts. I want the bite of pain from you gripping my hair as you fuck my mouth. I want your hand around my throat, squeezing so hard that I struggle to breathe. I want to feel you in every hole I have. I want you to need me so badly that you can't wait, so you take me no matter where we are. I want you mindless with lust and desperate enough to give me those things, not only because I want you to give them to me, but because *you* want me to have them."

"Fuck," he growls a mere second before he smashes his lips to mine.

I moan into his mouth, desire ravaging me like a category five hurricane. My mind spirals, pushing away the unwanted images of a past too painful to remember and replacing them with Hunter. A husband who has put up with way too much shit from me. It may be shit he's willing to deal with, but it's not something I want to put him through anymore. He's hurt too much because of me.

I wrap my legs around his waist, and the moment my feet lock together at the small of his back, he forcefully thrusts his hips forward. The impact of suddenly being full is deliciously painful.

A loud cry escapes me, and I dig my fingers into his biceps. Hunter stops with his hips pressed against the back of my thighs.

"Shit, baby. I'm sorry," he groans.

"Don't you dare apologize, Hunter St. James," I tell him heatedly, lifting my hips to show him I want more. "I want all of you. Every dirty and twisted part. Now take me," I squeeze my inner muscles, "and show me I'm yours in every single way."

He growls, the deep and guttural sound making my pussy gush around his cock. He hikes one leg up on his waist and wraps his other arm around my back from underneath so his hand is curled around my shoulder. His firm grip keeps me in place as he pulls back his hips and slams forward. Our chests remain pressed together, only his hips moving. With every forceful move he makes forward, I lose my breath.

This is what I wanted. The unhinged version of Hunter.

His face falls forward and his lips meet the spot between my neck and shoulder. His lips are sweet and gentle for all of two seconds before they latch onto the skin and he takes a bite. The sting is almost too much, just on this side of pain, but I lap it up.

He lets go, his tongue licking the spot before he moves his mouth to my ear. "Is this what you wanted, baby? Taking you like an animal? Needing you so fucking much I can't control what I do to you?"

"Yes," I hiss, arching my back. "Give me more."

"Goddamn it, Cat." He picks up speed, his hips hitting the

back of my thighs with enough force that I should have bruises later. I look forward to seeing them.

Hunter's deep groans and my loud cries of pleasure are mixed with the bed banging against the wall and the sound of flesh slapping together. Our sweat-slick bodies slide together.

Suddenly, Hunter's warmth is gone as he pulls away from me. Before I can protest, he's off the bed and pulling me with him. Picking me up as if I weigh nothing, my legs instinctively wrap around his waist. When the tip of his cock meets my entrance, and I slide down his shaft, my mouth drops open and my eyes roll back. With my weight coming into play in this new position, he hits deeper.

"Oh, God, Hunter," I moan.

I tighten my legs around him, and with the help of his strong arms, I lift up until just the tip is left inside and then impale myself again. He feels deliriously good.

I've never had complaints about the way Hunter has taken me. Our sex life has been incredible, and if we ever only have sex the way we have in the past, I would be perfectly fine with it. But this, *dear Jesus, is divine*.

From the look in his beautiful green eyes and the tense lines around his mouth, it's clear just how much he's enjoying this too. My mouth drops to his, taking his lips in a kiss not intended for lovemaking, but for pure raw fucking. My breasts scrape against the coarse hairs on his chest as he lifts and drops me up and down his cock.

The telltale sign of my impending orgasm hits me hard and fast, but I'm not ready yet. There's something I want to try first. It's something I've been curious about, especially since Hunter told me about Scarlett.

Sliding my fingers through Hunter's hair, I grip the strands and move my mouth to his ear. "Fuck my ass," I pant.

With him fully inside me, he jerks to a halt and pulls his head back to see my face. My eyes show him how much I want him to do this. It's not just a want, it's a deep-seated need.

"I don't want to hurt you," his deep voice rumbles.

"Sometimes a little pain can feel good."

"And sometimes it can do irreparable damage," he retorts.

I scrape my nails against his scalp. "I trust you won't hurt me that much. You won't go too far."

The muscle in his jaw twitches and indecision mixed with wanton need flares in his eyes. After a slight moment of contemplation, he unhooks my legs from his waist, and I drop my feet to the floor.

He grabs my hair and tilts my head back, forcing my eyes to his. "If it becomes too much, we stop. Swear to me, Cat, that you'll tell me to stop. I don't need to take you that way."

He may not need it, but it still feels good to him. Whatever he does with Scarlett, I want to offer it to him as Cat. Nevertheless, I give him what he wants.

"I promise."

He drops his head and presses his lips against mine in a bruising kiss before spinning me around. His breath whispers against my ear when he says, "Stay here."

After he leaves me, I hear him enter the bathroom and emerge a minute later. I breathe faster and my body vibrates and hums with excitement.

"Bend over, baby, and show me that gorgeous ass."

The desirous cadence of his voice sends shivers down my spine. I bend at the waist and place my hands on the end of the bed. The sound of a bottle opening fills the room, and I jerk involuntarily when something cool drips down my ass crack. His finger touches my hole next and my muscles automatically tighten on reflex.

"We're gonna take this slow," Hunter says, applying a tiny bit of pressure. "I won't take you like Scarlett likes, uncaring if it hurts." The tip of his finger slips inside, and I can't help but moan at the foreign feeling. "We'll do this my way at first, slow and steady, until I fit every inch of my cock inside you. After that, once you get used to having your ass full, then I'll fuck you fast." Inch by inch, he wedges his finger inside. "You understand?"

I can't concentrate on words right now, so I don't respond to his question.

"Do. You. Understand, Cat?" He punctuates each word with a sharp thrust. "Don't push me on this. It's not something I'm willing to give in on."

"Yes," I moan, pushing back against his finger. "Please give me more."

He adds a second one and my breath catches. Going just as slowly as he did with the first finger, he slides them in until his knuckles press against the flesh of my butt.

All too soon, but not soon enough, he removes his fingers from my hole and replaces them with the tip of his cock. I hold my breath, waiting on tenterhooks as he presses forward. My fingers dig into the blanket and my stomach muscles tighten when the tip slips past the tight bundle of nerves.

"Oh!" I moan.

Hunter pauses, running his hand down my back to rest his palm on one ass cheek. "You good?"

"More than good," is my breathy reply. "More, please."

His chuckle fills my ears, and it adds to the exquisite feeling coursing through me.

Another inch slips inside, and a little pinch of pain flares in my backside. I welcome the feeling, surprised at how much more I want.

Hunter does just as he said he would and takes his time filling my ass. I soak up every groan he releases, loving that I'm giving him something new. Giving him a part of me he's never gotten from me before. Technically, anal sex with me is not new to him. However, I do not have those memories, and the woman he took as Scarlett is very different from me.

"Sweet Jesus," he mutters once he's buried every bit of his length inside me. His fingers bite into my hips. "So goddamn tight, Cat. Fucking incredible."

I have to agree, but I can't do so out loud, because I've forgotten how to talk. So instead, I show him my appreciation by pushing back against him, telling him without words that I want him to move.

He slides out, only to slide back in again. He does this several times before picking up speed, taking me faster, going deeper with each thrust. I love it. At first it was a little intense, but now I don't want to stop.

"You ready for more?" Hunter asks, keeping his pace steady.

"Oh God, yes."

As soon as the words leave my lips, he pulls back and suddenly slams forward. I wasn't ready. There was no way I could have prepared myself for the onslaught of pleasure that grips me as he fucks the holy hell out of me. If I thought it felt good when he took it slow, this is beyond my imagination.

A long cry escapes my lips, his name shouted hoarsely, and my inner muscles tighten around him, my stomach muscles spasming. My head falls forward, too weak to hold it up. My body wants to slump forward like Jell-O. Only Hunter holding me up by my hips keeps me on my feet.

"Holy fuck," he growls. "You like this, baby?"

"Yes!" I cry.

"You like having your ass full of my cock?"

"Yes." I moan this time.

"That's a good thing, because now that you've given it to me," he slams his hips forward, jolting me, "I'm going to want it all the time."

He thrusts so hard that I'm lifted off my feet.

"You going to give it to me anytime I want it?"

"Yes, Hunter. You can have it whenever you want it."

He hooks one of his hands around my stomach and pulls my body upward. My back meets his hard chest as I stand impaled on his cock.

"That's my good girl," he whispers, then bites the side of my neck hard enough to leave a mark.

I whimper, the pleasure of everything Hunter is doing and making me feel is almost too much. He pulls away and pounds his way back inside. Over and over again, he fucks me, using my body for his own pleasure, but giving me the same in return.

Turning my head, I seek his lips, and blessedly, he gives them to me. Our teeth clash from his pounding, but we stay connected.

Lifting one arm, I reach behind me and wrap it around his neck. The changed position pushes out my chest and Hunter takes advantage, pinching and pulling hard on my nipples. His other hand finds mine, sliding his fingers through them and taking them both down my stomach, over the thin line of hair covering my mound and straight to my soaked pussy.

I yank my mouth away and toss my head back on his shoulder. A low moan drifts from my lips when he pushes the middle and ring finger of both of our hands into my slick hole. With his cock in my ass and four fingers in my pussy, I'm almost too full. He uses both of our hands to fuck me, all the while his hips steadily thrust. A flood of overwhelming sensations clouds my vision and ignites my body. The heel of my palm, pressed inward by Hunter's hand, grinds against my clit, intensifying those sensations.

Hunter's hot, panting breath flutters across my ear. "Is this what you've been wanting, Cat?" he rasps. "Your ass full of my cock and your pussy filled with our fingers?" I nod, unable to form words. "Bet I could get another finger inside that tight cunt," he grits out, shoving our fingers in as far as they can go and punching his hips forward.

His crass words and the mental image they evoke send a shockwave of pleasure through me. Arching my back, I grind my hips against the fingers and cock filling me up.

"Mmm... You like that idea, don't you?" he murmurs darkly, his voice rumbling against my neck. "After all these years, who knew I married such a dirty girl."

"Please, Hunter," I moan, desperate for something, anything, to take me over the edge.

He slips our fingers out of my pussy, and I whine in protest. His chuckle tickles my ear. "Don't worry, baby. You'll get what you need."

With his fingers slick with my juices, he moves my hand up so the tips of my fingers hit my clit. "Rub that clit, Cat, and I'll take care of the rest."

His hand travels back down to my hole, inserting three of his fingers this time. His other hand trails up my torso, between my breasts, and he wraps his fingers around the base of my throat. My breath stutters, not because of the exquisite pleasure wracking my body, but from the harsh grip Hunter has around my throat. I can still breathe, but only barely. Little white spots dance behind my closed eyelids as euphoria filters through every cell in my body.

Little whimpers erupt from my lips, barely heard over the loud slap of flesh hitting flesh. My head falls back on Hunter's shoulder and my legs weaken. It's only his grip around my throat and his fingers and cock that keep me standing. My fingers swirl over my clit, chasing a high that's just centimeters away.

Hunter's thrusts become more forceful. My body is so lax, I feel like a rag doll being tossed around. But holy hell, the pleasure is more than anything I could have dreamed of.

Hunter's fingers curl inside me, hitting a spot that makes my stomach muscles tense. My release hits hard and fast, stealing the last of my energy. My toes curl against the floor and my mouth drops open, a hoarse cry, restricted by Hunter's grip around my neck, pierces the air.

My arm around his neck falls limply by my side, my bones feeling like they're made of jelly.

He releases my neck, placing a kiss on the side, and moves his arm to wrap around my torso just below my breasts. His chest presses against my back, bending me slightly at the waist. Then, with his fingers still inside me, and my ass still full of his cock, he thrusts hard and fast, using his arm around me to pull me back to him. His grunts fill the room, along with my low cries.

Shockingly, the moment I feel Hunter stiffen, another orgasm hits me, holding me in its tight grip, refusing to let me go.

Hunter's arm still holds me up, despite my body wanting to fall to the bed in a pile of mush. His chest is pressed against my back, both slick with sweat, and I feel his heartbeat hammering erratically.

My gentle husband is back when he carefully slides out of me and eases me down on the bed. "Stay right there," he says, kissing my bare shoulder.

Even if I wanted to move, I couldn't, so I remain on my side with my feet hanging off the end of the bed. I hear the water run in the bathroom and a moment later, the bed dips as he climbs on the end.

"On your stomach, baby," he murmurs gently.

With the last of my energy, I roll to my stomach. My legs are moved apart and a warm washcloth is pressed between them.

After the washcloth is tossed away, he pulls me up to the top of the bed. Hunter settles on his back and drapes me over his chest with the covers pulled up over us. His big hand rests on my back just above my butt. The other hand tips up my chin until my eyes meet his.

"You okay?"

I curl my lips. "Okay is an understatement. Fantastic is closer, but still not accurate."

His eyes crinkle when a deep chuckle leaves his lips. "You always manage to surprise me, even after all the years we've been married."

I press a kiss against his chest, right over the spot where his heart beats.

"Why have you never told me you wanted something like that?"

I lift my eyes back to him. "Because I was worried it was something you didn't want."

"Baby, I want anything you want. You only have to let me know."

I smile again. "Well, now you know."

He tilts my head back further and dips his down. "Now I

know," he says against my lips. When he pulls back, his expression is serious. "About your nightmare."

I'm already shaking my head before he finishes his sentence. "Please not tonight." I fight hard at pushing away the images of my nightmare, wanting to forget about them for as long as I can. "Can we talk about it tomorrow?"

Concern pulls down his eyebrows, but thankfully, he doesn't push. "Yeah."

I lay my head back down on his chest, my eyes so heavy they close before I'm comfortable. I concentrate on the steady rise and fall of Hunter's breathing.

I can feel the images, the *memories*, fighting to come back to the forefront of my mind. I know the wall I've kept them behind won't ever be rebuilt. Now I must find a way to prevent them from crippling me.

Chapter Thirty
Hunter

What feels like minutes after I close my eyes after taking Cat like I never have before, a loud piercing noise jerks me awake. I spring up in bed and instinctively reach for the gun I keep on the nightstand. It's not the same sound as Cat's screams that woke me earlier. It's the fucking house alarm.

The bed jostles beside me, and I stretch out my arm—the one not holding the gun—to wrap around Cat's waist. As I slide off my side of the bed, I take her with me.

"What's going on?" she asks over the jarring sound of the alarm, her voice trembling with fright.

I let Cat go to pull on the pair of jeans that had been tossed on the chair by the window. Grabbing the robe hanging over the back of the same chair, I hand it to her.

"I don't know."

Someone broke into the house or attempted to break in. Cat isn't stupid. She's aware of this as well. The fear that darkens her eyes gives away that knowledge. Nevertheless, I keep my thoughts to myself.

As soon as she has the robe tied around her waist, I grab her hand and pull her toward the closet. It's not the safe room in the basement, but with the reinforced bedroom door, it's the best place to put Cat on the second floor. Taking her downstairs when I don't know what's waiting down there isn't an option.

"Stay here," I demand, swooping down and giving her a quick kiss.

She tightens her fingers around mine when I attempt to let her hand go. "Stay," she begs.

Fucking hell. I hate seeing fear plastered all over her face. I hate even more not giving her what she thinks she needs. There isn't much I could ever deny Cat.

"Baby, you know I can't," I tell her quietly.

Her eyes say she wants to argue, but Cat knows me better than anyone, so she knows it would be futile. I'm not a cower-in-a-closet-and-wait-for-the-police kind of guy. I'll confront any bastard who thinks they can fuck with me or mine in any way.

Cat's eyes glisten, and for a moment, I worry she's going to beg me to stay anyway, but she blinks back the tears, straightens her spine, and pushes back her shoulders.

"Okay."

Before I can back out of the closet, she smashes her palms against my cheeks and pulls my head down until my lips collide with hers. The kiss is short, but hard, with a hint of desperation.

"Please be careful," she whispers against my lips. "You better come back to me in one piece with not even a scratch, or I'm going to kick your ass."

If the situation were different, I might have smiled at her demand. But since it isn't, I drop a peck on her lips. "You got it, baby." I step back and close the closet door.

When I hear Cat lock the door, I silently move across the bedroom floor and grab a t-shirt from the hamper. It's still dark outside, but my eyes have long since adjusted. The door, which is mostly closed, doesn't so much as creak as I pull it open and peer out into the hall. With the alarm blaring, I can't hear shit, so I rely on sight as I move down the hall. The doors to the kids' rooms are still closed, so I move past them and check the spare bath, the linen closet, and the guest bedroom. I pause at the top of the stairs for a moment before I slowly take them one at a time.

The entryway to the front door is only a few feet away from the bottom of the stairs, so I go there first to shut the alarm off. The sudden silence is deafening. I hold still for a moment, listening intently for any sounds that don't belong. The only sound I hear is the whirl of the ceiling fan in the living room and the low hum of electricity.

Instinct tells me that Cat and I are the only ones in the house, but I still check every room and every window with the gun loaded and ready to shoot any fucker I see. Nothing is out of place.

Frustration slides through my limbs as I make my way back through the house toward the stairs. As I reach the bottom one, there's a loud knock on the door. I peer through the peephole, not surprised to see two uniformed officers on the other side. Flipping the safety back on my gun, I slip it into the waistband of my jeans before pulling the door open.

"Hello, officers," I say.

I recognize Officer Spiel from my few visits to the police department. The other, who looks too young to be wearing a badge, I've never met before.

"Good morning, Mr. St. James. I'm Officer Spiel and this is Officer Lanson. We're here as a courtesy visit. Monroe Security said the alarm at this address went off and when they tried to call to inquire about it, there was no answer. They notified us immediately."

I lost faith in the River Heights Police Department when they failed to inform me of Henry Stephens's release. Seeing them on my doorstep right now doesn't help my opinion, but at least they're doing something right.

Even though I don't want them in my house, I still step back and gesture with my arm, "Come inside."

Officer Spiel looks around as I lead them into the living room, his eyes alert. "Did the alarm trip by accident or was there an intruder?" he inquires. Based on the way he stands and the tenseness of his body, I can tell he's ready to act if necessary.

"I don't know if someone was in the house or not, but there was at least an attempt to come inside. My wife and I were asleep when the alarm went off, so it wasn't accidentally tripped." Spiel stiffens, his eyes darting around the room. "If you'll excuse me for a moment, I left my wife in our bedroom closet while I looked around. I need to let her know everything is okay. I've checked each room and nothing seems to be missing or disturbed, but you're more than welcome to check yourself."

While I'm confident that if there was a person in the house, they're not anymore. The sooner the police check it themselves, the easier it will be to get rid of them.

I take the stairs two at a time and walk swiftly down the hall to the master bedroom. My knuckles rap against the door of the closet. "Cat, it's me."

The words barely leave my lips before the door is thrown open and Cat is throwing herself into my arms, shoving her face into my chest. My grip on her is just as tight.

"Did you find anything?" she asks, pulling back to look up at me.

"No. But the police are here. The alarm company called them when I didn't answer my phone." I look across the room to the nightstand, where my phone still sits.

Her head jerks up and down as she exhales a shaky breath. It is astounding how much this woman can endure and still remain sound of mind.

As much as I hate to bring up a subject that could upset her, the incident tonight proves I need to address it. It's something we need to discuss. For her safety, I have to take the chance and believe she can handle what I throw at her. She needs to understand the extent of the danger she's in.

But that can come later. Right now, we need to get back downstairs.

I dip my head and press a kiss against her lips. "Put some clothes on, baby."

As she does that, I grab my phone and check the screen, seeing two missed calls from Monroe Security. I pocket the device and wait by the door for Cat. A few minutes later, we walk out together. As we pass Ryder's room, Cat stops. I turn to her, seeing a frown forming on her face.

"What's wrong?" I ask.

Hesitantly, her hand lifts and she sets her palm on the white door. "I don't know. Something doesn't feel right," she answers so quietly I barely hear her words. "Something isn't right behind this door."

I stiffen, and the hand I have wrapped around hers impulsively pulls Cat until she's behind me. The only two rooms I didn't check were this one and Eliana's. Considering how close they are to our bedroom, an intruder would be foolish to hide there. Besides, if anyone did come into the house, they didn't have time to make it up the stairs and into one of the rooms before the alarm went off, and I was out of the master bedroom checking the house.

As I open the door, my other hand moves to my back to grip the gun, ready to pull it out at a moment's notice. A sudden rush of cold air hits me, sending a chill running down my spine. My eyes move to the window when the red and blue Captain America curtains billow.

The fucking window is open. Cat doesn't come in here, so I know it wasn't her who opened it. We're on the second floor, and there aren't any trees close enough to the window that someone could climb up or down. There's no way someone could have broken into the house, made it up to this room, opened the window, and made it back down the stairs before I left the bedroom. The only logical explanation—and this shit has my blood boiling—is that they disarmed the alarm when they broke in, stayed in the house doing God knows what, while we slept, and then purposefully set off the alarm when they left.

Motherfucking hell.

How in the hell is that possible? We have a top-notch security system. The best money can buy and it's supposed to be unhackable.

Fucking Whisper.

It has to be. It's rumored that he's a genius when it comes to computers. Can break into damn near any system, so long as it's connected to the internet.

The bastard who tortured my family was in my fucking house. Was in my son's room. Only feet away from my wife.

As I slam the window down, rage radiates through me so strongly that my hands shake. When I turn away to leave the room, my eyes are drawn to the mirror above the chest of drawers.

I walk over to look closer and blood roars through my ears when I see the scrawled words written in red on the mirror.

My hands broke him. His blood still coats my tongue. I was his ending, just as I shall be yours.

Before I can stop myself, my fist smashes against the mirror. I barely register glass slicing into my flesh, my mind too focused on the violent rage filling every cell in my body, threatening to consume me and push me over into a rampage.

In the black haze seeping into my mind, only the gentle hands on my back and the sweet scent of vanilla and roses pulls me back.

"Hunter." Cat's gasp jerks my gaze from the shattered mirror to find her standing in front of me, her head bent as she takes my bloodied fist gently into her hands. "What did you do?"

My eyes briefly lift to the ruined mirror, satisfied it's destroyed enough that you can't make out the words.

There's no point in answering Cat's question since it's pretty obvious what happened.

I'm not sure if she's in a hurry to doctor my hand or if she wants out of the room as soon as possible, but she tugs hard on my forearm until I follow behind her.

Before she can pull me toward our room, I stop her by planting my feet against the floor. "We'll take care of this in a few minutes. The police are still downstairs."

As she bites her bottom lip, her eyes fly back to my hand, where I'm certain blood drips onto the hardwood floor from the tips of my fingers. She pulls out a hand towel from the linen closet. Lifting my hand, I allow her to gently wrap the cloth around it.

The muscles in my jaw ache from clenching my teeth so hard

as we come up to Eliana's room. I stop and crack the door open. The window is closed, but a quick glance at the mirror on the wall above the vanity shows more writing. I don't have time to look at it right now, but I'm sure it's another message.

I blow out a huff of heated air and close the door. I'll come back here later to see what was written.

Officers Spiel and Lanson are just leaving the kitchen when Cat and I get downstairs. I introduce them to my wife. As I expected, neither found anything in their walkthrough.

Spiel's eyes fall on my wrapped hand, blood already seeping through the cloth. "What happened there?" he asks.

"I punched a mirror." His eyebrows rise. "It kinda pisses a man off when someone breaks into or attempts to break into his house. Even more so when he and his wife are sleeping and are unaware."

He jerks his chin up in acknowledgement and looks briefly at Cat, huddled against my side.

"Do you mind if we take a look upstairs?" Spiel asks.

"I would prefer you didn't," I tell him. Although I haven't dealt much with Spiel, Trevor has mentioned him a few times, and he seems alright. There's nothing here that could implicate me in a crime, but I don't like cops nosing around in my shit. "The upstairs has already been cleared. You'll find nothing up there, just like you found nothing down here."

Lanson doesn't like my answer, but there isn't shit he can do about it.

Cat and I walk the officers to the front door, and Spiel hands me a card with his number. "Call me or the station if anything else happens."

Nodding, I shove the card into my pocket, crumpling it. I'll toss it in the trash later. As a kid growing up on the streets, you quickly learn you can't depend on the police, which was reinforced by recent events. I take care of my own, have for years, and don't plan to change now.

Once the door is closed behind them, Cat grabs my wrist and pulls me into the kitchen. She's silent as she pushes me down into a chair, though her eyes look haunted.

When she approaches with the first aid kit we keep under the sink, I take it from her and set it on the table. With my hands on her waist, I pull her forward, so she's straddling my lap with her legs on either side of my thighs.

"Are you okay?" I ask, cupping my uninjured hand against her cheek.

"Yes." She lifts a shoulder. "No." Her eyes drop from mine. "I don't know."

My chest aches with her uncertain response. "I'm so sorry, baby."

Her gorgeous eyes meet mine once again. "Why are you sorry? None of this is your fault."

She's wrong. It's all my fault. If I had been home when those bastards broke into my house, my family would still be intact, and my wife wouldn't be close to a mental breakdown. If I had gotten my hands on the boys who tortured my family before they were arrested and convicted, they'd be dead, and one of them wouldn't be walking free. If only I had gotten my hands on Whisper, my wife wouldn't be in danger.

Instead of acknowledging her statement, I make my own. "There are things we need to talk about, Cat."

Once again, she avoids my eyes by grabbing the kit from the table and lifting the lid.

"I know," she finally says quietly, pulling out a roll of gauze and a pair of tweezers. "And we will. Later." She lifts my hand, unwraps the cloth, and begins carefully plucking the glass from my knuckles.

Later could be minutes from now, but something tells me Cat's definition of the word in this instance is hours or days. She has an appointment with Dr. Armani this afternoon, so I'll wait until we get home before I force the conversation we're both dreading.

Chapter Thirty-One
Caterina

"How have the headaches been?" Dr. Armani asks, steepling his fingers as he peers through his square-rimmed glasses at me. Having salt and pepper hair, kind blue eyes, and a slim body, Dr. Armani has always reminded me of my grandfather. It's why I immediately felt comfortable with him when I started seeing him years ago.

I tuck a piece of hair behind my ear. "About the same."

"Hmm..." He tips his chin down. "No difference since you found out about Athena, Scarlett, and Presley?"

"Not really."

It's my first time seeing Dr. Armani since Hunter told me about the three people I share my mind with. He was surprised when I told him I knew about the other identities, but I also saw approval. Perhaps he thought I wouldn't be calm knowing about them. Honestly, I'm surprised myself. I keep waiting for the other shoe to drop and for me to go into a meltdown. I know I'm toeing the edge of sanity. One slight shift in the wind could blow me off, leaving me spiraling into something unrecognizable.

"That's good." He nods again and smiles. His eyes briefly flick to Hunter before returning to me. Hunter doesn't always join me for sessions, but I asked him to this time. "And the nightmares?"

I hate talking about my nightmares. The horrible sounds they leave in my head are sounds I want to forget.

"Any changes?"

I shift in my seat, suddenly feeling like I'm sitting on jagged rocks. Hunter's hand, with his thick fingers laced through my slender ones, twitch and tighten in mine.

"My last nightmare was different. I remember more," I say, my voice small.

"Do you want to talk about it?"

I shake my head. "No."

I haven't even told Hunter about my most recent nightmare. I keep hoping that if I don't talk about it, it'll fade and become another forgotten memory.

"That's okay. We're here when you're ready."

I nod, grateful he doesn't push.

"Is there anything else either of you would like to discuss before we call it a day?"

"No," I respond. Even though Dr. Armani makes me feel relaxed and comfortable, I'm tired after not getting much sleep last night, so I'm ready to leave. Thankfully, my hour is almost over.

"Okay. I'll see you next month, Cat. Should you need anything before then, you only have to call the office."

Hunter and I get up from the couch. "Thank you, Dr. Armani."

"Always a pleasure, my dear."

We leave, and I breathe a sigh of relief when we walk out into the fresh air.

Hunter pulls on my arm, turning me toward him. My hand is

placed on the firm muscle over his heart as he observes me with his green eyes.

"You okay?"

"Yeah." I smile. "I was just getting a little twitchy in there, but I'm okay now."

Using his other hand, he tips my chin up and drops his head, laying his lips softly against mine.

"Hunter? Cat?"

We both look over when our names are called. I smile when I see Jimmy Simons approaching. Hunter tucks me under his arm as we face him.

"How are you, Jimmy?" I ask.

"Never better." He grins.

Every time I see Jimmy, he always has a smile on his face. Being a marine for ten years, injured, discharged from the military because of the injury, having no family, and ending up on the streets, you'd think he'd be more bitter and not the happy man he is today. I'm not exactly sure how it happened, but apparently, a few years ago, Hunter helped him get back on his feet.

"That's great." I say with a big grin. "It's been too long since I've seen you. Why don't you come over for dinner soon?"

"Wouldn't miss it." He gives me a sly grin. "So long as you make your delicious apple turnovers."

I can't help but laugh. Last time we had Jimmy over for dinner, I thought he would fight Hunter for the last apple turnover. "You got it. I'll even make an extra for you to take home."

He raises his hand to his chest. "A woman after my own heart." He flashes his teeth at Hunter. "I tell you, Hunter, if she weren't so attached to you, I'd try to steal her away."

Hunter laughs, his arm around my waist flexing, pulling me closer. "Get your own woman."

One cheek pokes out more than the other when he smirks. "I'm working on it."

"Now that sounds interesting," I say, laying my hand on Hunter's lower stomach. "Do tell."

"Maybe over dinner. Don't want to jinx it." He winks. "I'll let you two get going." He holds out his hand for Hunter to shake. "Call me about that dinner invite, Hunter."

"See you later, Jimmy."

Jimmy walks in the opposite direction from us. I stay tucked into Hunter's side as we make our way to his SUV. Fatigue from a restless night leaves my limbs sluggish, so I'm grateful for the added support.

Soon after, we pull into our driveway beside my car. The sun has already set and the temperature has dropped several degrees. A chilled shiver races down my spine as we walk up the steps to the front door.

My phone pings in my purse, so I pull it out while Hunter unlocks the door. It's a text from my sister telling me she'll drop off her boys at two in the afternoon on Friday. I'm babysitting the rugrats for her while she goes to a doctor's appointment.

While I type my reply, I follow Hunter into the house, barely registering the beep of the alarm as he disarms and resets it.

A harsh curse pulls my attention away from my phone. At first, I'm confused as to why Hunter is standing so stiffly in front of me. But then I notice the pictures on the walls. Pictures I've never seen before. Or rather, pictures I haven't seen in years and pretend they don't exist.

Except, these pictures aren't the same. They've been altered.

I walk to the one closest to me. Hunter tries to stop me, but I shake off his hand. It's a big picture, set in an elegant gray frame. Hunter and I are sitting on a bench in what appears to be a public park. One of his arms is wrapped around my shoulders. My eyes well up with tears when I see his other arm wrapped around the shoulders of a young girl. My gaze moves to my lap, where I'm holding a baby boy. I don't need to guess the kids' ages or names. Ryder was just over a year old when this was taken, and Eliana was eleven.

In the distance, Hunter yells my name, but I'm too absorbed in the picture. A low buzz starts, ramping up in volume in my ears, as I take in what was done to the faces of the two beautiful children. *My* beautiful children.

Their faces have been gouged out, and red marks replace them.

A sob forces its way up my throat and through my dry lips.

As I move to the next picture, I feel Hunter's presence just behind me.

This picture is of me in the hospital right after I delivered Ryder. Hunter lies squished up on the bed beside me, half of his body hanging off the side. In my arms is a newborn Ryder, wrapped in a blue checkered baby blanket. What's supposed to be his little scrunched up face is scratched out with red.

Another low cry creeps past my lips.

My feet lead me to another picture frame. In this one, which has always been one of my favorites, Hunter is reclining back against a big tree. I'm sitting between his legs, and Eliana is between mine. Ryder is between hers. Ryder just turned two and Eliana was twelve. Once again, their faces are marked with red.

As I look around, every picture appears to be the same.

Something sharp pierces the center of my chest, stealing all of my breath. I try to suck in air, but it's like my lungs are clogged with sludge. Black spots dance across the edges of my vision, and my legs wobble, threatening to collapse. I teeter forward, my arms too weak to lift and catch myself so I don't hit the wall.

One second I'm standing there, suffocating from the pain that fills every inch of my body, and the next, I'm falling into a void of darkness. Screams, loud and excruciating, reverberate inside my head. I try to block them out because I know what they are, but no matter how much I attempt to shove them behind the weak wall in my mind, they still tumble out, refusing to be silenced any longer.

Visions follow the screams. Those visions lead to nightmares of a past that I wish I could banish forever, but I can't. I can't keep pushing them away. Pushing them away doesn't make them disappear. They're still there, and will always be there, to torture and torment me.

My two beautiful children don't deserve to be forgotten. If they are forgotten, it means that they never existed, and every moment spent with them should be cherished. I love Eliana and Ryder with all my heart and soul. They were my precious treasures, my angels. For years, I kept their memories locked away in my mind, because of the pain of losing them. The pain of not being able to save them, not being strong enough, not giving the bastards who took them from me what they wanted, was too much to bear.

No more.

There'll always be guilt over what I couldn't do, but my babies won't be hidden away any longer.

"*Don't do it, Cat,*" a voice says in my head. Athena. "*It hurts too much to remember. Once you let them out, they won't be pushed away again.*"

Loud banging rattles the inside of my skull. I feel her presence trying to break free. Athena tries to protect me from the pain when she knows I'm no longer able to handle it.

"*NO!*" I mentally shout, refusing to let her steer me away from what I must do. She shoves harder, and I almost give in. Only my determination and sheer willpower allow me to keep her at bay. "*My babies will not be silenced. They're mine, Athena.*"

"*With the good, always comes the bad. Are you willing to remember them as you saw them last?*" she asks, her voice becoming weaker. "*Can you really live with those memories, with that pain, or will it consume you so completely, you'll do anything to make it go away? To end it permanently? Think of Hunter, Cat. Think of what it'll do to him, should your mind fracture beyond repair.*"

Her question makes me pause. As painful as those memories were the last time I was with my children, I will endure them again if it means I can have all their good memories.

"*Yes,*" I whisper back to her. "*I'm strong enough. I can do it.*"

Athena retreats, but I still sense her presence. She's not gone forever, just for the time being.

I open my mind, preparing myself for the paralyzing pain I know is coming, but before I can fully open myself, another stronger presence makes itself known.

"*With pain comes more pain. Let them in, and know you'll have the harsh hands of your husband when punishment becomes your only escape. Know that he'll always give you what you need, even when that means making you bleed.*"

A wail slides past my lips with Scarlett's statement. Pain is her escape. She luxuriates in it and uses Hunter as a tool to seek it out. While I hate what she makes Hunter do to us, I also understand her. And we are an us. Scarlett is as much a part of me as Athena and Presley.

I won't let her stop me, any more than I will let Athena. I am stronger than them. This is *my* body, *my* mind, *my* soul. They may have access to them, but I won't let them control me anymore. They may slip through during my weaker moments, but right now, with what's most important, I'm the one making the decision.

Scarlett says no more, but stays in the background, her ominous presence residing by Athena's.

A new voice comes, this one so sweet and innocent, it brings tears to my eyes.

"*It's time, Cat,*" Presley says gently. I feel the warmth of her touch on my hand. "*Let them out. It's time to bring them back into the light.*"

A soft smile slowly lifts my lips.

It disappears when I open my eyes, and I'm standing in the corner of our living room. In front of me is a chair with the me of five years ago tied to it. I'm naked, every inch of my body covered in cuts, blood, and bruises, with tape covering my mouth.

It's like I'm there, back in that place. Time has not passed, and I'm reliving the event as though it were happening for the first time.

I try to move, to go to her, but I'm frozen in place, unable to move or make a sound.

The me in the chair tries to scream, but her throat is so raw from screaming so much that nothing comes out. As if drawn by a magnet, we both look across the room. My daughter, naked and bleeding, lies on her side on the floor. She's turned toward us, so I can clearly see her face. Blood slides from the side of her mouth and out of her nose. One of her eyes is black and swollen shut, and she has a cut above her eyebrow. Purple lines her neck from a bruising grip. Blood covers her thighs, and I know more bruises will be hidden beneath the bright red.

A deep grunt pierces the air, and I watch in horror as a masked boy gets up from the floor. Beneath him, my two-year-old toddler lays limply on the floor on his stomach, his limbs spread out from his bloody and abused body. The other two boys stand over him, having already found their sick pleasures and are fixing their clothes.

The past me gags, bile rising in her throat, and I remember swallowing it down because of the tape covering my mouth. If I allow it up, I'll choke on my own puke and die. I can't die. I have to find a way to save my children. I don't care about myself. They can cut me up into a thousand pieces, torture me, rape me for hours, so long as my babies live.

Even though I know what's going to happen next, I'm still not prepared.

A fourth person, bigger than the boys, enters the room wearing a crisp black business suit. His mask differs from the others. There are no x's covering the eyes. Instead, a big white x cuts across the whole mask.

The man stands there with his hands casually shoved into his pockets. He glances from my daughter, lying on the floor, to my son, who's lying there motionless. The few whimpers slipping past his lips in his unconscious state are the only indication that he is still alive.

The man approaches, and I freeze in my seat. My eyes are nearly swollen shut and my whimpers are scratchy from crying so much and screaming so hard.

He walks behind me and puts his mouth at my ear. I shiver in revulsion. He lifts the mask and sinks his teeth so hard into my neck that he pierces the skin and blood trickles out. The scar from that bite stings. The little I can see of the guy's face is blurred since I never actually saw him.

"Seems like my boys had a little too much fun." I tremble as the voice and hot breath slides over my ear. Even though the words are said to the past me, the present me still hears them loud and clear, like he's behind me right now. "Looks like they've still got a little fight left in them though."

As if hearing his words, both of my kids stir, the pain in their bodies bringing them back to consciousness.

I begin to struggle against the ropes, not registering the blood dripping from my wrists from the ropes digging into my flesh. I cry behind the tape, my pleas muffled and unrecognizable.

A dark chuckle fills my head. Fingers wrap around my throat, squeezing so hard my vision becomes blurry. "I typically don't go for ones so young." I whimper when he runs his tongue up the column of my neck, hitting the wounds from his teeth, making them sting. "But they do look incredibly tempting."

Behind the tape, I let out a cry, horror thrashing through my body as I struggle against my bonds. My eyes fall on my two precious children, already used and beaten so severely that they're barely recognizable.

"But don't worry your cute little head, my dear Caterina." He says my full name like he knows me. "I like my toys to fight back and those two brats don't have enough left in them."

His hot breath leaves me, and after slipping the mask back in place, he comes around to the front of me. I don't have to see his face to know he's smiling a nasty and cruel smile. It's in his eyes. The twisted pleasure of what he's doing. I've never seen someone look so sinister and depraved.

"I'm feeling generous tonight and giving you a choice."

He walks to Eliana, grabbing her by the hair and yanking her to her feet. She's so weak she can barely stand on her own. She fights as hard as her body will allow, but it's no match for his strength. While he drags my poor beautiful daughter across the floor, I scream behind the tape. Nausea rises again when he stops with her facing me only a few feet away.

He grabs a fistful of her long, dark brown hair, then yanks her head back so I can see her battered face. "Your beautiful daughter." He shoves her head forward and she slumps to the floor. Another muffled cry leaves me.

My chest caves in on itself, and I worry I may choke to death because I can't take in enough air. My hands, bound by rope, are numb and my arms are sore and weak from pulling at the joints. But I still try. I try so hard to pull my hands free that I have no doubt the strands of the rope are sawing against bone and tendons.

The man walks to Ryder, grabs him by the arm, and carelessly drags him over to Eliana. My poor, sweet daughter, after having suffered so much, senses her little brother beside her and tries to wrap her arm around him. But she's so weak she can't even lift her arm. Instead, she scoots closer to him.

"Your innocent little boy," the man says, standing just beyond my children. "You get to choose which one lives and which one dies."

I can't comprehend what he's saying because the idea of it is so abhorrent. It's impossible. How can a mother, or any parent, make a choice like that? How can anyone choose one child's life over the other?

The answer comes immediately, and it's simple. I can't.

There's no way I can force myself to respond to this man, so I don't even consider what to say.

So, I sit there and die inside. Life drains out of me, seeping through my eyes as my tears flow. Flowing from my pores to the blood-stained floors. My soul withers and crumbles to dust, never to be revived again. My heart stutters, still beating, but sluggish. I know down to the very depths of me, if by some miracle Hunter's and my children survive this, they truly wouldn't survive. No person could. Even if their bodies healed, their minds never would.

His henchmen stand off to the edges of the room, silent and unmoving the entire time.

"What's it to be?" the man asks, his voice too casual for the situation, like he's asking me what I want for dinner, not what child I want to live and which one dies. He walks to me and rips the tape from my mouth. Skin comes off with it, leaving my lips stinging. "The boy or the girl?"

I shake my head, tears and snot slinging from my face.

His hands slide into the pockets of his slacks as he rocks back on his heels. "One dies, and one lives, Caterina. You're powerless in everything but this. Make your choice, or I'll make it for you, and I promise you'll live to regret it."

"Why?" I croak, barely getting the words out through my dry and swollen throat.

Behind the mask, his eyes light once again with sinister delight. "Because I can. Because I get immense fucking pleasure from it." His eyes narrow. "My patience is running thin. Your answer, now."

"I c-can't," I say, shaking my head again. "How c-can you," I hiccup on a sob, "expect me to make a decision like that? P-please, just let my babies go. Do w-whatever you want to m-me."

"That's not how this works. You see," he grips my jaw between two harsh fingers, shoving my chin up as he steps closer until he's standing between my tied legs and looming over me, "I want to witness the pain on your face as you give me a name. I want to watch your expression as I drain the life of something you love." His fingers squeeze painfully. "To see a part of you die along with them."

A great sob shutters my body. "P-please," I beg again. "I'll do anything you w-want."

What happens next will haunt me for the rest of my life and will follow me into death.

It happens fast, while I sit frozen in the chair. He spins on his heel and walks to one of the guys who's holding a knife. Then he goes over to my daughter, grabs a handful of her hair, and pulls back her head so far that her mouth is forced open. Her beautiful eyes, one swollen shut, the other filled with busted capillaries, meet mine. I scream and scream and scream, both the past me and the me stuck in the corner, as the man doesn't hesitate even a fraction of a second before he runs the knife across my daughter's throat. A river of red blood gushes from the wound.

Unable to comprehend what just happened, I watch as he untangles his fingers from her hair and she falls forward. My baby was dead before she hit the floor in her own pool of blood.

He moves to my son, and I know before it's even done, his fate is the same.

"NOOO!" I scream so loud and forcefully that my throat cramps, and I can feel the blood vessels in my eyes pop.

The man ignores my plea and wraps his big fingers through my son's baby soft, dark brown hair and yanks him up from the floor as if he weighs nothing.

I yell and screech and pull and tug on the ropes holding me to the chair, but no matter what I do, it's not enough.

As he holds up my son by his hair, the man looks at me, his eyes through the mask meeting mine. "You had your chance,

Caterina. You fucked it up. I told you that you wouldn't like my choice."

He barely finishes his words before my youngest child is taken from me.

I don't remember much after that, and even as I watch from my corner as the scene plays out before me, it blurs and not much registers. I can't look away from the two bodies on the floor, their blood seeping into the wood.

Catatonic state.

That's what the doctors said I fell into after my children were murdered right in front of me. Over and over again, I prayed that it was all a nightmare, and I would wake up and find my babies alive and well. I stared at their still bodies, my mind fracturing.

I remember the sting of the first stab to my abdomen and the second to my chest. I was stabbed four more times, but I don't remember the rest.

I blink, and time seems to have passed because I'm no longer tied to the chair. I'm on my hands and knees, weakly crawling toward Eliana and Ryder, blood slick and sticky on the floor. They're lying right next to each other. When I reach Ryder, who is the closest to me, I curl up on my side, wishing death would take me to the same place where my kids are.

I lay with my arms wrapped around them both.

Chapter Thirty-Two
Hunter

There have been less than a handful of times in my life when I truly felt fear. The first time it happened was when I was eight years old and one of my foster fathers came into my room. My eyes were squeezed tight, but slit open enough to see him standing over my bed with his dick in his hand. I laid there frozen, terrified out of my fucking mind that he would touch me, force me to do things I didn't want to do. As young as I was, I knew exactly what he was doing. Living in foster care from the time I was two years old, I learned things from the other kids early on.

The first time I saw someone having sex, I was six. My foster brother, Dustin, and his girlfriend were lying on his bed with him on top. They were both naked, and he was lifting and dropping his hips between her legs. After he caught me watching them, he ordered me to stand beside the bed until they finished. After that, he explained what sex was. Occasionally, he had me watch them do other things as well. Though I had no interest in experiencing any of it myself, I found it oddly fascinating to my young mind. He never touched me or asked me to participate. He said it was my education, so when I was ready to do those things, I would know how.

So I knew what my foster father was doing, and it scared me shitless. I was so frightened that I peed the bed while he shot his load on my blanket. The next morning, I was beaten with a strap for soiling my sheets. The sticky residue on my blanket was never mentioned.

Another time I felt true fear was when Cat, who was pregnant with Eliana, awoke one night with blood between her legs. She went into labor two months early and nearly bled to death. The placenta detached and there was no stopping our daughter from entering the world early. Thankfully, she was as healthy as a baby born eight weeks early could be. A few weeks in an incubator allowed her to fully develop, and then we brought her home.

The time I felt the most fear, which literally brought me to my knees, was when I was informed that my home had been invaded. My kids were gone and my wife was in an ambulance on her way to the hospital, fighting for her life. When I stormed into the hospital, demanding an update, the nurse could only tell me Cat was in surgery and it was possible she wouldn't survive. In front of God and everyone around, I fell to my knees when my legs buckled under the heavy weight of my body.

Never, in all the years of my life, through everything I saw and experienced living in foster care and then on the streets, have I felt such fear and helplessness. It took seven excruciating hours for the doctor, his face drawn and pale with fatigue, to emerge through the set of doors to tell me my wife had made it through surgery. Though she wasn't out of the woods yet, the surgeons managed to stop the internal bleeding and patch up her insides as best they could. I had to wait another ninety minutes before I could see her. It felt like I hadn't taken a breath in those hours, and it was only when I walked into the sterile room, the beep of the machines barely heard in the background, and saw my battered and bandaged wife lying on the hospital bed, tubes and needles stuck all over her, that I filled my lungs.

Tears I hadn't shed since I was a child filled my eyes as I slowly approached her bed. The sheet was pulled up to just below her breasts. Her arms were mostly bare, except for the heavy bandages around both wrists and the IV line taped to the back of one hand. Purple and black bruises covered the skin around her neck, like someone had wrapped their hands around it and squeezed. To this day, she still has a faint mark on the side of her neck where she was bitten. Bandages and medical tape covered most of her face, but the exposed skin was discolored or marked with small cuts and scrapes.

Thankfully, there was a chair already sitting beside the bed, because my ass landed there a second later.

I gently took my wife's hand into mine and kissed the back of it. It wasn't until then that I felt the full force of grief over what had happened.

Our children were gone. And from the looks of Cat, they were taken in a way even the sickest of minds couldn't conjure. I didn't know the details of what had happened yet. I refused to speak to the police until I knew my wife's condition, so I had no idea what they went through was much worse than I imagined. I only knew they were gone, taken from us, their lives stolen.

Those were the worst hours of my life, and they'll remain the worst until the day my life ends.

However, as Cat stared at the pictures on the wall and her legs gave out from under her, tipping her forward, that moment was a close second.

Luckily, I was standing close by to catch her before she hit the ground.

"Cat." Her name grated through my sandpaper throat. My heart felt like it was in my fucking toes as I dropped to the floor with her in my arms. "Baby."

No movement. There wasn't even a flicker of her eyelids or a change in her breathing. But she *was* breathing, the little puffs of air leaving her lips came faster than normal.

I goddamn knew I shouldn't have let her see those pictures. It even turned my stomach when I saw what was done to them. Just like their lives were wiped out of existence, their faces were scratched out and marked over with red marker.

Another of Whisper's games.

Another tick on the number of hours he'll suffer once I find him.

How in the fuck does he keep getting past the alarm system? Before we left this afternoon for her appointment, I had the code for the system changed. Did he figure out the new code, or is he somehow bypassing it?

One thing's for damn sure, the alarm company better figure out what the hell is happening and fix it or heads will roll. Quite fucking literally.

While I sit beside the bed, holding Cat's hand, I don't wonder what she's thinking. I know she's there, her mind filled with memories of that night, unable to escape. Dr. Armani warned me it could happen at any moment, so I knew it was a possibility. Just as her headaches were increasing, her nightmares were becoming more frequent, and she was remembering more than she had since they began. Discovering the truth about her other personalities and the warning from Presley.

All of it led to this.

After she fell, I brought her upstairs to our bedroom and called Dr. Armani. He was knocking on the door fifteen minutes later. He didn't seem as concerned about her unconscious state as I was, telling me to let her rest, and she would wake up soon. He said her mind was trying to heal and it was up to her whether she allowed it.

For the first time since Cat began seeing the doctor five years ago, I wanted to slam my fist into his face and break the fragile bones.

I didn't want to wait for her to decide. I wanted him to wake her up. I needed to see her eyes to assure myself that she was okay, because until then, I couldn't fucking function properly.

That was three hours ago. Dr. Armani left after checking on Cat with instructions to call him when she awoke. My ass hasn't left this chair and won't until Cat gives me those beautiful blue eyes of hers.

I pull out my phone to call Silas to inform him we need to find Whisper before I tear the city apart. My phone drops to the floor when a soft whimper has me jerking my eyes to Cat. Her eyebrows are pinched and her face scrunches, as though in pain.

"Cat, baby." I gently call her name. I move to the side of the bed and grab her clammy hand in mine. "Can you hear me?"

Her eyelashes flutter, and for a moment, I think she's only reacting to something in her head, but when her eyelids slowly open, her gorgeous blue eyes focus on mine.

"Hunter?" she croaks, like she's been screaming for hours and her throat is too raw to speak. Her face crumples as tears fill her eyes. A loud wail erupts from her throat. "They're gone! Our babies are gone!"

I'm lying on the bed and have her pulled into my arms in the next second. Her sorrowful cries and deep sobs of pain break something inside me. She clings to me, her nails digging into my chest so hard they'll leave little crescent marks. While holding her tightly, her slender body shudders and her sobs fill our room.

I know how hard this fresh wave of hell is for her. I've had five years to deal with my own grief. It still hurts as much as the day it happened, but I've learned how to deal with it. Cat only had a few months before her mind put up a protective wall. She was never given the chance to heal.

We stay like this for a long time. My shirt is soaked with Cat's tears, and the only thing I can do is hold her as she wails out her grief. Being helpless isn't something I'm accustomed to feeling, but when it comes to knowing what to do to help my wife, it seems like it's all I feel. I can't take away this pain. I can't even fucking lessen it.

After what seems like hours, Cat lifts her head. Her face is red and splotchy and her eyes are puffy, her lashes soaked.

But it's my Cat looking back at me. Not a woman who looks like her, but goes by another name. For that, I breathe a sigh of relief.

"I couldn't save them," she says tearfully. "I tried, Hunter. I swear I tried so hard, but I wasn't strong enough."

I brush the wet hair off her cheeks. "I know you did, baby. Nothing could have saved them."

She shakes her head adamantly. "I should have been able to. It's my fault they're gone."

"No," I bark.

I quickly sit up in bed, plant her ass on my lap, and grab her cheeks in my hands. I force her head up so she sees how serious I am.

"I never want to hear those words come out of your mouth again, Caterina." I give her head a gentle shake. "There is nothing, absolutely fucking nothing, you could have done differently to save our children. Those bastards broke into our house knowing exactly what they had planned. What was done to them wasn't random or spur of the moment. They had every intention of," I grit my teeth and push the next words out between them, "brutally forcing their touch on them and taking them from us." I bring her face closer to mine. "And I fucking swear to you, I haven't forgotten my promise to make them all pay."

"I want to help."

Her words are spoken quietly, and for a moment, I'm speechless. Cat, my innocent, sweet, gentle wife, wants to get her hands dirty and bathe in the blood of those who wronged us.

She didn't say those exact words, but I see them in the harshness in her gaze, in the hatred she can't hide, the way her body suddenly tightens.

Even though I want to give her what she wants, I won't let my wife's hands get dirty.

"No, baby," I say. "This isn't for you. Let me take care of it."

Her nostrils flare as she presses her lips together. "I will always blame myself for not saving our children, Hunter, regardless of what you say. I was there. I watched as those men touched them in vile ways. Their screams of fear and pain still burn my ears. They begged me to save them, and I couldn't do a fucking thing." Tears glisten in her eyes, and a new wave falls down her cheeks when she squeezes them shut. Determination mixes with the wetness when she opens them again. "You won't take this from me," she says, her eyes sparking a lightning blue. "It is my right as their mother. A mother who failed them when they needed me the most. A mother who was forced to sit through the brutality of their deaths. A mother they looked at," a sob slides from between her lips, "as their throats were slit."

A fresh round of anger ignites, and I drop my hands from her cheeks to ball them into fists.

"Please, Hunter," Cat whispers.

I agree only because I know how important this is to her, and if it helps with her healing, then all the better. Aside from that, she's right. She *does* deserve to watch as the men responsible for tearing our world apart are put down.

"Okay."

Her tongue darts out, licking the tears from her lips. "Thank you."

We don't say anything else after that, despite the fact that there's a lot to be said. She may or may not remember the letter she received about Henry being released, but this needs to be addressed. Her life is in danger and she needs to be prepared as much as possible.

But as she falls against my chest, her face going to my throat, I hold the words back for the time being.

Right now, the only thing I need to do is hold my wife.

An hour later, I stroke Cat's back as she lays curled up to my side. Her head is on my chest and she hasn't moved or spoken for the last fifteen minutes, but I know she's still awake.

I dislike the quietness. It means she's thinking too much, and with everything that's happened over the last few hours, it's impossible to know where her mind is.

I'm shocked as shit that she's handling things as well as she is. I've lived in fear for nearly five years. Fear of what would happen should Cat remember the past. What it would do to her mentally. It just goes to show just how fucking strong she is.

Before I can utter a word to get her to open up to me, she moves from my chest. Sitting up, she draws her knees to her chest and wraps an arm around her legs as she stares at me. Her eyes, once they meet mine, aren't the same. Behind the bright blue color lies darkness and pain.

"I'm sorry," she says, filling the silence in the room.

Her finger covers my mouth as I try to reprimand her for once again apologizing for something that is not her fault.

"No. Let me speak."

Despite knowing I won't like what she says, I nod anyway. Her arm loops back around her legs and she rests her chin on her knees. She looks so young and innocent in the pose.

"I'm sorry that I hid them away," she continues, her voice low and filled with so much sadness that my chest physically hurts from it. "I'm so sorry, Hunter. I not only kept them in the dark from myself, I forced you to do the same. Our babies," a tear drips down her cheek, "deserve so much more than what I've given them for the last five years. They should have never been forgotten. They should be remembered and talked about and cherished every single day."

"Cat." The one word comes out hoarse, my chest tight. "Baby."

When I reach out for her, she tightens her arms around her legs and shakes her head. My hand falls to the bed, my jaw clenching.

"For so long, I was lost in my own grief, unable to cope with what had happened, afraid to even try. It was selfish and wrong of me to do that. You were hurting too, but instead of grieving with you, I blocked it out." She sweeps away the tears flowing down her cheeks. "Realizing that, I'm still unsure if I can handle it. Even right now, I feel grief seeping into my bones, weighing me down, trying to pull me back into oblivion. I don't want that, but I'm so scared I won't be able to fight it." Her lips pinch together and her eyes squeeze shut. "Please," she whispers brokenly, eviscerating my heart, "please don't let me go. Please don't let me do that to our children again. Don't let me forget them."

Whether she wants to be there or not, the choice is taken out of her hands when I grab the tops of her arms and haul her onto my lap. Her legs go around my waist, her arms around my shoulders, and she buries her face in my neck. I wrap myself around her just as tightly as she's wrapped around me. Still, it's not enough. If she crawled inside of me, she still wouldn't be close enough.

"I will never let you go, my sweet Cat," I say against her ear. "You want our children's memories to stay with you, I'll make sure they do. Every single day, we'll talk about them. The pictures will be replaced and rehung. I'll never let you forget them again."

Her sobs become heavier, her body wracked by tremors, and I hold her through them until she gradually calms.

She looks exhausted when she lifts her head. Today has been a hell of a day, but it could have turned out so much worse.

"Henry, one of the boys, was released from prison not long ago," I say, closely watching her face.

"I know. I remember getting and hiding the letter."

"He left town as soon as he was released. I have a couple guys looking for him." I pull her closer until her front is plastered to mine and only inches separate our faces. "You don't need to worry about him, but I still want you to be cautious."

She nods.

"There's something else," I say cautiously.

"Whisper." She says the name so low I barely hear it.

It's been years since the name was used in her presence. I

purposely didn't say it around her because I wasn't sure how she would react. I'm mildly surprised she remembers it.

"He sent the box. The one with the clothes."

I nod, the muscle in my jaw twitching. "Yes. I've been on his trail. I'm so fucking close, baby."

She stares over my shoulder as her brows drop and a wrinkle forms between them. Something dark and painful fills them when they return to me.

"He was there that night."

I suspected as much, but I wasn't sure until she confirmed it. I would have known for sure if I had watched the thumb drive in its entirety.

"He's the one who," another pause, "killed them. I didn't remember until my memories came back tonight. I couldn't see his face because he was wearing a mask like the others, but his was different."

After the attack, Cat's memories were splotchy. The doctor claims she blocked out certain details of the incident because it was too traumatic, so she only remembered bits and pieces.

We always believed Terry was the one who killed my children. It's what he, Henry, and Howard told police and claimed in court. Why in the fuck would Terry admit that, knowing it would add more to his sentence? What was the purpose of keeping Whisper being there a secret? He was just as guilty as the others because he gave the order, but his actual presence and participation in the killing made him even more responsible.

The thumb drive.

He sent it, knowing I would watch it. But I didn't. Not all the way through. I stopped because I would have killed someone if I hadn't. Didn't matter who. I just needed to feel blood on my hands.

Having this confirmed changes nothing. Except for the amount of pain Whisper will feel.

As soon as I get a chance, I'll watch the thumb drive all the way through, even if it kills me. Maybe there will be a clue as to who the bastard is, and I can finish this once and for all.

Chapter Thirty-Three
Caterina

"Mom, I swear I'm okay," I say, pulling back from her. "At least right now I am," I add, because there's no telling if that may change.

Athena and Scarlett are constantly in my head, tempting me to let them out. So far, I've held them back. What worries me more is the darkness. That darkness, a place I can go to and forget about the pain, is far more tempting.

I can barely breathe when I think about the horrors Eliana and Ryder endured. The pain I feel consumes every part of me, body and mind. But I don't want to forget them again. Forgetting that part means forgetting all the good too. Every minute I spent with them, except for the hours we all endured hell, was precious and special to me. I wouldn't trade any of those moments for anything. Even if it means facing my demons every day.

Mom looks at me the way moms look at their daughters when they're looking for lies or hidden meanings. I keep my expression as relaxed as possible, not wanting her to see the worry I constantly feel.

I guess I succeed, because seconds later, she nods and smiles. "Okay."

Dad steps up when she lets me go. Thankfully, he doesn't ask how I am. Just gives me a tight hug and says in my ear, "Don't let her get to you, sweetheart. You know she just worries."

With a smile, I kiss his cheek and pull back.

When we turn to enter the living room, I find Mom standing in front of one of the pictures on the wall. Since the pictures we originally had hanging on the wall years ago were destroyed, we had others printed. I wanted to fill every inch of space with pictures of our children and family, but I limited it to a few. There are also some on the entertainment center by the TV and a few on the end tables. We have more on our nightstands and on my dresser upstairs. It hurts every time I see them, but they also make me happy. For so long, I've kept their memories locked away.

I walk up to Mom, who has her hand over her mouth and tears in her eyes. Wrapping my arm around her waist, I rest my head on her shoulder and look at the picture. It's a black and white picture of Hunter lying on the couch in my parents' house with baby Ryder tucked in his arms against the back of the couch. I'm lying between his legs on my side, my head on his lower stomach with my hand resting on Ryder's back. On the other end of the couch, Eliana is leaning against the arm with her legs tossed over mine and Hunter's. All four of us are asleep. The picture was taken right after we had Thanksgiving dinner.

"I woke up with a crick in my neck from how I was sleeping," I say quietly, tracing my eyes over every inch of my beautiful children's faces. "But it was one of the best naps I ever had."

Mom laughs, the sound strained because I know she's fighting back tears. My own eyes water, but I force them back.

"I remember you saying that. Ryder had colic and had been keeping you and Hunter up at night."

"Yeah. It was mainly Hunter. Anytime Ryder would cry, it was Hunter who heard him first and was adamant he attend to him."

Her arm comes around my waist and she squeezes me. "I'm not sure if there were ever any children who had the most loving and caring parents as you and Hunter were."

My eyelids flutter, blinking rapidly to keep the tears at bay. I still wasn't strong enough to protect them, no matter how loving and caring we were.

We spend a few minutes in silence as we take in the photos hanging on the wall, both of us left to our own thoughts.

"I wanted to talk to you about something," Mom says, taking a seat on the couch, and I sit beside her. "Your dad and I were thinking of traveling to Max and Emily's for Christmas this year, but I don't want to leave you and Hunter alone. Ginger and her crew are already on board to go as well. How do you and Hunter feel about joining us?"

I look at Hunter and he shrugs. "Up to you, baby."

"What about Slate?"

"Silas and Katie's families are here, so they always stay in the area. We're closed on Christmas Eve and Day, so they won't be put out."

I look back at Mom. "Alright. Count us in."

Mom smiles brightly, "Excellent! It'll be nice to have a white Christmas for once. Tennessee is so unpredictable, so you never know if there will be snow or not."

I laugh at her excitement. "It's settled then. Does Max know?"

"I spoke with him about it yesterday. It works out perfectly, because he just finished the guest house a few weeks ago. Ginger,

Mason, and the boys will take the guest house, and we'll have the two guest rooms in the main house."

I nod my agreement.

"We also wanted to let you know that we've dropped the yacht idea."

"Really?" I lift a brow. "Why the change of heart?"

"Because," she takes my hand, her eyes shifting to Dad's for a moment before coming back to me, "I don't like the idea of being so far away from all of my kids."

"Mom," I try to protest, but her tight grip on my hand halts my words.

"No. Your dad and I spoke about this. While we still love the idea of living on a boat, we'll settle for taking a vacation for a week or two on one and having a captain on board. Dad wasn't too keen on learning to navigate a boat anyway."

"Are you sure? Ginger and I would be fine without you guys here. I hate for you to give up on something you want to do because you're worried about us."

"Nope. We've already made our decision. While it may have been a sudden spur of the moment dream, I just cannot imagine, and I don't want to, being away from my girls. I already hate Max being so far away."

I dip my chin down. "Okay."

Mom and Dad only stay for a few more minutes since one of Dad's old friends is in town and they're meeting him and his wife for lunch. There is no mention of Scarlett, Athena, or Presley, which I'm grateful for. Talking about Eliana and Ryder is already difficult, but I refuse to keep them hidden. It's still hard for me to believe I'm not losing my mind when I think about my other personalities. They're a sensitive subject, and I'm not sure I'm ready to discuss them with anyone other than Hunter.

When my parents leave, I leave Hunter in the living room and go upstairs to grab a pair of socks. I've always had a problem having cold feet, something I hate.

Instead of grabbing a pair of my socks, I root through Hunter's sock drawer in the closet. He always has the warmest and softest thick socks. He picks on me because I steal them all the time.

After rummaging through his neatly folded sock drawer, I find my favorite pair. As I turn to leave the closet, I'm stopped by something on the top shelf. My stomach plummets and my heart squeezes tight in my chest. As if having a mind of their own, my feet take me further inside the closet, and I reach up, my fingers grazing the dark wood of the box on the shelf.

I should leave it alone. I'm not sure I'm ready to look at the contents. Yet something inside me urges me to pull the box down.

So, that's what I do.

Raising to my tiptoes, I tug the box to the edge of the shelf and into my hands. Looking at the beautifully carved initials on the top, my eyes sting.

E. P. S. and R. H. S.

Eliana Presley St. James and Ryder Hunter St. James.

My fingers run over the name Presley, our daughter's middle name. Although I forgot about my babies, I couldn't ignore them completely. The name I give the young girl I become sometimes reflects that.

Hunter's socks are forgotten on top of his dresser as I pull the box out of the closet. I start for the bed, but change directions at the last minute. Taking the box out of our bedroom, I go to the room across the hall. One of the rooms I forced myself to ignore for years.

As soon as I open the door I smell the familiar innocent scent of a little boy. Even after all these years, this room still has the faint aroma of Ryder.

I take a deep breath, and then another and another, desperate to breathe in that scent as much as possible. While it hurts, it also soothes my frayed nerves.

I smile when I see Ryder's Captain America comforter. Ryder loved all superheroes, but Captain America was his favorite.

Sitting on the side of the bed, I set the box beside me. My eyes catch on the mirror that Hunter punched the other day. Even though the shattered glass has been cleaned, the mirror's frame remains. Based on Hunter's violent reaction, I deduced that someone had written something on the mirror. I haven't asked Hunter what it was. I don't want to know.

Looking down at my hands, I run my fingers over one of the scars on my wrists. Hunter said the first time I was Athena, I tried to kill myself. I don't really have Athena's memories, but if I think hard enough, I can barely catch a glimpse of red covering my wrists and the slight niggle of pain that accompanied the attempt. Shame heats my face when I think about what I tried to do, even if I wasn't myself at the time. I hate what I put Hunter through, and I hate that I almost left him all alone.

With a deep breath, I push those thoughts aside and lift the lid of the box. The first thing I see is a light blue checkered baby book with Ryder's name written in calligraphy.

Setting it on my lap, I flip it open to the first page.

Ryder Hunter St. James

Birthdate: March 3, 2016

Weight: 7 lbs., 9 oz.

Birthplace: River Heights, TN.

My throat closes, and I force myself to swallow the lump.

Ryder would be seven years old. It's been five years since I've seen his beautiful innocent face, held him in my arms.

On to the next page, I read, lovingly, but painstakingly, all the things that made Ryder so special.

The color of his hair when he was born, with a small lock of strands taped to the page.

A description of his first outfit. Light blue with white elephants.

The first thought that came to mind when I first saw him. How utterly perfect he was.

I devour every word. Not because I've forgotten, but because it makes me feel closer to him.

Midway through Ryder's baby book, I notice movement in the open doorway. As tears stream down my cheeks, my eyes meet Hunter's. His brows are dipped in concern, but his expression is soft.

"Baby," he says gently, taking a seat beside me on the bed. He sits so close that his thigh touches mine.

I'm amazed at how gentle and soft Hunter can be with me, when to most people he seems hardened and unfeeling.

So we can both see, I slide the book over so half of it is on Hunter's thigh. "Look with me."

That's what we do. We look at each page, stopping every so often to reminisce over a memory. We laugh, I cry, and Hunter's there to wipe away my tears. My heart breaks at the thought of pushing away the memories of our children as if they never existed.

When we're done with Ryder's baby book, I set Eli's on our lap.

I gently trace her name. "When I forgot about them, do you

think I, without realizing it, gave Presley her name so I wouldn't truly forget?"

Hunter takes my hand and laces our fingers together. "Yes, baby. It was your mind's way of keeping them with us."

More tears are shed as we look at Eli's baby book. She would be seventeen today. She'd be looking at colleges and fighting her father over the boys she dates. I'd be helping her pick out her senior prom dress and stressing over her leaving the house once she graduated.

My lungs fill with sadness when I think about all that we have missed and will continue to miss in their lives.

Rage sits beside sadness. Pure and raw, and so all-consuming to the point that I would relish in peeling the flesh off the bones of the people who took them away from us. I'd delight in seeing pain fill their eyes and bask in the screams of terror that would flee from their throats.

I'm not a violent person. I've never wished death upon anyone. I've always believed all people can be redeemed no matter what they do.

But not the man and three teens who tortured, abused, and murdered our children. It wouldn't matter if they felt true remorse for their crimes. No one, not even God, can stop me from delivering exactly what those bastards deserve when Hunter finds them.

It won't simply be payback. It won't even be about revenge.

It's wiping the bastards from a world they never should have been born into.

After looking through both baby books and returning them to the box, Hunter takes out a piece of paper from his back pocket. I take it from him, unfolding it to see what it is. I smile when I see the familiar handwriting. I find it strange looking at it now, because although my own hand wrote the words, the handwriting resembles that of a child.

It has always been a pleasure to receive the short stories Presley wrote me each time she visited. What I love even more is the subject matter of the stories. At the time, I didn't realize her words were so significant.

"When did you get this?" I ask, glancing up from the sheet of paper.

"The day Presley came to see me at Slate."

My brows pucker. "Why wait until now to give it to me?"

He grabs my hand into his big one and brings it to his lap, lacing our fingers together. "It was before your memories came back. For years, your mind has blocked out anything related to that night. Truthfully, I've been terrified what state you'd be left in if your memories returned. What you experienced would drive even the sanest person crazy." He lifts my hand and kisses the back of it. "Don't misunderstand me, Cat," he says when he notices my frown deepening. "No matter how you reacted, I love any and all forms of you, so it wouldn't have changed anything, but I wanted to spare you that heartache."

Grabbing the front of his shirt, I pull him down until our lips brush. "I love you," I murmur.

"And I love you."

After letting him go, I turn my attention back to the paper. It becomes clear why Hunter was concerned after reading the first few lines. Presley held nothing back. No masking of her words or changing things to make the reader believe these are the thoughts of a child.

The thing I loved most about Presley's stories was her memories and thoughts of her childhood. But they aren't *her* memories or thoughts. They're mine. Every single story she's written was inspired by moments I've shared with Eliana, Ryder, and Hunter. She was telling me the story of my life, and I didn't even know it. She kept their memories alive when I couldn't.

Although I don't need to read these stories anymore since I have the actual memories, I absorb every word. And the more I read, the more guilt rises inside me.

What kind of mother forgets her own children?

I try to give myself some grace. What I experienced—watching the brutal rape of our children and then being asked which one I want to save, while the other dies and then watching both die—was more horrific than what the most disturbed person could conjure up.

My grace is always short lived.

I'll never forgive myself for not saving them. And I'll never forgive myself for letting them slip my mind for even a moment in time.

Chapter Thirty-Four
Hunter

From outside the bathroom door, I hear my phone ring. I finish running soap over my body before I rinse and shut off the shower. Following a quick wipe down with a towel, I exit the bathroom naked and grab my phone from the nightstand. Mathias's number appears on the screen just as it begins to ring again.

"What's going on?" I bark into the phone.

"Cat just left the house."

"Shit." I press the speaker icon on the phone and drop it on the bed. "You got someone on her, right?" I ask, grabbing a pair of slacks from the top of the laundry basket and quickly putting them on.

"Yes. Damon's tailing her. Want me to follow or stick to the house?"

Loud pounding in my ears mixes with Mathias's answer. "Follow, but send a couple more guys to the house. I want them inside to make sure no one else gets inside."

We still don't know how Whisper has been breaking into the house, and I don't want any more surprises when Cat and I return. Unfortunately, watching the thumb drive all the way through didn't enlighten me about Whisper's identity. It only further fueled my rage.

"Got it."

I pull on a shirt and stomp my feet into my shoes. "Which way is she headed?"

I take the stairs two at a time. Knowing the danger she's in, Cat wouldn't have left if she were herself, so there's only two places she would be headed.

"Toward The Grove."

"Stay on her. Do not let her out of your sight," I demand, my fucking heart lodged in my throat. "Go inside and tell the staff who you are. Tell them I sent you and that I'm on my way. And Mathias," I pause, "if something happens, shoot to fucking kill."

Though I'm eager to get my hands on Whisper and Henry, I would rather see them dead than take the risk of them getting to Cat.

After grabbing my keys, I turn off the alarm and run out the door without resetting it. Mathias's men will be here any minute.

I break every fucking traffic law as I speed through the darkening streets. Just as Scarlett and Presley did recently, Athena has gone off script. Athena usually appears during the day, whereas Scarlett appears at night.

The whole situation reminds me of the first time Cat's alternate personalities appeared. My nerves were shot then, just as they are now, because I had no idea when or how they would return. All three are becoming unpredictable, and I don't like it.

I didn't stop looking over my shoulder until a year and a half after the first one appeared because I was afraid she would appear as someone else. And perhaps the new one wouldn't seek me out like the others had.

I screech to a halt in the gravel parking lot at The Grove,

seeing Cat's red car parked along the side of the building. Flinging my car door open, I barely stop long enough to slam it closed behind me. When I see Mathias and Damon's cars at the back of the parking lot, the heavy pounding in my chest lessens slightly. Ginger's car is there as well, which is odd since she normally works the mid-afternoon shift because Athena usually arrives around that time.

I dart up the steps, but before I reach the door, it's flung open and Ginger's worried gaze meets mine.

"She got here ten minutes ago," she says. "She's never come this late before."

"I know." I shoulder my way past her into the reception area. "Where is she?"

"In her room." Ginger grabs my arm before I can head toward the stairs. I don't turn, too impatient to get to Cat, but I look at her over my shoulder. "Why the sudden change, Hunter? Mom said she'd gotten her memories back and she knows about the others. Is that why?"

I pull Ginger's hand from my arm and turn halfway around. "I think so. Dr. Armani believes that since she allowed herself to fully remember, her emotions are heightened and out of whack. I'll explain more later. Right now, I need to go see her."

I don't give her a chance to reply before I rush for the stairs, taking them three at a time. Mathias stands outside Cat's door, out of sight.

"Damon is patrolling the outside," he says when I approach.

"Good," I grunt. "Not sure how long this is going to take."

"I'll stick around if you need me."

"Thanks," I say before leaving him.

As I step into the room, I don't see Cat at first, but then I notice her on the floor in a corner. Her legs are drawn up to her chest and her chin rests on her bent knees as she leans against a wall. Her forlorn expression as she stares down at the floor sends shards of ice straight to my heart.

"Athena?" I ask, approaching her slowly so I don't startle her.

Her head jerks up, her surprised gaze meeting mine. "Hunter?"

When I'm only a few feet from her, I squat down. "Why are you sitting on the floor?"

Her fingers dig into her legs where she's resting her hands. "I don't know," she says evasively.

"Is everything okay? Why do you look so sad?"

She licks her lips and her voice dips. "Because there's so much to be sad about."

Her answer pierces through my chest, leaving a gaping hole behind. Scooting around, I lean against the wall beside her. Not too close, but close enough that when she lifts her hand, I place mine in hers and put them both on the floor between us.

"But there are also things to be happy about, right?" I ask.

"Maybe." She gazes down at our hands for a moment before lifting her head. "But sometimes I feel like the bad stuff far outweighs the good. So much so that I feel like I'm drowning in it, and I won't ever resurface."

I squeeze her fingers. "Sometimes I get sad too."

"You do?"

I nod. "Yes."

"How do you make it go away?"

"I think about the person I love most in the world. The only person capable of making my heart beat fast one moment and slow the next. She takes my breath away, but is the reason I breathe. She's my heart and owns my soul so completely that I would no longer exist without her by my side."

Some of the melancholy fades from Cat's face as she takes in my words. "She must be pretty special."

"She's more than just special. She's everything."

"Who is she?" she asks hesitantly.

I wait a few seconds before I say her own name. "Caterina."

Something flickers in her eyes, and I wonder if Athena will acknowledge the name. But after a moment, she turns her head forward and rests her chin back on her knees.

It's difficult to tell if Athena is truly aware of who Cat is or if she's protecting herself by forgetting, just like Cat did with the memories of our children.

"I did something horrible." Cat's sorrowful voice has me looking at her closely.

I have a feeling I know what she's about to say, but I ask her anyway. "What did you do?"

"I forgot about them." She turns her head so her cheek lays on her knees and her eyes are directed at me.

"You had your reasons," I say quietly.

"There is no good enough reason to forget your children, Hunter. Nothing can excuse that." A tear leaks from the corner of her eye and splashes on her knee.

"Sometimes we don't have control of our minds, Athena. Sometimes our choices are taken from us. And in some cases, our bodies go into protective mode, doing whatever possible to avoid harm. You didn't forget them because you didn't love and care for them. You did it to protect yourself. You did it because you had no other choice if you wanted to survive."

Hope flashes in her eyes. "You really think so?"

"Yes."

She's quiet for a moment, then replies, "Maybe."

We sit for a few more minutes without saying anything. Occasionally, Ginger pops in to check on her sister, but I wave her off.

I get to my feet, keeping her hand in mine. "Come on. Let's get you off the floor."

Using her hand, I help her to her feet then walk her to the bed. I smile when she crawls on top of the mattress like a kid would. She catches my smile when she turns and sits.

"What?"

I wipe the look off my face and mutter, "Nothing."

She settles back on the pillows, her eyes following me as I pull the chair by the window beside the bed. It's after nine at night, so I know Cat has to be exhausted. Whenever one of her personalities emerges, it always exhausts her. Since it's usually during the day when Cat comes to The Grove, I'm not sure how this is going to play out.

After a few minutes, Athena's eyes close and her breathing evens out. Seeing her like this, asleep in a room that's not ours, reminds me too much of when Athena was here before. Back when she considered dying a better choice than being haunted by the memories of that horrific night.

Those were some of the darkest nights of my life, and I don't wish to relive them.

I sit for a few more minutes before getting up. As I bend over the bed, I breathe deeply, letting the unique scent of vanilla and roses fill my lungs.

Taking care not to startle her, I brush my lips across her soft ones. I don't want to leave her, I hate doing it each time she's here. However, in order for her to come out of this, the sooner I'm away from her, the better.

"I'm heading down to my car. Stay up here until she leaves,

then follow us home," I tell Mathias and receive a nod in return. "Text Damon and tell him to stay close."

"On it."

Ginger is waiting for me down at reception, her expression filled with concern.

"She dozed off. Not sure how long it'll be before she wakes up and goes home."

Her eyes move to the stairs before sliding back to me. "I'll keep an eye on her."

"I'll be out in my car. I'm going to wait until she leaves and follow her home. I have a couple of men here if anything happens."

For the most part, I've kept Cat's family informed. They know about Whisper and Henry's freedom. They're aware of the shit we've gotten in the mail and the times someone's broken into our house. They know mostly everything because those things affect Cat and there's no way to keep it from them. I haven't told them that I'm actively searching for Whisper and Henry, or what I intend to do when I find them. As far as they're concerned, I'm leaving it up to the police to find Whisper. They don't know about the people Silas and I killed over the years, and that's the way I plan to keep it.

"Why are you here so late?" I ask.

"Betty called in. Her daughter is sick so she's staying home with her. I offered to take her shift."

I nod, grateful that she's here. Even though I trust every single staff member employed, when it comes to family, it's different.

I leave her inside and walk out to my SUV. I see Damon's dark figure walking around the side of the building where Cat's car is parked. He'll patrol the area over and over again until it's time to leave.

I keep an eye on the building's front door. More often than not, Cat stays here for only an hour or two at most. When Cat switches from one of her personalities back to herself, she falls into a sort of trance. At first, I was concerned about her driving, but Dr. Armani explained that she's completely aware of her surroundings and will function normally. She just doesn't remember those short periods of time. Neither herself or the personality she just switched from.

When three hours pass and Cat hasn't appeared, worry sets in. I text Mathias for an update inside, and he replies that she's still asleep. She never stays this long.

Another hour passes, and then another. Ginger appears in the dim yellow light of the porch and walks over when she spots my SUV.

I push the button to roll down my window. "If your shift is over, you should head home to Mason and the boys," I tell her. There's no need for her to stick around when I'm here.

"I'd like to stay," she replies. "I don't like that she's been here for so long. I want to be here if something happens. Mason will be fine with the boys until I get home." She pauses for a moment. "How is she doing at home?"

My hands grip the steering wheel tightly. "For the most part, she's fine. She has moments though where things get to her. She's doing better than I thought she would with her memories back and knowing about Athena, Scarlett, and Presley."

"Have the others shown themselves more since she found out?"

"No, but they've changed their usual routine. You obviously know about Athena showing tonight, and Presley came to me while I was at Slate."

Her eyes widen. "Slate? With her mind being so young, I bet that was awkward."

"Thankfully, she was in my office when it happened and Katie was there with her so she didn't wander off and come across anything inappropriate."

"Close call. I can't imagine what she would have thought had she walked into the bar area and seen the girls on stage."

Ginger grabs the edges of her coat and pulls them closed when a gust of wind whips past.

"You should go inside before you catch a cold."

"Yeah." She turns to leave, but spins back. "She sent me her manuscript a few days ago. Have you had a chance to read it yet?"

The hand I have resting on my thigh tightens into a fist. "Yes," I reply.

When Ginger speaks again, her voice cracks. "I never knew." She stops, her head dropping as she clears her throat. "I mean, I did, but only what you told us and what was said in court." She lifts her head again and tears are sliding down her cheeks. "Jesus, Hunter. The details... I can't..." She shakes her head. "Does she realize what she did?"

"I don't know."

"She needs to before her agent moves further with it."

When Cat sent me the manuscript to read, I expected it to be her usual gory psychological thriller. I certainly wasn't prepared when I realized it was *our* story she was telling in vivid detail.

Before her memories came back, I wasn't sure how I should approach her with my concerns, but now that they are, it won't be as much of a shock. I'll leave the decision up to her whether or not she wants to publish the work. I just want to make sure she's aware before it gets that far.

"Any updates on Whisper?" Ginger asks.

"No," I grunt.

She nods, her lips pressing firmly together. She doesn't like my answer any more than I do.

After she returns inside, I text Mathias for another update, knowing the answer already. Had she woken up, he would have alerted me.

Two hours later, the sun peeks over the horizon and Cat still hasn't awoken. Fatigue has my body sagging in the seat, but my eyes stay alert on the front door. As tired as I may get, sleep will have to wait until my wife is safely back home.

Chapter Thirty-Five
Hunter

Cat spent two days at The Grove.

Thankfully, Dr. Armani was already on his way when I called. It didn't make me feel any less concerned when he explained why Athena had been staying around so long. He believed that Athena, the more emotional of Cat's personalities, was closer to the surface because of all the changes lately and the heightened emotions she's been feeling.

I stayed at The Grove the entire time. Nothing could have pulled me away. The few hours of sleep I managed to get were in the room beside hers.

Ginger wanted to stay until Cat was Cat again, but I sent her home to her family. She only agreed when I promised to call her if anything changed. I also called Peggy and Jacob to inform them of the situation. They wanted to visit, but since Cat had never met them as Athena, I didn't want to introduce anyone new to her.

We're finally home and everything seems to be back to normal. Cat's parents just left after stopping by for a couple of hours and having a late lunch. If I had my way, I would have waited a few more days before having family over—I wasn't ready to share her just yet—but I knew how worried Peggy and Jacob were. I did draw the line at Ginger and her crew coming over. Instead, Cat and I made plans to visit them soon.

Since we've been home, I haven't let Cat out of my sight. Literally, with the exception of when one of us has to use the restroom. Wherever she goes, I follow. I'm fucking terrified that if I lose sight of her something will happen or she'll disappear again.

I'm sitting at the bar in the kitchen, glass of whiskey in hand, while Cat wipes down the counters. I've been watching her for the last five minutes and in those minutes I've seen several emotions cross her face.

"Come here," I say, downing the rest of my drink and setting the glass on the counter.

After throwing the rag in the sink, she walks around the bar. When she's within reach, I swivel my stool and pull her between my legs.

"What are you thinking?" I ask.

She tucks a chunk of hair behind her ear, her eyes moving to mine before darting away, only to come back. "I have a doctor's appointment in a few days."

"With Dr. Armani?"

"No. Dr. Wells."

Dr. Wells is Cat's primary care physician. Unless she's sick, she sees her once every six months for regular checkups. She last saw her about three months ago, so she shouldn't be due yet.

"What are you seeing Dr. Wells for?"

She doesn't answer right away. Instead, she chews on her lip with a frown wrinkling her forehead.

"Cat?" I prompt.

"I'm late."

Immediately, I understand what she means. Her statement can only mean one thing.

"How late?" I ask, trying like hell to keep my body relaxed.

"I didn't realize until this afternoon that I'm over a month past my period. My birth control isn't due for another three months though."

"It could just be stress."

Though she nods slowly, her troubled expression suggests she doesn't truly believe it. "It could be."

"Either way, we'll get through it." I wrap my arms around her waist and pull her closer to me.

In the five years since our children were taken from us, having more is one subject we've never discussed. Of course, until recently, Cat believed we never had children. With what happened, I believe she never thought about having children because it might have brought back memories of Eliana and Ryder.

For myself, I've thought about it occasionally over the years, but never seriously. I'm not opposed to having more children, but I also don't need them to feel fulfilled. My only concern is what it would do to Cat. Ryder and Eliana could never be replaced, but would having a baby help or hinder her healing?

Cat looks as if the idea of her being pregnant weighs heavily on her mind.

"How would you feel if you were pregnant?" I ask cautiously and watch her expression.

Her lip goes back between her teeth. "I'm not sure," she replies slowly. "In a way, it feels like we just lost Eli and Ryder, so it's still so fresh." Her eyes glisten and she sniffs and blinks back tears. "It kind of feels like I would be using a new baby as a crutch, and that's no reason to bring a baby into the world."

"True." I slip my thumbs under the edge of her shirt and rub them along her lower back. "But you wouldn't love them any less than you love Eli and Ryder."

"No, I wouldn't." Cat's eyes drop to the button she's playing with on my shirt and she lowers her voice. "I also worry I would fail like I did with Eli and Ryder."

My thumb and forefinger press against her chin as I tilt her head back. Her eyes shine with unshed tears and the look obliterates my fucking heart.

"Don't ever think you failed, Cat," I tell her, my voice firm. "Our children were lucky to have you as a mother. I don't know another woman alive who loved and cherished their children more than you. And they loved you just the same. No one blames you for what happened. Not even Eli and Ryder, if they were here."

It's not hard to see she wants to believe me, desperately so, but she still doesn't. I'm not sure she ever will. Just as I'll always blame myself for not being there when my family needed me. It's a burden we'll both bear for the rest of our lives. But it's one I'm determined we'll overcome.

I pull her forward and brush my lips against hers. "I know having another baby is scary to think about. Eli and Ryder are special in every way children can be special. They'll always be in our hearts and no matter how many children we may have one day, they'll never be replaced or forgotten."

As a tear slides down her cheek, I know I've touched on one of Cat's biggest fears. She still feels guilty about pushing our children's memories away, and now that she has them back, she worries their memories will fade if we have more children.

"Any new child we have will know everything there is to know about the two beautiful babies we lost. We'll talk about them every day. Their big brother and sister won't be with them, but they'll still be a part of their lives. All of our lives."

Her cheeks turn red as she fights back more tears. She loses the battle when several manage to slip free down her cheeks. I gently kiss them away, wishing I could erase all the bad things that have ever happened to Cat. She deserves only the best things in life. Not the ugly and depraved.

We stay like that for a while, with her face pressed against my front and her forehead resting on my shoulder. My thoughts are filled with what it would be like to have another child, and I'm sure Cat's are as well.

Our tender moment is interrupted by the doorbell ringing. I press a kiss on the top of her head before I gently push her back.

"I'll be right back," I tell her before leaving the kitchen.

I check the camera beside the alarm before I press the code to disarm it. Jimmy's smiling face is there when I open the door. He's dressed in a pressed suit and his hair is slicked back, his face shaved clean. It's strange seeing him in this get-up. Usually he wears jeans and a T-shirt, with his hair less nicely kept and at least a couple days worth of growth on his face.

"Hey, Jimmy. What brings you by?"

"My piece of shit car broke down a block away," he says, pressing his hands into his pockets and rocking back on his heels. "The tow company won't be able to pick it up for a couple of hours. I figured I'd stop by for a visit since I've got time." His expression turns sheepish. "And I was hoping you wouldn't mind if I stayed while I waited for the tow truck."

Although it's not the best time, I can't turn away the man who saved my wife.

I open the door wider and gesture with my hand. "Sure. Come on in. Cat will be happy to see you."

"Thanks, Hunter."

Before I close the door, I tip my chin to Damon, who's sitting in his car out front, to let him know everything is fine.

Jimmy follows me down the hall and into the kitchen. Cat smiles brightly when she sees him.

"Jimmy! This is a pleasant surprise."

Getting up from her seat, she walks toward him, wrapping her arms around his middle. Her affection for him is unusual, but then I realize this is the first time she has seen him since she allowed her memories to surface. This man saved her life and she's just now remembering it.

Jimmy looks at me over her shoulder, his expression full of confusion, but he still wraps his arms around her.

"Hey, sweetheart," he says, patting her back awkwardly.

When she pulls back, she quickly brushes away a couple of stray tears and offers him a smile. "Just ignore me." She laughs. "Hormones."

They both sit at the bar.

"Can I get you a drink?" I ask Jimmy, reaching across the bar for my glass to refill.

"Actually, I was hoping you still had that bottle of Merlot I dropped off a while back."

I grab the bottle of Masseto Jimmy gave us for our anniversary several months ago from the cabinet by the refrigerator. The price tag for something like this is steep, so I was surprised Jimmy could afford it. Since Cat and I don't drink merlot, the bottle has sat untouched in the cabinet. I decided to keep it to share with Jimmy during one of his visits. He spent his hard-earned money when he shouldn't have, so he deserves to enjoy a glass.

"Perfect!" he says when I set it on the counter between us.

"What are we drinking to?" I ask as I grab two glasses and pour each of us one.

I slide one across the bar in front of Jimmy. He takes it and looks over at Cat. "You aren't having any?"

Cat glances at me, unsure how to answer, so I do it for her.

"There's a possibility that she may be pregnant."

Jimmy looks between the two of us, a slow smile forming on his face. "*That* is what we're toasting to." He holds his glass up. "To new beginnings."

Cat smiles as she lifts the glass of juice she poured for herself earlier. We each touch glasses.

"So, Jimmy, how have you been? Are you still seeing the woman you teased us with the other day?"

He sets his glass down, a proud smile splitting his lips.

"Sure am, and things are getting serious. I'll actually be seeing her tonight."

"That's great." Cat beams. "She's lucky to have you."

Jimmy laughs. "I'm not sure if she would agree with you, but I'm glad to have her in my life."

"When do we get to meet her?"

I lift my glass, holding in my grimace when the bitter taste hits my tongue. I can barely tolerate the stuff, but I let the rest slide down my throat to get it over with.

"You'll meet her soon enough, and I have no doubt you'll love her. She actually reminds me of you."

"Oh yeah? How so?"

He spins his glass by the stem. "She has the same quiet disposition as you have. She's really smart in an unassuming way. She's sweet and caring like you. And believe it or not, she's a big fan of thriller novels. She's actually read all of your books. When I told her I knew you, I thought she was going to pop my eardrums from her screaming so loudly."

Cat laughs, a light blush covering her cheeks. She's never been comfortable taking compliments about her work.

"That's sweet. I'll have to sign a couple of books for you to give to her."

"She would love that."

He grabs the bottle and offers me more wine, but I shake my head. "I've had enough." More than enough, if the headache forming between my eyes is any indication.

"Anyway," Jimmy says, picking up his glass and swirling the liquid. "I really appreciate you letting me sit for a while. I wasn't looking forward to waiting for the tow truck in my car." He lifts his glass, but before he takes a sip, he sets it back down. "Heard the temps are supposed to be dropping over the next couple of hours."

"It's really no problem," Cat responds.

I glance at her when her voice seems to be drifting away. She wobbles on her seat. After a minute, I realize it's not her who's unsteady, but me. I slam my hand on the counter to keep myself upright as my vision blurs.

My eyes jerk to Jimmy, the small movement making my swaying body stumble to the side. I barely catch myself from ass planting on the floor.

"Hunter? Are you okay? What's wrong?"

I ignore Cat's question, unable to look away from Jimmy. His lips are curved into a smile I've never seen on his face before. It's nasty and filled with twisted glee.

"What in the fuck have you done?" Even to my own ears, my voice sounds warbled, like I'm talking through a ton of cotton.

"Giving you what you've been wanting." He gets up from his seat.

From my peripheral vision, I see Cat get up, but Jimmy grabs a handful of her hair before she makes it far. Her scream is cut short when Jimmy shoves her against the bar, smashing her head down on the granite.

He runs his hand down her hair like she's his fucking pet. "I heard you've been looking for me."

My whole fucking world crashes down on me. Even as my vision becomes hazy, red still bleeds across the edges. I've been so goddamn stupid.

I fight the darkness closing in around me, but whatever Jimmy slipped into the wine bottle is too strong. I grit my teeth, my legs losing their battle to stay upright.

Just before I crash to the floor, I say one word.

"Whisper."

Chapter Thirty-Six
Hunter

My mouth feels like it's full of cotton and a thousand drums beat along the inside walls of my skull. As I lift my head and open my eyes, the brightness of the room blinds me, making my head pound harder.

I try to raise my arms, but they won't move. Dropping my chin to my chest, I stare down at the reason. I'm sitting in a chair with my arms pulled behind me. It's then that I feel the roughness of a rope around my wrists. My legs are also attached to the chair.

Memories of Jimmy in the kitchen, sitting beside Cat at the bar, flash through my mind. Soon after comes the revelation I made right before I blacked out.

Whisper.

This whole fucking time, he was right under our goddamn noses.

Lifting my groggy head, I survey the room. Our living room. And across from me only a few feet away is my wife. She's lying on her back on the coffee table. Her arms are pulled above her head with a rope wrapped securely around her wrists, which is attached to the legs of the table. Her body is pulled down to the other end until her butt nearly hangs off the edge. Her legs are spread and kept open with rope wrapped around the top by her knees all the way down to her ankles. Like her wrists, she's bound to the legs of the table. A piece of duct tape covers her mouth.

My only consolation is she still has her dress on. But how long will that last?

As if sensing my gaze, she turns her head. Her beautiful blue eyes are wide and filled with terror.

"It's okay, Cat," I say, my voice scratchy from whatever drug Whisper put in the bottle of merlot. I thank Christ that Cat didn't have any of it. "I'm going to get you out of here."

"It's not nice to lie to your wife, Hunter," a voice says off to my right. Jimmy or Whisper or whatever the fuck his name is, comes into view. "After all, Caterina is lying in her final resting place."

I tug on the ropes around my wrist to no avail. They're so tight it's damn near cutting off blood circulation.

"You're Whisper," I state needlessly. We've well past established that he is, but if I keep him talking it might buy me time to figure a way to get Cat and me out of this shit. "I underestimated you."

I move my gaze to the window, which faces the front of the house. The curtains are closed, meaning no one can see inside, including Damon.

Whisper grins and walks over to where Cat's lying. "You did." Cat whimpers and jerks against the rope when he touches her knee. He trails his fingers up her thigh, moving the dress upward. His head swings back to me. "I have to say, watching you this whole time, looking for me, seeing the life you have with Cat, witnessing the struggles she goes through, knowing there wasn't a damn thing you could do, gave me much more enjoyment than I thought it would."

"Get your filthy fucking hands off her," I growl. I don't look at Cat when her whimpers become muffled cries. If I do, I won't be able to keep my cool, and that's what I need to do right now.

"It's amusing that you demand I remove my hands like I'll actually do what you want. I'll be doing much more to Cat than this." He punctuates his words by grabbing her roughly between the legs and squeezes. Cat cries out behind the tape and wiggles on the table as she tries to get away from his touch. "She and I have unfinished business and it's well past time we complete it."

"What in the fuck are you talking about?" I grit out, yanking harder on my wrists and turning them raw.

Thankfully, he removes his hand as he answers. "The night I so deliciously took your beautiful daughter and cute little boy from you, your dear wife wasn't supposed to survive. She was to die right alongside them."

Warmth trickles down my fingers. "Then why pretend to save her?"

"Because I realized I could prolong your torture." He walks around the table and takes a seat on the couch, his position at the center of Cat's torso and putting him in my direct line of sight. "Because I wanted to watch you try and fix your beautiful Cat, and just when you thought you might succeed, I'd be there to snatch her from you again."

He grabs a lock of Cat's hair, rubbing it between his fingers. His eyes lift and meet mine. "And you know what's so damn delicious about that night?" I don't take the bait. He's going to tell me whether I want to hear it or not. "The fire at Slate—the reason you left the house." His lips twist into a sinister smile. "I staged it to get you away so me and my boys could spend hours with your precious little family."

The pressure in my head feels like it's going to explode at any moment.

"Why?" I snarl. "Why target my family? What in the hell have I ever done to you?"

He pulls out a knife from a sheath by his ankle. "You took everything from me," he says quietly, his gaze mesmerized by the blade in his hand. "You took everything away and left me with nothing."

"What are you talking about? I had no idea who you were until the night you and those bastards broke into my house."

His eyes lift, and for the first time since I met Jimmy, I know I'm finally seeing what he truly is. Hatred at its purest and deepest. A devious monster, filled to the brim with sick intentions. How did he hide himself so well from me?

"Oh, you know me. You know me really well actually. So well, in fact, that you should call us family."

My limbs lock, and I cease my struggles. I throw his words around in my head, trying to comprehend them. I'm unable to because what he's saying is too fucking absurd. I have no family. The only family I had, before they died when I was two, was my mother and father. That's what the reports say, at least.

A portion of the inheritance I received after turning eighteen was used to search for my family. Patrick and Summer St. James were my only two relatives. No other relatives were associated with those two names, which must have been a lie since they had to have come from somewhere. Despite my efforts or the money I handed over to private investigators, nothing could be found.

After a couple of years, I stopped looking because it didn't really matter. I didn't need to know my background. It had no impact on where I was going.

I sit there and stare at Whisper, my expression blank and keeping my mouth shut, refusing to give him the satisfaction of my curiosity.

The bastard chuckles when I continue to keep silent after several minutes.

"You can try and hide it, but I see your interest, Hunter. I've been watching you a lot longer than five years and know every little detail there is to know about you. Including your facial expressions." He places the tip of his blade on the hollow of Cat's neck. She sucks in a breath and holds it. "Like right now, you're imagining taking this knife," he moves the tip down her neck, "and jamming it down my throat." His lips curve into a cruel smile. "Am I right?"

Pretty fucking close, but not quite. I'd first use it to cut off his dick and shove that down his throat before forcing the blade down afterward.

"Anyway," he says as he uses the knife to pick up one of the straps on Cat's dress. "Back to what I was saying before. You believe Patrick and Summer St. James were your parents, but they were fictitious." He flicks his wrist and the strap easily cuts in two. I clench my jaw, my teeth nearly snapping at the pressure. He does the same to the other strap. "Created by our parents, Nicholas and Teresa Monroe."

"How do I know you're telling the truth?" I grind out.

I keep my eyes on his, but in my peripheral vision, I see him slowly begin sawing Cat's dress down the middle. Behind me, my hands are slick with blood as I continue to try to loosen the ropes.

"I have birth records."

"Those can be forged, just as you implied the same with Patrick and Summer St. James."

"And pictures," he continues as if knowing what I was going to say. He looks up, his eyes moving to my right forearm. "You have a birthmark on your right arm in the shape of a dragonfly."

He sets the knife down on Cat's stomach and pulls up the sleeve of his dress shirt, showing the exact same birthmark on his left arm. I've never seen that mark on another person, and the chances of it being on someone else are damn near impossible. Unless we're related.

"Who in the fuck are you?" I growl.

"Your big brother," he answers.

"Why was it hidden where I came from?"

"Because our father dabbled in shit that wasn't legal. He was part of the Chicago mafia. He set it up so that if anything ever happened to him, his wife and children would be given new identities. He didn't want anyone coming after his family. The same was set up if only his children survived."

I file that information away for later.

"This still doesn't explain why you targeted my family. I was two years old when they died. How in the fuck could I have stolen anything from you?"

"I'm getting to that," he replies. "But first, I want to refresh my memory of the handy work my boys left on this beautiful body." He pulls the two pieces of the dress apart, exposing Cat's torso. There are six scars on her stomach and chest and he traces every one with his fingers, looking at them with glee and sick pleasure in his eyes. "A work of art, if I do say so myself."

My blood boils, heating me from the inside out. Rage surges through me and my arms tense, the sockets in my shoulders threatening to pop as I struggle against the ropes binding me. Cat squeezes her eyes closed, a whimper slipping through the tape. When she turns her head toward me, her face is red and her eyelids slide open. For a moment, I stare into her eyes before moving my gaze to Whisper.

"When I get free—and I will, one way or another—I'm going to kill you slowly."

His eyes lift to mine and one side of his mouth curves up. "That'll be a neat trick, considering your current lack of control of the situation."

"Remove your fucking hands from my wife or you'll lose them."

I need to calm my shit if I have any hope of getting Cat out of this. I've failed her once. Doing so again is not an option.

"I believe I like them where they are," he taunts. "Actually, that's wrong. I like them better right here." He yanks the cup of her bra down on one side and wraps his filthy hand around her breast. He squeezes it so hard, the parts that stick out between his fingers are red. Cat screams and thrashes against the table.

"Jimmy!" I roar, jerking and pulling, but all it does is dig the rope further into my skin. Maybe if the rope digs in far enough, it'll loosen enough for me to slip free.

He lets Cat's breast go and she stops moving, her eyes still pinned on me.

"Actually, my name is Nico, named after dear old Dad. I was the apple of both of our parents' eyes." The look on his face turns to loathing. "Until the day you were born. I was six. The moment they brought you home, you became their new favorite. I hated you from the moment I saw the way they looked at you. I tried and tried to regain their attention, but it was always you they flocked to."

"I was a fucking baby."

He leans over Cat and yells. "It didn't fucking matter!" His eyes flare and he takes a deep breath, seeming to calm himself. "They were my parents first and you got in the way."

He picks up the knife again and moves the tip down Cat's stomach. She stops breathing, too afraid to move in fear it might sink inside. He slips it underneath the band of her panties and easily slices it down the center of the silk material.

Jimmy continues talking as he watches his handy work. "I used to slip into your room at night and drag a stool over to your crib. I'd watch you sleep and pray you'd never wake up, but every fucking morning, you'd wake the house with your cries." His lips curl in disgust. "One night, I decided I was done praying and would take care of it myself. Mom caught me right as I shoved the pillow over your face. They never trusted me around you after that, but it didn't stop me from trying a few other ways to get rid of you. I put bleach in your bottle once, but Mom smelled it before you had any. And there was one time, right after your first birthday, you managed to climb out of your crib. You were in the hallway, wobbling toward the stairs. As your helpful big brother, I was going to help you down them, but the stupid nanny found you first."

I'm not even listening to what he says. My sole focus is on what he's doing to Cat.

My body vibrates in the chair, my chest pumping, and sweat coats my skin. Cat's panties have been cut away and the bastard uses the flat part of the knife to press it against her pussy. How in the fuck he hasn't cut her already, I don't know.

"The scar you have on your thigh, right above your knee. That happened when I pushed you down on a fork I purposely placed on the floor. You were supposed to land on your fucking head so the tines punctured your skull, but I was still an amateur killer at the time." He shrugs.

"What do you want, Nico?" I ask, using his real name. Everything he's told me so far could be lies. Even the birthmark on his arm and the scar on my thigh could have been fabricated. But deep down, I know it's all true. This man may be unhinged, but he's smart. Too smart to not have all the facts. "Leave my wife out of this, and I'll give you whatever the fuck you want. Money? Me dead. Whatever, you can have it."

From the corner of my eye, I see Cat's eyes widen with panic at my words.

"You think I want your money?" he asks with laughter in his eyes. "I've got plenty of my own. There's something you don't know about me, Hunter. I'm smart. Really fucking smart. So smart I was able to break into one of the most prestigious IT colleges in the nation and give myself a free pass through college. After I graduated, I started my own company with the money I had filtered off one business after another. Can you guess the name of the company?"

My gaze is flat as I stare at him without answering.

"Monroe Security."

Motherfucker.

So that's how he's been breaking into our house without setting off the alarm.

"So what I want is more than you're willing to give," he says, while I still process what he just revealed. "Which is why you'll sit there and watch me take it from you. I thought your kitty Cat was the last thing you had to offer. But then you gifted me with the pleasure of knowing you may have another little one on the way." His grin is pure evil. "Isn't it fucking grand that I can take another child from you before it's even born?"

He presses harder on the knife and this time it does cut into Cat. She screams, the sound, even through the tape, is ear-piercing.

"Goddamn it!" I roar. "Fucking stop!"

The bastard laughs. "I wonder how long I can fuck her with a knife before she bleeds out."

Cat screams louder, and I become frantic, jerking and pulling with every bit of strength I have left. Just as my hand starts slipping through the rope, Cat's screams abruptly cease and her frightened eyes dart over my shoulder. A second later, the barrel of a gun is pressed to my temple by someone who must have stepped from the hallway.

"You didn't honestly believe I came alone, did you?" Jimmy asks, his lips twisting into a cruel smirk. "After all, Henry deserves to be here after he spent so much time in jail."

Henry Stephens steps forward just enough for me to see him. He wears the same sick smile as Jimmy. I'm not surprised to see him. My guess is he went straight to Jimmy the moment he got out of prison. Which means he, Terry, and Howard lied when they said they didn't know who Whisper was.

The muscle in my jaw pulses and my hands ball into fists, itching to wrap them around the fucker's throat.

"I don't believe you two were ever properly introduced. Hunter, meet Henry Stephens, your nephew."

"Your son?" I ask. How many more fucking surprises will he come out with today?

Jimmy grins. "Yes."

"And Terry and Howard?"

"My adopted boys. Well, not technically," he shrugs, "but they were friends of Henry's, and I took them in when their shit parents left them on the streets."

"How fucking generous of you," I grate out.

"I thought so. Anyway, they were all too happy to play their part when I told them what I had planned for you. Especially when I showed them pictures of your children. Apparently, it was a fantasy the boys shared to rape and break a child."

Red coats my vision with his taunt.

"And you loved them so much that you just let them rot in prison," I state.

"Only for as long as it took to get them out. Of course, since Henry is my blood, I had to get him out first."

"Terry and Howard are still in the pen."

"Their time is coming."

Not if I have anything to do with it. That's if I can get us out of this.

"So, you staged a break-in, tortured my family, killed my children, and were going to kill my wife all because you were a jealous spoiled brat when we were kids?"

"Of course not. That would be insane."

I grunt. The guy is definitely off his fucking rocker.

"After the fourth time I tried to kill you, our parents took me to a shrink. They thought something was wrong with me." He rolls his eyes, for the moment not touching Cat. "They put me on medicine, but it only made me angrier. I wasn't just angry at you anymore, though, but at them. I hated them for choosing you over me. Life was fucking perfect before you came along."

My joints lock as he looks down at Cat and something ugly crosses his face. The knife is put down on her stomach again and he pulls out a gun from the back waistband of his pants. He presses the barrel of it against her pussy, pushing the tip inside.

Before I can say anything—what can I really say?—he

continues talking. I keep my eye on the gun, hoping like fuck he doesn't have twitchy fingers.

"I overheard them talking one night about sending me away to a boarding school. So, I killed them," he says, casual as you fucking please. "Our father kept a gun in his nightstand. I took it out, shot him first, and then shot our mother. I knew from watching our father kill a man once that I needed to wipe the gun down so the cops wouldn't know I did it. It never occurred to them that it was an eight-year-old boy." He laughs maniacally, as if it was the funniest thing he's ever seen. "I thought since we were brothers they would put us with a family together, and I'd bide my time before I finally killed you, but that didn't work out. We were separated. I was willing to let it go, until I found out years later that our parents left you a fucking fortune and me not one fucking dime. Oh, and since we're clearing the air, once I found out about the inheritance and the people who took you in who informed you of the money, I had the brakes cut on their car."

I grit my teeth. "You killed Thomas and Sandra?"

"With fucking pleasure."

Just another reason to enjoy killing this bastard once I get free. I didn't spend enough time with Thomas and Sandra for me to get close to them, but they were the only people who had given me anything good. Through them, my life changed for the better.

"The inheritance came from Patrick and Summer St. James. Another fabrication," I add more to myself than to him. I look at Jimmy. "How in the fuck was that my fault?"

He jams the gun further inside Cat and she cries out. I hear the click of the hammer, and I freeze, my blood running cold.

"It wasn't," he says frostily.

For the first time since this shit started, Jimmy looks as though he's coming unglued. A red flush spreads over his face and the hand holding the gun shakes. Him becoming unhinged is bad. Very fucking bad with the gun shoved inside Cat. Just a twitch of his finger and she's dead.

"It should have been mine. You took my parents from me. You turned them against me. I killed them because of you." Spit flies from his mouth, landing on Cat, who's barely breathing. His voice rises. "You took everything that was supposed to be fucking mine," he finishes on a roar.

The echo of his scream barely fades from the room when a loud knock sounds against the front door. I tense, preparing to spring forward.

His eyes move to Henry's over my shoulder. "Go see who it is and take care of it," he barks.

I'm not sure if Henry never noticed that my hands are nearly free or if he's just stupid. He moves around me, and I keep one eye on him as he leaves the room while the other stays on Jimmy and his gun.

Thankfully, Jimmy gets up and pulls it free from her then sets it on the couch. The reprieve lasts only a second because his hands move to the waistband of his slacks. Unbuttoning and sliding down the zipper, he pulls out his hard cock and fists it. His lecherous eyes move to Cat laid out before him.

"I always regretted not fucking you myself that night." He tugs on his cock. "Out of all the women I've had over the years, your pussy would have been the tightest. My son says you were his favorite, while Terry favored your boy and Howard favored the little bitch. Having you for only one night won't be nearly enough. Too bad I can't take you with me to play with at my leisure, but I don't have time for that."

With one hand around Cat's throat and one gripping his dick

between her legs, he leans down, resting most of his weight on her. His head swivels toward me, his crazed eyes meeting mine with a twisted smile.

"I have just enough time for you to watch as I squeeze the life out of your bitch while I fuck her," he says, bending his knees, the tip of his dick an inch from Cat.

My jaw cramps at how hard I'm clenching my teeth. Behind me, I pull my blood-slicked hand free from the rope.

Everything happens at once. When I stand to my feet, ready to charge Jimmy to break his fucking neck, Henry stumbles backward into the living room, his hand around his throat. Red oozes from between his fingers and he falls back onto the floor. Just as he lands, the window across the room shatters and a figure dives inside. Jimmy, who's momentarily stunned by the events, pauses long enough for me to reach him.

I briefly register Cat's muffled scream as my roar fills the room. I have my hand wrapped around Jimmy's neck in the next second, and I pick him up, slamming him to the floor and follow him down.

I'm blinded by rage. All I can see, my every fucking thought, is to continue squeezing until his eyes pop out of their sockets. To feel the life leave his body.

Jimmy will die a brutal death, but not at this moment. He deserves a death much more painful and prolonged.

Cat's whimpers draw my attention away from Jimmy, whose face has turned red from lack of oxygen. Seeing fear and pain in her beautiful blues, I immediately let go of Jimmy.

I notice Silas, who must have been the person at the front door, standing over a deathly still Henry, and I jerk my chin at Jimmy. "Secure him and put him in the basement at Slate," I growl, barely containing the rage still roaring through my veins.

"Station Kurt outside the room. No one goes in unless it's you or me."

Dropping to my knees beside the coffee table, I gently remove the tape covering Cat's mouth. As soon as it's gone, she bursts into tears.

"It's okay, baby," I whisper hoarsely. I start working on the ropes around her wrists, but it's taking too fucking long. A knife appears over my shoulder.

The second the ropes are cut away, I'm pulling Cat from the table at the same time she's scrambling to get onto my lap. With her arms around my neck and legs around my waist, I fall to my ass. We're as close as two bodies can get, but it's still not enough. I want to absorb her into my skin and never let her free.

I look up when a blanket is set over Cat's shoulders and meet Mathias's eyes. "Thanks," I grunt.

He walks away without a word.

I bury my face in Cat's hair, breathing in her scent, reassuring myself that she's really okay. Her body begins to shake, so I tuck the blanket around her more tightly, leaving smears of blood from my wrists on the material. I'm not sure if she's cold or her shivers are because of the events over the last couple of hours.

I pull my head out of her hair and gently tip her head back, needing to see her face.

"Are you okay?" I ask, forcing the words out through my dry throat.

Her chin jerks up and her tongue darts out, licking away a fallen tear sliding down her lip. "Yes. I think so."

My chest hurts, like someone punched me in the solar plexus. My eyes roam her face. Her cheeks are splotchy and red, her eyes are swollen and bloodshot, and there's a cut on her bottom lip from when Jimmy slammed her face on the counter. There's also a bruise forming on her left cheek, and blood drips from her nose.

My eyes move to the man lying on the floor on his stomach only ten feet away. My anger renews, not that it's lessened all that much. I want to set Cat aside and pummel the bastard until every bone in his body breaks beneath my hands.

"Hey," Cat says, laying her hand against my cheek and turning my head back to her. "Don't look at him. Look at me."

I inhale a shaky breath and let it out slowly. Careful not to hurt her, I pull her toward me again. She comes willingly, tucking her head back into my neck.

I close my eyes, letting the closeness of her body soak into my bones, calming the unspent rage still radiating through me.

Chapter Thirty-Seven
Hunter

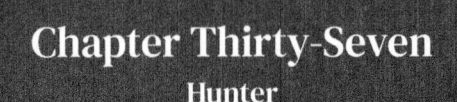

I sit in a chair beside the bed with my elbows on my knees, my hands dangling between them. Keeping my gaze on Cat, I watch her chest rise and fall steadily. She's asleep, her face relaxed and peaceful. But I know the calm is fleeting. Only temporary until the nightmares invade or the memories resurface.

This woman has been through hell and back. She's fought for her life far too many times. She's faced evil and beat its ass more often than most. How much more can she take before she breaks irreparably? Cat's one of the strongest women I know, hell, she's stronger than most men, but the mind can only handle so much.

Will what happened tonight finally push her over the edge? Will she awaken as someone else? Will her mind decide that enough is enough and hide forever?

It doesn't matter what state she's in. I will love this woman and protect her with my life until the end of my days on this earth. Nothing and no one will take her from me, and that includes Cat herself.

A light tap sounds against the door, and I release the breath I've been holding. Getting up, I lean over Cat and brush a soft kiss against her lips. "I'll be right outside the door," I whisper in case her subconscious can hear me. I don't want her to wake up wondering where I am.

My eyes linger on her face when I pull back, but she doesn't so much as flutter an eyelid.

Walking across the room, I open the door and step outside, leaving it cracked open a couple of inches so I can see inside. I turn and face Silas.

"How is she?" he asks, concern written in his expression.

I sigh, dragging a hand down my face. "Sleeping for the moment."

"Sleeping is good." He nods. "Probably the best thing for her right now."

Dr. Armani left thirty minutes ago after speaking with Cat. I pulled him aside and explained what happened. He wanted to talk to Cat alone, but gave up that notion when I told him there wasn't a chance in hell I was letting her out of my sight. Instead, I stood across the room to give them as much privacy as possible. I couldn't hear what they were saying, but I was close enough if Cat became upset.

When I hired the doctor to oversee Cat's mental care, I quadrupled the pay he was making at the practice he was at. Now he only sees Cat and the patients at The Grove. While he still has a private office in town, he spends most of his time at The Grove, except when Cat has an appointment. His fat paycheck was not without conditions, however. The doctor/patient confidentiality can be broken if the patient becomes a danger to themselves or others. With what I fork out, it ensures he keeps his mouth sealed tight, no matter what he hears or encounters. When I informed him of what happened tonight, I knew he'd keep quiet when the police weren't involved.

While Dr. Armani took care of Cat's mental state, she also needed to be seen for her injuries. That's where Dr. Savers comes in. She's another doctor I have on payroll and oversees any medical issues I need kept under wraps.

I managed to hold my shit together when Dr. Armani and Cat were talking quietly, but when Dr. Savers examined Cat, I broke out into a cold sweat. I damn near stormed the house on a hunt to find and destroy Jimmy. Only Cat's pain and fear kept me rooted by her side, her hand tightly clasped in mine. I fucking hated that for the second time tonight, she had to lay there with her legs open. However, the doc needed to make sure there was no internal damage. Thankfully, there wasn't. There were a few minor cuts that would heal on their own within a few days. God help Jimmy if they had been more severe, because there was no chance I would have been able to hold back.

With Cat's consent, Dr. Armani sedated her, explaining that she needed unrestricted rest at the moment. In response to my concern that she may be pregnant, he assured me that the medication was safe. She refused to take a pregnancy test, saying she didn't want the results on the same night Jimmy terrorized her.

"Where is he?" I demand, shoving my fisted hands into my pockets.

"Basement of Slate, like you requested."

"How's Damon?"

"Lucky to be alive. He made it through surgery. His doctors say he should make a full recovery."

I nod.

Damon was found outside his car with a knife wound to his chest. Due to the extent of his injuries, Mathias took him to the hospital under the pretext that he had been jumped from behind down an alley.

"I want to thank—"

"Fuck off," Silas growls, cutting me off. "Shove your gratitude up your ass, Hunter." His hands delve into his pockets, mirroring my position. "You know damn well I don't want it or need it. Your wife has been through more shit than most men, and so have you. It's offensive to me and the friendship we've had over the years for you to think even for a second, I wouldn't do everything in my power to take down the bastards who stole so much from you and Cat. To give your two children the revenge and justice they deserve. I only wish we had gotten here sooner."

"Regardless, you still have it," I say gruffly. "I still have my wife because of you and Mathias, so you'll accept my gratitude for what it is."

Last week, I had the feed coming from the cameras in my house split to go to a bank of computers at Silas's house. As we knew Whisper was breaking into our home undetected, I wanted Silas to have access just in case something went wrong that I wasn't aware of. His games were becoming more frequent and escalating, so I expected him to make a move soon. I just had no fucking clue it would be a man I trusted.

A fucking brother I knew nothing about. A sick psychotic brother. One who murdered our parents when he was eight and attempted to kill me multiple times as a baby.

My jaw tics at the reminder.

The video feed at Silas's house wasn't monitored constantly, but Silas happened to check the feed and saw what was going on in the living room. His first move was to call Mathias, knowing a couple of his men were watching the house. Our best guess is Jimmy had learned the schedule of when Mathias's men switched shifts, which included about an hour of only one man on duty. He made his move when only Damon was present. After Jimmy knocked on the door, Henry snuck up on Damon and stabbed him as he was getting out of his car. Our assumption is that Henry thought it was a kill shot, but he was wrong.

Silas, Mathias, and his men arrived at the house ten minutes before they busted through the place. Silas knocked on the door as a distraction while Mathias and his men waited at other points of entry outside the house.

We were goddamn lucky Silas happened to check the camera feed when he did. Had things happened even a moment later than they had, shit could have ended differently.

Regardless of how much he resists accepting my apology, claiming he doesn't need it, I'll always be in his debt.

"I'll be here for another hour or two in case you need anything," he informs me. "Do you want me to call Cat's family?"

"No. I want to give her a little longer before I let them know. I won't be able to keep them away once they learn what happened. I'll call them later." I look into the room and see Cat in the same position as when I left. I glance back at Silas. "Go home. There's nothing we'll need for the rest of the night."

He nods, his eyes moving to the crack in the door. "Call if that changes. We'll give you a few days before we stop by. I won't be able to keep Katie away longer than that."

After he leaves, I open the door and close it quietly behind me. Reaching over my shoulder, I grip the neck of my shirt and rip it over my head, tossing it to the chair I was sitting on earlier. After dropping my jeans to the floor, leaving me in only a pair of boxer briefs, I peel back the covers and climb into bed. When I reach for Cat, she slides into my arms as if sensing that I'm close.

She puts her head to my chest, still asleep, and I wrap my arms tightly around her. I could have lost her tonight. I damn near *did* lose her.

I close my eyes and take a deep breath. The restricting band around my chest, which has been tight since the moment I realized Jimmy is Whisper, finally loosens its hold.

It's over. Fucking finally.

But not for Jimmy. His suffering hasn't even begun.

I KNOW THE MOMENT SHE WAKES UP. HER BODY STIFFENS against mine, and I know she's remembering what happened just hours ago. She'll always have those memories, just as I will. But then she relaxes back against my chest, realizing she's safe in our bed.

A small string of light filters into the room from the inch of space between the heavy curtains. The sun rose hours ago. I haven't slept. I haven't even tried, opting to stay awake just to feel Cat against me. I've watched her sleep, waiting for the nightmares to come, wanting to be awake when they do so I can pull her out of them.

But they never came. She slept peacefully except to shift around a couple of times.

When she rolls onto her back, I lean up on my elbow, hovering just a few inches above her. A piece of hair lays across her cheek, the one with the nasty bruise, and I reach up and gently swipe it away. My gaze moves to the cut on her lip and the bruises around her eyes.

"How are you feeling?" I ask, keeping my voice low.

She lays her hand on my cheek, and I close my eyes at the soft touch. "I'm okay." She's quiet for a moment. "How are *you* feeling?"

My eyes open, and I stare down at her. "*Not* okay." She frowns at my answer. "I'm so goddamn sorry, baby," I say gruffly.

"You keep apologizing for things you don't have to apologize for." Her fingers slide into my hair. "No matter how you justify those apologies in your head, you've got it wrong, Hunter. There was nothing you could do to prevent what happened. Five years ago or last night."

"I was gone that night. I should have been here. I let that bastard fool me. Not only for the last five years, but also that night."

She shakes her head against the pillow. "You being there wouldn't have changed anything. There were too many of them. They would have still done what they did, or killed you, or orchestrated some other way to get you out of the house. I'm glad you weren't there to see what I did. I have to live with those memories. I'm glad you don't."

"Cat—"

She presses a finger against my lips. "And last night wasn't your fault either. Nor believing that he was a good man. Jimmy...." She stops and her throat bobs, as if fighting back her emotions. She clears her throat before she continues. "He had us all fooled. Someone as deranged as he is, there was nothing anyone could have done to stop him. You've got to stop taking responsibility for things out of your control."

She uses her other hand and the one on the back of my head to pull me down. Our lips meet.

"I'm okay," she whispers. "I'm right here with you. It's over now."

I drop my forehead to hers, taking several deep breaths. I'll never get over the fact that I almost lost her for the second time. I'll never stop seeing her lying on that table with Jimmy hovering over her. I will never truly believe there was nothing I could have done either time. I'll never stop blaming myself for not saving our children.

But seeing how much it bothers Cat, I'll force those feelings away and keep them hidden from her.

"Come take a shower with me," she suggests, and I lift my head from hers.

Last night, after everything was done and the doctors left, she fell asleep before she could shower. Dr. Savers and I changed her clothes and cleaned her as best we could, but nothing beats a shower.

I press another gentle kiss against her lips before I get up from the bed. Before she can rise on her own, I scoop her up into my arms. In the bathroom, I set her down by the shower to turn the water on. As we wait for the water to warm, I help her take off her clothes. I stare at her wrists, which are covered in bruises caused by the ropes. They're so dark, they almost hide the thin white scars. I pick up each one and brush my lips against them.

Cat notices my wrists, which are wrapped in bandages. It wasn't until Cat was treated that I allowed Dr. Savers to see to my injuries. The skin was damn near rubbed raw to the bone. She cleaned them as thoroughly as she could and insisted she slap some gauze around them.

With a frown, Cat lightly traces a finger over one of them.

"I'm fine, baby. They'll heal."

Nodding, she runs her tongue over her lips, a frown still pulling down her eyebrows.

I turn my attention to the scars on her stomach and chest. Both sets of scars almost took her from me. One done maliciously. The other to escape pain. I kiss those as well.

To avoid her thinking I expect anything sexual, I quickly get up and move us to the shower.

After the attack five years ago, it wasn't until Cat's mind shifted into protective mode and suppressed her memories that we had sex again.

She reaches for a washcloth on the shelf, but I take it from her. After pouring some of her body wash onto the cloth, I gently rub it over her body, taking extra care when I run it between her legs.

I have no idea where we go from here. I don't know how this will affect Cat's mental state. She seems fine right now, but that could change at any time.

The only thing I do know is that whatever happens, we'll get through it together.

Chapter Thirty-Eight
Caterina

Picking up my phone, I swipe my finger across the screen and bring it to my ear. "Hey, Max."

"Jesus, Cat, you're going to put me in an early grave," my older brother's words growl against my ear. "Can you hold off for a while on the dramatics and let my damn heart heal before something else happens?"

I laugh. Only my brother would request such a thing, like I had any control over what happened. I know he's joking though. "I'll try."

His breath crackles in the speaker when he exhales. "Are you okay?"

"Yeah," I tell Max, unsure if it's the truth.

"Let's try this again. Are you okay, Cat?" he presses quietly, knowing me all too well.

I stare down at my coffee sitting in front of me. Am I okay? I honestly don't know. It feels like I'm waiting for the other shoe to drop. Sure, last night's events were horrifying. Just thinking about what Jimmy did and what else he wanted to do freezes my blood in fear. With what I went through the first time, coupled with last night, you'd think I'd be a catatonic mess, barely functioning.

I'm fine, though. Or as fine as I'm capable of being. Maybe it's because I know it's over. Henry is dead. I don't know where Jimmy is, but I know Hunter will take care of him. Perhaps those five years I spent hiding the truth have actually helped me to build my mental strength.

Athena, Scarlett, and Presley still tap on the walls in my head, but they seem content right now. As if they're letting me call the shots, but they're there if I need them. Maybe it was them who have been making me stronger this whole time, instead of keeping me weak like I first assumed.

"I'm getting there," I say, giving him only what I can.

"Emily, Skylar, and I are coming down next month. We'd be there sooner, but I need to organize someone to take over the ranch while we're gone."

"Max, you don't need to come. I'm fine, I promise. And if I wasn't, I've got Hunter, Mom, Dad, and Ginger. Don't uproot your life for me."

"I'm not doing it for you," he replies. "I'm doing it for my own peace of mind."

Sighing, I pick up my coffee and bring it to my lips. It's cool enough now to take a sip without burning my lips off.

"Fine. But no hovering. I get enough of that from Hunter."

"He loves you, little sister, so he worries about you. Especially with everything that's happened and your unique situation."

My nose wrinkles. "You mean when someone else takes over my mind when the stress becomes too much?"

He chokes on a rumbling laugh. "To put it bluntly." His laughter dies off. "You need anything, call me."

"Will do." I hear voices coming down the hall. "I've got to go. Mom and Dad just got here."

"Love you, Cat. We'll see you soon."

"Love you too."

Just as I set the phone down on the counter after hanging up, I'm spun around and yanked off my stool. I let out a huff of air when I'm forcefully pulled into Mom's arms.

"My baby," she cries in my ear. I can already feel her tears wetting the shoulder of my shirt.

I wrap my arms around her, hugging her tight. "I'm okay, Mom."

After a moment, she grabs my arms and pulls back from me. When she sees the damage on my face, more tears glisten in her eyes.

"Mom, stop. I'm fine, okay?" I smile even though it hurts, hoping it'll lessen her worry.

She doesn't respond. Just snatches me forward for another nearly suffocating hug. I let her do her thing because she's a mom and it's what she needs to do.

As soon as she lets me go, Dad reaches out and pulls me into his firm arms. He handles his emotions better, but I know he's just as worried as Mom, and just as relieved.

I do this a couple more times with Ginger and Mason, although Mason's embrace is shorter than the others. I get hugs from the boys too, and their curious eyes latch onto my face, but they don't say anything. Ginger probably talked with them before they arrived.

After everyone has seen that I'm okay, Hunter walks over and takes the stool next to the one I was sitting on. Grabbing the waistband of my jeans, he pulls me backward until I'm wedged between his legs.

Since last night, he's been touching me constantly and keeping me in view all the time. I'm surprised he left me in the kitchen to answer the door a few minutes ago. I fully expected him to toss me over his shoulder and cart me around with him. I don't complain. This whole ordeal has been hard on him, and if hovering makes him feel better, then he can do it to his heart's content.

"Ginger, why don't you and Mason take the boys into the living room? Mom and I want to talk to Cat and Hunter alone."

As I look at Dad, I see his eyes firmly fixed on Hunter. Ginger doesn't argue as she collects Aiden and Josh from the kitchen and she and Mason take them to the living room.

As soon as they clear the doorway, I ask, "What's going on Dad?"

He doesn't look at me, but keeps his keen gaze over my shoulder at Hunter. "I want to know what's happening?"

"We've already told you," Hunter replies, resting his hand on my waist.

"Don't take me for a fool, Hunter," Dad says, a scowl forming on his face. "What happened here last night was never called in. I would have heard about it."

I glance over my shoulder at Hunter. His lips are flat, and I can see indecision in his eyes. Dad's right. One of his hunting buddies works for the police department. William would have called Dad as soon as the call came in. If that had happened, my parents would have been here last night.

"It's being taken care of. That's all you need to know," Hunter responds, his voice firm.

"How?" Dad asks anyway.

"Let's just say Jimmy is no longer a threat and leave it at that. And Henry isn't an issue either."

"Hunter—"

"With all due respect, Jacob, I'm going to insist you leave it alone. The only thing you need to know is that Cat is safe and no one will ever touch her again."

Dad seems poised to argue, but his mouth snaps shut and he jerks his chin up. "That's all I can ask for." He pauses. "But I'm still going to make a request. Make it slow," he adds.

Everyone in the room knows what he's saying.

"It will be my pleasure." A shiver runs down my spine at Hunter's dark response.

"And painful."

Shocked, my head snaps to Mom. Hunter and Dad look at her too, but either they aren't surprised or they're concealing it. Mom is one of the most gentle people I know. But right now, she looks like she could easily pluck out Jimmy's eyes and jam them down his throat without batting an eye.

Her gaze moves to me. "That bastard has hurt my baby too many times. He's taken far too much from my family, and I know he'd take more if given the chance. No matter how badly he suffers, it'll never be enough."

"Mom," I croak, leaving Hunter and walking to her. I pull her in close. "He'll never hurt me again. He'll never take anything from any of us again."

She sniffs and pulls back. "I know he won't. Because Hunter will ensure it." She looks at him over my shoulder before bringing her eyes back to me. "Justice will be served the way it's supposed to be."

I nod.

She dashes away her tears and gives me a tremulous smile. I can still see the pain and anger in her gaze, but she drops the subject and turns to Dad. "Go grab the groceries from the car, dear." She smooths her hands down her navy blue slacks and walks around the bar. "I'm making spaghetti lasagna."

AFTER MY PARENTS HAVE LEFT AND HUNTER AND I ARE getting ready for bed, my phone rings. At first, I consider ignoring the call, but when I see the name on the screen, I accept it. As much as I want to fall into bed and sleep for a week, I can't leave my best friend worrying about me.

"Hey, Megs," I say, leaning back into the pillow against the headboard.

"Are you okay?"

The sound of tears in her voice makes my chest spasm. I would be just as worried and upset if I were in her position and she was the one hurt.

"I'm okay, I promise," I tell her softly, hoping she can hear the truth in my words.

She lets out a muffled sob that crackles through the speaker. "I called as soon as I heard. Peggy let me know everything. I wish you had called me. I want to be there for you."

"I was planning to call you tomorrow. I just... needed another day. Mom and Dad came by earlier with Ginger and her family and they were about all I could handle right now. I'm sorry."

"No, no." She sniffs. "I get it. When can I come see you?"

I smile. I knew she would understand, even if she wants to rush to my side. "Can you give me a couple more days?"

"Yes." Her voice drops. "But promise me that if you need anything, you'll call me."

God, I miss my best friend so much. "I promise."

Hunter emerges from the bathroom wearing only boxer briefs,

his concerned eyes moving toward me. I mouth Megan's name and he nods, taking a seat on his side of the bed.

"Is this Saturday okay?" she asks, and I focus back on our conversation.

"That's perfect. And you can tell me the latest news about Wyatt."

Her laugh is strained. "There's a lot to tell. I'm actually at his place right now, but we'll talk about it this weekend."

If I weren't so tired, I'd insist she tell me right now. But what I really want is to curl up in bed with my husband wrapped around me. I've had my fill of socializing today.

"I'll call you in a couple of days," I tell Megan.

"Okay. Love you, Cat."

The sincerity in her voice brings tears to my eyes. "Love you, too."

Once my phone is on the nightstand, I'm pulled across the bed into a firm chest. Instead of staying with my back facing him, I roll over and smash my face against his chest. As if knowing exactly what I need, Hunter's arms tighten around me, securing me against him in his protective bubble.

Chapter Thirty-Nine
Hunter

When we make it down the stairs and arrive at the metal door, I grab Cat's hand and turn her to face me. A few feet away, Kurt stands with his beefy arms crossed over his chest. For a week now, he and one of Mathias's men have been vigilantly watching over the scum behind the door.

"Are you sure you want to do this? It's not going to be pretty."

With her brows dropping, she looks at the door, and I know the wheels are turning in her head. As she straightens her spine, she swivels her eyes back to me. "Yes, I'm sure," she says.

Things are about to get messy. I wasn't exaggerating when I said it wasn't going to be pretty. In fact, it'll be downright ugly and would make even the strongest stomach weak. It's not something a woman should ever see. But if there's anyone who deserves to be part of this, it's Cat.

I know it's not a black and white decision for her. It's not what she *wants* to do, but what she *needs* to do.

I pull her closer, dropping my chin to look down at her. "If at any time you want to leave, let me know, and I'll get you out of there."

She rolls to her toes and brushes her lips against mine before rolling back down. "Stop, Hunter. I'll be fine. I need to do this." Something hard passes over her eyes. "I want to see that man suffer and bleed. I need to see the pain in his eyes. Because I won't truly believe it's over until I'm standing over his cold, dead body."

As fucked up as it may be, Cat's words have my cock twitching. I'm not blood thirsty. I don't kill people for sport. I do it because if I don't, another innocent person will be hurt. Silas and I don't truly make a difference in the world, but even if we only save one person from suffering, then that's enough for us. What matters is how we make a difference in that person's life.

What fills my cock with blood are the emotions she is letting out. Fear and pain have been so much a part of Cat's life for years. Even when she refused to acknowledge what happened, I could still see it lurking in the depths of her eyes. Cat has never been weak in any way, but seeing the fight and determination on her face right now reminds me of the woman I married. I'm so goddamn proud of her.

Twisting the knob, I push open the door. The putrid smell of sweat and piss hit us first, the stench so strong that it makes my eyes water. Cat coughs beside me.

Across the room, Jimmy sits on an old wood chair. I refuse to call him Nico. We may have the same blood running through our veins, but he's not family. He's Jimmy Simons, the sick bastard who stole my kids and tortured my wife. Nothing more, nothing less.

I haven't seen him since he was carted out of my house a week ago. The anger that's been slowly brewing inside me slams back tenfold.

Behind me and Cat, I feel another presence step into the

room, and I know it's Silas. He asked to be here, and I wasn't going to deny him.

Slowly, my eyes take in Jimmy. He's been stripped down to nothing but an undershirt and a pair of silk boxers. He looks fitter than I expected when I thought he was homeless for ten years. However, after sitting in this room for days, rotting, and getting only the bare minimum to survive, he's lost weight.

His arms aren't tied to the arms of the chair. They don't need to be. With thick nails anchored to the back of his hands and buried in the wood, he won't be going anywhere. However, rope is wrapped around his ankles and the chair's legs. His torso is also held in place by rope.

When we entered the room, his head was lying limply on his chest, but now it's slowly rising. His face looks gaunt. His eye is slightly swollen with a cut on his brow, and he has a line of dried blood from the corner of his mouth. He sees me first, his expression blank, but then he notices Cat beside me. A creepy as fuck smile splits his lips.

"Cat," he rasps, his voice scratchy from either not talking or screaming. "I see you've missed me as much as I've missed you. I'm glad you came."

Cat stiffens, out of fear or hatred, I'm not sure which.

She takes a step forward. "I'm here because I won't miss the opportunity to watch you suffer. To see your life drain from your eyes."

Jimmy chuckles, the sound rusty. "I guess you're saying the time we spent together *wasn't* enjoyable for you?" He licks his cracked lips. "I have to admit, it wasn't as pleasurable for me either, since I didn't get a chance to shove my dick into your pussy like my boys did. That's my biggest regret."

My feet are moving before the last syllable leaves his filthy fucking mouth. I swing my arm back and strike him in the jaw with my fist. My knuckles split from the tooth that flies across the room. His head whips around, but he brings it back. An evil smile splits his lips, showing off a gap where the tooth used to be in the front.

"You can hit me, stab me, torture me as much as you want, Hunter, but I still won. I took from you something precious that you'll never get back. Your two perfect little children were my son's and his friend's play things. They ripped them to shreds and gobbled up the delicious pieces. But that's not the most exciting part. What makes this so enjoyable and ensures I'll always win is that you'll never be rid of me. Your pretty little Cat will always think of me and my boys. I'll always be in the back of both of your heads, taunting you, reminding you of what you had and what you lost." He laughs like a mad man because that's what he is. A fucking lunatic. "You can kill me, but you'll never be rid of me."

The more he talks, the higher my blood pressure rises and the darker the red seeps into my vision.

It's obvious what he's doing. He wants me angry. Enraged. He wants me to lose control and end his life fast. To remove the option of making him suffer. He knows he's not leaving this room alive. He believes that if he can control the situation, shit will go his way.

A rabid scream comes from my left, followed by a flash of black hair. Before I can stop her, Cat has buried a knife in Jimmy's thigh. He howls in pain. Her chest heaves as she twists the blade, digging it deeper.

I let her have her moment before stepping up and wrapping my arms around her waist. I pry her fingers away from the knife handle. "Let go, baby. This is what he wants. For us to put him out of his misery quickly."

She blinks, the enraged scowl slowly fading from her face. She looks down at my hand covering hers which is still wrapped around the knife. Slowly, her fingers relax and she lets go. Her eyes move to Jimmy, who's trying his best to hide the pain he's currently experiencing. By the time I'm done with him, he'll be begging for death.

What he said was true though. Neither Cat nor I will ever forget what he did. It will always loom over our heads, haunting us. But he's also wrong. Jimmy may have changed our lives forever, but we'll use it to strengthen ourselves. We will use it to ensure that something like this never happens again. What Jimmy took hasn't made us weaker. It's made us stronger and wiser. In time, he will fade from our memories and be replaced by the beauty we had before he came along. The children we had will be remembered for who they were during their time with us, not for who Jimmy made them.

Cat straightens, and I pull her back across the room. She'll remain close enough to witness what's coming, but far enough away so she doesn't get dirty.

I turn back to Jimmy. Sweat pours down his temples and his cheeks are flushed red.

"How's Presley doing?" he asks with a toothless grin and dribbles of blood sliding down his chin.

Ignoring his taunts, I glance at Silas, who's standing silently off to the side, his eyes blazing with his own anger on Cat's and my behalf. "Wheel that cart over here, will you?" I ask him.

He immediately moves to the cart with a single gas burner. A pot sits on the burner with the temperature set as high as it'll go. Kurt came in earlier to set it up so it was ready when we arrived.

Silas maneuvers the cart across the smooth concrete floor, careful not to spill the contents in the pot. He stops the cart beside

Jimmy's chair. Jimmy eyes the pot and his throat convulses when he sees what's inside.

His eyes jerk back to me. He tries to hide it, but it's not easy to fake bravery when everything in you is quaking in fear.

"No matter what you do to me, it'll never match the pain I've caused you," he says, his last ditch effort to force my hand prematurely.

"You're right." I grab a rubber oven mitt and slip my hand inside. "Nothing I or anyone else could do to you will ever give you even a small glimpse of what I feel every fucking day for what you did." Picking up a ladle, I dip it into the boiling oil. Carefully, I lift it out and hold it over the knife still buried inside his thigh. His breathing, which was already labored from Cat stabbing him, becomes erratic. His eyes widen and his legs try to move beneath the tight bindings of the rope. He can't move even an inch. "But I'll fucking enjoy trying my best."

His screams of pain rent the air when I start pouring the boiling oil over his bare thigh. I don't keep it in one spot because the nerves die after a few seconds. I want him to feel as much as possible, so I make sure to coat his entire leg. After dipping the ladle in the pot again, I repeat the process on the other. He's panting, and if I'm not careful, he'll pass out from shock.

Dropping the ladle back in the pot, I look over at Cat. She's leaning back against the wall, her face pale. If it wasn't for the hard look in her eyes as she glares at Jimmy, I'd say this is too much for her. My first instinct is to get her out of here, but I decide against it. She'll tell me if it becomes too much.

Turning back to Jimmy, I find his incensed stare on me. His jaw is tight as he clenches his teeth against the pain. His greasy hair is drenched in sweat, and his once red cheeks have turned ghostly white. Still, he's fighting it. I want him scared and begging. Only when he's a broken, slobbering mess will I finish him off.

I grab a small box from the table by the wall. It opens like a match box. Pinching one of the small three-inch sticks inside, I examine it as I slowly walk toward Jimmy.

"Bamboo torture was perfected by the Japanese," I say absently as I twirl one of the sticks between my fingers. "They used it on American Prisoners of War in World War II. Bamboo grows fast. Up to several feet a day, and it can pierce through the toughest materials. Even concrete."

I stop in front of Jimmy, his wary eyes fixed on the stick in my hand. He's a smart guy. I'm sure he already knows what I'm telling him, which makes this more enjoyable because he knows what's coming.

"It's rumored that one method the Japanese used was tying a person down over growing bamboo. The sharp ends of the bamboo would slowly pierce through the person until it came out the other side. The torture was extremely painful and slow."

Jimmy instantly starts wriggling in his seat, his grunts of pain filling the room from the pain of the nails pounded through his hands. His fingers are already spread out on the flat arms of the chair and he can't ball them inward because the fat head of the nail was hammered all the way down.

"Fuck," he hisses, knowing there's not a thing he can do to stop what's about to happen.

Holding his middle finger still, I press the bamboo tip under his fingernail. I push it in a quarter inch and hear his grunt of pain.

"Unfortunately, I don't have the time or inclination to sit and watch that particular form of torture," I continue, "so I'll improvise." Leaving him, I turn to grab a small hammer from the table and walk back. "Not as torturous, but still just as effective."

I lightly tap the bamboo stick under his nail and it moves a centimeter deeper. Jimmy grunts louder. When only an inch remains on the outside, I stop tapping the stick. Plucking out another from the box, I set the tip under his ring fingernail and push until it stays when I let go. Likewise, that one is tapped in further. As I reach Jimmy's thumb, having completed the other four fingers, his face has lost all its color, and his undershirt is drenched with sweat. Little rivulets of blood seep from the tips of his fingers and the pungent smell of piss intensifies.

"How am I doing so far?" I ask, pausing to look up at him. "Do you think I've come even close to the pain you've caused me and Cat?"

"Fuck you," he spits through his heavy panting.

I chuckle, digging the stick beneath his thumb nail and start tapping. "Doesn't matter. Everyone eventually breaks."

"I'll never fucking break."

I shrug. "We'll see."

Jimmy lasted for another thirty minutes before he was howling and pleading. Tears ran rivers down his ruddy face, while snot oozed from his nose, mixing with the slobber and blood seeping out of his mouth. He withstood all ten fingers being impaled with bamboo sticks, which was longer than I expected.

It was when I started stripping off layers of skin on his chest that he broke. His screams of agony filled my ears and it was fucking glorious.

Cat stayed throughout. After the first layer of skin hit the floor, I went to her and made her sit in a chair. She looked sick to her stomach, but when I asked her if she was ready to leave, she kept her eyes on Jimmy and shook her head. I let her stay. When Jimmy finally broke, the look on Cat's face was serene. Her eyes were closed and her head was tilted back, an almost smile on her face. She looked like she got just as much enjoyment out of hearing Jimmy's agony as I did. I didn't doubt that she did.

In the end, I didn't kill Jimmy. He's still in the basement of Slate. To suffer until he dies, which should take only a few days at most. Afterward, he'll be taken to the same pig farm that Henry was sent to.

At the moment, I'm driving Cat and myself home. She hasn't spoken since we left Slate. I've allowed the silence because I know she's still processing what happened. I have never hidden this dark part of myself from her, but I've kept her away from it. This is the first time she's actually witnessed it. She's seen the ugly the world has to offer through Jimmy and those boys, but she hasn't seen it from me. It makes me wonder if she views me differently now.

We enter the house through the garage door. I drop my wallet and keys on the kitchen counter. While torturing Jimmy, I managed to keep most of the blood off of me, but I have a few splatters on my dress shirt and pants. Cat doesn't have a speck of blood on her, but regardless, we both need a shower. First, I need to make sure she's okay.

When I turn around, I see her standing at the bar, her hands resting on the granite top. She stares across the room with unfocused eyes. Unease trickles through me as I wonder what she's thinking.

Walking around the island, I approach her slowly until I'm

right behind her. A small part of me wonders if she'll flinch away if I touch her.

I reach out with both hands, wrapping my fingers around her slim waist. Stepping forward, I press my front against her back. She doesn't move or acknowledge that I'm there and my apprehension grows.

"Cat," I say quietly, watching the side of her face.

She blinks and a rush of relief flows through me when her body relaxes back against mine.

"Does it make me a bad person to have enjoyed that?" she asks, her voice small, like she's afraid to even ask the question. "I feel like it should."

I turn her around and use one hand to tip her chin until she's looking up at me. "It makes you human," I tell her.

"It doesn't feel like it." Her tongue runs across her bottom lip. "It makes me feel less than what I should be."

I tuck her closer against my chest and slide my fingers through her hair to the back of her head. "Would you have felt safe if he had been taken to jail? Even if he was convicted and spent the rest of his life in prison with no chance of parole, would you have felt safe?"

She immediately shakes her head. "No."

"If he's alive, there's a chance he could be set free. And if that happened, he would come after us both and possibly hurt someone else. After everything he's done, do you think he deserves to live?"

She shakes her head again.

"Do you think what I did to him tonight was justified?"

This time she nods. "Every. Single. Bit. of it."

Her answer almost makes me smile.

"If he had done this to someone else's family, the exact same thing, and he was punished in the same way, would you fault the woman for watching and enjoying it? Would you blame the husband for ensuring he never touched his family again?"

This time, she takes a moment to answer. Her eyes move to the specks of blood on my shirt, and instead of disgust, her expression turns pensive. Slowly, she returns her gaze to mine.

"I could never blame you for what you did to Jimmy. You protected me from someone who was a threat, and would always be a threat, so long as he breathed." Her hands move to my sides where she curls her fingers into the material of my shirt.

"It's okay to have enjoyed what happened, Cat." I run my thumb across her cheek. "It doesn't make you a lesser person. He's hurt us in unimaginable ways. To watch him suffer, knowing he'll never get another chance to do more damage, is normal, because you know the threat of him is gone forever. It's a step to moving forward."

"Thank you."

My brows pinch. "For what?"

"For being the man you are. For loving me as much as you do. For staying by my side, even when I know it had to be difficult at times."

I dip my knees, bringing my face closer to hers, lowering my voice. "Loving you is the easiest thing I'll ever do in my life. Staying by your side is the only place I'll ever be. And I'm the man I am today only because of you."

Chapter Forty
Caterina

I stare at the little white stick, my eyebrows drawn down and my stomach spinning like it has been through a speed cycle in a washing machine. I'm not sure how I feel about the results. Having a baby right now probably isn't the best idea. I'm still very much in the grieving stage of losing Eliana and Ryder, despite it being five years since they were taken. My head was protecting me from a horrific past, but it also hindered my healing process.

My eyes return to the stick and its single blue line.

Not pregnant.

There's a part of me that's relieved that we won't have a baby in the next however many months. Yet, a bigger part of me, one I didn't even realize existed, aches with longing.

Having a child, a little baby to cherish and love, would be a blessing. Hunter was a wonderful father to our children. He was a natural from the first moment he held Eliana in his arms. The look in his eyes told me she would have him wrapped around her little finger in no time. And she did. He would have done anything to make our daughter smile and laugh. But she was always my little princess. Each morning, she sat at my vanity as I dressed and got ready for the day. We'd talk and laugh about anything and everything. She was my best friend, and I was hers.

Ryder was my little man. When he started walking, he followed me around the house, babbling away in toddler gibberish. He loved helping me bake desserts. His favorite was when he got to help with the blender. He'd giggle because the vibrations of the machine tickled him.

He was also very much a daddy's boy. Hunter would take him outside whenever he did yard work. Most of the lawn maintenance was handled by a gardener, but Hunter always insisted on mowing because Ryder loved riding the mower with his daddy.

We were all happy. The perfect family.

Until it was all ripped away.

A tear slips down my cheek, and I swipe it away. I feel lost without Eliana and Ryder in our lives, but I'm finally starting to remember that as much as I miss them and wish they were here, *I'm* still here. Hunter is still here. And we need each other to fully heal. To move past this.

I feel the bed dip beside me and it's only then that I realize Hunter has walked into the bedroom. I was so focused on my thoughts I didn't see him come in.

Before he can say anything, I hand over the pregnancy test. He looks down as he takes it. He pulls in a breath, and I'm not sure whether he's relieved or disappointed.

"Are you upset?" he asks, setting the test down on the bed and grabbing my hand.

"I don't know." I glance at the test before looking at him. "I think a part of me is, and I don't know how to feel about that."

"You can feel however you want, baby. No feeling is wrong."

I nod and tuck a piece of hair behind my ear. "What about you? Are you disappointed it was negative?"

He tugs at my hand, so I get to my feet. Pulling me forward, he spreads his legs so I stand between them. His hands touch the back of my thighs, and his head tips back so his eyes meet mine.

"What I feel is that I would love to have another baby with you. You have so much love inside you, Cat. Me, Eli, and Ryder are not the only ones you're supposed to give that love to. God built you to love more than us." He leans forward and kisses my stomach over my shirt. "And one day, when it's meant to be, we'll have that other person you were meant to love." Tears spring to my eyes and he reaches up, rubbing his thumb over one when it falls down my cheek. "I don't know if right now is the time for that. I would have been happy if it were. But that doesn't mean I'm sad because it didn't happen."

He's right. I know that. We still have some time to have more children. We need to spend right now healing, making sure we're whole when we do decide to add to our family.

I sniff and give him a watery smile. "One day."

He returns it with one of his own. "One day."

When I hear growls from beside me, I jerk upright in bed. My heart dives to my toes when I see Hunter thrashing beneath the sheets. His brows are pinched low and his forehead is dotted with a light sheen of sweat.

Taking care not to startle him, I lay my hand over his heart. It beats a mile a minute beneath my palm.

"Hunter," I call quietly, trying to gently wake him from his nightmare.

They've been happening since Jimmy did what he did nearly a month ago. Almost every night. My own nightmares have diminished. Maybe it's because I now remember what happened, so I don't need them to try and remind me. Or perhaps it's because Hunter is suffering through his own nightmares and now it's my turn to be there for him.

I hate to see him going through this. I realize now just how emotionally draining it must have been for him when I woke him up with my own nightmares. It's almost more debilitating for the person witnessing the struggle. It makes them feel helpless because they can't do anything to lessen the pain and fear.

I get no reaction when I call his name, so I get to my knees and bend over him. As I cup his cheek, a lump forms in my throat, threatening to choke me when I see the pain crippling his face.

"Hunter," I call again, a little louder this time.

His eyes snap open and instantly, they find me in the dark. The next thing I know, he's sitting up and pulling me onto his lap. I straddle his thighs and he buries his face in my neck. His hot and heavy breath warms the chill in my bones.

"Jesus," he mutters, his voice muffled against my neck.

I run one hand through his hair and the other up and down his back, giving him the comfort he's given me so many times over the years. "It's okay. It was just a nightmare."

He pulls back, but puts both of his hands on my cheeks to bring our foreheads together. When he speaks, his voice is raw. "It was real. You were laid out on that fucking table with Jimmy lying over you. Except this time, he got what he wanted. I was stuck in that motherfucking chair and had to watch him rape you and then slit your throat right as he finished."

His words evoke an image in my head of when Ryder and Eliana were killed the same way. I push the unwanted vision away.

Hunter's breathing is hard and his eyes look frantic. It's

almost like he's still stuck in his dream, watching the nightmare play out.

I drop my head, laying my lips against his, hoping to distract him.

"I'm right here," I tell him quietly. "Jimmy's gone. He's dead. He can't hurt us anymore. And I'm right here. Safe with you." Taking his hand, I place it around my throat, making sure his fingers touch the spot I want him to feel. "Feel me, Hunter. No blood. No gash. Only my pulse."

Some of the panic leaves his eyes and he lets out a long breath. "Yeah."

With my fingers running through the hair on his head, I tilt his head back and drop my mouth to his. As our lips meet, mine open automatically, seeking out his tongue. He doesn't disappoint.

I moan, loving his taste. We haven't had sex since Jimmy hurt me. I've wanted to, but Hunter insisted we wait until I'm completely healed. I only suffered a few minor cuts around the opening of my vagina and some light bruises. It only took a few days to heal. I think Hunter was more worried about my emotional state.

Now I worry about him. I want to take the visions of his nightmare and replace them with something good.

"I want you," I murmur over his lips.

He pulls his head back, his eyes searching mine. "Are you sure?"

"Yes," I say, then grind my ass against him to be sure he understands. He groans and grips my hips, moving me back an inch so he's rubbing against my pussy.

His hands slide upward under my shirt, and he whips it off. Once the material is over my head, his head drops and his lips surround my nipple. He sucks deep, his teeth scraping across the sensitive flesh. I arch my back and push more of myself against his mouth. I scrape my nails down his muscular back and grind down harder, feeling the length of his cock rubbing against the soft cotton of my shorts.

I need him deep inside me. I want his warm flesh against mine. I want to be full of him and never again know what it's like to be empty.

I fall back on my butt and lift my legs, grabbing the hem of my shorts to pull them off. Hunter helps me, and as soon as they are down my legs and tossed to the floor, I'm back on my knees with my legs on either side of his. Reaching down between us, I slide my hand into his briefs and wrap my fingers around his swollen cock. He's rock hard, but smooth, and I feel a little pulse on the underside of the head.

After I tug him free of the material, I lift up and touch the head against my opening. My eyes remain fixed on him as I pant, my heart fluttering with anticipation. As I slide down his shaft, he groans, his fingers digging into the flesh of my ass.

"So goddamn tight, baby," he says roughly. "I could stay in you for days and still want more."

With my hands on his shoulders, I lift up until he's halfway out and then fall back down. A little cry leaves my lips. "Don't ever leave."

"Never," he growls.

I fuck him slowly for a few strokes before picking up speed. My boobs bounce between us, the tips scraping along the coarse hairs on his chest, adding to my pleasure. As his hands dig into my ass cheeks, he picks me up and lets me fall back down. Over and over. Up and down. In and out. His cock rubs against my smooth inner walls and with each glide, my desire heightens.

He lifts up so he's on his knees. My legs lock around his waist and my arms encircle his neck, holding him tightly. Grunts fill the room as he continues to slam me down on his length, his fingers biting into my ass so hard I expect to see marks later.

It only lasts a moment before I'm falling back to bed with him on top of me. As he goes deeper, I let out a hoarse cry when he hits a spot that shoots sparks of delicious electricity through me.

"So fucking beautiful."

I open my eyes and look at my husband. There's so much heat and love shining in the green of his.

"In every way a person can be beautiful," he continues.

I've always counted myself lucky to have such a special man like Hunter.

I slide my hand across his cheek, the little prickles that've grown overnight abrading my palm. "Hunter," I say softly. "Love me."

"Always," he groans, pushing his hips forward and smashing his pubic bone against my clit. Just how he knows I like it.

With one hand, he laces our fingers together then lifts our arms so both of them are wrapped around the top of my head. The other hand slides down one of my legs until it reaches the back of my thigh. He lifts it so it's over his shoulder. His weight drops down on me as he wedges his arm under and up my back so he curls his fingers around my shoulder. This new position is almost suffocating, but I love it, because I'm completely surrounded by him.

Moving his hips, he lifts a few inches before pushing back inside and grinding against me. He holds me by my shoulder, keeping me in place as he fucks me slow and deep. My breath catches, and I let out a long moan, feeling the tingles begin in my belly and work their way down my legs and shoot up my torso.

"Oh God, Hunter," I whimper. "That feels...."

"Fucking incredible," he finishes for me.

"Yes."

He takes me like this, slowly and softly, until we're both shouting out our release. He releases my leg, and I hug it around his waist like the other. He stays inside me as he rolls to his back with me lying on his chest.

And that's how we drift off to sleep.

Chapter Forty-One
Hunter

Having checked the front door and all the windows, I head to the fireplace to add a few more logs. While Jimmy is no longer a threat, there are always other people who are willing to hurt you or take what you have. This has been my routine for five years, and I have no intentions of changing it.

I'm stirring the glowing ashes when my phone pings with an incoming text. I pull it out and see a message from Mathias.

> Mathias: It's done. Check the news tomorrow.

The small knot that's been slowly getting tighter since we found out Jimmy had plans to have Terry and Howard somehow released or orchestrate their escape finally unravels.

Although the fee I paid Mathias was hefty, I owe him a bonus. Thanks to him and his contacts, we were able to find someone in the same pen who could take care of the pair. I didn't care how it was done, I just wanted the bastards in the ground, their corpses rotting.

Despite the worry I know she still feels, I haven't told Cat of my plans. I wanted to wait until it was finished. Now I can put that worry to rest.

Over the last month, I had Marcus search for information on Nicholas and Teresa Monroe. He didn't find much. My father did a damn good job of making sure their lives were erased if anything happened to them. Marcus was only able to confirm that they were real and had two boys named Nicholas Cooper Monroe Junior and Hunter James Monroe. The boys were eight and two when their parents were killed in a suspected home invasion. Both boys disappeared after that.

Nothing was found about how I got to Tennessee from Chicago. Considering Thomas and Sandra moved to River Heights a few months after my parents were killed, and I was placed in my first foster home soon after, I believe they had something to do with it. I've gathered that my fabricated last name, St. James, comes from the middle name I was given at birth.

Marcus also managed to find a picture of my parents on their wedding day. Dressed in the finest clothes money can buy, the couple in the photo were young. They couldn't have been older than their late teens or early twenties. Both looked happy as they smiled at the camera. What I found interesting was the protective way Dad held Mom's barely-protruding stomach. In accordance with the date on the back, she was pregnant with their first child. There wasn't a doubt in my mind that they both loved the child she was carrying. Furthermore, I didn't doubt their love remained strong after their second child was born.

When Jimmy was a child, he probably saw shit that wasn't there and fell off the deep end because he wasn't the center of attention anymore. Alternately, something happened between the time he was born and when I was born that pushed them away.

I know there's more information out there, but I'm letting it go. The whole fucked up situation has messed with my and Cat's lives for long enough. The last piece of the puzzle was having Terry and Howard dealt with, and now that they have been, we can put that shit to rest.

After tossing in a few small logs, I walk out of the living room and down the hallway to the bedroom in the back. We're in a small cabin in the mountains. Cat and I bought the place years ago when Eliana was a baby. It's over thirty miles to the nearest village and deep in the woods. I brought Cat here to get away. We both needed a reprieve.

The door creaks when I open it, and I find the room empty. The bathroom light is on, and steam billows from the open doorway. I check the fireplace and find enough wood burning to last for the next few hours. The cabin has central heating, but Cat prefers a fire. The temperatures are expected to drop into the thirties in the next few days, so I spent the afternoon chopping wood.

Reaching back, I pull my shirt over my head as I walk into the bathroom. My hands are working to remove my jeans as I watch Cat's silhouette behind the fogged glass enclosure of the shower.

Without fail, every single fucking time I look at her, my heart rate picks up. This woman is my life, and I'd die a painful death without her.

Opening the shower door, I walk down a few steps and close it behind me. The shower is huge, big enough to fit four or more people. When we toured the cabin and Cat saw the bathroom, she spun around and demanded we buy it. Grey, black, and white tiles take up most of the walls. A stone bench sits at one end. Standing facing away from me, Cat runs a sudsy sponge down her arm as the rainfall showerhead rains water down on her. My eyes trace the pink dotted scars littering her back and my gut tightens.

Taking a step behind her, I wrap my arms around her waist,

pressing my chest against her back and my groin against her backside. I watch the side of her face and see her lips form a smile.

She lifts the sponge to her chest, but I take it from her. "Let me."

As I smooth the sponge down over her breasts and taut stomach, her head falls back on my shoulder, her eyes closing. As soon as it meets the dark layer of curls above her pussy, I drop the sponge and let my hands do the work. I slip my fingers between her lips, feeling the slickness of her juices seeping out of her. My other hand moves up her stomach to palm her breast. Her tight nipple pokes my palm, and I squeeze the plumpness.

Her inaudible moan vibrates against my chest. As I slip two fingers inside, I hook them and apply pressure to her clit with the heel of my hand. I drop my lips to the crease of her neck and take little nibbling bites.

Lifting her arm, she grasps my hair, pulling my face closer while her other hand slides down my arm until her fingers mesh with mine inside her. My hard cock wedges between the soft globes of her ass, and I pump my hips.

She turns her head and lifts her chin, offering me her lips, which I readily accept. She tastes like a beautiful spring morning. I pinch her nipple and swallow her soft cry.

Without lifting my lips from hers, I reach over to a shelf and grab the bottle of lube I placed in here earlier.

I haven't taken Cat's ass since the first time she asked me to. I know she enjoyed it, and I damn sure want to fuck it again. I'm the one who needed time though. To come to grips that Cat may not be as sweet and innocent as I always thought she was. Sex with her has always been gentle and soft. I'm a different man when I'm with her. The stuff I did with Scarlett couldn't be more different. I've always felt guilty that, other than giving her the type of pain that leaves permanent marks, I enjoyed the raw and rough way Scarlett wanted me to take her.

Before I met Cat, sex never came with feelings. I liked it that way. And I liked it hard. Flesh pounding flesh hard enough to leave bruises. Fingermarks left by a tight grip. Bites deep enough that they nearly pierce skin. A tight throat gripping the head of my cock as I force it down, using their hair to guide their movements.

Once Cat came along and completely captivated me, I could have spent the rest of my life giving it to her the way she deserved. Sweet. Loving. Tender. Soft caresses and endearing words whispered in her ear.

Our sex life has never been boring or stale. We weren't a vanilla couple that only engaged in missionary sex with no adventure. The passion between us was intense and real. We explored and played and we were both more than satisfied. And if Cat should want to revert back to the way things were, I'd still die a completely satiated man.

But knowing there's a darker side to her, a side that likes to get down and dirty and to be taken and dominated....

Fuck yes, I'm game. Anything and everything she wants. Any way she wants it. Whenever she wants it.

Flipping the cap of the lube open, I pull my hips back until my cock sticks out straight, the head pressing against Cat's ass crack. I dribble some on my length.

"What are you doi—"

Her words die off when she turns her head and sees the tipped bottle in my hand. I move my eyes to hers long enough to see something dark flare behind the pretty blue. She licks her lips as she draws a long breath of air.

I close the bottle and toss it on the shelf. Putting one hand around her waist, I wrap my other hand around my long length and give it a few strokes, making sure the lube covers every inch, because I plan to give her every inch.

Rather than going straight for her tightest hole, I set the tip just outside of her slick pussy and push forward, letting it slide through her lips and nudge her clit. I press my thumb against her asshole, pushing just the tip inside. Her breath hitches and a low moan mixes with the sound of the shower.

"Please, Hunter," she whimpers, thrusting her ass backward.

I give little pumps of my hips, repeatedly hitting her clit and applying more pressure against her hole with my thumb. "Where do you want me, baby?"

"You know where," she pants.

I hold her hips still when she pushes back, trying to force more of my thumb inside her.

"Tell me." I grunt. My control is slipping fast.

She turns her head, looking at me over her shoulder. Her cheeks are a cute shade of pink. Not from the heat of the water, but from the words I'm asking her to say. Her bottom lip rolls between her teeth before she lets it pop free. "My ass. Fuck my ass."

I grit my teeth, my cock pulsing and squirting out a drop of precum at the explicit words.

We lean forward together, my front plastered to her back, until our hands meet the wall in front of her, directly under the falling water. With my other hand, I guide the head of my swollen cock and notch it at her asshole. Pushing forward an inch, the head pops inside. I groan and stop moving. I'm ready to shoot my load, and I'm barely fucking inside her.

I trail a line of kisses down her neck and over her shoulder as I wait for myself to calm the hell down. I want this to last longer than two minutes, but goddamn, her ass feels incredible strangling my cock.

I groan and grind my molars together when she pushes back into me. "Fuck, baby, don't do that. I need a minute here." I drop my forehead between her shoulders.

I give myself another moment before I push in another inch. Cat's moans match my groans. Pulling out, I plunge back in deeper.

"You feel so fucking perfect," I growl. "So tight and warm."

"More, Hunter. Give me more."

As I slide in another couple of inches, she rises to her toes. Her fingers, wrapped through mine, flex against the shower wall. With my other hand, I reach down and slide my fingers through her pussy lips, then press my middle finger against her clit. She bucks her hips.

Using my hold against her pussy, I hold her still as I force my cock in the rest of the way, bottoming out until my hips meet the flesh of her ass.

"Put your other hand on the wall and keep both of them there," I tell her, letting her hand go and standing straight.

When she complies, I bend slightly and hook her right leg over my arm. This new position opens her up more and gives me better access. After swiveling my hips against her ass, I pull out halfway and slide forward slowly.

The muscles in my jaw ache from clenching my teeth. Back and forth, I fill her ass, retreat, and fill her again. I play with her clit as I fuck her, picking up speed and ramming deep. If it weren't for the little cries of pleasure coming out of her, I'd worry I was being too rough. But Cat eats it up and even demands more.

As soon as she clamps down on me and shouts out her release,

I'm right behind her, fucking her hard and fast until I've emptied every bit of myself inside her.

Later, after I finish washing her and she does the same to me, we're both in bed. She's snuggled up to my side with my hands running through her damp hair. Her breathing is even, but I know she's not asleep because she's gently playing with the hair on my chest.

"Terry and Howard are dead," I say in the quiet room.

Her fingers stop moving and her body stiffens against my side. She doesn't say anything at first, but after a moment, she resumes twirling her fingers.

"Good. I'm glad they're dead." She kisses my chest before tipping her head back to look at me.

"I needed you to know that they're no longer a threat."

"Thank you."

"You never have to thank me for protecting you."

I roll to my side, keeping my arm under her head as I curl it so I can lay my head on my palm. Our faces are only inches apart. Wrapping my other arm around her waist, I tuck my fingers between her and the mattress.

"You became mine from the first moment I saw you, and you'll be mine until the day we both take our last breath. And even then, I'll find you in the afterlife." I smile and lean forward to kiss her curled lips. "Sorry, baby, but you're stuck with me for eternity."

She entwines our legs together, her eyes sparkling with her smile. "I guess that's something I can learn to live with."

Epilogue
Hunter

Sometime later...

The first thing I see when I open my eyes is a pair of beautiful blue pools. Her smile is small, the curl of her lips barely noticeable, like she's holding back a secret.

Cat's sitting on the bed with her legs crossed, facing me, like she's been watching me for some time.

Except when I look closer, I notice something. She's not Cat right now.

I stiffen when she reaches for my hand that's lying on my stomach. Picking it up, she holds it in her small hand as she places it on her lap. Her eyes are drawn to the black wedding band on my ring finger. She twirls it around, that small smile still in place.

"Presley." Her name comes out gruffly.

Due to her innocence, Presley has always been the easiest one to be around. She's also the one I struggled with the most. She's my wife. Looks like her, sounds like her, smells like her. However, her mind is that of a child. It feels fucking wrong for my body to still want her. For me to look at her and see the womanly curves and know how good they feel beneath my hands.

Rolling to my side, I pull the sheet further up my chest. Morning wood is a real thing, and the last thing I want to do is make Presley curious about the tent beneath the sheet. Especially considering I don't know if it's really morning wood or if it's because of the way Presley is lightly playing with my fingers and how close our hands are to her....

My thoughts trail off when she giggles. It's so girly that it reminds me once again how inappropriate our current situation is. I wince, wanting to pull my hand away, but leaving it in hers instead.

"It's okay, Hunter," she says, her laughing eyes drifting to mine. "I know all about penises and the nasty things guys do with them with girls." Her pert nose wrinkles in disgust.

"What do you mean, *you know?*" My question comes out a growl. "*How* do you know?"

She lifts a hand and taps the side of her head. "They're foggy and not very clear, but I do have her memories floating around up there."

"Jesus," I mutter.

I assumed Presley, Scarlett, and Athena were unaware of Cat, or at least, didn't carry her memories. Just as Cat doesn't carry theirs. Except for vague visions of seeing Presley, Cat never remembers when they come to the surface, so it was safe to believe the same applies to them.

"*All* of her memories?" I ask.

Her head bobs up and down, her lips twitching.

Fuck.

So this twelve-year-old female child has had front row seats to a fucking porno, starring Cat and me.

Jesus Christ, I'm going to be sick.

"She's ready, you know."

My eyes snap back to Presley. She gazes at me, her expression looking thoughtful and more adult-like than her young years.

"What do you mean?"

"Cat," she says. "She's ready for a baby. She wants one so badly, but she's afraid to tell you."

My gut drops and a heavy weight settles over my heart.

"Afraid, why?"

Presley puts my hand down on the bed, the tips of my fingers still touching her shin. Dropping her elbow to her knee, she plops her chin in her hand.

"She's worried that you'll think she's not ready. She is though." A small smile curls her lips. "She was always meant to be a mother longer than she was. And you were meant to be a father longer than you were." She pauses for a moment. "Eliana and Ryder were so lucky to have parents like you and Cat. The children you still have yet to have will be even luckier, since you'll know what a precious gift they are and how easily it can be taken away."

My throat tightens, and I'm forced to clear it before it chokes me.

"Thank you," I say gruffly.

There is no need for me to elaborate. Presley knows what my gratitude is for. If it wasn't for her and the other two women, I'm not sure Cat would have survived the shit that was forced on her. Scarlett was the darkest part of her that felt like she deserved pain for what happened to our children. Athena was the loner. Rather, she felt as if she should be alone. Like no one could ever love her after what happened, and even if they did, she didn't deserve it.

Both women took their places and carried the burden of those emotions so Cat wouldn't have to.

But it was Presley who kept that spark of life inside Cat. She kept the light on while the others navigated through the darkness. Through Presley, the innocence, the love of a child, the need to be loved, she held Cat's hand and guided her so she would never get lost.

"I don't know if I'll ever be back." My brows drop at Presley's softly spoken words. "But know that I'll never be far away."

Even though I want Cat to be whole again, I will miss Presley. Scarlett and Athena have only made a few appearances over the last year, which is a lot less than usual. Presley has shown herself more, but I don't think it's because Cat really needs her. I think Presley just likes to come out and play. To visit the world and see what we're up to.

Her deep blue eyes gaze into mine. "I'm going to miss you."

Rising to an elbow, I lean over and press a kiss against her forehead. "I'm gonna miss you too," I say quietly.

When I pull back to look at her, her eyes are closed and she has that small smile on her face again.

Seconds later, when her eyes flutter open, Presley is gone and my beautiful wife is back.

Some more time later...

Standing with my shoulder propped against the doorway, my hands shoved in my pockets and my ankles crossed, I watch what's going on across the room.

A single lamp on the nightstand between the two twin beds illuminates most of the room, leaving much of it in shadow.

"Tell us a story, Mommy," Everly, our four-year-old daughter, requests with a hopeful look in her eyes.

"Yeah, Momma, please," chimes in River, Everly's twin brother, who's lying beside his sister.

When the twins were old enough to leave their cribs and have bigger beds, we put them in separate rooms. However, they weren't having it. Each night, one of them snuck into the other's room and climbed into their bed. They didn't like being separated. After six months of this, we moved them into the same room. They were okay sleeping in their own beds, so long as they were still close to each other. Even so, each night, they lay together while Cat or I tell them a story.

Cat laughs as she sits on the edge of Everly's bed. Picking up the framed photo of Eliana and Ryder, she brings it to her lap and gazes down at it, her eyes full of love.

"There once was a little girl," Cat begins. "A beautiful little girl with long brown hair that almost reached her waist. Her name was Eliana. She was sweet and kind and she loved her baby brother, Ryder, so much. The day her momma and daddy brought him home from the hospital, Eli sat for hours outside his bassinet and just watched him. Anytime Ryder moved or made the tiniest of sounds, Eli was right there, making sure he was okay."

She smiles and looks from Everly to River, both of whom were captivated by their mother's story.

"Eli used to tell her mother that she was going to have a baby just like her brother one day."

A twinge of pain hits my chest as her smile slips a fraction, but it's back a moment later.

"But sissy never got to have a baby, right?" Everly asks.

Cat reaches out and brushes hair from Everly's cheeks. "No, she didn't." She taps the end of River's nose and he giggles. "But you know what? Everything ended up the way it was supposed to."

I know how difficult it is for Cat to say those words, and for her to actually believe them. Eli and Ryder were prematurely taken from us. They should have both lived long and happy lives. We should have been given a chance to watch them grow and start their own families.

But sometimes things happen for a reason. While I would love to have our lost children with us, if we did, we may not have Everly and River. How do you choose one child over another? Jimmy tried forcing that decision on Cat. She wasn't able to choose, just as I wouldn't have been able to, because no good parent could.

"Eli's not sad though," Cat continues. "Because right now, she's up in Heaven with her baby brother, still looking after him. And you know what else?" she asks, lowering her voice and bending closer to our children. "She's looking down on her little sister and her other baby brother."

River and Everly look up at the ceiling with grins on their faces, loving that idea.

This is what we do every night. Through hundreds of different stories, Everly and River know all about their older brother and sister.

"Alright, time for bed, you two," Cat says, getting to her feet.

Before she can coax River from Everly's bed and into his, I walk across the room and scoop up our son. His slender arms go around my shoulders and his face sinks into my neck. I press my face into his thick black hair and inhale.

"Goodnight, Daddy," he mumbles sleepily.

I kiss his cheek before laying him down. "Goodnight, buddy." I pull the covers over him. "I love you."

"Love you too."

As part of our routine, I move from River's bed to Everly's while Cat goes to our son. Putting my fists on the pillow on either side of Everly, I drop down and press my lips against her cheek. My eyes slide closed when her arms wrap around my neck and she squeezes me tight.

"Love you, Daddy."

"Love you too, princess. Goodnight."

"G'night," she replies, her eyes already drifting closed.

The lamp is turned off and Cat and I back out of the room, but we stay in the doorway for several long moments. I wrap my arms around her waist and she lets her weight fall back against me. I drop my chin to her shoulder and we stand there, simply watching our beautiful family as they drift off to sleep.

Also by Alex Grayson

JADED HOLLOW SERIES
Beautifully Broken

Wickedly Betrayed

Wildly Captivated

Perfectly Tragic

Jaded Hollow: The Complete Collection

THE CONSUMED SERIES
Mine

Sex Junkie

Shamelessly Bare

Hungry Eyes

The Consumed Series: The Complete Collection

HELL NIGHT SERIES
Retribution

Vindication

Vengeance

Wrath

The Hell Night Series: Complete Collection

WESTBRIDGE SERIES

Pitch Dark

Broad Daylight

Salvaged Pieces

BULLY ME SERIES

Treacherous

Malicious

ITTY BITTY DELIGHTS

Heels Together, Knees Apart

Teach Me Something Dirty

Filthy Little Tease

For I Have Sinned

Doing Taboo Things

Lady Boner

Lady Boss

Lady Balls

Lady Bits

Itty Bitty Delights: 1-5

Itty Bitty Delights: 6-9

STANDALONES

Whispered Prayers

Haunted

Dear Linc

Just the Tip

Uncocky Hero

Until Never

About the Author

Alex Grayson is a USA Today bestselling author of heart pounding, emotionally gripping contemporary romances including the Jaded Hollow Series, The Consumed Series, The Hell Night Series, and multiple standalone novels. Her passion for books was reignited by a gift from her sister-in-law. After spending several years as a devoted reader and blogger, Alex decided to write and independently publish her first novel in 2014 (an endeavor that took a little longer than expected). The rest, as they say, is history.

Originally a southern girl, Alex now lives in Ohio with her husband, three cats, and one dog. She loves the color blue, homemade lasagna, casually browsing real estate, and interacting with her readers. Visit her website, www.alexgraysonbooks.com, or find her on social media!